Praise for *Look Again*

"Bestseller Scottoline (*Lady Killer*) scores another bull's-eye with this terrifying thriller about an adoptive parent's worst fear—the threat of an undisclosed illegality overturning an adoption. . . . Scottoline expertly ratchets up the tension."
—*Publishers Weekly* (starred review)

"Scottoline's best novel to date will have faithful fans and new readers singing her praises."
—*Library Journal* (starred review)

"Her best book yet." —*Kirkus Reviews* (starred review)

"*Look Again,* if I may be so bold, is probably Lisa Scottoline's best novel. It's honest and hugely emotional, with very real characters who you care about and will remember long after you finish this terrific book." —James Patterson

"Scottoline still sticks to what she knows in this taut standalone. . . . A surefire winner." —*Booklist*

"A pulse-racing novel." —*USA Today*

"In *Look Again,* Scottoline has created a tension that draws the reader in from the first page." —*Deseret News*

"In *Look Again,* Scottoline resembles a figure skater who . . . executes a fine sequence of laybacks, sit spins, and double lutzes." —*The Washington Post*

"Scottoline has set up a plot that will suck readers in—and make them shiver a bit the next time they get a 'Have You Seen This Child?' card in the mail."
—*San Antonio Express-News*

Also by Lisa Scottoline

LOOK AGAIN

Lisa Scottoline

St. Martin's Paperbacks

This is a work of fiction. All of the characters, organizations, and events portrayed in this novel are either products of the author's imagination or are used fictitiously.

LOOK AGAIN

Copyright © 2009 by Lisa Scottoline.
Excerpt from *Come Home* copyright © 2012 by Lisa Scottoline.

For information address St. Martin's Press, 175 Fifth Avenue, New York, NY 10010.

Library of Congress Catalog Card Number: 2008043924

ISBN: 978-0-312-38074-8

Printed in the United States of America

St. Martin's Press hardcover edition / April 2009
St. Martin's Griffin trade paperback edition / February 2010
St. Martin's Paperbacks edition / February 2013

St. Martin's Paperbacks are published by St. Martin's Press, 175 Fifth Avenue, New York, NY 10010.

10 9 8 7 6 5 4 3 2 1

For my beloved daughter

Where did you come from, baby dear?
Out of the everywhere into the here.
Where did you get your eyes so blue?
Out of the skies as I came through.
   —George MacDonald
   At the Back of the North Wind

Where have you been, my blue-eyed son?
   —Bob Dylan
   "A Hard Rain's A-Gonna Fall"

Chapter 1

Ellen Gleeson was unlocking her front door when something in the mail caught her attention. It was a white card with photos of missing children, and one of the little boys looked oddly like her son. She eyed the photo as she twisted her key in the lock, but the mechanism was jammed, probably because of the cold. Snow encrusted SUVs and swing sets, and the night sky was the color of frozen blueberries.

Ellen couldn't stop looking at the white card, which read HAVE YOU SEEN THIS CHILD? The resemblance between the boy in the photo and her son was uncanny. They had the same wide-set eyes, smallish nose, and lopsided grin. Maybe it was the lighting on the porch. Her fixture had one of those bulbs that was supposed to repel bugs but only colored them yellow. She held the photo closer but came to the same conclusion. The boys could have been twins.

Weird, Ellen thought. Her son didn't have a twin. She had adopted him as an only child.

She jiggled the key in the lock, suddenly impatient. It had been a long day at work, and she was losing her grip on her purse, briefcase, the mail, and a bag of Chinese takeout. The aroma of barbecued spareribs wafted from the top, setting her stomach growling, and she twisted the key harder.

The lock finally gave way, the door swung open, and she dumped her stuff onto the side table and shed her coat, shivering happily in the warmth of her cozy living room. Lace curtains framed the windows behind a red-and-white-checked couch, and the walls were stenciled with cows and hearts, a cutesy touch she liked more than any reporter should. A plastic toy chest overflowed with plush animals, Spot board books, and Happy Meal figurines, decorating never seen in *House & Garden*.

"Mommy, look!" Will called out, running toward her with a paper in his hand. His bangs blew off his face, and Ellen flashed on the missing boy from the white card in the mail. The likeness startled her before it dissolved in a wave of love, powerful as blood.

"Hi, honey!" Ellen opened her arms as Will reached her knees, and she scooped him up, nuzzling him and breathing in the oaty smell of dry Cheerios and the faint almond scent of the Play-Doh sticking to his overalls.

"Eww, your nose is cold, Mommy."

"I know. It needs love."

Will giggled, squirming and waving the drawing. "Look what I made! It's for you!"

"Let's see." Ellen set him down and looked at his drawing, of a horse grazing under a tree. It was done in pencil and too good to be freehand. Will was no Picasso, and his go-to subject was trucks. "Wow, this is great! Thank you so much."

"Hey, Ellen," said the babysitter, Connie Mitchell, coming in from the kitchen with a welcoming smile. Connie was short and sweet, soft as a marshmallow in a white sweatshirt that read PENN STATE, which she wore with wide-leg jeans and slouchy Uggs. Her brown eyes were bracketed by crow's-feet and her chestnut ponytail was shot through with gray, but Connie had the enthusiasm, if not always the energy, of a teenager. She asked, "How was your day?"

"Crazy busy. How about you?"

"Just fine," Connie answered, which was only one of the reasons that Ellen counted her as a blessing. She'd had her share of babysitter drama, and there was no feeling worse than leaving your child with a sitter who wasn't speaking to you.

Will was waving his picture, still excited. "I drew it! All by myself!"

"He traced it from a coloring book," Connie said under her breath. She crossed to the coat closet and retrieved her parka.

"I *drew* it!" Will's forehead buckled into a frown.

"I know, and you did a great job." Ellen stroked his silky head. "How was swimming, Con?"

"Fine. Great." Connie put on her coat and flicked her ponytail out of the collar with a deft backhand. "He was a little fish." She got her brown purse and packed tote bag from the windowseat. "Will, tell Mommy how great you did without the kickboard."

Will pouted, a mood swing typical of toddlers and manic-depressives.

Connie zipped up her coat. "Then we drew pictures, right? You told me Mommy liked horses."

"I *drew* it," Will said, cranky.

"I love my picture, sweetie." Ellen was hoping to stave off a kiddie meltdown, and she didn't blame him for it. He was plainly tired, and a lot was asked of three-year-olds these days. She asked Connie, "He didn't nap, did he?"

"I put him down, but he didn't sleep."

"Too bad." Ellen hid her disappointment. If Will didn't nap, she wouldn't get any time with him before bed.

Connie bent down to him. "See ya later . . ."

Will was supposed to say "alligator," but he didn't. His lower lip was already puckering.

"You wanna say good-bye?" Connie asked.

Will shook his head, his eyes averted and his arms loose at his sides. He wouldn't make it through a book tonight, and Ellen loved to read to him. Her mother would turn over in her grave if she knew Will was going to bed without a book.

"All right then, bye-bye," Connie said, but Will didn't respond, his head downcast. The babysitter touched his arm. "I love you, Will."

Ellen felt a twinge of jealousy, however unreasonable. "Thanks again," she said, and Connie left, letting in an icy blast of air. Then she closed and locked the door.

"I DREW IT!" Will dissolved into tears, and the drawing fluttered to the hardwood floor.

"Aw, baby. Let's have some dinner."

"All by myself!"

"Come here, sweetie." Ellen reached for him but her hand hit the bag of Chinese food, knocking it to the floor and scattering the mail. She righted it before the food spilled, and her gaze fell on the white card with the photo of the missing boy.

Uncanny.

She picked up the bag of Chinese food and left the mail on the floor.

For the time being.

Chapter 2

Ellen put Will to bed, did a load of laundry, then grabbed a fork, napkin, and a cardboard container of leftover Chinese. She took a seat at the dining-room table, and the cat sat at the other end, his amber eyes trained on her food and his tail tucked around his chubby body. He was all black except for a white stripe down the center of his face and white paws like cartoon gloves, and Will had picked him because he looked so much like Figaro from the *Pinocchio* DVD. They couldn't decide whether to name him Figaro or Oreo, so they'd gone with Oreo Figaro.

Ellen opened the container, forked chicken curry onto her plate, then dumped out the leftover rice, which came out in a solid rectangle, like sand packed in a toy pail. She broke it up with her fork and caught sight of the Coffmans, her neighbors across the shared driveway, doing their homework at their dining-room table. The Coffman boys were tall and strong, both lacrosse players at Lower Merion, and Ellen wondered if Will would play a sport in high school. There had been a time when she couldn't imagine him healthy, much less wielding a lacrosse stick.

She ate a piece of chicken, gooey with bright yellow

curry, which was still warmish. It hit the spot, and she pulled over the mail, sorted out the bills, and set them aside. It wasn't the end of the month, so she didn't have to deal with them yet. She ate another bite and was about to daydream her way through the Tiffany catalog when her gaze fell on the white card. She paused in midbite and picked it up. HAVE YOU SEEN THIS CHILD? At the bottom it read, American Center for Missing and Abducted Children (ACMAC).

Ellen set her fork down and eyed the photo of the missing boy again. There was no blaming the lighting this time. Her dining room had a colonial brass candelabra that hung from the ceiling, and in its bright light, the boy in the photo looked even more like Will. It was a black-and-white photo, so she couldn't tell if they had the same eye color. She read the caption under the photo:

Name:	Timothy Braverman
Resides:	Miami, Florida
DOB:	1/19/05
Eyes:	Blue
Hair:	Blond
Stranger Abduction:	1/24/06 *

She blinked. They both had blue eyes and blond hair. They were even about the same age, three years old. Will had just turned three on January 30. She examined the photo, parsing the features of the missing boy. The similarity started with his eyes, which were a generous distance apart, and the shape, which was roundish. They both had small noses and shared a grin that was identically lopsided, turning down on the right side. Most of all, there was a likeness in their aspect, the steady, level way that they looked at the world.

Very weird, Ellen thought.

She reread the caption, noticed the asterisk, and checked the bottom of the card. It read "Timothy Braverman, Shown Age-Progressed to Three Years Old." She stumbled over the meaning of "age-progressed," then it registered. The picture of Timothy Braverman wasn't a current photo, though it looked like one. It was an approximation of how the boy would look right now, a projection done by computer or artist. The thought eased her, unaccountably, and she remembered the day she'd met Will.

She'd been doing a story on nurses in the pediatric cardiac intensive care unit at Dupont Hospital in Wilmington, and Will was in the CICU being treated for a ventricular septal defect, a hole in his septum. He lay at the end of the sunny unit, a tiny boy in a diaper, in an institutional crib with high white bars. He was undersized, failing to thrive, and it made his head a bobblehead doll's on a bony frame. His large blue eyes were his most prominent feature, and he took in everything around him, except people. He never made or held eye contact with anyone, which Ellen later learned could be a sign of neglect, and his was the only crib with no plush toys or colorful mobiles attached to the bars.

He was between heart operations when she first saw him—the first procedure was to patch the hole with a Dacron graft, and the second to repair the graft when one of the stitches came loose—and he lay silently, never crying or whimpering, surrounded by monitors that relayed his vital signs to the nurses in glowing red, green, and blue numbers. So many tubes led to him that he appeared to be tethered; an oxygen tube was taped in place under his nose, a feeding tube disappeared into a nostril, and a clear tube popped grotesquely from the center of his naked chest, emptying fluids into a plastic canister. His IV snaked to his hand, where it ended, adhesive-taped to a board and topped by half of a plastic cup, jury-rigged to make sure he didn't pull it free. Unlike the other babies, Will never tried.

Ellen kept doing research for the story and found herself visiting Will more frequently than necessary. The story became a series, and the angle changed from the nurses to the babies, among them, Will. But amid the cooing, gurgling, and crying babies, it was the silent one who held her attention. She wasn't allowed to approach his crib because of CICU regulations, but she would watch him from a short distance, though he always looked away at the blank white wall. Then one morning, his eyes found her, locking in and latching on, their blue as deep as the sea. They shifted away, but after that stayed on her longer and longer, connecting with her in a way she began to sense was heart to heart. Later, when everyone asked why she'd wanted to adopt him, she would answer:

It was the way he looked at me.

Will never had any visitors, and one of the mothers, who had a baby girl awaiting a heart transplant, told Ellen that his mother was a young girl, unwed, who hadn't even seen him after his first operation. Ellen followed up with his caseworker, who investigated and told her that adoption was a possibility, and she'd gone home that night, elated and unable to sleep. She'd been elated ever since, and in the past two years had come to realize that even though Will wasn't born to her, she was born to be his mother.

Her gaze fell again on the white card, and she set it aside, feeling a pang of sympathy for the Braverman family. She couldn't imagine how any parent lived through such an ordeal, or how she would cope if someone kidnapped Will. A few years ago, she'd done a piece in which a father had kidnapped his children after a custody dispute, and she toyed with the idea of calling the mother, Susan Sulaman, and doing a follow-up. She had to keep the story ideas coming if she wanted to keep her job, and it would give her an excuse to meet with her new editor, Marcelo Cardoso, a sexy Brazilian who'd come to the paper a year ago, having left behind the *L.A. Times* and a model girlfriend. Maybe a single mother would make a nice change, and if he'd seen enough of the fast lane, she could show him the checkout lane.

Ellen felt a smile spread across her face, which was embarrassing even though the only witness was a cat. She used to think she was too smart to crush on her boss, but Marcelo was Antonio Banderas with a journalism degree. And it had been too long since the man in her life was older than three. Her old boyfriend had told her she was a "handful," but Marcelo could handle a handful. And a handful was the only woman worth handling.

She scraped curry from a few chicken pieces and slid her plate over to Oreo Figaro, who ate with a loud purr, his tail bent at the tip like a crochet needle. She waited for him to finish, then cleaned up the table, put the bills in a wicker basket, and threw away the junk mail, including the white card with the missing children. It slid into the plastic kitchen bag, and the picture of Timothy Braverman stared at her with that preternatural gaze.

"*You're a dweller,*" she heard her mother say, as surely as if she'd been standing there. But Ellen believed that all women were dwellers. It came with the ovaries.

She closed the cabinet door and put the white card out of her mind. She loaded the dishwasher, pushed the Start button, and counted her blessings again. Butcher-block counters, white cabinets with glass fronts, and a hand-painted backsplash with painted wildflowers, matching walls of pinkish white. It was a girl kitchen, down to the name of the wall color—Cinderella. Though there was no Prince Charming in sight.

She performed her final chores, locking the back door

and retrieving the used coffee filter from the coffeemaker. She opened the base cabinet and started to throw the grinds away, but Timothy Braverman looked back at her, unsettling her all over again.

On impulse, she rescued the white card from the trash and slipped it into her jeans pocket.

Chapter 3

The alarm went off at six fifteen, and Ellen got out of bed in the dark, staggered in bare feet onto the cold tiles of the bathroom, and hit the shower, letting the hot water wake her. Even people who counted their blessings never counted them in the morning. For one thing, there wasn't time.

She finished dressing by seven so she could get Will up and dressed before preschool, which started at eight thirty. Connie would arrive at seven thirty to feed and take him, and Ellen would hand Will to her on the fly, like a domestic relay. Mothers ran this race every morning, and they deserved the gold medal in the most important event of all—life.

"Honey?" Ellen switched on the Babar lamp, but Will was sleeping soundly, his mouth partway open. His breathing sounded congested, and when she stroked his forehead, it felt hot to the touch. She told herself not to worry, but once you've had a sick kid, you hold your breath forever.

"Will?" she whispered, but was already wondering if she should send him to preschool. A crust had formed around his nostrils, and his cheek looked pale in the soft light from the lamp. His nose was a ski slope that was the beginner version of hers, and people often mistook him for her biological child, which she liked more than she should. She found herself wondering if Timothy Braverman looked like his mother, too.

She touched Will's arm, and when he didn't move, decided not to send him to school. Perspective was in order, and construction-paper snowflakes could wait another day. She didn't kiss him because she didn't want to wake him and instead patted Oreo Figaro, sleeping at the foot of the bed, curled into a Mallomar. She switched off the lamp, tiptoed from the bedroom, and went back to her room, to use the extra fifteen minutes.

"Don't you look nice!" Connie said with a smile, coming out of the dining room, and Ellen grinned as she tiptoed down the stairs. She had used the time to change into a tan corduroy jacket, nipped at the waist, and brown suede boots worn on top of her jeans. She had even done a better than usual job on her makeup, blown her hair dry, and put her liquid eyeliner back in rotation. She was going to see Marcelo this morning and wasn't sure if she wanted to look hot, employable, or both.

"Will's running a low fever, so I figured he'd stay home today."

"Good decision." Connie nodded. "It's twenty degrees out."

"Yikes." Ellen crossed to the closet and grabbed her black down jacket. "So stay inside, take it easy. Maybe you can read to him?"

"Will do." Connie set down her tote bag and slid out her newspaper, folded in half. "I loved your story today, about the old man who trains pigeons."

"Thanks." Ellen tugged her coat on and fought to get

into her sleeves. Maybe the cropped jacket had been a bad idea.

"The other sitters all read your articles, you know. I'm like a celebrity."

"Sell autographs," Ellen said, with a smile. She knew that the sitters were curious about her, the single reporter with the adopted kid. Like that song on *Sesame Street,* she was the thing not like the others.

"You'll be home regular time?"

"Yes. Thanks for everything." Ellen felt a familiar tug inside her chest. "I hate when I don't get to say good-bye to him. Give him a kiss for me, will you?"

"You know I will." Connie reached for the doorknob.

"Tell him I love him."

"Gotcha." Connie opened the door, and Ellen stepped reluctantly outside. A frigid wind bit her cheek, and the sky was a dull pewter. She wished she could run back inside, send Connie home, and take care of her own child, especially when he was sick. But the front door was already closing behind her, leaving her outside.

She didn't remember about Timothy Braverman until she got into work.

Chapter 4

Ellen entered the building with a lunch-truck coffee and flashed her laminated ID at the security guard. She wanted to hit the ground running on that follow-up story, but her thoughts kept returning to Timothy Braverman. She made her way through the dim hallways of the old building and finally popped out into the newsroom, an immense, bright rectangle that ran the length of a city block, its ceiling three stories high.

Sunlight filtered in from tall windows covered with old-fashioned blinds, and blue banners that read CITY, NA-TIONAL, BUSINESS, NEWS DESK, ONLINE, and COPY DESK hung over the various sections. She started down the aisle to her desk, but everyone was collecting in front of the glass-walled editorial offices that ringed the newsroom, gathering around Marcelo.

This can't be good.

She caught the eye of her friend Courtney Stedt, who detoured to meet her midway up the aisle. Courtney was her usual outdoorsy self in a forest green fleece with jeans, but her expression looked uncharacteristically grim. The office earth mother, Courtney was the one who got sheet cakes for everybody's birthdays. If she was worried, something was wrong.

"Please tell me this is a surprise party," Ellen said, and they fell into step.

"I can't. I have a journalist's respect for the truth."

They reached the back of the crowd, and staffers filled the aisles between the desks and borrowed each other's chairs. The crowd was collectively restless, with low talk and nervous laughter. Ellen leaned back against one of the desks next to Courtney, and thoughts of Timothy Braverman flew from her head. Unemployment had a way of focusing the brain, because of its direct connection to the mortgage lobe.

Marcelo motioned for order, and everyone quieted, a sea of heads turning to him. He was tall enough to be seen over everyone, with a lean frame, and his thick, dark hair curled unprofessionally over his collar, in a raggedy line. Strain showed in his dark brown eyes, and a fork creased his forehead. His eyebrows sloped down unhappily, and his pursed lips spoke volumes.

"First, good morning, friends," Marcelo said, his voice deep and soft, with a pronounced Portuguese inflection. "I'm sorry to surprise you first thing, but I have bad news. I'm sorry, but we have another round of layoffs to make."

Somebody cursed under his breath, and the crowd stiffened. Ellen and Courtney exchanged glances, but neither said anything. They didn't have to, which was the friends part.

"I have to make two cuts today and one more by the end of the month."

"Two, *today*?" someone repeated, echoing Ellen's thoughts. Her chest tightened. She needed this job. Someone else called out, "No chance of a buyout?"

"Not this time, sorry." Marcelo began rolling up his sleeves in a black shirt, European-cut, which he wore without a tie. "You know the reasons for the cuts. No newspaper has the readers it used to. We're doing everything we can here, with blogs and podcasts, and I know you guys are working very hard. None of this is your fault, or management's fault. We can't dance any faster than we are."

"True, that," someone murmured.

"So we have to deal with the reality of more cuts, and it's terrible, because I know you have families. You'll have to find another job. Relocate. Take kids out of schools, spouses from jobs. I know all that." Marcelo paused, his somber gaze moving from one stricken face to the next. "You know, when my mother used to spank me, she would always say, 'This hurts me more than it does you.' But, *sabia que nao era verdade.* Translated? I knew it was bullshit."

The staff laughed, and so did Ellen. She loved it when Marcelo spoke Portuguese. If he could fire her in Portuguese, she would be happy.

"So I'm not going to tell you it hurts me more than it hurts you. But I *will* tell you that I know how you feel, and I do." Marcelo's smile reappeared. "You all know, I've been laid off by some of the best papers in the world. Even by the *Folha de São Paulo,* my hometown paper."

"Way to go, boss," a page designer called out, and there was more laughter.

"But still I survived. I'll survive even if this paper lets me go, and I'll never quit the newspaper business, because I love it. I love this business. I love the feel of the paper." Marcelo rubbed his fingerpads together, with a defiant grin. "I love the smell of a good lead. I love finding out something nobody else knows and telling them. That's what we do, every day, on every page, and I know you love it, too."

"Hear, hear!" somebody called out, and even Ellen

took heart. She loved the business, too. She'd grown up with the newspaper on the kitchen table, folded into fourths for the crossword, next to her mother's coffee cup, and she still got a charge when she saw her own byline. She had never felt so right for any job in her life, except motherhood, where the pay was even worse.

"But this business doesn't love us back, all the time, and especially not lately." Marcelo shook his glistening head. "After all we do for her, after how much we love her, she's a faithless lover." He flashed a killer smile. "She goes home with other men. She's always looking around. She strays from us."

Everybody laughed, more relaxed now, including Ellen, who almost forgot she could lose her job.

"But we love her still, so we'll stay with her, as long as she'll have us. There will always be a place for the newspaper, and those of us, the crazy-in-love ones, we will put up with her."

"Speak for yourself!" cracked one of the business reporters, and everybody laughed, relaxing as Marcelo's expression changed, his forehead creasing again, so that he looked older than his forty-odd years.

"So I will make the hard decisions, and I have to cut two of you today, and another one at the end of the month. To those of you I have to let go, please know I won't hand you off to human resources and forget about you."

Somebody in front nodded, because they all had heard that he had helped place one of their laid-off business reporters at the *Seattle Times*.

"I think you're all terrific journalists, and I'll do everything in my power to help you find another job. I have friends all over, and you have my word."

"Thank you," a reporter said, and then another, and there was even a smattering of applause, led by Courtney. Ellen found herself clapping, too, because Marcelo reached her at a level she couldn't explain merely by good looks, though it helped. Maybe it was his openness, his honesty, his emotionality. No other editor would have talked about loving the business or taken the reporters' side. Marcelo's eyes swept the crowd, meeting hers for a brief moment, and Ellen got so flustered she barely felt the nudge in her side.

"Down, girl," Courtney whispered, with a sly smile.

Chapter 5

A ladies' room is a girl headquarters, so it was only natural that Ellen, Courtney, and another reporter, Sarah Liu, would end up talking about the layoffs by the sinks. A photographer had been let go after the meeting, so they were waiting for the other shoe to drop. Courtney and Sarah were in News, but Ellen was in Features, traditionally the most dispensable of reporters. She washed her hands, and the water felt hot, though it could have been her imagination.

"Marcelo won't fire anybody in Sports," Sarah said, and anxiety speeded up even her normally fast speech. She was slim and petite, with pretty eyes and a small, lipsticked mouth that never stopped moving. "I think it's going to be a reporter, either News or Features."

"One more to go today," Courtney said, and her Boston accent made it, *One ma ta go taday.* "I think it'll be News."

"No, it can't be. They need us." Sarah raked a hand through her glossy black hair, layered around her ears. Diamond studs twinkled from her earlobes, and she looked typically chic, in a tailored white shirt with black slacks and a skinny, ribbed black sweater. "They can't get it all off AP."

"That's why God invented Reuters." Courtney chuckled, without mirth.

Ellen reached for a paper towel and caught sight of herself in the mirror. Her lips flattened to a grim line, and she'd swear she had more crow's-feet than when she got up. Her extra makeup emphasized the hazel green of her eyes, but she felt like she'd dolled up for her own firing.

"You're just wrong, Courtney," Sarah was saying, and it reminded Ellen of why she'd always disliked her. Aggressiveness was an occupational hazard in journalism, and Sarah never knew when to turn it off. She said, "They need news reporters, with Iraq and the new administration."

"Why? It's not like we have somebody in the White House pressroom." Courtney shook her head. "And it's our turn, because they already cut in Features. Remember Suzanne?"

"She deserved it," Sarah said, and Ellen tossed away a paper towel, her stomach a clenched fist.

"Suzanne didn't deserve it. None of us deserves it."

"If it's News, it won't be me, it can't be." Sarah folded her arms. "I'm too well sourced in City Hall, and they know it."

"It'll be me," Courtney said, and Ellen turned to her, hating the sound of it.

"No, Court, they can't let you go."

"Yes, they can, and they will. Bet me." Courtney's gaze, devoid of eye makeup, looked resigned. "Look, it is what it is. My uncle used to set hot type with Linotype machines, and he and his friends lost their jobs when computers came in, in the seventies. The cuts that everybody went through in production have come to editorial, that's all." She shrugged. "I need a vacation, anyway."

"It won't be you." Ellen managed a smile, but she knew the truth. "It'll be me, and we all know it. Marcelo thinks Features is kitten-up-a-tree, so I'm outta here. At least I'll get canned by somebody hot."

"There's the upside." Courtney smiled. "I heard he made *Philadelphia* magazine's list of the most eligible bachelors."

Ellen rolled her eyes. "I can't believe they do those stupid lists."

"I can't believe they use the word 'bachelor.' "

Courtney and Ellen laughed, but Sarah was deep in thought, then she looked up.

"It's gonna be you, Courtney."

"Sarah!" Ellen frowned. "Don't sugarcoat it or anything."

"She said it herself," Sarah shot back.

"That's not the point." Ellen turned away, ashamed of her next thought. Courtney's husband owned three summer camps in Maine, and Sarah's was a thoracic surgeon. She was the only one who didn't have a husband, like a salaried safety net.

"El, you look kinda sick." Courtney eyed her. "You gonna barf?"

"No, Boston, I'm not gonna *bahf.*" Ellen shook her head. She was going to lose her job today, and that damn white card gnawed at the edge of her thoughts. "Look, let's calm down, okay? We'll know any minute which one of us is getting let go. It doesn't help to obsess."

Sarah turned to her. "Oh, get real. You know Marcelo will never let you go. He's hot for you."

"He is not." Ellen felt her face flush.

"He looks at you from his office, like you're the one

behind glass, like a fish in a bowl." Sarah's eyes flickered. "Like a little blond fishie."

"That's ridiculous," Ellen said, but Courtney placed a hand on her shoulder.

"El, here are my famous last words. You're single, he's single, and life is short. I say, go for it."

Suddenly there was a knock at the bathroom door.

And the three women looked over.

Chapter 6

Filling the newsroom were fifty-odd L-shaped desks furnished with computers, multiline phones, and atmospheric clutter, but only a few were occupied. Ellen had been at the paper long enough to remember when all the desks were full and the newsroom had the self-important hustle-bustle depicted on TV and the movies. There had been an electricity in the air then, from working at the epicenter of breaking news. Now the epicenter of breaking news had moved to the Internet, leaving too many of the desks vacant, now one more. Courtney's.

The room felt so much emptier to Ellen, even though she knew it wasn't possible. Mostly everybody had gone out on assignment, fleeing the scene of the crime. Sharon Potts in Business and Joey Stampone in Sports were at their desks, writing away and avoiding each other's eyes, stricken with survivor's guilt. Only Sarah chatted happily on her cell phone, the sound incongruous as laughter at a funeral.

Ellen set down her cold coffee and sat at the computer, checked her email, and opened her address book. She was supposed to be starting her follow-up story and looking for

Susan Sulaman's phone number, but she felt shaken. Courtney hadn't shed a tear when she'd packed her desk, which only made it harder, but they'd hugged and promised to stay in touch, even as they both knew they'd get too busy.

You're single, he's single, and life is short. I say, go for it.

Her thoughts circled back to Timothy Braverman, and she reached into her purse, slid out the white card, and looked at the photo in the middle. The likeness between Will and Timothy struck her again as unmistakable, even for an age-progressed depiction. The bottom of the card read ACMAC, and she Googled it, then clicked through. American Center for Missing and Abducted Children, read the screen, and Ellen skimmed "About Us." ACMAC was a national organization to recover abducted children and runaways, and the page listed Amber Alerts.

She found the search button, typed in Timothy Braverman, and pressed Enter. The screen changed.

And Ellen almost gasped.

Chapter 7

On the screen was a color photo of Timothy Braverman as a baby, and his features were identical to Will's, especially the eyes. Timothy had blue eyes, a shade she had never seen in anyone's eyes but Will's.

My God.

She read the webpage. The top said, **Timothy Braverman**, and underneath were two photos, side by side. On the right was the black-and-white thumbnail, the age-progressed picture from the white card, but on the left was the color baby photo of Timothy that had made Ellen gasp.

Timothy at one year old, read its caption. The photo had been cropped, a close-up of the baby's face in excellent focus, and it was taken outdoors in front of a lush green hedge. Timothy's blond hair caught the light, his highlights ablaze in the sun, and he grinned broadly, with his mouth turned down on the right, showing only two front teeth. Ellen had seen that very same grin on Will, after he'd finally gotten healthy.

She studied the screen, wondering what Will looked like when he was that little. She hadn't met him until he was a year and a half old, and the shape of his face then had been more elongated than Timothy's, due to his illness. He had been paler, his skin thin and curiously aged. Timothy had the exact same face, only healthier, his cheeks a rosy hue under a cheery layer of baby fat.

Ellen read on, avoiding a creeping sense of unease. The page said, **For further information, please see www .HelpUsFindTimothyBraverman.com.** She clicked on the link. The screen changed, and the top of the page read: Help Us Find Our Beloved Son, Timothy Braverman. It was a homemade website with Thomas the Tank Engine chugging around the perimeter. Her heart fluttered, then she dismissed it. It didn't mean anything that Will loved Thomas the Tank Engine, too. All little boys did, probably.

She scanned the webpage. It showed the same baby picture as the ACMAC site, but the photo hadn't been cropped, and she could see the whole picture. Timothy was dressed in a blue Lacoste shirt and jeans, and his legs stuck out straight in front of him, his feet in new white Nikes, their bottoms clean. His pudgy fingers grasped an oversized set of Fisher-Price plastic keys, and he was sitting very straight in his navy blue stroller. Will used to sit that way too, remarkably erect, as if he didn't want to miss anything.

Ellen reached for her coffee, then set it down without taking a sip. It was so damn eerie, like seeing Will's double. Was it possible that he had a twin somewhere? A brother she hadn't been told about? Those things happened, at least according to Oprah.

She clicked the link for the next page. There were more photos of Timothy as a baby; nine in all, a chronological progression from birth to his first birthday. She scanned the photos of Timothy as an infant, swaddled in a white receiving blanket, then flopped on his tummy, next propping himself up on soft arms, and finally ensconced in a bucket car seat. She had never seen Will as an infant, so she had no idea how he'd looked, but at about ten months old, Timothy began to look exactly like Will. She read the text below the photos:

> We, Carol and Bill Braverman, will be eternally grateful to anyone who can help us find our son, Timothy Alan Braverman. Timothy was kidnapped by a Caucasian male, about thirty years old, approximately five-foot-ten and 170 pounds. The man stopped the Mercedes driven by Carol, pretending to be a motorist in distress. He pulled a gun on Carol, carjacked the Mercedes, and shot and killed Timothy's nanny, Cora Elizondo, when she began screaming. He drove away, with Timothy still in the car seat. The suspect called with a ransom demand, which we paid in full, but Timothy was never returned. For a composite drawing of the suspect, see below.

Ellen shuddered. The wrong place at the wrong time; a car driven away with a baby inside. It was every parent's nightmare. Guns, screaming, murder, and in the end, a kidnapped child. She looked at the composite drawing, sketched with simple pencil lines and only slight shading. The suspect had a thin face with narrow eyes, a long nose, and high cheekbones, like your average scary guy. She continued reading:

> Carol Braverman says: "In the year God shared Timothy with us, we came to know him as a loving, happy, joyful little boy who adores Thomas the

Tank Engine, his cocker spaniel Pete, and lime Jell-O. As his mother, I will never stop looking for him and won't rest until he is back home."

Ellen would have felt exactly the same way, if it had happened to her. She never would have given up on finding Will. She returned to the webpage:

The kidnapper is currently wanted by federal and state authorities. The Braverman family has posted a reward of $1,000,000, payable to anyone who has information that leads to finding Timothy. Please do not call with false leads or pranks, or you will be prosecuted to the fullest extent.

Ellen's heart went out to the Bravermans, maybe because of the similarity between the boys. A million bucks was a huge amount for a reward, so the family must have been wealthy, but all the money in the world hadn't kept them safe from harm. She clicked back to the first page of the website and looked again at the baby photo of Timothy. On impulse, she scrolled over the picture and hit the Print button.

"Hey, girlfriend," said a voice at her shoulder, and Ellen reflexively clicked the mouse, so her screensaver of Will popped back onto the monitor. Standing next to the desk was Sarah Liu, who shot her a quick smile. "How you doing?"

"Fine."

"What's up?"

"Nothing, why?"

"You don't look good. Courtney was right. You sick or something?"

"Nah." Ellen felt unaccountably nervous. The photo of

Timothy edged in noisy increments from the printer on her desk. "I just feel bad about Courtney."

"She'll be fine. She knew it was coming."

"No, she didn't." Ellen frowned.

"She said as much in the bathroom."

"But she didn't mean it. And still, it's a shock when it happens."

Sarah lifted an eyebrow. "She was the obvious choice. She wasn't sourced that well, and her writing wasn't as good as yours or mine."

"That's not true," Ellen shot back, hurt for Courtney, even in absentia. Meanwhile, the photo of Timothy slid from the printer tray, showing a rectangle of clear blue sky.

"What are you working on, anyway?"

"Research." Ellen was a bad liar, so she asked, "How about you?"

"An embezzlement piece, if Marcelo okays it." Sarah wiggled some papers in her hand. "The police commissioner just agreed to meet with me. An exclusive, which he never gives. So, what are you researching?"

"A follow-up on an old abduction story." Ellen wondered why she kept lying. She could have just told the truth. *Funny, I just saw a picture of a kid who looks exactly like Will.* But something told her to keep it to herself.

"What abduction story?"

"Sulaman, a family abduction I did a while ago."

"Oh, right, I remember. It was so *you*." Sarah snorted, and Ellen hid her annoyance.

"What do you mean?"

"It was heartfelt. Unlike me, you can pull it off."

"You can do heartfelt," Ellen said, though she wasn't so sure. The photo of Timothy had almost finished printing, and suddenly she wanted Sarah gone. "Sorry, but I have to get back to work."

"Me, too." Sarah's gaze fell on the printer just as the photo shot out, and she plucked it from the tray. "Aha! You're not working."

Ellen's mouth went dry as Sarah scanned the photo of Timothy.

"You took more baby pictures than anybody I know."

"Guilty." Ellen didn't know what else to say. Obviously, Sarah had mistaken Timothy for Will.

"See you later." Sarah handed her the photo and took off, and Ellen bent down and slid it into her purse.

Then she picked up the phone to call Susan Sulaman.

Chapter 8

Fifteen minutes later, Ellen had hung up the phone, and Marcelo was motioning to her from his office doorway.

"May I see you for a minute?" he called out, and she nodded, seeing through his glass wall that Sarah was still sitting in one of the chairs across from his desk.

"Sure." She rose and walked to his office, which was lined with colorful photographs that he had taken in his native São Paulo. One was a series of exotic stone arches in warm gold and tan hues, and another of weathered doors painted germanium red, vivid orange, and chrome yellow, with a pot of magenta petunias on one threshold. Ellen realized she had a crush on Marcelo's office, too.

"Please, take a seat." He gestured her into a chair, and Sarah smiled quickly at her. He took his seat behind his desk, uncluttered except for stacked screen shots beside his laptop and a pencils-and-pens mug with a soccer ball on it that read *Palmeiras*. He sighed. "First let me say, I know it's hard on you both, losing Courtney. If I could have avoided it, I would have. Now, Sarah just told me a great story idea." Marcelo brightened, nodding at Sarah. "You wish to explain or shall I?"

"You can."

"Fine." Marcelo faced Ellen directly. "We all know that Philly's homicide rate is among the highest in the country, we cover some angle of it every day. Sarah's idea is that we do a major think piece on the issue, not treat it as episodic news. Sarah, this is where your editor steals your idea." Marcelo flashed Sarah a grin, and she laughed.

Ellen, confused, couldn't even fake a smile. Sarah had told her she was going to Marcelo with an embezzlement piece, but that wasn't true. She had gone to him with a think piece, which was a much bigger deal. With one lay-off to go at the end of the month, Sarah was making damn sure it wasn't her.

Marcelo continued, "We need to explain why this is happening here, as opposed to other big cities in the States. What's more important? It's life or death."

"Exactly," Sarah said, and Ellen felt a half step behind, like a middle schooler during a pop quiz.

Marcelo nodded. "I see this as a cause-and-effects story. A thoughtful, in-depth examination. I will assign Larry and Sal to analyze the causes. Talk to social scientists and historians."

Ellen blinked. Larry Goodman and Sal Natane were the A-team, finalists for the Pulitzer for their investigative series on municipal bonds. All of a sudden, she was playing in the hard-news bigs.

"I'd like to get you two started on the effects, and it has to be good, new work. Sarah, I want you to look at the effects from the perspective of costs. How much does violent crime cost the city in law enforcement, cop and court time, lawyer time? How about in tourism, lost business, and prestige, if you can quantify that. Crunch the numbers, as they say, but make it understandable."

"Will do." Sarah took notes, her glossy head down.

"Ellen." Marcelo turned to her again, and she guessed that if he had a crush on her, either he hid it well or the murder rate had killed the mood. "I want you to put a human face on it. The homicide rate has to be more than a number. Don't be politically correct about it. We can't fix it if we don't tell the truth."

Sarah interjected, "I have good stats on the race issue, and that's the part I already wrote. Maybe I should take that angle, too."

Marcelo dismissed her with a wave. "No, please give your notes to Ellen. As far as deadlines, today is Tuesday. Let's talk on Friday, before the weekend. Can you both do that?"

"No problem," Sarah answered, then rose, papers in hand.

"Okay by me." Ellen may not have studied for the quiz, but she was a fast learner. "By the way, can I ask you about another story?"

"Sure. Go ahead." Marcelo leaned back in his chair, and Ellen became aware that Sarah was lingering behind her in the threshold. Marcelo seemed to read her mind because he raised his gaze. "Thank you very much, Sarah. You don't have to stay around."

"Thanks," Sarah said, and left.

"Okay, what is it?" Marcelo asked, his voice almost imperceptibly gentler, and Ellen wondered if he really did like her.

"I did a story once on the Sulaman family, a wife whose kids were taken by her ex-husband. I just got off the phone with Susan and I'd like to do a follow-up."

"Why? Did she get the children back?"

"No, not yet."

"Then what happened?"

"They're still gone, and I thought it would be interest-ing to let Susan tell us how it feels, as a mother."

Marcelo frowned, with sympathy. "It feels horrible, I assume."

"Right."

"Well." Marcelo opened his palms on the desk. "A mother who grieves the loss of her children, still. It's ter-rible for her, but there's no story there."

"It's more than that." Ellen couldn't explain the pull of the story, but then again, she never could with any of her stories. She sensed that the idea was connected to the Braverman baby, but she wasn't about to tell that to Mar-celo. "Why don't I go see Susan, then write it up and see what you think? It might pay off."

"I don't understand you." Marcelo shifted forward on his chair, an incredulous smile playing around his lips. "I just asked you to make our readers feel the tragedy of murder. Isn't that enough to keep you busy, Ellen?"

She laughed. Humor was as strong an aphrodisiac as power, and the man had both. Also that accent, with the soft esses like a whisper in her ear.

Marcelo leaned further forward. "I know you're feel-ing unhappy about me today."

"What do you mean, unhappy?"

"Sarah told me you were no longer a fan of mine, be-cause I let Courtney go. I made the best decision I could." Marcelo's expression darkened. "Please, try to under-stand that."

"I do understand." Ellen didn't get it. Why would Sarah tell him such a thing? Time to change the subject. "So what do you say, about the Sulamans? Gimme a chance?"

"No. Sorry."

"Okay." Ellen rose, hiding her disappointment. It

wouldn't do to give him a hard time. She had to get out of the office before she got herself fired.

"Good luck with the homicide piece."

"Thanks," Ellen said, leaving to talk to Sarah.

She felt a catfight coming on.

Chapter 9

Sarah's desk was empty, and her coat wasn't on the hook, so Ellen went to the desk nearest hers, where Meredith Snader was on her computer, her short gray hair barely visible above the monitor.

"Meredith, excuse me, have you seen Sarah?"

Meredith looked up over her tortoiseshell glasses, though her eyes remained vague, her thoughts with whatever she'd been writing. "She left."

"Where to, did she say?"

"No, sorry." Meredith focused on Ellen belatedly, her gaze sharpening like a camera lens. "So how are you, now that Courtney is no longer?"

"Sad. How about you?"

"Terrible." Meredith *tsk-tsk*ed like everybody's favorite aunt. "You know, they say war is hell, but I've been in a war and I've been in a newsroom. To me, you pick your poison."

Ellen smiled, grimly. Meredith had been a nurse in Vietnam, but she rarely mentioned it. "You have nothing to worry about. You're an institution around here."

"I hate it when people call me that. Institutions close at three o'clock." Meredith mock-shuddered.

"They'll never cut you, ever."

"Brings me no joy. I feel like you do, that cutting one of us cuts us all. Courtney was a real sweetheart and a helluva reporter." Meredith shook her head. "I heard how upset you are."

"What do you mean?"

"Sarah said you took it hard."

Ellen could barely hide her pique, and Meredith leaned over her keyboard, lowering her voice.

"She also mentioned that you blame Arthur. By the way, so do I. It's corporate greed of the highest order."

Ellen stiffened. Arthur Jaggisoon and his family owned the newspaper, and it was career suicide to bad-mouth him. In truth, she didn't blame him for the layoffs at all. "She said that?"

"Yes." Meredith's phone rang, and she turned away. "Pardon me, I've been waiting for this call."

"Sure." Ellen went back to her desk, glancing around the newsroom. Sharon and Joey, on the phone, looked pointedly away, and she wondered if Sarah had been talking to them, too.

Ellen's face burned as she sat down in her chair. Marcelo's back was to her, so there were no more eye games, and she wasn't in the mood anyway. On top of her computer keyboard sat a messy stack of printed notes with Sarah's name at the top.

Ellen picked up the pages and thumbed through them, and they included a draft, research, and stats. She wanted to confront Sarah, but didn't know her cell phone number. She reached for her coffee and took a cold sip. Her distracted gaze met Will's on her screensaver, but his face morphed into Timothy Braverman's.

She had to get her head back in the game. She rose, grabbed her purse, and got her coat.

Chapter 10

Ellen sat in a lovely family room that had everything but the family. Susan Sulaman sipped water from a tumbler, curled up in a matching chintz couch opposite her, in jeans, a pink crew neck, and bare feet, a remarkably down-to-earth woman who looked oddly out of place in her own home. An Oriental rug covered a floor of resawn oak, and the couches faced each other in front of a colonial-era fireplace that had authentic cast-iron hooks and a swinging iron bracket inside. A perfect circle of cherrywood table held the latest magazines, a stack of oversized art books, and a tape recorder, running, now that the small talk was over.

"So you've heard nothing about the children at all?" Ellen asked.

"Nothing," Susan answered quietly, raking fingers through thick brown hair that curved softly to her chin. Her pretty eyes were brown, but her crow's-feet went deeper than they should for her age. Two lines had been etched in her forehead, over the bridge of a perfect nose. Susan Thoma Sulaman had been Miss Allegheny County when she became the trophy wife of her worst nightmare, multimillionaire builder Sam Sulaman.

"What have you done to find them?" Ellen asked.

"What haven't I done?" Susan smiled weakly, a fleeting glimpse of a dazzling grin. "I hound the police and the FBI. I hired three private investigators. I posted on the missing kids sites on the web."

"Like the ACMAC site?" Ellen was thinking of the white card.

"Of course, that's the main one. Nobody's turned up anything, scam artists, but no leads. I offered a fifty-thousand-dollar reward. Real money."

"Sure is." Ellen thought of the Bravermans and the million-dollar reward.

"I'll never forget the day he took them. It was October, a week before Halloween. Lynnie was going as a fish." Susan's smile reappeared. "We glued glitter to a piece of blue oak tag, and she was going to wear it like a sandwich board. It was from *The Rainbow Fish*."

"I know the book."

Susan's eyes lit up. "Oh, right, you have a son now. How old is he?"

"Three."

"Goodness, already?"

"I know, right?" Ellen didn't have to say, *time flies,* though it was her favorite mommy conversation. Some things never got old.

"I read that. I loved the articles you wrote about his sickness."

"Thank you. Anyway, you were saying."

"Yes, well, Sam Junior was going as a turtle. He had this chicken-wire shell we made"—Susan stopped herself—"well, never mind about the costume. My ex picked the kids up, loaded them in the car, and I never saw them again."

"I'm so sorry." Ellen lost her bearings, momentarily. Now that she'd become a mother, it was even harder to imagine. Maybe her mind simply refused to go there. "Does it get easier with time?"

"No, it gets harder."

"How so?"

"I think about all that I'm missing with them. All that time, with each of them. Then I start to think that, even when I get them back, I'll never be able to catch up." Susan paused, a stillness coming over her. "I worry they won't remember me. That I'll be a stranger to them."

"Of course they'll remember you," Ellen rushed to say, then switched tacks. "Is it easier because at least you know they're with their father? That they're not abducted by some stranger, who could be doing them harm?" She was thinking of the Bravermans again.

"Honestly, no." Susan frowned. "Sam was a terrible father. He lost the custody battle and he didn't like the settlement, so this is the way he got me back. At the end of the day, they need me. I'm their mother."

"So you're hopeful."

"I am, I have to be. The FBI thinks like you do, that it's less of a priority because it's family. Not all victims are alike." Susan pursed her lips. "Anyway, the theory is that he took them out of the country. His money is all off-shore, and they think he told the kids I died."

"Would he do that?" Ellen asked, aghast.

"Of course, he's an egomaniac, a narcissist." Susan sipped her soda, and ice rattled in the tumbler. "I don't agree with the FBI, and if I tell you what I think, it'll sound crazy."

"No, it won't, and honestly, I don't even know if this will run. It depends on my editor."

Susan frowned. "Any press at all could help find them. You never know."

"I'll try my best. Please, go on."

Susan shifted forward on the cushion. "I believe my

kids are in the country, nearby even. Maybe not in Philly, but in Jersey or Delaware. Near here. I think it because I feel them, inside. I feel my children, close to me." Certainty strengthened Susan's voice. "When they were babies, if someone took them out of my sight, I felt nervous. When we were in the same room, I knew it. I *feel* them here, still." Susan put a hand to her heart. "I carried them, they were *inside* me. I think it's a mother's instinct."

Ellen reddened. Was there such a thing? Could she have it if she had never been pregnant? Evidently, not everything came with the ovaries.

"I've posted their photos everywhere. I had somebody design a website and made sure it comes up first if they ever search their own name. I go on the Internet all the time, checking out all the sites where they might go, even the gamers' sites, because Sammy loved Nintendo."

Ellen watched Susan, who slumped in the soft couch as she continued.

"I drive around the neighborhoods, the schools. I check out the Gymboree for Lynnie and the T-ball leagues for Sammy. In summer, I troll the beaches in Holgate and Rehoboth. Sooner or later, I'll spot one of them, I just know it." Susan needed no encouragement to keep speaking, her words flowing from a pain, deep inside. "There's not a minivan that goes by that I don't look in the backseat, not a ball field I don't look on the bench and the bases. I stop by pet stores because Lynnie liked kittens. If a school bus passes, I look in the windows. I drive around and call the kids' names at night. Last week I was in Caldwell, in New Jersey, calling them, and a woman asked me what kind of dog Lynnie was."

Susan stopped talking abruptly, and a sudden silence fell.

And Ellen understood firsthand that after the loss of a child, a mother would be haunted for the rest of her life.

Chapter 11

Back in her car, Ellen stopped at a traffic light, dwelling. She'd had a glimpse of Susan Sulaman's world, and it made her want to drive home and hug Will. Her Black-Berry rang in her purse, and she rooted in her bag until she found it, then hit the green button.

"Elly Belly?" said the familiar voice.

"Dad. How are you?"

"Fine."

"What's the matter?" Ellen could tell he was upset by the way he said he was fine.

"Nothing. I'm about to have lunch. You free? I just got back from the doctor's."

"Are you sick?"

"Nah."

"Then why'd you go to the doctor?"

"A checkup, is all."

"You had a checkup in September, didn't you?" Ellen remembered because it was near her birthday.

"This was just a thing, a routine thing."

Ellen glanced at the car's clock, then did a quick calculation. Her father lived in West Chester, forty-five minutes from the city. Being closer to her parents was the reason she had come here from the *San Jose Mercury.* "Are you home today?"

"Yeah, doing email and expenses."

"Why don't I drop by? I'm actually in Ardmore."

"Great. The door's open. Love you."

"Love you, too." Ellen hung up, then slid the phone back in her purse. She cruised to the corner in light traffic, turned around, and headed back down Lancaster Avenue. She felt a pang of guilt, realizing she hadn't been to visit her father in almost a month. She just hadn't had the time, between work and Will. Every week, she mentally shifted the hours of her days, as if her life were a handheld puzzle with tiles that slid around to make a picture. The tiles fit differently every week, and no matter how hard she tried, the picture didn't come together. The lines connected to nothing.

She accelerated.

Chapter 12

"Hi, Dad." Ellen entered her father's kitchen, which overlooked the golf course at Green Manor, which billed itself as a Community for Active Adults. Her father had moved here after her mother died, which was when he got Active, especially in the Adult Department.

"Hi, sweetheart," he said, standing at the counter, absorbed in slicing a tomato onto a plate. His wrinkled forehead knit over his brown eyes, set close together and hooded now, and his nose had a telltale bulb at the tip from the drinking he'd given up, years ago. Even at sixty-eight, her father had enough black in his thinning hair to make people wonder if he colored it, and Ellen was pretty sure he didn't.

"Dad, are you gonna die?" she asked, only half-joking.

"No, never." Her father turned with a broad smile that served him well on the back nine and the road, where he drove a thousand miles a week as a sales rep for an auto-parts company.

"Good." Ellen slid out of her coat and purse, dumped them on a kitchen chair, and kissed him on the cheek, catching a whiff of strong aftershave. None of her perfume lasted as long as her father's aftershave. She fleetingly considered picking up a bottle of Aramis.

"You look nice, honey. Dressed up."

"I'm trying not to get fired."

"Succeeding?" Her father sliced another pink-red tomato. Already on the table sat a plastic tub of Whole Foods tuna fish, a loaf of multigrain bread, and a pitcher of green tea, permanent fixtures in Don Gleeson's Antioxidant Heaven.

"So far." Ellen crossed to the counter, plucked a floppy tomato slice from the plate, and plopped it into her mouth. It tasted like nothing, a winter tomato.

"Don't let the bastards get you down. How's my grandson?"

"He has a cold."

"I miss him. When am I gonna see him?"

Ellen felt a guilty twinge. "Soon as I can. So, what's up with the doctor? You're scaring me."

"I waited lunch for you."

"I see that, thanks. You're avoiding the question."

"Sit down like a civilized person." Her father carried the tomato plate to the table and set it down, then eased into the chair with a theatrical groan. He always moaned for comic effect, though he kept in great shape, fit and trim in his pale yellow polo shirt, Dockers, and loafers.

"Dad, tell me." Ellen sat next to him, worried. Cancer was the worst sort of coward, sneaking up on people, and her mother had died from lymphoma, having lived only three months after her diagnosis.

"I'm not sick, not at all." He untwisted the tie on the plastic bag of bread, extracted two slices from the center of the loaf, and set them on his plate, open-faced.

"Then why did you go to the doctor?"

"Make yourself a sandwich, then we'll talk."

"Dad, please."

"Suit yourself, but I'm hungry." Her father popped the plastic lid of the tuna, then picked up the serving fork, speared himself a small mound, and patted it onto his bread with the tines of the fork, making crosshatches.

"You're stalling, Dad. It's tuna fish, not rocket science."

"Okay, here it is. I'm getting married."

"What?" Ellen was dumbfounded. "To who?" She had no idea. He was dating four women here. He was Romeo, with an enlarged prostate.

"Barbara Levin."

Ellen didn't know what to say. She didn't even know the woman. Her parents had been married forty-five years, and her mother had passed a little over two years ago. Somehow this meant her mother was really gone. As if someone had put a period on the sentence that was her life.

"El? I'm not dying, I'm getting married."

"Why, is she pregnant?"

"Ha!" Her father laughed, then stabbed the tuna with the serving fork. "I'll tell her you said that."

Ellen hid her ambivalence. "This is kind of a surprise."

"A good one, right?"

"Well, yes. Sure." Ellen tried to get a grip, but a hard knot in her chest told her she wasn't doing such a great job. "I guess I just wasn't sure who the lucky lady was."

"Barbara's the one that matters." He picked up a tomato slice with the serving fork. "You gonna congratulate me?"

"Congratulations."

"I needed a cholesterol check. That's why I went to the doctor's."

"Oh. Thank God you're not sick."

"You got that right." Her father placed his tomato on top of the tuna, added a piece of bread, then lined up the two pieces, leaning over as if he were sizing up a putt. He pressed his sandwich closed, lowering his hand, then eyed her. "You don't look happy, El."

"I am." Ellen managed a smile. She loved her father, but he had spent her childhood on the road. The truth was, everybody had a go-to parent, and with him away from home so much, Ellen's had become her mother.

"El, I'm entitled to be happy."

"I didn't say you weren't."

"You're acting it."

"Dad, please."

"I don't like to be alone and I'm not getting any younger."

Silence fell between them, and Ellen made no move to fill it. The ugliest of thoughts popped into her head—the wrong one had died. She felt ashamed of the very notion, and confused. She loved her father.

"I guess I knew you'd get upset. You and your mother were two of a kind. Peas in a pod."

Ellen couldn't speak for a moment. Her mother had been her best friend in the world. That said it all.

"Life goes on."

Ellen felt the knot again, then flipped her thinking. "So when's the wedding? I need to get a dress and all."

"Uh, it's in Italy."

"Italy? Why?"

"Barbara likes it there, near Positano." Her father cut his sandwich and took a bite, leaving Ellen to fill in the blanks.

"Am I going? Is Will?"

"Sorry, but no." Her father looked back at her over his sandwich. "It's not a big deal, not at our age. We're just doing it, no muss, no fuss. We're getting on a plane end of the week."

"Wow, that soon?"

"I told her you'd be fine with it. Her kid's fine with it."

"I understand." Ellen tried to shrug it off. "I'm officially fine with it."

"She has a daughter, too. Year older than you. Abigail."

"I thought she had a boy in the Peace Corps."

"That was Janet."

"Oh." Ellen smiled. It *was* kind of funny. "Well, good. I always wanted a sister. Can I have a pony, too?"

At that, he smiled, chewing.

"What does she do, my new sister?"

"Lawyer in D.C."

"I always wanted a lawyer, too." Ellen laughed, and so did he, setting down his sandwich.

"Ha! That's enough, wise guy."

"I think it's good, I really do." Ellen felt better saying it, and her chest knot loosened just a bit. "Be happy, Dad."

"I love you, kitten."

"I love you, too." Ellen managed a smile.

"You gonna eat or what?"

"No, I'm waiting for the wedding cake."

He rolled his eyes.

"So tell me what she looks like."

"Here, I'll show you." Her father leaned over, slid a brown wallet from his back pocket, and opened it up. He flipped past the second plastic envelope, which had an old photo of Will, and the third, he turned sideways and set down on the table. "That's Barbara."

Ellen eyed the woman, who was attractive, with her hair in a short, classy cut. "Mommy!"

"Gimme that." Her father smiled and took the wallet back.

"She looks nice. Is she nice?"

"Of course she's nice." He leaned over to put the wallet into his back pocket. "What do you think? She's a jerk, that's why I'm marrying her?"

"Are you going to move in with her, or is she moving in here?"

"I'm selling the house and moving in with her. She's got a corner unit with a deck."

"You gold digger, you."

He smiled again, then leaned back in his chair, regarding her for a moment. "You know, you gotta move on, kid."

Ellen felt the knot again. Time to change the subject. "I interviewed this woman whose husband kidnapped her children. Susan Sulaman, if you remember the story I did."

He shook his head, no, and Ellen let it go. Her mother would have remembered the story. She'd kept scrapbooks of Ellen's clippings, starting with the college newspaper and ending three weeks before she died.

"Anyway, Susan thinks there's an instinct that mothers have about their children."

"Your mother had that in spades." Her father beamed. "Look how good you turned out, all because of her."

"Hold on, let me show you something." Ellen got up, opened her purse, and extracted the photo of Timothy Braverman as a baby, then handed it to her father. "How cute is this baby?"

"Cute."

"Do you know who he is?"

"What am I, stupid? It's Will."

Ellen stood over him as if suspended, not knowing whether to tell him. He and Sarah had both mistaken Timothy for Will. She felt funny about it, and not good funny. It made her uncomfortable. She realized now why she was missing her mother so much. She could have told her mother about Timothy Braverman. Her mother would have known what to do.

"He's grown up a lot since then, hasn't he?" her father asked, holding up the photo with unmistakable pride.

"How so? I mean, what differences do you see?"

"The forehead." He circled the area with an index finger knotted from arthritis. "His forehead got a lot bigger, and his cheeks, they're full now." He handed her back the photo. "He just grew into his face."

"He sure did." Ellen lied more easily than she thought, for a bad liar. She folded the paper, put it back inside her purse, and sat down, but her father was looking reflective, pouring them a glass of tea.

"You were like that, too, just like that. When you were little, your face was so wide. I used to say you looked like a salad plate. Will's the same way. He gets it from you."

"Dad, he's adopted, remember?"

"Oh, right." Her father laughed. "You're such a good mother, I always think you're his real mother."

Ellen let that go, too. She usually felt like Will's real mother, until someone told her she wasn't. But she knew what he meant.

"You got that mother instinct from your mother. You're every inch her daughter. That he's adopted, it doesn't matter. That's why we keep forgetting. It's like proof."

"Maybe you're right." Ellen nodded, oddly grateful.

But then again, Don Gleeson could sell anybody anything.

Chapter 13

Ellen finally got home and closed the front door behind her. "How is he?" she asked Connie, keeping her voice low.

"Hanging in. I gave him Tylenol at two." Connie checked her watch. "He's been asleep since four."

"Did he eat?" Ellen shed her coat and hung it in the closet as Connie reached for hers, the domestic changing of the guard.

"Chicken soup and crackers. Flat ginger ale. We took it easy today. All he wanted to do was stay in bed." Connie slipped into her coat. "I read to him after lunch until he got sleepy."

"Thanks so much."

"Don't know how much he heard of it, though. He was just lying there." Connie zipped up her coat and picked up her tote bag, which was already packed.

"Poor thing."

"Give him a kiss for me." Connie got her purse, and Ellen opened the door, said her good-byes, then shut the door and locked it, preoccupied. If Will had just gone to sleep, she had a window of time to do something that had been bugging her on the ride home. She kicked off her boots and hurried upstairs.

Half an hour later, she was sitting cross-legged on her bed, bent over her task. A blown-glass lamp cast an ellipse of light on two photos of Timothy Braverman, the age-progressed picture from the white card and the computer printout of his baby photo from ACMAC.com. Next to those were a pile of ten photos of Will, chosen because they showed his features the best. Oreo Figaro sat beside her like the Sphinx, keeping his own counsel.

Ellen arranged Will's photos in two rows of five, in chronological order. The top row was a younger Will, the first year she had him, at age one-and-a-half to two-and-a-half. The bottom row was the second year she'd had him, ages two-and-a-half to present. She looked at them all, examining his face over time, from its thinnest and least healthy to a beaming little boy. It was like watching a sunflower open and thrive, turning to the sun.

She returned to the top row of photos and picked the youngest one that was the most representative of Will's features. It showed him at about one-and-a-half years old, in a flannel shirt and overalls, sitting next to an oversized pumpkin at Halloween. Suddenly, Susan Sulaman broke through Ellen's consciousness.

It was October, a week before Halloween. Lynnie was going as a fish.

She shook it off, staying the course. She picked up the Halloween photo of Will and held it next to the photo of Timothy, taken at about a year old. He was also sitting, but in his stroller, and when Ellen put the photos side by side, she felt an undeniable jolt.

Their faces looked so much alike as babies that they could have been identical twins. Their blue eyes were the same shape, size, and hue, their noses carbon copies, and their mouths plastered with the same goofy smile, in which the right corner turned down. Both boys were sitting in the exact same way; oddly upright for such young children. No wonder Sarah and her father had mistaken them. She held the photos closer to the lamp, and it spooked her. She shook her head in disbelief, yet couldn't deny what she was seeing.

She set the photos down and went to the second row, of older photos of Will. She picked one of the most recent, in which Will was sitting on their front porch on the first day of preschool, wearing a new green T-shirt, green shorts, and green socks. It was an unfortunate choice for a favorite color, unless you were a leprechaun.

She picked up the age-progressed photo of Timothy and held it next to the photo of Will. They were almost dead ringers, even though the photo of Timothy was only black-and-white. Their eyes were the same shape, round and wide set. The smiles were similar, though she couldn't see all of Timothy's teeth and she knew Will's were perfect. The only slight difference was their hair, because Timothy's was described as blond, and Will's was dark blond. There was a likeness, too, in the configuration of their features, and again, their very aspect.

Ellen set the photos down, but she had one more thing she wanted to try. She picked up the baby photo of Timothy and held it next to the older photo of Will, starting preschool. She eyeballed them, and it was almost as if Timothy got older and turned into Will. Eyes, nose, mouth; all were the same, but bigger, older, more mature. Ellen felt her stomach tense.

Then she got another idea. She set down the photos, then picked up the older photo of Will going to preschool and the baby photo of Timothy in the stroller. She compared them, and before her eyes, Will regressed back into Timothy as a baby. Ellen's mouth went dry.

"Connie!" Will called out from his bedroom.

"Coming, honey!" she called back, leaping from the bed so quickly she almost tripped on the duvet. Oreo Figaro jumped out of the way, objecting with a loud meow. The photos scattered, unwanted, to the floor.

Chapter 14

"It's Mommy, honey." Ellen went over to Will's bed, and his sobs intensified, cranky wails in the dark room.

"I'm hot."

"I know, baby." Ellen scooped him up and hugged him close, and he flopped onto her, resting his head sideways on her shoulder and clinging to her like a baby koala. His face was damp against her neck, and she rocked him as she stood. "My poor baby."

"Why am I hot?"

"Let's get you out of these clothes, okay?" Ellen lowered him back into the bed, and he was too listless to squirm. He had fallen asleep in his turtleneck and overalls. "I'm gonna turn the light on, so be ready. Cover your eyes. Ready?"

Will slapped two small hands over his eyes.

"Good boy." Ellen leaned over to the night table and switched on the Babar lamp. "Okay, move your hands away from your eyes, nice and slow, so they can get used to the light."

Will moved his hands away, then came up blinking. "I'm getting used."

"Right, good." Ellen retrieved the board books that had gotten wedged inside the bed frame and set them on the night table. She unhooked the fasteners at the top of his straps, then shimmied him out of his overalls. "You had a big, long nap."

"Mommy." Will smiled shakily at her. "You're home."

"I sure am," Ellen said, with a twinge. "I'm so glad you got such a good rest. That's going to help you feel better. Reach for the moon, partner." She pulled off his damp shirt as Will raised his arms, and she could barely see the thin white line that divided his little-boy chest down the center, though he felt embarrassed enough to wear a T-shirt when he swam. Once it had been a knotted zipper of flesh, in days she would never forget. "You hungry?"

"No."

"How about soup?" Ellen placed her palm on his forehead. She couldn't remember the last time she'd used a thermometer, as if it proved her motherhood bona fides.

"No soup, Mommy."

"Well, then, how about bugs and worms?"

"No!" Will giggled.

"Why, did you have that for lunch? Are you sick of bugs and worms?"

"No!" Will giggled again. Oreo Figaro appeared in the threshold and sat silhouetted in the hall light, a fat cat with a back hump like Quasimodo.

"I know, how about you eat some cat food? I bet Oreo Figaro would share with you." Ellen turned to the cat. "Oreo Figaro, would you share your dinner?" Then she turned back to Will. "Oreo Figaro said, 'No, get your own food.'"

Gales of laughter, making Mommy feel like a comic genius. "He *has* to share."

"Oreo Figaro, you have to share. Will says so." Ellen

turned to Will. "Oreo Figaro says, 'I make my own rules. I'm a cat, and that's how cats roll.' "

"Oreo Figaro, you're gonna get a time-out."

"Right." Ellen got the liquid Tylenol from the night table, unscrewed the lid of the small bottle, and sucked some into the dropper. "Here's medicine. Open up, please, baby bird."

"Where's Oreo Figaro?" Will opened his mouth, then clamped down on the dropper.

"In the doorway. Did you swallow?"

"Yes. Get him, Mommy."

"Okay, hold on." Ellen put the sticky dropper back in the bottle, closed the cap, and went over and picked up the cat, who permitted himself to be carried to the bed and placed at its foot, curling his tail into a shepherd's crook.

"Oreo Figaro, you gotta share!" Will wagged a finger at him, and Ellen rooted around on the night table for a bottle of water.

"Drink this for me, please, sweetie." She helped him up to sip from the bottle, then laid him back down. A slight, pale figure in his white undies, he took up barely the top half of the bed, and she covered him lightly.

"No books, Mommy."

"Okay, how about we cuddle up, instead? Scoot over, please." Ellen turned off the light, eased herself over the side of the guardrail, and gentled Will up and onto her chest, where she wrapped her arms around him. "How's that feel, baby?"

"Scratchy."

Ellen smiled. "It's my sweater. Now, tell me how you are. Does your throat hurt?"

"A little."

Ellen wasn't overly worried, she hadn't smelled strep on his breath. You didn't have to be a good mother to smell strep. Even a drunk could smell strep. "How about your head? Does it hurt?"

"A little."

"Tummy?"

"A little."

Ellen hugged him. "Did you have fun with Connie today?"

"Tell me a story, Mommy."

"Okay. An old or a new one?"

"An old one."

Ellen knew the one he wanted to hear. She would tell it and try not to think about the photos in her bedroom. "Once upon a time there was a little boy who was very, very sick. He was in a hospital, all by himself. And one day, a mommy went to the hospital and saw him."

"What did she say?" Will asked, though he knew. This wasn't a bedtime story, it was a bedtime prayer.

"She said, 'My goodness, this is the cutest little boy I have ever seen. I'm a mommy who needs a baby, and he's a baby who needs a mommy. I wish that little boy could be mine.'"

"Oreo Figaro's biting my foot."

"Oreo Figaro, no, stop it." Ellen gave the cat a nudge, and he went after her foot instead. "Now he's got me. Ouch."

"He's sharing, Mommy."

Ellen laughed. "That's right." She moved her foot away, and the cat gave up. "Anyway, back to the story. So the mommy asked the nurse, and she said, 'Yes, you can take that little boy home if you really, really love him a lot.' So the mommy said to the nurse, 'Well, that's funny, I just happen to love this baby a whole lot.'"

"Tell it right, Mommy."

Ellen got back on track. She'd been distracted, thinking about Timothy Braverman. "So the mommy said to the nurse, 'I really love this baby a whole lot and I want to

take him home,' and they said okay, and the mommy adopted the little boy, and they lived happily ever after." Ellen
hugged him close. "And I do. I love you very much."

"I love you, too."

"That makes it perfect. And oh, yeah, they got a cat."

"Oreo Figaro's head is on my foot."

"He's telling you he loves you. Also that he's sorry
about before."

"He's a good cat."

"A very good cat," Ellen said, giving Will another
squeeze. He fell silent, and in time she could feel his skin
cool and his limbs relax.

She remained in the dark bedroom, listening to the occasional hiss of the radiator and looking at a ceiling covered with phosphorescent stars that glowed WILL. Her
gaze fell to shelves full of toys and games, and a window
with the white plastic shade pulled down. On the walls,
cartoon elephants lumbered along in a line, knockoff
Babars holding onto each other's tails and balancing one-
legged on bandbox stands. She had put the wallpaper up
herself, with the radio blasting hip-hop. It was the child's
room she'd always dreamed of, ready just in time to bring
Will home from the hospital.

Her gaze returned to the WILL constellation, and she
tried to count her blessings, but failed. Until that damn
white card had come in the mail, she'd been happier than
she'd imagined she ever could be. She hugged Will gently, but her thoughts wandered back down the hall. Then
she got another idea, one that wouldn't wait.

She eased Will from her chest and shifted out of bed,
clumsily because of the stupid guardrail. She got up, covered him with his thermal blanket, and padded out of the
room on fleece socks.

Oreo Figaro raised his head and watched her sneak
off.

Chapter 15

Ellen went into her home office, flicked on the overhead light, and sat down at her fake-wood workstation, a floor sample from Staples that held an old Gateway computer and monitor. The room was tiny enough that the Realtor had called it a "sewing room," and it barely accommodated the workstation, an underused stationary bicycle, and mismatched file cabinets containing household files, research, appliance manuals, and old clippings Ellen kept in case she had to get a new job.

I'll have to cut one more by the end of the month.

Ellen sat down, opened her email, and wrote Courtney an email telling her she loved her, then logged on to Google and typed in Timothy Braverman. The search yielded 129 results. She raised an eyebrow; it was more than she'd expected. She clicked on the first relevant link, and it was a newspaper story from last year. The headline read, CORAL BRIDGE MOM KEEPS HOPE ALIVE, and Ellen skimmed the lead:

Carol Braverman is waiting for a miracle, her son Timothy to come home. Timothy, who would now be two-and-a-half years old, was kidnapped during a carjacking and is still missing.

"I know I'll see my son again," she told this re-porter. "I just feel it inside."

It sounded like what Susan Sulaman had said. Ellen read on, and another paragraph caught her eye.

Asked to describe Timothy in one word, Carol's eyes misted over, then she said that her son was "strong." "He could get through anything, even as a baby. He was smaller than most one-year-olds, but he never acted it. At his first birthday party, all of the other babies were bigger, but nobody got the best of him."

She printed the interview, then went back to the Google search and read the line of links, scanning each piece on the Braverman kidnapping. There was a lot of press, and she contrasted it with Susan Sulaman, who had to go begging to keep the police interested. She learned from the articles that Timothy's father, Bill Braverman, was an investment manager, and his mother had been a teacher until her marriage, when she stopped to devote herself to being a mother and doing good works, includ-ing fund-raising for the American Heart Association.

The Heart Association?

Ellen saved the articles, logged on to Google Images, searched under Carol and Bill Braverman, then clicked the first link. A picture appeared on the screen, showing three couples in elegant formal wear, and her eye went immediately to the woman in the middle of the photo.

My God.

Ellen checked the caption. The woman was Carol Braverman. Carol looked so much like Will, she could easily have been his mother. The photo was dark and the focus imperfect, but Carol had blue eyes the shape and color of Will's. Her hair was wavy and dark blond, almost his color, and she wore it long, curling to her tanned shoulders in a slinky black dress. Ellen scanned Bill Braverman's face, and he was conventionally handsome, with brown eyes and a nose that was straight and on the small side, a lot like Will's. His smile was broad, easy, and confident, the grin of a successful man.

Her stomach clenched. She closed the photo, went back to Google, and clicked the second link, which retrieved another group picture in shorts and T-shirts at a poolside party. The photo was dark, too, taken at night, but Carol's hair had been cut around her ears in a boyish style that made her look even more like Will. And Bill's body looked lean but cut, with muscular arms and legs that showed the same wiry build that Will had.

"This is crazy," Ellen said aloud. She shoved the computer mouse away, got up from her chair, and went to the first file cabinet. She slid open the top drawer, moved the green Pendaflex files aside, skipping folders hand-labeled Bank Statements, Car Payments, Deed, until she found the Will file. She slid the file out, took it back to her chair, and opened it on her lap.

On top were folded clippings of the series she'd done on the CICU nurses, then the one she did on adopting Will. She leafed through them, pausing at an early photo of Will in his crib. The paper had run it on the first page, and Will looked nothing like himself then, so thin and sick. She moved it aside, shooing away the memories. Finally she found Will's adoption papers and slid out the packet.

At the top of the final adoption decree, it read, "The Court of Common Pleas of Montgomery County, Pennsylvania, Orphans' Court Division," and the order was in bold: **"The Court hereby orders and decrees that the**

request for adoption is hereby approved and that the above-captioned adoptee is hereby adopted by Ellen Gleeson."

She felt satisfied, in an official sort of way. Will's adoption was all sewn up, legal, certified, and irrevocable. The court proceedings had been routine, and she had appeared on the second floor of the courthouse in Norristown, for the first time in public with Will. The judge had pounded the gavel, then issued the decree from the bench with a broad smile. She would never forget his words:

I have the only happy courtroom in the entire courthouse.

It gladdened her to remember that day, holding baby Will in her arms, her first day as a mother. She read the decree again. **"The needs and welfare of ADOPTEE will be promoted by approval of this adoption and all requirements of the Adoption Act have been met."** So her adoption was a done deal, and it was closed, meaning that she didn't know the identity of the birth mother and father. They had consented to relinquish their parental rights, and their written consent forms had been submitted to the court by Ellen's lawyer, as part of the adoption papers. The lawyer's name and address were at the bottom of the page:

Karen Batz, Esq.

Ellen remembered Karen well. Her office was in Ardmore, fifteen minutes away, and she had been a smart, competent family lawyer who had guided her through the adoption process without overcharging her, the thirty-thousand-dollar fee in line with a standard private adoption. Karen had told her that the birth mother was thrilled to find someone with the desire and the means to care for such a sick child, and that taking a sick baby would be her best chance to adopt as a single mother. Even the judge had commented on the unusual facts of the case:

It was a stroke of luck, for all concerned.

The paperwork had been completed without a hitch, and Ellen became responsible for Will's medical expenses to the tune of $28,000 and change, but the hospital permitted her to pay in installments. She had just paid off the last penny, and in the end, she got Will, safe and sound, and they became a family.

She sighed happily, closed the file, and put it away behind the others. She shut the file drawer, but stood there, lost in thought for a minute. On the wall over the cabinets hung a Gauguin poster she'd had framed, and she found herself staring at it, the tropical blues and greens blurring her thoughts. The house was quiet. The wind whistled outside. The radiator knocked faintly. The cat was probably purring. Everything was fine.

Still, she was thinking about her lawyer.

Chapter 16

The next morning, Ellen's wardrobe was back on autopilot, and she slipped a down coat over her jeans-sweater-clogs trifecta. Her hair was still wet from the shower, her eye makeup only perfunctory. She felt raw and tired, gone sleepless after a night of quality dwelling.

"You're leaving early?" Connie asked, shedding her coat by the closet. Bright sunlight shone through the window in the door, warming the living room.

"Yes, I have tons of work," Ellen lied, then wondered why. "He didn't have a fever this morning but he slept badly. I still wouldn't send him to school."

"We'll take it easy."

"Good, thanks." Ellen kept her back turned, grabbed her bag and the manila envelope, then opened the door. "I told him good-bye. He's playing in bed with his Legos."

"Ouch."

"I know, right?"

"Looks like the snow's holding off," Connie said, cheery.

"See you, thanks." Ellen went to the door and left, catching a glimpse of the babysitter's puzzled expression through the window, then she pulled her coat tighter and hit the cold air, hustling across the porch and toward the car.

Ten minutes later, she reached the two-story brick building behind Suburban Square and pulled up at the curb in front of the sign that read PROFESSIONAL BUILD-ING. She'd called Karen Batz's office from her cell phone this morning, but no voice mail had picked up, so she'd decided to drop in. It was on the way to the city, and she was hoping Karen would see her. Even a feature reporter knows when to be pushy.

Ellen grabbed her bag and the envelope and got out of the car. She walked down the walkway and went inside the blue door, which they kept unlocked. There was a colonial-style entrance hall with a hunting-scene umbrella stand, and she opened the door on the right, which read, LAW OFFICES, and went inside. She stood, disoriented, for a minute.

Karen's office was completely different. There was a navy carpet and a paisley couch and chairs she didn't remember from before. The huge bulletin boards blanketed with baby photos had been replaced by beach-and-surf scenes and a mirror framed with fake seashells.

"May I help you?" a receptionist asked, coming out of the back room. She was about sixty-five, with red reading glasses and her brown hair cut short. In her hand she held an empty Bunn coffeepot, and she had on a cardigan embroidered with stick-figure skiers and a long corduroy skirt.

"I was looking for Karen Batz," Ellen answered.

"Her office isn't here anymore. This is Carl Geiger's office now. We do real estate."

"Sorry. I called Karen's old number, but they didn't pick up."

"They should disconnect the line. I keep telling them

to, but they don't. You're not the first one to make this mistake."

"I'm a client of hers. Do you know where she moved to?"

The receptionist's eyes fluttered briefly. "I'm sorry to have to tell you this, but Ms. Batz passed away."

"Really?" Ellen asked, surprised. "When? She was only in her forties."

"About two years, maybe a year and a half ago. That's how long we've been here."

Ellen frowned. "That would be right around the time I knew her."

"I'm so sorry. Would you like to sit down? Maybe have some water?"

"No, thanks. What did she die of?"

The receptionist hesitated, then leaned closer. "Frankly, it was a suicide."

Ellen felt stunned. "She *killed* herself?" Memories came back to her. Karen's desk had photos of her three sons. "But she was married, with kids."

"I know, such a shame." The receptionist turned toward a noise from the back room. "If you'll excuse me, I should get ready. We have a closing this morning."

Ellen was nonplussed. "I wanted to talk to her about my son's adoption."

"Maybe her husband can help you. I've directed her other clients to him." The receptionist went to the computer and hit a few keys, the bright monitor screen reflected in her glasses. She pulled a pen from a mug, then scribbled on a piece of paper. "His name's Rick Musko. Here's his office phone."

"Thanks," Ellen said, accepting the sheet, which had a 610 phone number, the Philly suburbs. "Do you have the address?"

"I'm not authorized to give that out."

"Okay, thanks."

Back in her car, Ellen was on the cell phone to Karen's husband before she pulled away from the office. It was only 8:10, but a man answered the phone.

"Musko here."

"Mr. Musko?" Ellen introduced herself and said, "I'm sorry to bother you, but I'm, er, was, a client of Karen's. I'm very sorry for your loss."

"Thank you," Musko said, his tone cooler.

"She helped me adopt my son, and I had wanted to speak with her. I have a question or two about—"

"Another lawyer took over her practice. You should have gotten a letter. I can give you his information."

"I just wanted my file. Does he have the files, too?"

"How old is the case?"

"It was about two years ago." Ellen winced at the coincidence of timing, but if Musko noticed it, he didn't miss a beat.

"I have the dead files in my garage, at the house. You can come by and look for your file. That's the best I can do."

"Wonderful. When could I come by?"

"I'm busy this month, we have a project at work."

"Please, could it be sooner? This is important." Ellen heard anxiety thin her voice, surprising even herself. "If I could just come over this week? Tonight, even? I know it's short notice but I won't make any trouble for you, I'll just go out to the garage and find it myself."

"*Tonight?*"

"Please?"

"I suppose the housekeeper can let you into the garage. Her name's Wendy. I'll call her."

"Thanks so much. I'll be there by six." Ellen prayed Connie could stay late.

"Make it seven, then the kids will have eaten. Look for

the U-Haul boxes in the garage. Wendy will show you. You can't miss them." Musko gave Ellen an address, and she thanked him and hung up, then typed it into her BlackBerry.

As if she would forget it.

Chapter 17

"Ellen, come on in!" It was Marcelo, calling from his office as she hustled into the newsroom.

"Sure." She waved to him, masking her dismay as she spotted Sarah sitting inside his office. She slipped off her coat and stuffed it under her arm with her bag and envelope.

"Good morning." Marcelo stood smiling behind his desk, in dark pants and a matte black shirt that fitted close to his body, showing broad shoulders tapering to a trim waist. Either he'd been working out, or Ellen was in lust.

"Hi." Sarah nodded at her, and Ellen took a seat, barely managing a smile.

Marcelo sat down. "Sarah was just telling me she spent the afternoon with the new police commissioner. Great, no?"

Grrrr. "Great."

"He was willing to talk on the record about the homicide rate. Wait until you see her draft, it's terrific." Marcelo turned to Sarah. "Make sure you copy Ellen. I want you two to keep each other up to speed."

"You got it." Sarah made a note on her pad, but Marcelo was already turning to Ellen.

"How's the story going?" His dark eyes flashed expectantly.

"Nothing significant yet." Ellen had to think fast. "I have a lead but nothing to get excited about."

"Fair enough." Marcelo nodded, and if he was disappointed, it didn't show. "Let me know and copy Sarah whenever you get something drafted."

Sarah asked, "Ellen, did you see those leads I listed on page three? The top one, Julia Guest, said she'd love to talk to us. You might want to start with her."

"Maybe I will." Ellen hid her annoyance, and Marcelo clapped his hands together like a soccer coach.

"Okay, ladies," he said, but his gaze focused on Ellen, and not in a come-hither way. More in a you're-gonna-get-fired way.

"Thanks." She left the office behind Sarah, who slid a sleek BlackBerry from her waist holster and started hitting the buttons. Ellen dumped her stuff on an empty desk on the fly and caught up with Sarah before she started the call. "Hold on, wait a sec."

"What?" Sarah turned, her cell to her ear.

"We need to talk, don't you think?"

"Maybe later," Sarah answered, but Ellen wasn't about to let it go. She snatched the phone from Sarah's hand and pressed the End button, then turned on her heel.

"Meet me in the ladies' room if you want your toy back."

Chapter 18

"Give me back my phone!" Sarah held out her palm, her dark eyes flashing. "What's your problem?"

"What's *my* problem?" Ellen raised her voice, and the sound reverberated off the hard tiles of the ladies' room. "Why are you talking to everyone about me?"

"What do you mean?"

"You told Marcelo I was upset about Courtney, and you told Meredith that I was bad-mouthing Marcelo and Arthur."

"I did no such thing and I want my phone back." Sarah wiggled her hand impatiently, and Ellen slapped the Black-Berry into her palm.

"Meredith told me, and so did Marcelo. *Marcelo,* Sarah. Our *editor.* You can get me fired, talking me down to him."

"Oh please." Sarah scoffed. "Meredith misunderstood. I didn't say you said anything bad about them, specifically."

"I didn't say *anything* about them."

"You called them bastards!" Sarah shot back, leaving Ellen incredulous.

"What? When?"

"In here, before they came for Courtney. You said, 'Don't let the bastards get you down.'"

"Gimme a break, Sarah. It's an expression. My father says it all the time."

"Whatever, you said it." Sarah snorted. "I only told one person in the newsroom."

"One is enough. That's why they call it a newsroom."

"Meredith never talks."

"Everybody talks, these days."

Sarah rolled her eyes. "You're overreacting."

"And what about Marcelo? You told him, too. You said I wasn't a fan of his."

"He asked me how was morale in the newsroom after Courtney got fired. I told him it was bad and that you felt the same way. That's all." Sarah put her hands on her hips. "Are you telling me you didn't feel that way? That you're happy Courtney got fired?"

"Of course not."

"Then what are you whining about?"

"Don't talk to the boss about me, got it?"

Sarah waved her off. "Whatever I said, it's not gonna hurt you. Marcelo wants you around, and you know why."

Ellen reddened, angry. "You know, that's insulting."

"Whatever. We need to talk about the think piece." Sarah straightened up at the sink. "Do us both a favor and use my lead. Call Julia Guest. My job's riding on this, and I'm not about to let you screw me up."

"Don't worry about it. I'll do my part, you do yours."

"You'd better." Sarah brushed past her for the door, and Ellen heard her mutter under her breath.

Ironically, they were saying the exact same thing:
Bitch.

Chapter 19

Ellen worked on the homicide piece through lunch, reading Sarah's notes and doing her own research before she made any contacts, but she found it almost impossible to concentrate, distracted by thoughts of Karen Batz. Tonight she'd find the file on Will's adoption, and it had to help fill in some of the blanks. She'd already called Connie, who'd agreed to stay late.

Her gaze returned to the notes on her desk, and she told herself to focus on the task at hand. She had to look busy, too, aware that Marcelo was in his office, holding meetings. She glanced up, and at the exact same moment, Marcelo was looking at her through the glass.

Ellen smiled, flushing, and Marcelo broke their eye contact, returning to his meeting, gesturing with his hands, his shirtsleeves folded carelessly over his forearms. She put her head down and tried to focus. She had only a few hours of daylight left.

She picked up the phone.

Chapter 20

Night came early to this neighborhood, the sun fleeing the sky, leaving heaven black and blue, and Ellen circled the block, scribbling notes as she drove. Trash blew in the gutters, swept along by unseen currents, stopping when it flattened against older cars. Sooty brick rowhouses lined broken sidewalks; some houses had graffitied plywood where windows used to be, and others had only black holes, unsightly as missing teeth. Porch roofs sagged, peeling shutters hung crooked, and every home had bars covering its doors. One house had encased its entrance in bars, curved inward at the top like a lion's cage.

A boy had been shot to death on this block of Eisner Street, only two weeks ago. Lateef Williams, age eight.

Ellen turned right onto Eisner, where only one streetlight worked, and it threw a halo over a pile of trash, rubble, and car tires dumped on the corner. She stopped at number 5252, Lateef's house, and his memorial out front was bathed in darkness, the shadows hiding a purple bunny rabbit that sat lopsided against Spider-Man figurines, crayoned drawings, a king-size box of Skittles, sympathy cards, and a mound of spray-painted daisies and sweetheart roses, still in plastic wrap. A sign hand-written in Magic Marker read WE LOVE YOU, TEEF, and a few candles sat around it, unlit in the cold and wind. Lateef Williams was denied the smallest measure of warmth and light, even in death.

Ellen felt a wrench in her chest. She didn't know how many children had been killed in the city last year, but she could never get used to the idea. She never wanted to get to the point at which a child's murder was old news. She fed the car some gas and pulled into a parking space, then gathered her things to meet Lateef's mother.

Laticia Williams was twenty-six, with a slim, pretty face, narrow brown eyes, high cheekbones, and a promi-nent mouth, devoid of lipstick. Long earrings with wooden beads dangled from her earlobes, showing just under chin-length hair colored reddish. With her jeans, she wore an oversized black T-shirt that bore her son's photo and the caption, R.I.P. LATEEF.

"I appreciate you coming," Laticia said, setting a mug of coffee in front of Ellen as they sat at her round table. The kitchen was small and neat, the cabinets refaced with dark wood and the Formica counters covered with Pyrex oblongs of cakes, cookie tins, and two pies covered with tinfoil, which Laticia had said were "too ugly" to serve.

"Not at all, I appreciate your talking to me at a time like this," Ellen said, having already expressed her condo-lences. "The only thing I hate about my job is barging into people's houses at the worst time of their lives. Again, I'm so sorry for your loss."

"Thank you." Laticia sat down with a weary smile, showing the gold rim of her front tooth. "I want it to be in the paper, so everybody know what's happenin'. So they know kids are gettin' killed every day. So it's not just a number, like Powerball."

"That's the point. That's what I'm here to do. Make them see it and understand what it's like to lose Lateef this way."

"I cried all I can cry, we all have. But you know what they don't understand? What they're never gonna understand?"

"Tell me."

"That with me, and with Dianne down the block, who lost her child, it's different. We're mad, too. Mad as all hell. Sick to *death* of all this *dyin'*." Laticia's voice rose and fell, with a cadence almost like a prayer. "All the mothers are *sick* our kids are bein' shot at, like it's a damn shootin' gallery, and it makes no never mind. Ain't nothin' gonna change here, and this is *America*."

Ellen absorbed her words, and her emotion. She wondered if she could convey all that feeling in the piece.

"It's like *Katrina,* we're livin' in a different country. We got two sets of rules, two sets of laws, two things you can get outta life, whether you're white or black, rich or poor. That's the thing in a nutshell." Laticia pointed a stiff index finger at Ellen. "You live in America, but I don't. You live in Philadelphia, but I don't."

Ellen didn't know how to respond, so she didn't.

"Where I live, my kid can get shot on the street, and nobody sees nothin'. You wanna blame them, tell people to snitch, I know, but you can't blame people. I *can't* and I *don't*. If they snitch, they're *dead*. Their family's *dead*. Their kids are *dead*."

Ellen didn't want to interrupt Laticia with a question. Nothing could be as valuable as what she was saying and she deserved at least that much.

"So I could sit here and tell you all about Teef and how cute he was, 'cause he was." Laticia smiled briefly, light returning to her angry eyes, softening them for just an instant. "He was a funny child, a *goofball*. He cracked us *up*. At the last reunion, he was freestylin', he tore it *up*. I miss him every minute."

Ellen thought of Susan Sulaman, talking about her son. And Carol Braverman, praying for a miracle on her website.

"But even though Teef was mine, what matters is he isn't the only one killed here." Laticia put her hand to her chest, resting on the painted photo of her son's face. "Three other kids were killed in this neighborhood, all of them shot to death. Lemme aks you, that happen where you live?"

"No."

"And that jus' this year. You figure in the year before that and the one before that, we got eight kids killed. You can make a big pile outta those bodies."

Ellen tried to make sense of the number. Everybody counted bodies, to quantify the cost. But whether it cost nine kids or twelve, it was no worse than one. One child was enough. One body was one too many. One was the only number.

"We don't have kids walkin' around here, we got *ghosts*. This neighborhood's full a ghosts. Pretty soon they'll be nobody left to kill. Philly's gonna be a ghost town, like in the wild wild west. A *ghost* town."

Ellen heard the bitterness in her words, and she realized that Laticia Williams and Susan Sulaman, two very different women from two very different cities in the same city, had that much in common. Both of them were haunted, and they always would be. She wondered if Carol Braverman felt the same way, and it nagged at her. She thought of the files, waiting for her in the garage. Answers would be inside.

"You got a child?" Laticia asked, abruptly.

"Yes," Ellen answered. "A boy."

"That's good." Laticia smiled, the gold winking again. "You hold that baby close, you hear? Hold him close. You never know when you gonna lose him."

Ellen nodded, because for a minute, she couldn't speak.

Chapter 21

Ellen surveyed the garage, her breath chalky in the cold. Kids' bicycles stood propped up in front of metal shelves that held Nerf footballs, a black plastic mountain of Rollerblades and kneepads, and a spare jug of sea-blue antifreeze. There were greasy jars of Turtle Wax and Bug-B-Gone, and an exercise bicycle had been relegated to a corner, wedged behind a workbench. Fluorescent panels overhead cast light on the left well of the garage, where Rick Musko must park, because there were a few grease spots on the concrete floor. In the other well, where Karen Batz's car would have been, sat cardboard boxes piled like a Rubik's Cube. An old green tennis ball hung uselessly from the ceiling, resting on the top of the boxes, its string slack.

Dead files.

Ellen fastened her down coat, went over to the boxes, and started moving them aside. They were piled alphabetically, and she searched for the G's. Ten minutes later, boxes lay all around the garage floor, and she wasn't cold anymore. She wedged off the lid of a box labeled Ga–Go and looked inside. It held manila folders packed tight, and she took out a batch at the front, allowing them to move freely. Each file had a white label with the client's name, last name first. Ellen started at the beginning, and predictably, most of them were couples: Galletta, Bill and Kalpanna; Gardner, David, and Melissa McKane; Gentry, Robert and Xinwei; and Gibbs, Michael, and Penny Carbone. Her heart was pounding by the time she got to Gilbert, Dylan and Angela, but the next file wasn't Gleeson, Ellen. It was Goel, John, and Lucy Redd.

She thumbed past Gold, Howard and Mojdeh; and Gold, Steven and Calina, and even onto Goldberger, Darja. No Gleeson. Not even misfiled. She skipped ahead to Golden, Golen, Gorman, then to Grant and Green. Still no Gleeson. Puzzled, she looked up at the pile of boxes, then eyed the ones she'd left lying around the floor. There had been other G boxes, and Gleeson could be misfiled anywhere. She took a deep breath and got busy. She was finished two hours later, but still hadn't found her file.

What gives?

She was putting the Rubik's Cube back together when she heard the loud rumbling of a car engine, and the garage door slid up noisily, leaving her in the blinding glare of the high beams from an SUV. The driver stepped out, walked toward her, and introduced himself as Rick Musko.

"You're still here?" he asked, stepping into the fluorescent lights. He was tall and bald, in his fifties, older than Karen.

"Sorry, but I can't find my file. I'm almost finished putting all the boxes back."

"Wait a minute." Musko blinked. "I know you. Aren't you the reporter who did the story on the baby you adopted?"

"Yes, right." Ellen introduced herself again.

"Your name didn't register, when we spoke. I was in

the middle of something." Musko extended his hand, and they shook. "I was pretty rude to you, I wish I had known who you were. That story you wrote made Karen so happy."

"She was a great lawyer. I'm so sorry about your loss."

"Thank you."

"Do you know where my file could be?" Ellen picked up a box and heaved it on top of another. "Could it be with the lawyer who bought her practice? I figured I'd call him tomorrow morning."

"No, he won't have it." Musko picked up a box. "He went through all of Karen's files with a fine-tooth comb and took only her active files, mostly divorces and custody fights. Said he didn't have the space for the dead files. That, I believe." Musko straightened the tower of boxes and gave them a pat. "These have been sitting here all this time. I'm too cheap to put them in a storage space. I wonder where yours could be."

"No idea?" Ellen shelved another box, pressing the lid on tight. "It seems strange that it's missing."

"It should have been here." Musko's tone turned thoughtful as he reached for another box. "I have some of Karen's personal papers inside, from her desk drawers. Maybe your file is in there."

"Why would it be?"

"Because of the article?" Musko grabbed the last box. "She bought thirty copies."

Ellen felt touched. It was a secret pleasure of being a reporter. You never knew where your words landed.

"Maybe she saved the file. I haven't even looked in those boxes yet."

Ellen felt a twinge of guilt. "I hate to put you to this, if it's difficult."

"No, let's get it done. I'll set you up in my study. You can look through them there."

"That would be great," Ellen said, her hope surging. She grabbed her coat, and Musko parked the car.

Then they turned out the lights and went into the house together.

Chapter 22

Musko left Ellen in a home office that put hers to shame. His desk was a lustrous walnut, and he had a maroon leather chair with brass bolts around the edges. Built-in bookcases ringed the room, holding technical manuals and bound newsletters about structural engineering. The walls were lined with golf scenes and framed photographs of three towheaded boys. There were no photos of Karen.

Ellen turned her attention to the three boxes on the desk. She'd been running out of steam but the sight revitalized her, and she took off the first lid, which read Top Drawer. She felt nosy to be going through Karen's desk, but she wasn't about to hesitate. She started digging, and inside were a slew of Bic pens, pencils, Post-it pads, a ruler, loose change, a pink leather Filofax, and a stray lipstick. She found a few legal pads with notes and recognized the neat handwriting, with its detached capitals, as Karen's. She flashed on the lawyer, who had joked that her penmanship was so parochial school.

Odd.

Ellen was a lapsed Catholic, but even she knew that

suicide was one of the bigger no-no's. She wondered fleetingly what would have driven Karen to such an act, and she dug further in the first box. She reached the bottom, but there were no files inside. She closed the lid and moved to the second box, whose lid read Second Drawer. She dug through more legal pads, then checkbooks, piles of bills from Comcast, PECO, a web hosting site, old Filofax sheets with rubber bands, and dues invoices for various bar associations. Still no client files, and Ellen started to worry. She closed the lid and moved to the last box, which reminded her of a joke her father used to tell:

Why is the thing you're looking for always in the last place you look? Because after you find it, you stop looking.

She opened the box and looked inside. It was a hodge-podge of bills, stray invoices, reminders for continuing legal-education courses, and more legal pads. She started rummaging, then all of a sudden, spotted a letter from Karen to her, notifying her about Will's adoption hearing.

Bingo!

She felt her heart start to pound and kept searching, shuffling papers aside until she came across a printed email from her to Karen, asking questions about adoption procedures. She rummaged further, spotted some newsprint, and pulled it out excitedly. It was the front page of the Features section, and on the bottom right was Ellen's piece on Will's adoption. The headline read, HAPPY ENDING, and on the right was the photo of Will, looking so sick. She dug back into the box, and at the very bottom lay a manila folder. She grabbed it and read the label.

Gleeson, Ellen.

"Yay!" She tore it open, but it was empty, which is when she realized that the contents of her file folder were mixed up with the other papers.

"Did you get lucky?" asked a voice from the door, and

she looked up to see Musko in the threshold. His jacket was off, his tie gone, and he'd pushed up his shirtsleeves. He entered the study and sat down tiredly in the leather chair across from his desk.

"Sort of." Ellen held up the empty folder. "This is my file, but the papers are scattered all over the box."

"That's Karen. She wasn't the most organized person in the world. In fact, she was messy."

Don't speak ill. "The files in the garage were neat."

"That was her secretary's doing. They were made for each other." Musko leaned over and plucked Ellen's article from her hand, eyeing it. "You know, it wasn't too long after this article appeared that she was dead."

"When was it that she died, if I can ask?"

"July 13." Musko's smile vanished, and his crow's-feet deepened. He handed the article back. "Her secretary found her at her desk when she came in that morning."

"That was about a month after Will's adoption was final, on June 15. The article ran about two weeks after that." Ellen paused, puzzled. "I'm surprised I didn't hear. I paid my final bill, and the office didn't send me a letter that she was dead. I didn't even see an obit."

"I didn't run one. I kept it quiet, for the kids' sake. The funeral was just family. The neighbors know from the gossip mill, but I never told them." Musko gestured down the hall. "I still haven't told the boys how she really died, just that she got sick."

"Didn't they ask questions?" Ellen asked, surprised. She was thinking of Will, the question machine.

"Yes, but I just said she was sick and we didn't know it, then she died."

Ellen kept her own counsel. She'd made it a policy always to be honest with Will. She even felt bad lying to him about Santa Claus, but no child should have to live in a world without magic.

"I know, it was probably wrong, but what do you say—hey, guys, Mommy went to work today and put a gun in her mouth?"

Suddenly Ellen wished she could leave. The conversation was turning creepy, and she'd liked Musko better in the garage.

"Didn't mean to spring that on you." He laughed, but it sounded bitter. " 'How did she do it?' That's the thing everybody wants to know. Gas, gun, pills? The cops told me it was unusual for a woman to use a gun. I told them, 'But this woman is a lawyer.' "

Ellen stiffened. "I'm sure it's hard to deal with."

"You're damn right it is. They say suicide is selfish, and for once, they're right." Musko jerked a thumb behind him. "I got three kids who pray for her every night. What kind of mother abandons her kids like that? They were babies then. Rory was *two*."

"We can never really understand why people do the things they do." Ellen was trying to say something comforting but knew she sounded like a Hallmark card, or Yoda.

"Oh, I *know* why she did it. She did it because I caught her having an affair."

"Really?" Ellen said, shocked.

"He called her at the house one night, and I picked up. Then she went out and didn't get back until after midnight. She said she was at the gym, but it was the same night they had an electrical fire." Musko snorted. "She was getting her workout from her boyfriend."

Ellen didn't like the cruel twist to Musko's lips. She rose to go, but it didn't stop him from continuing.

"I confronted her, and she admitted it. She had to, I knew there was something going on. She'd been acting funny, moody. Anyway, she said she would stop seeing him, but I told her I wanted a divorce, that I'd fight her over the kids, too." Musko stopped abruptly, as if he'd just heard himself. "The next morning was, you know, when she did it." He leaned over, resting his head on his elbow, and began rubbing his eyes. "I quit therapy, but I better get back in, huh?"

"I'm sure it would help."

"So they say." Musko looked at her, then rose slowly. "You found the papers you needed?"

"Well, they're in the box somewhere but I didn't get a chance to go through and see which papers are mine."

"Then take the whole box. Take all three, for all I care. Take them with you."

"What if there's things in there you want?"

Musko waved her off. "I don't need anything in those boxes. I should get rid of the ones in the garage, too. I should just burn the damn things."

Ellen realized then why the dead files were still in the garage. It wasn't that he didn't want to spend the money on a storage space. It was that he wanted to keep them and he wanted to burn them, both at once.

"Thanks," she said. "I'll send you back what's not mine." She put a lid on the third box, shutting its secrets inside.

At least until she got home.

Chapter 23

The night was starless and black, and the windows dark mirrors that reflected Ellen at her dining-room table, sifting through the contents of the third box, sitting next to a glass of emergency merlot. Oreo Figaro sat in his spot at the far end of the table, watching with a disapproving eye.

She set aside bills and legal pads, then pulled out the papers that should have been in her file and read each one as she put them in chronological order, oldest to most recent, re-creating Will's adoption file. There was printed email correspondence to Karen and from the home-study people, who had come to see the house and interview Ellen before the adoption was finalized. She went back to the box, shoved aside pencils and a half pack of gum, and unearthed another typed letter to Karen, this one printed in a larger font, on thin paper. She read it with a start:

Amy Martin
393 Corinth Lane
Stoatesville, PA

Dear Karen,

   Here are the papers you asked me to get signed.
They are from the baby's father and he says he will
give up his rights to the baby. Please make sure the
woman who wants to adopt him takes good care of
him. He's a good baby, and it's not his fault he's
fussy and sick. I love him but I know this is what is
the best thing for him and I will remember him always and keep him in my prayers.

Sincerely,
Amy

   Ellen's heart thundered in her chest, and she read the
letter again, feeling a tingle just holding it in her hands. It
was from Will's birth mother, who had held this paper,
had written this note, and had printed it out. So her name
was Amy Martin. She sounded so sweet, and her pain in
putting Will up for adoption came through even her simple lines. It was all Ellen could do not to pick up the
phone and call her, but instead, she reached for her wine
and raised her glass in a silent toast.
   Thank you, Amy, for the gift of your child.
   Oreo Figaro looked over, blinking, and she set down
the wine, returned to the box, and kept digging, finally
reaching more court papers, with her caption at the top.
Consent of Birth Parent, read the heading, and the form
showed Amy's name and the Stoatesville address, and her
birth date, which was July 7, 1983, and marital status,
which read **single**. The paper was signed by Amy Martin
under the sentence, **I hereby voluntarily and uncondi-**

tionally consent to the adoption of the above-named child. The paper had also been witnessed by Gerry Martin and Cheryl Martin, from the same address.

Ellen skipped to the next form, which was the consent of the birth father, and she learned his name and address with her heart in her throat:

Charles Cartmell
71 Grant Ave
Philadelphia, Pennsylvania

She eyed his signature, a messy scrawl with barely comprehensible loops. So Charles Cartmell had been Will's father, and she couldn't help but wonder what he had been like. What he looked like. What he did for a living. How did he and Amy meet, and why did they never marry?

She returned to digging in the box but found nothing else relating to Will except his medical information sheet, which she already had in her file, stating that both birth parents had a history of high blood pressure. There was no mention of any heart problems, which was consistent with what she'd been told by the hospital, that Will's heart defect could have originated with him. The state had a voluntary medical registry online, but Will's birth parents had never registered. Still, the consent papers were a tangible answer to a question Ellen hadn't been able to articulate, even to herself.

"Well, that settles that," Ellen said aloud, startling Oreo Figaro. Her gaze fell on the papers on the table, and her thoughts strayed to poor Karen. She remembered that Karen had called to congratulate her on the day Will's adoption papers were processed. It was so hard to believe that she would be dead a little over a month later, by her own hand. Ellen shuddered and took a last sip of wine. It was so awful to think of Karen doing that, with three little kids at home. Musko had been right about that much.

Where was a mother's instinct then?

She couldn't think about it now. It was late and she had to get to bed. She'd done enough for one day, except on her homicide story. She'd normally have drafted something after her interview with Laticia Williams, but tonight she was too beat. She set the wineglass down next to the box, but a bright pink splotch amid the clutter caught her eye. She moved the papers aside. It was the hot pink of Karen's leather Filofax.

She picked it out and opened it, idly. It was a standard date book, a week on two opposing pages, and each page bore Karen's neat script, noting her appointments and meetings by client name. Ellen felt a pang, looking at the record of a woman's life, her time on earth divided into billable increments. What the diary couldn't show was that, in those increments, this woman had changed lives.

She flipped back in time through the Filofax, slowing when she reached the week of July 13, the day on which Karen had committed suicide. That week began on Monday, July 10, and the Filofax showed a neat lineup of appointments. The eleventh showed Karen had a client meeting in the morning and a Women's Way luncheon.

Ellen scanned the rest of the week, including the day Karen died. The lawyer had had appointments scheduled all day long, which made sense. Karen couldn't have known that the night before, her husband would find out about her affair. Ellen was about to close the book when she noticed that one of the appointments, on Wednesday, didn't have a name, but only an initial:

A, written next to the time: 7:15 P.M.

Ellen was intrigued. A nighttime meeting? Maybe A was Karen's lover? She skipped back to the week before that, but there was no A, and then the week before that. There, in the middle of the week, on Wednesday, June 28.

A, also at 7:15.

She flipped pages to the week before, and then the week before that, which brought her to Wednesday, June 14.

A, this time at 9:30 P.M.

She mulled it over. That was the day before Will's adoption was final, on June 15. She flipped back to earlier weeks, checking each one, but there were no other meetings with A. She sat back, thinking, and her gaze shifted to the letter on the table, from Amy Martin. The date on the letter was June 15.

Ellen thought a minute. There had been a meeting with A, and then the next day, a letter from Amy Martin. She put two and two together. "A" wasn't Karen's boyfriend. "A" could stand for Amy.

She sank into a chair at the table, her good mood evaporating. She looked again at the letter. It even said "in our meeting." So Karen had had a meeting with Amy. But Ellen didn't remember seeing Amy's name in the Filofax, anywhere. She paged through it again, around June, and double-checked. There was no notation of a meeting with Amy Martin or Charles Cartmell, though all the other client meetings had been noted.

Ellen set down the Filofax and reached for her wine. She took a sip, but it tasted warm and bitter. She knew what she had to do, first thing tomorrow morning. Finish this thing once and for all. Put an end to her dwelling. She was driving herself nuts.

"Why can't I leave well enough alone?" she asked, aloud.

But Oreo Figaro merely blinked in response.

Chapter 24

The next morning as Ellen put on her coat, she was already wondering how soon she could call Amy Martin. Will's fever had broken, and he was running around the living room with a new Penn State football that Connie had just brought for him. Ellen withheld the lecture on not introducing new toys before school. Working mothers had no time for spontaneity unless it was scheduled.

"He knows just what to do!" Connie said, delighted. "My Mark was like that, too."

"Look at me!" Will circled the coffee table with the blue football tucked under his arm. "Look, Mommy!"

"Watch where you're going, buddy," Ellen called back, and Oreo Figaro jumped out of the way as Will hurtled past him, turned left into the dining room, and ran into the kitchen. He ran through the kitchen, up and over the stairway, and ended up back in the living room, a circular floor plan designed for little boys and NASCAR drivers.

Connie said, "You know, he looks like a natural athlete."

"You think?" Ellen picked up her purse and briefcase, listening to the pounding of Will's feet through the kitchen. Whoever coined the expression pitter-patter-of-little-feet had a kitten, not a child.

"I should get Mark over here to throw the ball with him sometime."

Will came running back into the living room and looked up grinning, his cheeks flushed. "I did it! I made a yesdown!"

"You mean a touchdown?" Connie corrected him, and Ellen laughed and held out her arms.

"Gimme a hug. I gotta go to work and you gotta go to school."

"Mommy!" Will ran to her, and Ellen hugged and kissed him, brushing his bangs from his eyes.

"Love you. Have fun at school."

"Can I bring my football?" Will's eyes widened with hope.

"No," Ellen answered.

"Yes," Connie said, at the same minute.

"I WANT TO!" Will hollered, jiggered up.

"Hey, quiet down, pal." Ellen held his arm, trying to settle him. "No shouting in the house."

"I want to bring my ball, Mommy!"

"Fine, okay." Ellen didn't want to leave on a bad note, another axiom of Working Mother Guilt.

"Goody!" Will rewarded her with another hug, dropping the football and throwing his arms around her neck.

Ellen felt a twinge of separation anxiety, worse than usual.

Maybe because she knew what she was about to do, after she left.

Chapter 25

Ellen eyed the cars stacked ahead, their red taillights a glowing line, their exhaust trailing white plumes. The day was overcast and cold, and freezing rain had left an icy sleeve on the tree branches and a black veneer on the roads. The traffic stayed bad on the two-lane roads to Stoatesville, and in time, she found Corinth Street among the warren of rowhouses in a working-class neighborhood around an abandoned steel mill. She traveled down the street, reading the house numbers. Suddenly her cell phone started ringing in her purse, and she fumbled for it. The display showed a number she didn't recognize, and she hit Ignore when she realized that the house coming up was number 393.

Amy Martin's house.

A woman was standing in its driveway, scraping ice off the windshield of an old black Cherokee. Her back was turned, and she wore an Eagles knit cap, a thick black parka, jeans, and black rubber boots.

Amy?

Ellen pulled up in front of the house, grabbed her bag

and file, got out, walked up the driveway. "Excuse me, Ms. Martin?" she asked, her heart thumping like crazy.

She turned, startled, and Ellen saw instantly that the woman was too old to be Amy Martin. She looked to be in her late sixties, and her hooded eyes widened under the Eagles hat. She said, "Jeez, you scared me!"

"Sorry." Ellen introduced herself. "I'm looking for Amy Martin."

"Amy's my daughter, and she don't live here anymore. I'm Gerry."

Ellen tried to keep her bearings. Gerry Martin had been one of the witnesses on the consent form. She was looking into the eyes of Will's grandmother, the first blood relative of his she had ever seen. "She gave this address as hers, two years ago."

"She always does, but she don't live here. I get all her mail, all those damn bills, I throw 'em all away."

"Where does Amy live?"

"Hell if I know." Gerry returned to scraping the windshield, shaving fragile curls of ice, making a *krrp krrp* sound. She pursed her lips with the effort, sending deep wrinkles radiating from her mouth. Her black glove was oversized, dwarfing the red plastic scraper.

"You don't know where she is?"

"No." *Krrp krrp.* "Amy's over eighteen. It ain't my business no more."

"How about where she works?"

"Who said she works?"

"I'm just trying to find her."

"I can't help you."

For some reason, Ellen hadn't imagined there'd be an estrangement. "When was the last time you saw her?"

"A while."

"A year or two?"

"Try five."

Ellen knew it couldn't be true. Gerry had signed the consent form two years ago. Why was she lying? "Are you sure?"

Gerry looked over, eyes narrowed under the fuzzy hat, scraper stalled on the windshield. "She owes you money, right? You're a bill collector or a lawyer or somethin'?"

"No." Ellen paused. If she wanted the truth, she'd have to tell the truth. "Actually, I'm the woman who adopted her baby."

Gerry burst into laughter, showing yellowed teeth and bracing herself against the Jeep, scraper in hand.

"Why is that funny?" Ellen asked, and after Gerry stopped laughing, she wiped her eyes with the back of her big glove.

"You better come in, honey."

"Why?"

"We got some talkin' to do," Gerry answered, placing her gloved hand on Ellen's shoulder.

Chapter 26

Gerry went into the kitchen to make coffee, leaving Ellen in the living room, which was barely illuminated by two retro floor lamps, their low-wattage bulbs in ball-shaped fixtures on a stalk. Beige curtains covered the windows, and the air was thick with stale cigarette smoke. Flowered metal trays served as end tables flanking a worn couch of blue velveteen, and three mismatched chairs clustered around a large-screen TV.

Ellen crossed the room, drawn to photographs that ran the length of the wall. There were oversized school pictures of boys and girls in front of screensaver blue skies, photo montages cut to fit the various circles and squares, and a wedding photo of a young man and a woman in an elaborate bridal headdress. She shook her head in wonderment. They were Will's blood, but complete strangers, and she was his mother, known and loved by him, but having none of his blood. She went from one photo to the next, trying to put together the puzzle that was her son.

Which girl is Amy?

The photos showed girls and boys at all different ages, and Ellen tried to follow each child as he or she grew up, picking blue eyes from brown and matching young smiles to older smiles, age-progressing all of them in her mind's eye, searching for Amy. One of the girls had blondish hair and blue eyes, plus Will's fair skin, with just the hint of freckles dotting a small, pert nose.

"Here we go." Gerry came into the room with a skinny brown cigarette and two heavy glass mugs of murky coffee, one of which she handed to Ellen.

"Thanks."

"Siddown, will ya?" Gerry gestured at the couch, her cigarette trailing an acrid snake of smoke, but Ellen stayed with the photos.

"Can I ask, is this one Amy, with the blue eyes and freckles?"

"No, that's Cheryl, her sister. The girl with her is my oldest. I had three girls, one boy."

Ellen remembered the name Cheryl Martin as the other signature on the consent form.

"This one's Amy, the baby of the family in more ways than one." Gerry tapped a smaller photo in the corner, and Ellen walked over, feeling a frisson of discovery.

"So this is Amy, huh?" She leaned close to the photo of a young girl, maybe thirteen years old, leaning on a red Firebird. Her dark blond hair was in cornrows, and her blue eyes were sly. She had a crooked grin that telegraphed too-cool-for-school, and Ellen scrutinized her features. Amy and Will had the same coloring, but their features weren't alike. Still, one picture wasn't a fair sample. "Which of the other photos are Amy?"

"Uh, lemme see." Gerry eyed the photos with a short laugh. "None! I tell you, by the time you get to your fourth, you're a little sick of it, you know what I mean?"

Arg. "I only have the one."

"Oh, after the first, you stop springing for the forty-five-dollar pictures, the refrigerator magnet, the keychain, all that happy horseshit." Gerry motioned to the couch again. "Come on, sit."

"Thanks." Ellen walked over, sank into the couch, and sipped the coffee, which was surprisingly good. "Wow."

"I put in real cream. That's my secret." Gerry sat down heavily, catty-corner to the couch, pulling an ancient bean-bag ashtray onto the chair arm. Her expression looked softer, her hard lines smoothed by the low light. Her hair was a tinted brown with gray roots, the ends frayed, and she wore it tucked behind her ears. Her nose was stubby on a wide face, but she had a motherly smile.

"Why did you laugh outside?" Ellen asked, her fingers tight around her glass mug.

"First, tell me about Amy and this baby." Gerry took a drag on the brown cigarette.

"He was sick, in the hospital. I did a story on it, a series." Ellen reached into her purse, pulled out the clipping from her file, and showed it to Gerry, who barely glanced at it, so she put it back. "You may have seen them in the paper."

"We don't get the paper."

"Okay. Will, the baby I adopted, was in cardiac intensive care when I met him. He had a heart defect."

"And you think he was Amy's baby?"

"I know so."

"How?" Gerry sucked on her cigarette, then blew out a cone of smoke from the side of her mouth, meaning to be polite. "I mean, where'd you get your information?"

"From a lawyer, who died. My lawyer, mine and Amy's. It was a private adoption, and she brokered the deal between us."

"Amy brokered it?"

"No, the lawyer did. Karen Batz."

"It's a lady lawyer?"

"Yes. Does the name mean anything to you?"

Gerry shook her head. "You *sure* it's Amy? My Amy?"

"Yes." Ellen set the coffee down on the metal tray, reached into her envelope, and rifled through the papers. She found Amy's consent to the adoption and the letter with the Corinth Avenue return address and handed them to Gerry, who took them and didn't say anything for a minute, reading to herself and dragging on her cigarette. The smoke hit the court papers and billowed back on itself, like a wave crashing against a seawall.

"This is nuts," Gerry said, half to herself, and Ellen's chest tightened.

"Is that Amy's signature, on the consent?"

"It looks like it."

"How about on the letter?"

"There, too."

"Good. Now we're getting somewhere. So it's your Amy." Ellen reached over and turned the page to the consent form, pointing. "Is that your signature?"

"No way. I never signed this." Gerry's lips flattened to a grim line, again bringing out the wrinkles around her mouth. "And this other signature, it's not Cheryl's, either."

Ellen's heart sank. "Maybe Amy forged the signatures. Maybe she wanted to put her baby up for adoption and didn't want her family to know."

"That can't be it."

"Why not?" Ellen asked, and Gerry shook her head, the papers reflecting white on her face.

"Amy couldn't have kids."

Ellen's mouth went dry.

"She had an operation, when she was seventeen. She had a problem with her ovaries. What was it called?" Gerry paused a minute. "One day she woke up in cramps real bad, so I knew she wasn't fakin' to get outta school. We took her to the emergency and they said she had a twisted ovary, it was called. The ovary got all full of blood, and they had to take it out right away. They said she had almost no chance of getting pregnant."

Ellen tried to process it. "But not no chance. She still had one ovary left, right?"

"Yeah, but they said it was very—what did they say—*unlikely* she could have kids."

"But she had a child."

"I think if you take out an ovary, it affects the hormones, at least that's what they said, something like that, is all I remember." Gerry looked confused. "Whatever, if she had a kid, it's news to me."

"She didn't tell you?"

"No, like I said, we haven't talked. She didn't tell me nothin' anyway. I don't even know where she is. I was tellin' you the truth, outside."

Ellen couldn't accept that it was a dead end. "What about any of her sisters, or her brother? You never heard from any of them about her having a baby?"

"I don't think she talks to anybody but Cheryl, and she lives down in Delaware. I can call her and ask. I will, later." Gerry snorted, her nostrils emitting puffs of smoke. "Nice to know if I had another grandchild."

Ellen tried another tack. "Or maybe when the baby got really sick, that's the kind of thing you might tell someone."

"If Amy had a baby that got really sick, she couldn't handle it. She'd be lookin' for an easy out."

Ellen cringed at the harsh words. "That's the sort of thing that would overwhelm anyone, especially a young girl."

"It didn't take much to *overwhelm* Amy. If I asked her to take out the trash, that *overwhelmed* her."

Ellen let it go. She needed more information. "Can you just tell me a little more about her? What is she like?"

"She was always my wild child. I never could get a handle on that girl."

Ellen found it hard to hear. She had imagined Amy so differently. She wondered if all adoptive mothers had fantasy birth mothers.

"Smart girl, but got lousy grades. Didn't give a shit. I always thought she had, like, ADD, but the teachers said no." Gerry took another puff. "She did her share of drinkin' and drugs. I had no control with her. She was outta here after graduation."

"She ran away?"

"Not like that, just left."

"No college?"

"No way." Gerry smiled crookedly, and Ellen caught a trace of Amy's wisecracking grin.

"Why did she go, may I ask?"

"Didn't like my boyfriend, Tom. They used to get into it all the time. Now she's gone and so's he." Gerry emitted another puff. "I made her stay and graduate high school, but after that, she went off on her own."

"Hold on a sec." Ellen rifled through the papers and handed Gerry the father's consent form. "Look at this. My son's birth father is Charles Cartmell, from Philly. Do you know him?"

"No."

"The name isn't familiar at all? He lives on Grant Avenue in the Northeast." Ellen had checked online last night but couldn't get a phone number or find a listing of the address.

"I don't know the name."

"If Amy is twenty-five now and gave birth to Will three years ago, it means she had him when she was twenty-two. So maybe the father was someone from high school, or the area?"

"She didn't go steady in high school." Gerry shook her

head. "She saw a lot of different guys. I didn't ask no questions, believe me."

"Do you have her high school yearbook? Maybe we could look at it?"

"She didn't buy the yearbook. She wasn't the type." Gerry waved her off. "She was my baby, and I spoiled her, yes I did."

"Could I see her bedroom? There might be something in there that would help me."

"I cleared it out a long time ago. I use it for my son's girlfriend now."

Ellen began thinking out loud. "She must have stayed in the Philadelphia area, because she chose a lawyer in Ardmore. She even had meetings with the lawyer."

Gerry shrugged. "Cheryl might know."

"Can I have her number?"

Gerry hesitated. "Why exactly are you tryin' to find Amy?"

"It's a medical thing, about the baby," Ellen lied, having prepared for the question.

"Does she have to give it a kidney or something?"

"No, not at all. At most it's a blood test. His heart is acting up again, and I need to know more about her medical history."

"She didn't have no heart problems. None of us have heart problems. We got cancer, runs in the family."

"I'm sure, but the blood test will show more than that." Ellen was freewheeling. "If you'd prefer it, maybe you could give Cheryl my number and ask her to call me?"

"Okay, I'll do that." Gerry reached out and patted her hand. "Don't worry. I'm sure the baby will be okay."

"I don't want to lose him," Ellen added, unaccountably.

Chapter 27

Ellen got into the cold car, turned the heat up, and took off down the street under a cloudy sky. Her BlackBerry started ringing as soon as she left the block, and she steered the car with one hand and dug in her purse with the other, finding the device by its smooth feel. She pulled it out, and the screen showed the same unknown number as before, so she answered the call.

"Ellen, where are you?" It was Sarah Liu, sounding panicky. "I've been calling you. You missed the projects meeting. Marcelo asked about the think piece."

"Damn." The Thursday projects meeting. She'd completely forgotten about it, preoccupied with finding Amy.

"Where are you?"

"I wasn't feeling well this morning." Ellen was fast becoming an accomplished liar. "Was Marcelo pissed?"

"What do you think? When are you coming in?"

"I'm not sure, why?" Ellen checked the dashboard clock—10:37.

"We should meet about the think piece. I want to see your draft."

Ellen tensed. The week had flown. She hadn't even

transcribed her notes from Laticia Williams. "We don't need to meet and my draft isn't ready—"

"When will it be? Our deadline's tomorrow."

"Sarah, we're grown-ups. I don't have time to give you a draft, and I don't need yours. Don't tell Daddy."

"What the hell are you doing? You didn't call Julia Guest, and I greased it for you."

Ellen switched lanes to pass a VW Beetle, fighting annoyance. "Thanks, but I have my own leads. I won't need to talk to her."

"She's connected in the community, and she wants to talk to us."

"People who want to talk are never good leads. I don't need the community spokesperson."

"Why not call her, even for background?"

"I know what I'm doing." Ellen braked, checking the car on the way downhill. "Let me handle my end. You handle yours."

"Have it your way, but make that deadline."

"I will."

"Good-bye." Sarah hung up, and Ellen hit the gas. She had to make the deadline, or she was out of a job. She pressed the button for information, then took the ramp to the expressway.

Heading east under a threatening sky.

Chapter 28

Ellen got ahold of Lateef's teacher, Vanessa James, while her class was down the hall at the library. Tall and rail-thin, the teacher munched on a green apple as she moved quickly around the classroom, picking up stray books and crayons, straightening undersized chairs, and restoring a knit hat to its cubbyhole.

Vanessa asked, "It's all right with Laticia if we talk, right?"

"Yes, I called her on the way over. Sorry it's such short notice."

"No problem." Vanessa wore a long red sweater with black slacks and low heels. She had large eyes, a smile slick with lip gloss, and her hair straightened into a stiff bob, which showed off tiny diamond earrings winking in her earlobes. "We have fifteen minutes until they get back. What do you want to know?"

"Just a few things." Ellen slid her notebook from her purse and flipped over the cover, pen at the ready. "What kind of kid was Lateef?"

"Right to it, huh?" Vanessa paused in midbite, the apple at her mouth, her gaze suddenly pained. "Teef was like a light. You could say he was a class clown, but that wouldn't do him justice. He was the one who made everybody laugh. But he was a leader."

"Is there any example you can recall?"

"It hurts my heart to think about it." Vanessa tossed the apple into a scuffed brown wastebasket, where it made a loud *clunk*. "Okay, here's one. On picture day, he combed his hair flat as he could, which wasn't much, and he said he was Donald Trump. The photographer told him to cut it out, and he said, 'You're fired.'" Her pretty face relaxed into a smile, which vanished as quickly as it had appeared. "All the kids looked up to him. We just finished our unit on African-American history. It's part of the new core curriculum in social studies the SRC set up."

"SRC?"

"School Reform Commission. For Dr. King's birthday, Lateef was voted to be Dr. King. He memorized a few lines of 'I Have a Dream,' and he did a great job. He liked to be in front of the class." Vanessa paused at the memory. "He was quick as a whip. We do basic addition and subtraction, but he could have moved on to the third-grade curriculum, fractions and geometry. He was good on sentence structure, too; we have to get them ready for the PSSA's."

"What's that?"

"State tests. On our report cards, I have to pick from a lot of categories, like 'eager to try new things.'" Vanessa chuckled softly. "Lateef was my category buster. He was his own little category."

Ellen made rapid notes. "So how did the class deal with his murder?"

Vanessa shook her head, with a sigh. For a second, she seemed to focus on the large bulletin board on the wall, which was covered with red construction-paper hearts, each with a fold down the center. At the top of the board, gold glitter read, Get Ready For Valentine's Day In 2B!

Ellen waited for the teacher to respond. Experience had taught her that silence could be the hardest question to answer.

"These kids, they're used to death. We lost two kids already this school year, and it's only February." Vanessa kept her face to the bulletin board. "But Lateef, everybody knew him. Everybody *felt* him. The District sent us grief counselors. That child was too full of life not to be missed."

"Do the kids talk about it?"

"Some of them, and some of them cry. They'll never be the same. They're not innocent, like children are supposed to be." Vanessa turned to her, her lips forming a tight line. "What I see is a real deep sadness, and it goes all the way inside. These kids, they're *heartsick*. And those are the lucky ones."

Ellen didn't get it. "What you mean?"

"The unlucky ones, they don't even know what's bothering them. They can't express their feelings. They have an underlying grief and fear, but instead of expressing it in words, they act out. They fight. Bite. Kick. Bully each other. Their world isn't safe, and they know it." Vanessa pointed to one of the desks by the window, in the second row. "That was Teef's seat. It's there, empty, every day. I think about moving it, but that only makes it worse."

Ellen felt a pang. She thought instantly of Will's cubbyhole in his preschool, with his name card and a picture of Thomas the Tank Engine. What if one day that were empty, never to be filled again? "What will you do?"

"I'll leave it there. I have no choice. The first week, we made a little memorial and the kids brought flowers. Here, come look at this." Vanessa crossed to the desk with Ellen following her, and she lifted up the desk lid. Inside the well sat a huge pile of cards and dried red roses, their petals shriveling to black. "These are his Valentine's Day cards. Every day somebody comes by with another one. It kills me."

Ellen looked at the cards, thinking. *It kills all of us.*

"You know who you should talk to, if you really want to understand the effects of the murders in this city?"

"Who?" Ellen asked her, intrigued. The best leads always came from other leads.

"My uncle. He'll see you, if you can handle it."

Chapter 29

Ellen was standing in the Glade-scented entrance hall of the funeral home with its proprietor, Ralston Rilkey. He was a slight man with a compact frame, in his early sixties, and he wore his hair cut short and natural, with steel gray coils tangled at the temples. He had a short forehead, and his eyes were worried above a wide nose and neatly groomed mustache, also going gray.

"And what is it you want to know again?" Ralston asked. "I'm fairly busy. We have two viewings tonight."

"I'd like to know how you've been affected by the murders in the neighborhood. There's been so many lately, especially of children like Lateef Williams. Your niece told me you might help, and Laticia gave her permission to talk to me."

"I'll speak with you, but the interview must be respectful. Here at Ralston-Hughes, we practice dignity in death."

"I understand."

"Then follow me." Ralston left, and Ellen followed him across a red-carpeted hallway, through a paneled door that read EMPLOYEES ONLY, and downstairs into the basement of the converted rowhouse. The carpeting morphed into institutional gray tile, the temperature dipped slightly, and the fake-floral scents were eradicated by a starkly medicinal odor.

"Is that formaldehyde?" Ellen asked, making a note.

Ralston nodded, his bald spot bobbing as he walked ahead, and they reached a set of white double doors, which he opened. The odor grew stronger, and on the wall hung white smocks and plastic face shields. Stainless-steel shelves held boxes of cotton, jars, and bottles with labels that read Kelco Gold Series Arterial Embalming Fluid and Aron Alpha Instant Adhesive. Ellen made notes, trying not to shudder.

Ralston opened another door, and she found herself in a larger room with a glistening white table at its center, tilted at an angle. He stood behind the table in his suit of dark green, gesturing with evident pride. "This is our preparation room, one of them. You'll notice the table is porcelain. Porcelain doesn't react with the embalming chemicals."

"Would you fill me in on the procedure, generally?"

"The first step is washing and disinfecting the body. Embalming is simply the process of displacing blood with fluid, usually of formaldehyde preservative with a red dye, to give the flesh a lifelike appearance. Even African-American skin takes on a pallor once the blood is removed."

Ellen made a note.

"Then we inject the fluid, and this machine does its work, replacing the blood with fluid." Ralston rested his small hand on a yellowish pump at the head of the table. "We insert a trocar, which punctures the viscera and removes fluid. We disinfect the cavities as well, then inject preservative and we pack the orifices."

Ellen wasn't about to ask.

"We wash the body again and apply lotion, to protect against dehydration. After death, the eyes begin to sink into the skull, and we pack cotton into the eye socket, place a plastic eyecap under the eyelid, then pull back the eyelid to apply adhesive and keep the eye closed."

Ellen's stomach turned over.

"Death also causes the facial muscles to relax, and the jaw drops open. We make the eyes and mouth as lifelike as possible. As we say, we set the features."

Ellen tried to remain professional. "Now, how was the procedure in Lateef's case?"

"With Lateef, there were so many gunshot wounds on one side of his face that we had to use his school photo as a guide and build from that foundation."

Ellen tried to visualize it. That little face, smiling from his memorial T-shirt. "Couldn't you use the other side of his face?"

"No. With as many gunshots as he had, there was significant facial swelling, which distorted even the good side of his face. The trauma, you understand. We use chemicals to reduce the swelling."

"How did you cover the bullet wounds?"

"On his face?" Ralston frowned. "You misunderstand me. There was no covering. There was nothing there. So in his case, we reconstructed. We snipped away the excess tissue around the wounds and glued the skin that was left to his cheekbone and eye socket."

Ellen didn't want to know more. Nobody should know this stuff. It was unthinkable. She couldn't help but think of losing Will this way. Of him being the child on the table. Of his beautiful face being the one glued together.

"We poured wax into the bullet holes to fill the gap and used cosmetics to match the shade of the wax to his skin, which was lighter than his mother. Some mortuaries have airbrushes, but we don't need that. I'm forty-two years in this business, and my father had it before me. We don't airbrush."

Ellen rallied at the businesslike note in his tone.

"The result wasn't perfect, but it was acceptable to Laticia and the family, and it gave them comfort, to see him as they knew him in life. Even my niece gave us a good grade."

"That's wonderful," Ellen said, with an admiration she didn't try to hide, but Ralston shrugged it off.

"Even for a single gunshot wound, we wouldn't cover it, that would never work. The putty would simply sink into the wound." He held up an index finger. "That's one thing I've had to order more of, wax and putty. We've already used four times the amount that we did last year, and the manufacturer can't keep it in stock. I have a friend in Newark, he's in the same bind."

Ellen scribbled away. These would be the effects of murder that would flesh out the story, from a tragic perspective.

"And all the eyecaps I have are too big for children. For Lateef and the others, we have to resize the eyecaps. Cut them down with scissors."

Ellen wrote that down, too. "I hope the day never comes when they make eyecaps for kids."

"I hear that." Ralston nodded. "In addition, with Lateef, we didn't use a wire in his mouth. We sutured the muscle and used adhesive, and it worked very well. He had so much bruising, but luckily, the displacement during the injection cleared a lot of that. That's what we'd hoped for."

"You use the word 'we' a lot. Did you have help with Lateef?"

"My son John. We worked together." Ralston's tone softened. "We started at eight o'clock and we finished at dawn. My grandson, he's Lateef's age, and well, it wasn't easy for either John or me." He coughed slightly, and Ellen was about to ask a question, but held her tongue when she saw his head bow slightly and a stillness sweep over his slight frame. "Lateef, he's the one I'll never forget. I knew that boy. When he came in, looking the way he did, at first I didn't know what to do." Ralston shook his head, still downcast. "I didn't know what to do. I had to go outside. I stood in the back, by receiving. I asked the Lord to help me, to give me strength."

Ellen nodded. She didn't take a note. It would be off the record. It was too personal. Suddenly her cell phone rang, destroying the quiet and jarring them both. Embarrassed, she reached for her purse. "I'm so sorry," she said, digging. "I should have turned it off."

"Feel free to take the call." Ralston checked his watch, the moment having passed. "I should get back to work."

Ellen found the phone and switched it off, but not before she saw the area code. 302. Delaware.

Cheryl Martin.

Chapter 30

Ellen tore south toward Wilmington, racing the rush hour. The sky had turned black, and snow flurries had begun to fall, flecks of white lace frozen in her headlights. The radio news was predicting a storm, and she felt as if she were outrunning that, too. She was in an uneasy state, hyperexcited, even after the long, sad afternoon. She couldn't remember the last time she'd eaten, but it didn't matter. She found herself accelerating, going to seventy miles an hour, then eighty. She wondered if she was speeding toward something. Or away.

Ellen found the house, parked at the curb, and looked out her car window. Cheryl's home was a lovely Tudor with a white stucco façade and dark brown trim, set among plenty of open space. A white sedan sat in a circular driveway, and the evergreens and hedges landscaping the property were dusted by new flurries, so that the scene looked like a suburban snow globe. She grabbed her bag and her file and got out of the car.

They were sitting in a beautiful living room, on an L-shaped sectional couch in an oatmeal fabric that coordinated perfectly with a nubby sisal rug. The lighting was recessed and the walls were eggshell white, adorned with horsy landscapes that would undoubtedly echo the view from the picture window.

Cheryl was saying, "I have to admit, part of the reason I wanted to meet you is because I read your articles."

"Thank you." Ellen remembered the photos of Cheryl Villiers, née Martin, from her mother Gerry's house. Cheryl had been the pretty sister with large blue eyes and the sprinkling of freckles on a perfect nose, and in person, she resembled Will, despite the crow's-feet and the laugh lines bracketing her wide mouth.

"I even remembered the articles you wrote about adopting your baby, or Amy's baby. I reread them online after my mom called. I thought they were really good."

"Thanks."

"They had a photo of the baby in the paper. It's so strange to think that that little baby is Amy's. My new nephew. I just can't deal." Cheryl smiled uncomfortably, showing lightened teeth. "My mother said you showed her some court documents. Could I see them?"

"Yes, of course." Ellen dug in her purse and produced the adoption papers. "I really need to find Amy. I guess your mom told you, it's just to get some medical history. If you remember from the article, Will had a serious heart problem when I adopted him."

Cheryl read the papers, her head inclined at an inquisitive angle, so that her dark blond hair fell into her face. She had on a tan V-neck knit sweater, tight-fitting beige pants, and black leather flats.

"Do you think that's Amy's signature?"

"Yes, I do. It's absolutely her signature."

"How about on the consent form. Is that your signature?"

"No, I never signed this." Cheryl looked up, her eyes frank in light makeup. "She forged it."

"So what do you think's going on here?"

"Amy didn't want us to know about the baby, obviously."

Bingo. "What about this twisted ovary business?"

"Look, my mom thinks that Amy couldn't have had a baby, but I don't agree. All the doctor said was that she probably couldn't have a baby, and Amy made a big deal of that. Even my husband said she could conceive." Cheryl's tone resonated with resentment. "She's a major drama queen. She just used the twisted ovary to get attention."

"So do you think she had a baby?"

"Of course, it's certainly possible. We all stopped seeing her about the same time. If she had a baby three years ago, I have no way of knowing it for sure. I was married by then, and we don't see as much of my family." Something flickered behind Cheryl's eyes, but she guarded that emotion. "They all smoke, for one thing. We don't tolerate smoking around the house."

"Your husband's a doctor, you say?"

"Yes, a physician. He just left to take the kids to pizza for dinner. We have twin girls. We thought it wouldn't be a good idea if they were around while you were here."

"Right." Ellen considered it. Twins. They'd be Will's cousins. But back to business. "So do you have any idea where Amy could be? Your mom thinks she stays in touch with you."

"Amy does email, but hardly ever. When she needs money."

"Do you send her any?" Ellen wanted the address.

"No. My husband didn't think I should, so I stopped, and she stopped asking."

"May I have her email address? It really is important that I get in touch with her."

Cheryl frowned. "I should email Amy first and make sure that she wants to hear from you. After all, if she gave up her baby for adoption, she had a choice about whether she wanted to hear from you, didn't she?"

Damn. "Yes, but as your mom probably told you, the lawyer who brokered the adoption has passed away, and I have no other way to get this information."

Cheryl handed her back the papers. "My husband said that they can disclose medical information in an adoption, even if they keep the identity of the parent secret."

"That's true, but I find that I need to ask one or two more questions." Ellen tried another tack. "Tell you what. Would you give Amy my email address and have her contact me?"

"Okay."

"Thanks." Ellen hadn't come this far to be turned away. "What if she doesn't email me back? Will you give me her email?"

"Cross your fingers."

Ellen thought of her earlier request, which she'd made by phone. "I was wondering, too, if you were able to find any photos of her."

"Sure, I found two I had in the computer, one young and one more recent. I suppose it's okay if you have them." Cheryl turned to the end table, picked up two papers, and handed one to Ellen, pointing with a manicured index finger. "That's Amy, when she was little."

Ellen looked down at a photo of a cute girl holding an American flag and wearing an Uncle Sam hat. "How old is she in this picture, do you know?"

"She'd just turned five. Before she turned into a freak." Cheryl chuckled softly. "Does your son look like her?"

"Not that much." Ellen had to admit it. Amy's nose was wider than Will's and her lips fuller. "Frankly, he looks more like you."

"It must run in our family. I look nothing like my kids,

either. Can you imagine that, carrying twins for nine months and they don't look like you?"

"It doesn't seem fair." Ellen was too preoccupied to smile. "Will must look more like his father, but I don't know what his father looks like. Does the name Charles Cartmell mean anything to you?"

"No."

"According to the adoption papers, he's the father."

"Never heard of him. Amy dated tons of guys. She was never in a committed relationship."

"If she got pregnant, would she tell the father? I mean, would she feel as if she should?"

Cheryl scoffed. "Are you kidding? If I know my little sister, she probably didn't know who the father was. She could have made up the name on the form, couldn't she?"

Ellen leaned forward. "But why would she make up his name and not her own, or yours?"

"I don't know." Cheryl shrugged, but Ellen considered it for a minute.

"Wait, I bet I do. She couldn't make up her name because she had to produce ID at the hospital when Will got sick. But if she never married Charles, or Will's father, he never appeared. She could make up his name." Ellen's thoughts clicked ahead. "Tell me, did she have a boyfriend back then, three years ago, that you remember?"

"Oh, she had plenty. Is that the same thing?" Cheryl laughed, but Ellen didn't.

"No name you can recall?"

"No. Maybe this photo will help. It has a guy in it, and they look pretty chummy." Cheryl handed over the second photo. "This is the most recent picture I have of Amy. She emailed it to me, and you can see the date. June 5, 2004."

"That would be shortly before she had Will," Ellen

said, cheering inwardly. It was a picture of Amy, grinning on the beach, in a black bikini, with a brown beer bottle in her hand. Her arm was looped around a shirtless man who raised his bottle to the camera. If Will was born on January 30, 2005, she would have been about two months pregnant when the photo was taken, assuming it was taken when it was sent. But she had no baby bump, though maybe she wasn't showing yet, and there was that beer bottle.

"What are you thinking?" Cheryl asked.

"That if Amy was seeing this man around then, he could be Will's father."

"He's so her type. Amy went for bad boys."

Ellen eyed the man, who wasn't bad-looking for a bad boy, with narrow eyes and long brown ponytail. Something about him looked almost familiar, but maybe it was that he looked a little like Will. He had the smile, a little tilted down, but it looked like a smirk on him. The photo was too blurry to see more detail and it had been taken from a distance. "In the email, did Amy say who he was, or where they were?"

"No."

Ellen mulled it over. "It could be anywhere it's warm, which could be anywhere, in June. What did she say in the email, if I can ask?"

"Nothing. She just sent the photo. Nice, huh?" Cheryl scoffed again, but Ellen's gaze remained on the photo. She could be looking at Will's birth parents. Charles Cartmell, if it was him, had a sleeve of multicolored tattoos she couldn't read and he looked a little drunk, even in the fuzzy resolution.

"The focus is so bad on this."

"It could be my printer. Keep that copy and I'll email you another, if you want."

"Please, do." Ellen told Cheryl her email address. "Did Amy have any girlfriends?"

"She never got along with other girls. She hung with the guys."

Ellen made a mental note. "You said Amy emails you. Did she ever mention any men in her emails?"

"Not that I remember."

"Would you mind looking back at the emails, so we can check?"

"I can't, I deleted them." Cheryl checked her watch. "Well, it's getting kind of late."

"Sure, I should go." Ellen rose with her papers, hiding her frustration. "Thanks so much for meeting with me. Think she'll email me?"

"God knows."

Ellen said her good-byes and left, wondering if it was really Charles Cartmell in the photo. She hit the cold air outside and looked up at the sky, dark and starless.

Maybe it wasn't too late to take a drive.

Chapter 31

Ellen sat in her car with the engine off, watching the snow fall in the dark, holding the court papers. She was parked outside of an elementary school, a three-story red-brick edifice that had been there since 1979, according to its keystone. The school was at Charles Cartmell's address, but obviously, he didn't live here. He had never lived here. Amy must have pulled the address out of thin air and made up the name, too. She might as well have picked Count Chocula.

Ellen wasn't completely surprised. She had known that Grant Avenue was one of the busiest streets in the Northeast, in a commercial area, but she had been hoping that there would be an apartment house or maybe a converted rowhouse.

Cars rushed past her, their windshield wipers pumping and their red brake lights burning holes into the night. She looked again at the photo of Amy and the man on the beach. The streetlight cast an oblong of purplish light across his face, but his eyes remained in shadow.

"Who is my son?" she asked the silence.

Chapter 32

"Thanks so much for staying, Con." Ellen closed the front door behind her, feeling a wave of guilt. It was after eleven o'clock, and on TV, a bow-tied weatherman was sticking a yardstick into three inches of snow. "I really do appreciate it."

"S'okay." Connie rose tiredly from the couch, her Sudoku book in hand. "Everything go okay at your meeting?"

"Yes, thanks." Ellen got Connie's coat from the closet and handed it to her. "How's my baby boy?"

"Fine." Connie slipped into her coat. "But it was Crazy Shirt Day at school, and you forgot his shirt. I reminded you, last week. I thought it was in his backpack and just went."

"Oh no." Ellen felt another wave of guilt, which made two in two minutes, a record even for her. "Was he upset?"

"He's three, El."

"I should have remembered."

"No, I should've checked. I will, next time."

"Poor kid." Ellen kicked herself. Will hated to be the one who was different. The one who was adopted. The one with no dad. Neither she nor Will was like the other. "You even reminded me."

"Don't beat yourself up. It's easy to lose track. Crazy Hat Day, Snack Mom, Pajama Day, whatever. I didn't have to deal with that when Mark was little." Connie slid her puzzle book into her tote bag, picked up her things, then straightened up. "They're working you too hard."

"And I'm working *you* too hard." Ellen squeezed her shoulder. "Please tell Chuck I'm sorry for keeping you."

"He can get his own meal for a change. It won't kill him." Connie opened the door, letting in a blast of cold, wet air. "Snow's already stopping, isn't it?"

"Yes, but drive safe. Thanks again." Ellen held the door, then closed and locked it behind her. She took off her coat and hung it up, dwelling. She was screwing up left and right lately. Forgetting the crazy shirt. Missing the projects meeting. It had all started with the white card in the mail. She hoped Amy emailed her soon and she could put it all behind her.

Ellen went into the kitchen and brewed herself a fresh mug of coffee, pushing Amy to the back of her mind. She had a story to write and she was starved. She scarfed a bowl of Frosted Mini-Wheats over the sink, leaving her leftover milk to Oreo Figaro, who leapt onto the counter, purring deeply as he lapped it up. When he was finished, he looked up from the bowl, blinking his yellow-green eyes in a silent request for more. The tiniest droplet of milk clung to his chin.

"We have to get to work," Ellen said, taking back the bowl.

Up in her home office, she began as she did with any story. There were no shortcuts, at least none that worked. She built her stories from the bottom up, and her first step

was always transcribing her notes. If she needed to quote
directly, she'd go to the tapes. Then, usually, if she'd had
enough caffeine, her brain would lurch into action and an
angle for the story would suggest itself. She took a sip of
hot coffee, glanced at the notes beside her, and started
with the interview of Lateef's mother, typing:

**Pies "too ugly" to serve. She wants it in the paper,
so kids are not a number "like it's Powerball."**

Ellen kept going, trying to remember the mood of the
interview and how she felt sitting in Laticia's kitchen, but
her thoughts strayed back to Cheryl's house and the picture
of Amy and the man on the beach.

**"Ain't nothin' gonna change here, and this is _Amer-
ica_."**

Ellen flipped the page of her notebook and kept transcribing, but it was only mechanical. She'd learned a lot
about Will in one day. She'd met his mother, grandmother,
and aunt. She might have seen what his father looked
like. She tried to keep typing but her fingers slowed and
thoughts of the Martin family intruded. She found herself
wondering if Cheryl had emailed her a copy of the photo
of Amy and the man on the beach.

She minimized her Word file and opened up Outlook
Express. Incoming emails piled onto the screen, and she
ignored the one from Sarah with the attachment and subject line: FYI, I EMAILED MARCELO MY PIECE.
Suddenly an email came on the screen from twinzmom
373@gmail.com.

Ellen clicked it open. It was Cheryl's. The message
read, **Nice meeting you,** and there was an attachment.
She opened the attachment, and the photo of Amy and
the man on the beach popped onto the screen. Though
she'd seen it before, she couldn't wrap her mind around
the fact that Amy was Will's mother and the man on the
beach his father, glowing on her computer screen. She

looked over her shoulder in case Will had gotten out of bed, but there was nothing behind her except Oreo Figaro, his front legs stretched on the rug like Superman in flight.

She squinted at the picture. It was brighter online, but still blurry and the images too distant. She knew how to rectify that. She saved the photo to My Pictures and opened Photoshop, then uploaded the photo, drew a box around Amy's face, and clicked Zoom. The image exploded into pixels, so she telescoped it down a little, then examined Amy's features with care. The shape of her eyes didn't look much like Will's, though they were blue, but her nose was longer than Will's and too wide.

Not everybody looks like their mom.

Ellen zoomed out to the original photo, outlined the man's face with the mouse, then clicked. Her heart beat a little faster. The man did look a little familiar, and his smile was like Will's, with that downturn on the right. She sipped some coffee and clicked Zoom again, enlarging his face to fill the screen. She'd hoped the blur would let her sense the general configuration of his face, but it didn't. She set down her coffee, almost spilling it on her notes, so she moved the notebook out of the way. Sticking out from underneath was the white card with the photo of Timothy Braverman.

Hmmm.

She slid out the white card and looked at the age-progressed version of Timothy, then set the card down, went back into My Pictures, and found Will's last school picture. She enlarged it and set it up on the screen next to the photo of the man on the beach. Then she compared the two photos—the most recent of Will with the man on the beach—taking a mental inventory:

Will, eyes blue and wide-set; Beach Man, eyes close
     together and blue

Will, nose, little and turned up; Beach Man, long and
    skinny
Will, blond hair; Beach Man, light brown hair
Will, round face; Beach Man, long, oval face
Will, normal chin; Beach Man, pointed chin
Similarities—blue eyes, lopsided smile

Ellen reviewed the list, then leaned back and eyeballed
the photos from a distance. She wasn't able to reach a
conclusion, as much as she wanted to. Beach Man could
be Will's father, or maybe he was someone Amy was dating around the same time, or a random guy with a beer. Or
maybe Will didn't look that much like either of his parents. He looked like Cheryl, and that counted for something.

Ellen went back online. She clicked through to the
Braverman family's website, then captured the age-
progressed photo of Timothy and saved a copy to My Pictures. She was going to put it on the screen next to Will's
and Beach Man's, then compare all three of them when
something else on the Braverman family website caught
her eye.

The composite drawing of the carjacker.

On impulse, Ellen captured the composite and saved a
copy to My Pictures, then uploaded it and placed it next to
recent Will, age-progressed Timothy, and Beach Man—
all four images in a line. She blinked, and her heart beat a
little faster. She captured the composite drawing and the
photo of Beach Man, then placed them side by side on their
own page. The photos were different sizes, so she outlined
the composite drawing and clicked Zoom to enlarge it to
the approximate size of Beach Man, and clicked.

She froze. The composite drawing of the carjacker
looked like Beach Man. She double-checked, and there
was no doubt that they looked alike.

"Oh my God," she said aloud, and Oreo Figaro raised his chin, his eyes angled slits disappearing into the blackness of his fur.

Ellen looked back at the screen, getting a grip. It was impossible to compare a black-and-white pencil drawing with a color photo of a flesh-and-blood man. She flashed on Will's tracing of a horse from the other day, and it gave her an idea. She clicked Print, and her cheap plastic printer chugged to life. Then she got up and hurried downstairs, rummaged through the toy box, and ran back up with a roll of tracing paper.

The printer had spit out a copy of the composite drawing, and she took a black Sharpie and went over the lines of the carjacker's features, blackening them so they'd be darker and thicker. Then she took the piece of tracing paper and placed it on top of the composite drawing, tracing the image onto the crinkly transparent paper, ignoring the thumping in her chest. She set the traced composite aside, slid the copy of the Beach Man photo from the printer tray, then moved her computer keyboard to the side and set the printed photo on the desk.

Then she stopped.

She wanted to know and she didn't want to know, both at once.

"Get over it," she said under her breath, and she took the traced composite of the carjacker and placed it over Beach Man's face.

It was an exact match.

Ellen felt her gorge rising, and she jumped up and bolted for the bathroom.

Chapter 33

Ellen lingered on the threshold to Will's room, lost in her thoughts. She couldn't work any longer, not after what she'd learned, or what she thought she'd learned. She could barely give it voice inside her own head, but she couldn't ignore it, either.

Is Will really Timothy?

She tasted bile and Colgate on her teeth and sagged against the doorjamb, willing her brain to function. Tried to reason it out and spot any failures of logic.

Begin at the beginning. Remain calm.

Ellen thought a minute, trying to articulate the scenario she feared. If the composite matched the photo of the man on the beach, then Beach Man was the carjacker. He had shot Carol Braverman's nanny. Kidnapped Will. Taken the ransom money but kept the child. He had a girlfriend who pretended to be the baby's mother. Amy Martin.

Why not kill the baby right after the kidnapping?

Ellen shuddered, but she could guess at some answers. Amy wanted a baby and couldn't have one. Or they thought they could sell the baby on the black market. She folded her arms against her chest, hugging herself, and picked up the narrative in her mind, detecting another fallacy.

Why give him up for adoption?

That answer, Ellen knew for sure. Because he got sick. Will had a heart problem no one knew about. At least she assumed as much, because the Braverman site didn't mention that Timothy had any heart problems. The doctors at Dupont Hospital had told her that his murmur had gone undetected, which wasn't unusual. Will would have failed to thrive. He wouldn't eat well and he'd have been sickly. That would have overwhelmed Amy, even her mother said so, and it would have made it too risky to keep him. Too many blood tests, forms, and questions that could show Amy wasn't the mother and the boyfriend the father.

So what do they do next?

Ellen composed it like a nightmare news story. They'd take the baby to a hospital far from Miami, back to where Amy had grown up. They'd essentially abandon the baby in the hospital, and then a solution would come, in the form of a nice lady reporter, who falls in love with the baby. She adopts the baby and takes him home, where he sleeps under a sky of ersatz stars.

My God.

Ellen let her gaze wander around Will's bedroom, over the shadows of Tonka trucks and Legos, over shelves of skinny books and Candy Land and plush bears and bunnies, their soft pastels reduced to shades of gray. The window shade was up, and outside the sky was oddly bright, the world aglow with a new snowfall that insulated the house like a sheet of practical cotton, keeping her and Will safe inside.

"Mommy?" he asked sleepily, from the bed.

Ellen wiped her eyes, padded over to the bed, and

leaned over Will, brushing his bangs from his forehead in the light from the doorway. "Sorry I woke you."

"Are you home?"

"Yes, it's night and I'm home."

"Connie says you have to work hard."

"I do, but I'm home now." Ellen swallowed the knot in her throat, but she had a feeling it would only travel down to her chest and cause a heart attack, or maybe she'd just spontaneously combust. She eased onto the guardrail and tried to regain her composure. "Sorry I forgot your crazy shirt."

"It's okay, Mommy."

Ellen's eyes welled up. She reached down and stroked his cheek. "You're the best kid in the world, do you know that?"

"You brushed your teeth."

"I did." Ellen was uncomfortable, sitting on the guardrail. "I hate this guardrail. I'm taking it off." She stood up and began to slide the wooden rail from the bed, jiggling the frame.

"I won't fall out, Mommy."

"I know that. You're too smart to fall out of your own bed." Ellen jiggled one last time and finally wrenched the guardrail from the bed. "Sorry."

Will giggled.

"Stupid guardrail."

"*Stupid* guardrail!"

"See ya, guardrail." Ellen took the guardrail to the other side of the room and set it on the floor. "Wouldn't wanna be ya."

Will giggled again.

Ellen came back to the bed, where she could see Will wriggling in his bed. "Are you being a wiggle worm?"

"I am!"

"I'm coming in. We're having a slumber party."

"What's that?" Will scissored his legs.

"It's people having a party when they should be sleeping." Ellen eased onto the skinny bed, on her side. "Scoot over, wigglehead."

"Okay." Will edged backwards, and Ellen reached for him and wrapped him up in her arms. She didn't want to think about Amy Martin and the Bravermans anymore. She wanted to be where she was, right this moment, holding her son close.

"How's that feel? Good?"

Will hugged her back. "I made a snowball."

"You did? Cool."

"It's on the porch, did you see?"

"No." Ellen gave him a squeeze. "It'll be there tomorrow. I'll look at it in the morning, first thing."

"Do you have to go to work tomorrow?"

"Yes." Ellen didn't know what would happen at work tomorrow, with her story unfinished. Right now, she didn't care.

"I hate work."

"I know, sweetie. I'm sorry I have to work."

"Why do you?"

Ellen had answered this more times than she could count, but she knew it wasn't a real question. "I work so we have all the things we need."

Will yawned.

"Maybe we should settle down and go to sleep. Party's over, and slumber is beginning."

"I won't fall out," Will said again, and Ellen hugged him close.

"Don't worry. You won't fall out. I'm here to catch you."

"Good night."

"I love you, sweetie. Good night." Ellen cuddled him, and in the next minute, she could feel his body drifting back to sleep. She caught herself beginning to cry and willed herself to stop. If she went that way, she'd never come back, and this wasn't the time or the place anyway.

Flip it.

She really couldn't be sure that Beach Man was the carjacker. A tracing couldn't tell anything with accuracy, and composites were based only on a verbal description. Lots of men had narrow eyes and long noses. If the composite was too unreliable to prove that the carjacker was Beach Man, then there was no link between Will and Timothy.

Ellen smiled in the dark, feeling a tiny bit better. Maybe Amy would email her, tell her the story of Will's birth, and explain why she'd put him up for adoption.

Will shifted in his sleep, and she snuggled him. She couldn't resolve tonight whether her fears were founded or completely insane. But behind them lurked an unspoken question, one that she couldn't begin to acknowledge, much less articulate to herself. It had been lurking in the back of her mind from the moment she'd seen the infernal white card in the mail.

She hugged Will closer, there in the still, dark room, and the question hung in the air above the bed, suspended somewhere between mother, child, and the false stars.

If Will is really Timothy, what will I do?

Chapter 34

Ellen entered the newsroom the next morning, exhausted after only two hours of sleep. She hadn't been able to stop her brain from thinking about Will and Timothy, and she felt raw, achy, and preoccupied. She had on the same jeans and shirt she'd worn yesterday, but with a different sweater, and she hadn't had time to shower. She'd checked her email too many times on the way in, but there'd been no email from Amy Martin.

Get a grip.

"Good morning, dear," Meredith Snader said, passing her with an empty mug on the way to the coffee room, and Ellen managed a smile.

"Hey, Mer." She tried to put the Braverman business behind her, but her head was pounding. The newsroom was mostly empty, and she hustled down the aisle, trying to get her thoughts together for the meeting about the homicide piece. Through the glass wall of his office, she could see Marcelo at his desk and Sarah sitting across from him, laughing about something.

Great.

Ellen figured the laughter would stop when she told

them she'd be late with her end of the story. She dropped her handbag on her desk, shed her jacket, and hung it on the coatrack, seeing that Sal and Larry were entering Marcelo's office, holding styrofoam cups of coffee and looking like the journalists Ellen had grown up idolizing. She hated that she was about to crash and burn in front of the local Woodward and Bernstein. She girded herself and headed to Marcelo's office, where he looked up expectantly from behind his desk.

"Come in, Ellen." Marcelo smiled, his eyes flashing darkly. "I didn't get your draft. Did you email it?"

Ellen arranged her face into a professional mask. "Marcelo, I don't have the piece done. I'm sorry."

Sarah looked over. Larry and Sal turned around. Marcelo blinked. "You don't have it?" he asked, lifting an eyebrow.

"No, sorry." Ellen's temples thundered. "I got a little bogged down and I need a few extra days."

"Maybe I can help. That's what they pay me for."

"No, you can't," Ellen blurted out, but Marcelo was still smiling, his head cocked and his eyes sympathetic.

"Let me see what you have so far. I'm not looking for perfection. I can't be, with these two slackers on the story." Marcelo gestured at Larry and Sal. "Their draft needed the usual overhaul."

"Kiss my ass," Sal said, and they all laughed except Ellen, who had to come clean.

"Marcelo, to be honest, there is no draft. Not yet." She felt vaguely sick, unmasked and vulnerable. They were all looking at her in surprise, Marcelo most of all.

"Nothing?" Marcelo frowned, confused.

"No worries," Sarah chirped up. "I've got it covered."

"Please wait." Marcelo held up a large palm, but Ellen was looking over at Sarah, too angry to let it go.

"What do you mean, you have it covered?" she asked.

Sarah ignored the question. "Marcelo, Ellen refused to talk with my source, Julia Guest, so I did and wrote it up. I think it puts a human face on the issue quite nicely." She handed him some sheets from a stack she cradled against her chest. "Check it out."

Ellen felt stunned. Sarah had just stuck a knife in her back. The girl wanted her job and was taking no prisoners.

"Who's this source again?" Marcelo was asking, eyeing the pages.

"She's been active in the efforts to stop the violence and has organized the community on the issue. She knows all the players and she feeds to the Mayor's Office."

"What's her stake in this?"

"She organized last month's demonstrations and one of the vigils."

"Is she in local politics?"

"Not officially."

"Thanks, but that's not what I had in mind." Marcelo, troubled, handed her back the pages. "It sounds to me as if she has no stake. If she doesn't have a stake, she's not the story."

Ellen cleared her throat. "I interviewed one of the mothers who lost a son, a second-grader who was murdered. I also spoke with the boy's teacher and the funeral director who prepared his body."

Sal whistled. "Grieving mothers are a homerun."

Larry nodded. "I like the funeral angle, too. It's different. Original."

Marcelo looked relieved. "Okay, Ellen. Good. So you just don't have the draft yet. When can you finish it?"

"Next Friday?"

"She's been working on that Sulaman follow-up," Sarah interrupted, and Ellen turned on her, not bothering to hide her feelings.

"What are you talking about?"

"You've been working on Sulaman, right?" Sarah asked calmly, lifting an eyebrow. "That's the real reason you blew this deadline, isn't it?"

"That's not true!" Ellen shot back, but she could see that Sarah had gotten Marcelo's attention.

"Yes, it is," Sarah continued, her tone measured. "I know because Susan Sulaman called yesterday. She said she'd been calling you and couldn't reach you, so the switchboard sent the call to the newsroom, and I picked up. She said you'd interviewed her and wanted to know if you'd talked your editor into running the story."

Marcelo's eyes flared, and Ellen's face burned.

"You have no idea what I've been doing, so stay out of my business!"

"I knew you wouldn't make the deadline." Sarah remained calm, but Ellen raised her voice.

"Your story is separate from mine!" She couldn't stop herself from shouting even though everyone had fallen into shocked silence. Her head was about to explode. "It's not your concern whether I make my deadline or not!"

"Beg to differ." Sarah sniffed. "I pitched the piece in the first place and you're screwing it up. We're all ready, why aren't you?"

"Ladies, hold on." Marcelo stood up behind his desk, raising his hands. "Everyone, please, give Ellen and me a minute."

"Good luck," Sal said with a smile, plucking his coffee from the edge of the desk, and Larry followed suit, both of them edging past Ellen, who turned her head away when Sarah brushed by her, trailing perfume and adrenaline. After they had left, Marcelo put his hands firmly on his hips.

"Close the door, please," he said quietly.

Ellen did, then faced him.

"What's going on? You never miss a deadline." Marcelo looked mystified, and his tone sounded more disappointed than angry. "Is she right? Was it the Sulaman follow-up that delayed you?"

"No."

"Did you interview the mother?"

"Yes. Only once."

"When?"

Ellen could hardly remember. She rubbed her face. Everything before the white card was a blur, as if a line had been drawn down the middle of her life, dividing it into Before and After. HAVE YOU SEEN THIS CHILD? Her head hurt so much she felt dizzy. "Tuesday?"

"But I asked you not to." Marcelo's tone wasn't disappointed, Ellen realized, but hurt.

"I'm so sorry. I just had to."

"Why?"

"I was just curious, I had to see her again." Ellen knew it sounded lame, and Marcelo looked grave, his eyebrows sloping down.

"Ellen, let's be honest with one another. Ever since I let Courtney go, I feel you've been distant. You've acted differently toward me. It's as if we're on different sides."

"No, we're not, I swear."

"Please, don't work against me. We have too much work for anybody to be doing that. We're doing more with less, and every day it gets worse."

"I'm not working against you."

"But all this fussing with Sarah, it's not needed."

"It won't happen again."

Marcelo finger-raked his hair from his forehead and fell silent a moment, eyeing her. "I can tell something's wrong. You're not yourself. Is it Will? I know he was sick when he was little. Is he sick again?"

"No." Ellen couldn't tell him anything, as much as she

would have loved a sounding board. "I'll have the story to you early next week. I said Friday because I wanted to be realistic."

"Tell me what's wrong," Marcelo said again, his voice even softer. "You look tired."

"I don't feel that great." Ellen winced inwardly. *You look tired* was code for *you look ugly.*

"Are you sick?"

"I threw up last night," Ellen blurted out, then watched Marcelo's eyes flare in brief surprise. Throwing up was definitely not hot, and suddenly she felt like a frigging mess. Doing and saying the wrong things, exhausted and undone. "I should just go home. I really don't feel well at all."

"Okay, that's fine, of course." Marcelo nodded, walking around his desk toward her. "If you're sick, you must go home. Take care of yourself."

"Right, thanks." Ellen moved to the door, feeling oddly dizzy. She broke out into a sweat. Her head was light. She hadn't had time for breakfast. Even Connie had looked at her funny.

And in the next second, the office went black.

Chapter 35

"Surprise, I'm home!" Ellen called out from the doorway, slipping out of her coat. The living room was bright and peaceful, with a winter sun streaming through the windows, and the sight brought her back to reality, after having fainted in Marcelo's office. She'd blamed it on her mystery illness when she regained consciousness in his arms, their faces close enough to kiss. Or maybe she had imagined that part.

"Mommy!" Will zoomed from the dining room, his rubbery sneakers thundering on the soft pine floors.

"Honey!" Ellen let her coat fall to scoop him up and give him a big hug, and Connie came out of the kitchen, looking pleased. She was dressed to go to Happy Valley for the weekend in her Penn State wear, gray stretch slacks and a blue Nittany Lions sweatshirt.

"Hi, El. Is there much ice on the road?"

"No, and thanks for shoveling the walk."

"That's all right. Will helped."

"Good for you, sweetie." Ellen set Will down, and he hit the ground moving. She had called Connie on the way home, telling her she was taking the day off, though she'd edited out the fainting. "No school today, huh?"

"No, Mommy. We read four books!" Will held up four fingers, and Ellen grinned.

"Good for you!"

Connie said, "I don't know why they closed. It's a gyp, for what you pay."

"It's all right." Ellen smiled at Will, cupping his warm head. "I wanna have some fun, don't you, honey?"

"Fun!" Will started jumping up and down, and Ellen laughed.

"How about sledding? Is that fun?"

"YES!" Will shouted, jumping like crazy.

"Good idea." Connie reached for her coat, purse, and tote. "TGIF, hey?"

"Exactly." Ellen smiled, glad to give her the time off after she'd been working so hard. "Who are we playing this weekend?"

"Nobody as good as we are."

"So we're winning?"

"Of course. Mark might even start." Connie grinned.

"Go Lions!" Ellen raised a fist, and Will did, too, still jumping. She stroked his silky hair, beginning to feel better. "Will, say good-bye and thank you to Connie."

"Good-bye, Mommy!" Will shouted, throwing his arms around Connie's legs, and Ellen cringed.

"See ya later," Connie said, bending over and hugging Will back.

"Alligator," he replied, his face buried in her coat, and Ellen opened the door while Connie left, waving happily.

Ellen closed the door behind her with a grin for Will. "Hey, pal, did you eat lunch yet?"

"No."

"Me neither. How about we eat and then go sledding?"

"Sledding!"

"Not yet." Ellen glanced at the dining-room table, covered with crayons and coloring books. "Go pick up those crayons, please, and I'll get lunch ready. Okay, buddy?"

"Okay, Mommy!" Will ran into the dining room and thundered into the kitchen, where she could hear the scrape of the footstool as he pulled it up to the counter. Oreo Figaro jumped down from the couch with his characteristic chirp, and she bent over to pet him hello, then felt her BlackBerry vibrating on her waistband. She took the BlackBerry from its holster, and the screen showed a red asterisk next to the email.

She hit the button. The email was from twinzmom373, Cheryl Martin. Ellen felt her chest tighten. She opened the email and read:

> Ellen,
> I sent Amy an email about you and told her your email address. I'll let you know if I hear from her, but don't hold your breath. Hope your son gets better. Sorry I couldn't help more.
> Best,
> Cheryl

Ellen bit her lip, her gaze lingering on the tiny screen. At least Cheryl had gotten through to Amy. If the email hadn't bounced back, it was still a good email address. She'd have to hope for the best, but in the meantime, she was back to Before and After. Either the carjacker was Beach Man or he wasn't. Two choices. Do or die.

"Mommy, I'm done!" Will called from the dining room. He was kneeling on a chair, trying to hold a logjam of crayons. They were dropping everywhere, and Oreo Figaro was chewing Burnt Sienna.

"Let me help, honey." Ellen got up, putting the Black-Berry away.

During lunch, she tried to tuck her anxiety away in the back of her brain, but it kept coming to the fore, even as she got Will dressed in his snowsuit and retrieved the orange plastic saucer from the basement. She slid into her coat and took him in one hand and the saucer in the other, then went outside in the cold sun, inhaling a deep lungful of fresh air.

"Freezing, Mommy!" Will said, his breath making tiny puffs in the frigid air.

"Look, your breath looks like a little train. You're Thomas the Tank Engine."

Will giggled. "Choo-choo!"

"Here we go!" Ellen scanned the street, which was covered with a soft snow that blanketed the rooftops, filled the rain gutters, and lined the porch steps. The houses, mostly stone or clapboard, sat close together, and many of them shared driveways, like freshly shoveled Ys. Narberth was a stop-time neighborhood, where everybody looked out for each other.

They were making their way down the porch steps when Ellen realized something. Her neighbors must have gotten the white card in the mail, showing the photo of Timothy Braverman. They could have noticed how much he looked like Will, and everyone on the street knew that Will was adopted. They had all read her series, and she had even thrown a welcoming party for him when he was well enough. She used to be glad that Narberth was so chummy, but that was Before. After, it terrified her. She squeezed Will's hand.

"Ow, too tight, Mommy." He looked up in surprise, stiff in his puffy blue coat and snow pants, his arms sticking out like a gingerbread man.

"Sorry." Ellen eased her grip, shaken. She looked up

and down her block, worried about running into her neighbors.

Two doors away, Mrs. Knox, an older woman, was brushing snow from her sidewalk, and on the far side of the street, stay-at-home moms Elena Goldblum and Barbara Capozzi were talking while their kids played in the snow. All of them could have seen the white card, especially the moms. Ellen stood frozen on the sidewalk.

"Mommy?" Will asked. "Are we going?"

"I'm just looking at the street. It's so pretty with the snow, isn't it?"

"Go!" Will tugged her hand, but Ellen's thoughts raced ahead. They always went sledding a few blocks away at Shortridge Park, and the place would be packed with Will's friends, their mothers, and the occasional stay-at-home dad, probably Domenico Vargas, who usually brought an old-fashioned plaid thermos of Ecuadorian coffee. All of them would have gotten the white card.

"Will, guess what?" Ellen knelt to see him at eye level and held him by the shoulder. His face was a circle of adorable features—those blue eyes under a pale fringe of feathery bangs, upturned nose, broad smile—framed by the drawstring of his hood. "Today, how about we go to a new place to sled?"

"Where?" Will frowned.

"Valley Forge. I used to sled there when I was growing up. Did I ever tell you about that? I loved it there."

"What about Brett?" Will's lower lip puckered. "Is he there?"

"No, but we can tell him how great it is. It's good for a change. Why don't we give it a try?"

"I don't want to."

"Let's try it. We'll have fun." Ellen straightened up, took him by the hand, and walked him over to the car before he could object. She got her keys from her pocket, chirped the back door unlocked, hoisted him into his car seat, and locked him in, kissing his cold nose. "This will be an adventure."

Will nodded, uncertain. "We didn't say good-bye to Oreo Figaro."

"He'll forgive us." Ellen closed the car door, stuck the saucer in the trunk, and was going to the driver's side when Mrs. Knox appeared from nowhere in her black down coat, cackling.

"I know what you're up to!" she said, pointing with a red leather glove. "You're playin' hooky!"

"You got that right." Ellen opened the car door and got in. "It's a snow day for grown-ups, too. Gotta go!"

"Why're you drivin' to Shortridge? It's only around the corner."

"See you!" Ellen shut the door, started the engine, and backed out of the driveway, giving a disappointed Mrs. Knox a last wave.

"Mommy?" Will said from the backseat.

"What?"

"Connie doesn't like Mrs. Knox."

"Really?" Ellen backed out of the driveway and adjusted the rearview mirror to see him. He looked stuffed into the car seat, immobilized. "Why not?"

"Connie says Mrs. Knox is a busy-busy."

"A what?" Ellen steered the car down the street. "You mean a busybody?"

"Yes!" Will giggled.

Ellen hit the gas, hard.

Chapter 36

An hour later Ellen was still driving through Valley Forge Park, trying to find the sledding hill she remembered. She'd checked her BlackBerry at a few traffic lights on the way, but Amy Martin hadn't emailed yet. The road wound through snow-covered log cabins and lines of black cannons, passing George Washington's encampment from the Revolutionary War, but she had stopped pointing out the historical sites to an increasingly cranky three-year-old, kicking in his car seat.

"I'm hot. My coat is hot." Will pulled at his zipper, and Ellen steered right, then left, and finally spotted a packed parking lot.

"We're here!"

"Yay!"

"This is gonna be great!" Ellen turned into the lot and found a space next to a station wagon that disgorged a slew of teenage boys. The tallest one undid the bright bungee cords that fastened a wooden toboggan to the roof rack.

"He's a big boy!" Will craned his neck.

"He sure is." Ellen shut off the ignition, and the teenager slid the toboggan onto his head, where he struggled to balance it. The other teenagers hooted when it dipped like a seesaw.

"He's gonna drop it! Watch out!" Will squealed with delight. "Mommy, what is that thing on him?"

"It's called a toboggan. It's like our saucer." Ellen put on her sunglasses and gloves. "It goes down the hill."

"Why doesn't he have a saucer?"

"He must like a toboggan better."

"Why don't we have it?"

"Someday we will, if you want one. Now, let's rock." Ellen got out of the car, went around to his side, and freed Will from his car seat. He reached for her with his fingers outstretched, then wrapped his arms around her neck when she held him.

"I love you, Mommy."

"I love you, too, sweetie." Ellen set him down and took his hand, then went to the trunk and got the saucer. Laughter and shouting came from the hill on the other side of the road, the sound echoing in the cold, crisp air, and she and Will walked through the plowed parking lot, rock salt crunching under their boots. The teenage boys crossed the street ahead of them, but there was such a crowd on the other side that Ellen couldn't see the hill.

"Isn't this fun, Will?" Ellen held Will's hand as they crossed.

"So many people!"

"That's because they know it's a good place to sled." Ellen surveyed the view beyond the crowd, a gorgeous vista of snowy evergreens, stone houses, and horse farms surrounding the park. The sky was a cloudless blue, and the sun pale gold, and distant. "Isn't this pretty?"

"Very pretty," he answered agreeably, but Ellen realized he couldn't see anything for the kids in front of him, so she picked him up.

"How's that? Better?"

"Oooh! Pretty!"

"Here we go!" Ellen dragged the saucer by its rope and threaded her way through the crowd, noticing that they were older than she'd expected, high school and even college kids in Villanova hoodies. She and Will reached the front of the crowd and looked out over the hill, and Ellen hid her dismay. The hill was much steeper than she remembered it, if it was even the same hill. It dropped off as steeply as an intermediate ski slope, and the snow had been packed hard by the sledding, so its surface glistened, icy-hard.

"Mom, whoa!" Will shouted, blinking. "This is so BIG!"

"I'll say." Ellen watched with concern as the teenagers shot down the hill on sleds, toboggans, and inflatable rafts, laughing and screaming. Two rafts collided on a mogul, and boys popped out and went skidding downhill. It looked dangerous. "This is kind of big for us, honey."

"No, Mom, we can do it!" Will wiggled in her arms.

"I'm not so sure." Ellen was jostled by a snowboarder, who shouted an apology before he launched himself down the hill. She scanned the slope for younger children, but didn't see a one. She wanted to kick herself. They could have been having fun at Shortridge, but she had dragged him to Mount Everest.

"Now, Mom, put me down!"

"Okay, but hold my hand and let's move over, out of the way." Ellen set him down, and they moved aside. The hill didn't get less steep at the edge, but the crowd lessened. A brutal wind bit her cheeks, and her toes were already freezing. She looked ahead to a tree line of evergreens and scrub pines, and beyond them was a slope that was gentler, with only a few teenagers. "Wait, I think I see a better place for us."

"Why can't we sled here?"

"Because it's better there. Hold on to my hand."

Will ignored her and bolted ahead, along the icy crest.

"No, Will!" Ellen shouted, lunging forward and catching him by the snowsuit. "Don't do that! It's dangerous!"

"Mommy, I can do it! You said! I can do it!"

"No, we're going down the hill over there, so please be patient."

"I am PATIENT!" he yelled, and a group of teenagers burst into laughter. Will looked over, wounded, and Ellen felt terrible for him.

"Come here, sweetie." She took his hand and they walked with effort, dragging the saucer to the other hill, where they stood at the top, both of them sizing it up in silence. It was less of an incline, but no baby hill, like Shortridge.

"Let's go, Mommy!"

"Okay, we'll go together."

"No! I wanna do it by myself!"

"Not here, pal."

"Why can't I go by myself?"

"It's better if I go with you." Ellen placed the saucer on the ground and plopped into it cross-legged, yanking her coat under her butt. Wind whipped across the hill, and she pushed up her sunglasses as Will climbed onto the saucer and stuffed himself into her lap. She wrapped her arms around him like a seat belt, steeling herself. "We can do this."

"Go, Mommy, go! Like him!" Will was looking at another snowboarder in a red fleece dragon hat, about to go down the hill.

"Hold on to my arms, tight as you can. Keep your legs inside." Ellen gritted her teeth and paddled to give them a running start, setting the saucer sliding down the hill. "Ready, set, go!"

"Whooooo!" Will shouted, then Ellen started shouting too, holding him as tightly as she could until the saucer started spinning. All she could do was yell and hang on to him, watching the world fly by in a blur of snow, sky, trees, and people, completely out of control. Ellen prayed for the ride to be over and clung to Will as he screamed, and finally the saucer slowed toward the bottom of the hill, where they and the snowboarder hit a hard bump that jarred them all loose and sent them sliding downhill.

"NO!" Ellen shouted, as Will pinwheeled past her on his back, and when she finally stopped herself, she jumped to her feet and straggled down the hill after him.

"WILL!" she screamed, on the run. She reached him and fell to the ground beside him, but he was laughing so hard that he couldn't catch his breath, his smile as broad as his face, his arms and legs flat against the snow, like a starfish on the sea floor.

"Way to go, dude!" The snowboarder clapped his gloves together, and Will squealed.

"I wanna do it again, Mommy!"

Ellen almost cried with relief, and the snowboarder eyed her warily from under his dragon hat.

"Lady," he said. "You need to calm down. Seriously."

Chapter 37

Ellen trudged along the top of the hill carrying Will, who was crying and hollering in a full-blown tantrum. Teenagers hid their smiles as they passed, one young girl covered her ears with her mittens, and another looked over in annoyance. Ellen had long ago stopped being embarrassed by temper tantrums. She flipped it and wore it like a badge of honor. A temper tantrum was a sign that a mom said no when it counted.

"I want to . . . go again!" Will sobbed, tears staining his cheeks, snot running freely from his nose. "Again!"

"Will, try to calm down, honey." Ellen's head pounded at his screaming, and teenagers packed the hill, shouting and laughing, adding to the din. She sidestepped to avoid two older boys shoving each other, and she accidentally dropped the rope to the saucer.

"Mommy! Please! I want . . . to!"

"Oh no!" Ellen yelped, turning around, but before she could catch the saucer, it went spinning down the icy slope. She had no choice but to let it go. She needed to get both of them home and down for naps.

"I can . . . do it myself!" Will wailed.

"Please, honey, settle down. Everything's going to be all right." She finally reached the car, where she stuffed Will into his car seat, jumped behind the steering wheel, and pulled out of the parking lot with his crying reverberating in her ears.

"I . . . can, Mommy! I wanna go again!"

"It's too dangerous, honey. We can't."

"Again! Again!"

Ellen left Valley Forge Park, looking for the route back into the city. Traffic was congested because the Friday rush hour was beginning early, due to the snow. She slowed through the intersection, trying to read the route signs, which were confusing. Routes 202 and 411 were so close to each other, and horns honked behind her.

"I want to do it . . . again!" Will cried. "We only went one time!"

"We'll go home, and I'll make some hot chocolate. How about that? You love hot chocolate."

"Please . . . Mommy, please, again!"

"When you're older," Ellen said, but she knew it was the wrong thing to say the moment the words escaped her lips.

"I'M A BIG BOY!" Will howled, and Ellen didn't rebuke him, knowing it was disappointment and fatigue, a kiddie Molotov cocktail. She took a left turn, looking for the highway entrance when suddenly she heard the loud blare of a siren.

"Is it a fire truck, Mommy?" Will's sobbing slowed at the prospect, and Ellen checked the rearview mirror.

A state police cruiser was right behind her, flashing its high beams. She blinked, startled. She hadn't even known he was there. She said, "Perfect."

"What, Mommy?"

"It's a police car." Ellen didn't know what she had done. She'd been driving slow enough. Her headache returned, full blast. She waited for traffic to part and pulled over to the shoulder, with the police cruiser following.

"Why, Mom?" Will sniffled.

"I'm not sure, but everything's okay."

"Why do they make that sound?"

"So you know they're there."

"Why are they there?"

Ellen sighed inwardly. "Maybe I went too fast. We'll find out in a minute."

"Why did you?"

"Just rest, sweetie, don't worry." Ellen waited as the cruiser door opened and a tall cop emerged and walked along the side of her car, holding a small clipboard. She pressed the button to lower the window, letting in a blast of cold air. "Yes, Officer?"

"License and registration, please."

"Oh no." Ellen realized that she had neither, because she hadn't taken her purse. She had been going to Short-ridge before she changed the plan. She took off her sun-glasses and rubbed her eyes. "This isn't my day. I left the house without them."

The cop frowned. He was young, with light eyes under the wide brim of his brown hat, worn pitched forward. "You don't have any ID on you?"

"Sorry, no. It's at home, I swear it. What did I do?"

"You ran a stop."

"I'm sorry, I didn't see it. I was looking for the sign into Philly."

"What did you do, Mommy?" Will called out, and the cop bent from the waist and eyed Will through the open window.

Ellen felt a bolt of panic, out of nowhere. What if the state police had a registry of kidnapped kids? What if there was an Amber Alert out for Timothy Braverman? What if the cops got those white cards? What if the cop somehow recognized Will as Timothy? Ellen didn't know if the questions were paranoid or not, but couldn't stop them from coming.

"Cute kid," the cop said, unsmiling.

"Thanks." Ellen gripped the steering wheel, her heart beginning to thump.

"He looks unhappy," the cop said, his breath foggy in the frigid air. His gaze remained on Will, and Ellen told herself to stay calm. She was acting like a criminal and she hadn't done anything wrong.

"He's just tired."

"I'M NOT TIRED, MOMMEEEE!" Will screamed.

"I got a nephew hollers like that." The cop finally cracked a smile. "All right, Miss, this is your lucky day. I'll let you slide on the license but don't make a habit of it, we clear?"

"Yes, thank you, Officer," Ellen said, hearing the tremor in her own voice.

"Eyes front when you're driving, and no cell phones."

"I will, I swear. Thanks."

"Good-bye now, and be careful pulling out." The cop backed away from the car, and Ellen pressed the button to raise the window. She exhaled with relief as the cop rejoined the line of traffic, then she checked the rearview mirror. Will was falling asleep, his head listing to the side and his cheeks glistening with tear tracks, like tiny snail trails.

She looked for an opening in traffic, then pulled back onto the highway. Her forehead felt damp but her heartbeat was returning to normal. She fought the impulse to check her BlackBerry, but part of her knew that Amy Martin wouldn't be emailing her anytime soon.

Her head hurt, and she wished for the umpteenth time that her mother were still alive. She needed to talk to someone about Timothy Braverman, and her mother would have known what to do and what to think.

Ellen felt like she was losing her grip. Fainting in the office. Blowing her deadline. She could lose her job to Sarah if she didn't get her act together. She needed a saner head to prevail.

The traffic started to move, and she accelerated.

She had a new destination in mind.

Chapter 38

"Hey, Dad," Ellen said, closing the front door behind them.

"Pops!" Will raised his arms to her father, revitalized after his long nap in the car. Given the traffic, it had taken over an hour to get to West Chester.

"My little buddy!!" Her father's face lit up, his hooded eyes alive with animation. "What a nice surprise! Come here, you!" He reached for Will, who jumped into his arms, wrapping his legs around him like a little monkey.

"Dad, careful of your back," Ellen said, though her father looked fine, his face only slightly red.

"Are you kiddin'? This makes my day! I missed my grandson!"

Will hung on tight. "Pops, I went down the big hill!"

"Tell me all about it," her father said, carrying Will into the living room. Ellen took off her hat and coat, set them on the chair, and looked around. The rug was rolled up, leaving a dull yellow square on the hardwood floor, and cardboard boxes sat stacked all over.

"We only went down the hill one time, and Mommy wouldn't let us go down again." Will held up an index finger while her father set him down, then unzipped his coat, tugged it off, and tossed it aside, leaving the sleeves inside out.

"Why wouldn't she, Willy Billy?"

"She said it was too big."

"She's so mean!" Her father stuck his tongue out at Ellen, which sent Will into gales of laughter.

"Hope this isn't a bad time." She gestured at the boxes. "Did we catch you in the middle of packing?"

"Nah." Her father carried Will over to the couch and sat with him in his lap. "Barbara did all that. She's finished for today."

"You didn't put the house up yet, did you? I didn't see a sign."

"Nah, but it'll go fast. Frank Ferro was asking me about it already." Her father gestured to a small cardboard box on top of the TV. "That one has some things from your mother, pictures and whatnot. You might want to take it home."

"Sure, thanks," Ellen said, caught off-balance at the notion of Barbara, packing her mother into a box.

"Where's my Thomas the Tank Engine?" Will asked, looking around in bewilderment. The toy box that had been tucked in the corner was gone.

"I got the horse right here," her father answered. He got up, took Will by the hand, and crossed him to a large cardboard box, with the top flaps open. "Look inside, cowpoke. The gang's all here."

"My truck!" Will dug in the box, pulled out a red truck, and knelt and zoomed it back and forth on the floor, where its hard plastic tires made a satisfyingly rumbling sound.

Ellen said, "Will, I'm going to talk to Pop in the kitchen."

"Be right back, pal," her father said, straightening up, and they went into the kitchen, where her father leaned against the counter and faced her. He crossed his arms in a pale yellow golf sweater and khakis, with a smile. "God love that kid."

"I know."

"He got so big! He grows like a weed."

"He sure does."

"You gotta bring him over more, El. Barbara's dyin' to meet him."

"I will."

"He's so much smarter than her grandkids. They hardly talk, and him, you can't shut up!"

Ellen laughed, marveling at the emotion Will always brought out in her father. He became a different man when Will was around, and she loved it. Just not now. She had called him for a reason. "Dad, I need to talk to you."

"Sure. Right. What's on your mind, kiddo?"

"This is going to sound strange, so prepare yourself." Ellen lowered her voice, though Will was out of earshot. "What if I told you that Will might really be a boy named Timothy Braverman, who was kidnapped from a family in Florida, two years ago?"

"*What?*" Her father's eyes widened, and Ellen filled him in quickly, starting with the white card, going through to the composite drawing, and ending with the visits to Gerry and Cheryl. They were interrupted twice by Will, and Ellen sent him back to the toy box with a foil bag of potato chips, always a handy bribe.

"So, what do you think?" she asked, when she was finished.

"What do I think?" Her father looked mystified. "Are you serious?"

"Yes."

"I think you're just like your mother."

"What does that mean?" Ellen felt resentment flicker like an ember in her chest.

"It means you're a worrywart. You worry too much!"

"How am I worrying too much?"

He shrugged. "You dreamed this up. It's crazy."

"I'm not crazy, Dad."

"But you don't have any facts. You only have assumptions." Her father frowned, making deep wrinkles in his forehead. "You're assuming lots of things that may or may not be true. I'm surprised at you, a newspaperwoman."

Ellen hadn't heard that term in years. "What are the assumptions?"

"You can't tell anything from those stupid cards about the missing kids. I get them, too."

"Did you see the last one, with Timothy Braverman?"

"Who the hell knows? They're junk mail. I toss them out."

"Why? They're real people, real kids."

"They have nothing to do with me, or you. Or my grandson."

Ellen tried another tack. "Okay, remember that photo I showed you, last time I was here?"

"No."

"You said it was Will. You thought it was Will. Remember?"

He frowned. "Okay, whatever."

"It wasn't Will, it was Timothy Braverman. You thought it was Will."

"What was that, a trick, then?"

"No, Dad. Keep an open mind. I need you to take this seriously."

"But I can't. It's just silly."

"Dad." Ellen touched his arm, the cashmere soft under her fingertips, and the tight line of his mouth softened just a little. "It wasn't a trick, but the photo wasn't Will. It was Timothy. They look that much alike, exactly alike."

"So the kid looks like Will, so what?" He shrugged.

"They could be the same kid."

"No, they can't." Her father almost laughed. "You can't tell anything from those police drawings. I know, they're on TV news all the time." He pointed to the doorway. "They look like one of Will's coloring books, in that damn chest out there."

"They have an artist who does them. They're real tools the police use."

"There's no way in the world you can tell who a composite is by tracing a picture over his face." Her father looked at Ellen with a smile reserved for the delusional, and for a minute, she almost saw it his way. "You adopted that little boy in there—my only grandchild—legally. You had a lawyer."

"Who killed herself."

"So what? What are you saying?"

Ellen didn't even know. "It just seems strange. Coincidental."

"Bah!" Her father waved her off, chuckling. "Forget about it, it's crazy talk. You adopted that boy, and he loves you. He was half-dead. Nobody wanted him but you. Nobody was there for him but you."

Ellen felt touched, but that wasn't the point. "What matters now is whether he's Timothy."

"He is *not* Timothy. He's just a kid who looks like Timothy. He's not the same kid. He's Will. He's *ours*." Her father paused, then looked at her with a half smile. "El, listen to me. Barbara's grandkids, Joshie and Jakie, you could swap 'em out and nobody would know the difference."

"Are they twins?"

"No, but they look alike, and they look like Will, too. They're all little boys, and they all look alike."

Ellen burst into laughter, and it felt good.

"Well, it's the truth." Her father warmed to the topic,

moving closer. "Didn't anybody ever say to you, 'Hey, you look just like somebody I know?' That ever happen to you, Elly Belly?"

"Sure."

"Of course. It happens to me all the time. I look like people, who knows? Handsome men. George Clooney, maybe." Her father grinned. "That's all you got goin' on here. Don't worry about it."

Ellen's heart eased a little. "You think?"

"I know. They look alike but they're not the same kid. Will is ours, forever. He's *ours*." Her father gave her an aromatic, if awkward, hug, and Ellen knew he believed he had closed the deal.

"You sold me, Dad."

"I'm always selling somebody, kiddo." Her father grinned again. "But it's easy when you believe what you sell, and I believe this. Relax, honey. You're getting all worked up over nothing. Forget all this nonsense."

Ellen wanted to believe him. If Will wasn't really Timothy, then it all went away and they could be happy again.

"You seein' anybody?"

"Huh?" Ellen didn't know when the topic changed. "You mean, like a date?"

"Yes, exactly like a date." Her father smiled.

"No."

"Not since what's-his-name?"

"No."

"Not interested in anybody?"

Ellen thought of Marcelo. "Not really."

"Why not?" Her father puckered his lower lip, comically, and she knew he was trying to cheer her up. "A knockout like you? Why put yourself up on the shelf? You should go out more, you know? Live a little. Go dancing."

"I have Will."

"We'll sit for him." Her father took her hand in his, encircled her with his other hand, and started humming. "Let me lead, you follow."

"Okay, okay." Ellen laughed, finding the box step of the fox trot, letting herself be danced around the kitchen to her father's singing "Steppin' Out with My Baby" as he steered her from the small of her back, his firm hand a perfect rudder.

"Will, come see your ol' Pops!" he called over his shoulder, and in the next minute, Will came thundering into the kitchen.

"Ha, Mommy!" He ran to them, and they took his hands and the three of them shuffled around in a ring-around-the-rosy circle, with her father singing and Will looking up from one to the other, his blue eyes shining.

Ellen couldn't sing because of the sharp ache she felt inside, a sudden pain so palpable that she almost burst into tears, and she wished that her mother were still alive to take Will's hand and dance with them in a circle, all four of them happy and whole, a family again.

But it was an impossible wish, and Ellen sent it packing. She looked down at her child with tears in her eyes and all the love in her broken heart.

He's ours.

Chapter 39

It was late by the time Ellen got Will home, having had dinner at the clubhouse with her father. Will and his repertoire of napkin antics had been the focus of attention during the meal, which had helped her forget about Timothy Braverman, at least temporarily. She wondered if God had intended children to provide such a service for alleged adults. We were supposed to be taking care of them, not the other way around.

She read Will a few books before bed and tucked him in, then went downstairs to close up the kitchen. The cardboard box of her mother's things sat on the butcher-block counter, and Oreo Figaro crouched next to it, sniffling it in his tentative way, his black nose bobbing to and from the box.

Ellen stroked his back, feeling the bumpiness of his skinny spine, regarding the box with a stab of sadness. It was so small, not even a two-foot square. Could a mother be so easily disposed of? Could one mother be so quickly traded for another?

You could swap 'em out, and nobody would know the difference.

Ellen opened the lid of the box, and Oreo Figaro jumped from the counter in needless alarm. Stacked inside the box was a set of photographs in various frames, and the top one was an eight-by-ten color photo of her parents at their wedding. She picked it up, setting aside her emotions. In the picture, her parents stood together under a tree, her father wearing a tux and his I-made-my-quota smile. Her mother's smile was sweet and shy, making barely a quarter moon on a delicate face, which was framed by short brown hair stiffened with Aqua Net. She had roundish eyes and a small, thin nose, like the tiny beak of a dime-store finch, and at only five-foot-one, Mary Gleeson seemed to recede in size, personality, and importance next to her larger-than-life husband.

Ellen set the photo aside and looked through the others, which only made it tougher not to feel sad. There was a picture of her parents in a canoe, with her father standing up in the boat and her mother laughing, but gripping the sides in fear. And there was another of them at a wedding, with her father spinning her mother on the end of his arm, like a puppeteer.

Ellen set the photo down. She remembered seeing it and the others at their house, and now they were all being exiled, along with that part of his life. She resolved to find a place for them here. No mother deserved to be forgotten, and certainly not hers.

She went to the cabinet under the sink, got a spray bottle of Windex and a paper towel, and wiped the dust from the top photo. She cleaned all of them, working her way to the end of the stack until she noticed that between two of the photos was a packet of greeting cards, bound by a rubber band. The top one was a fortieth wedding anniversary card, and she took out the packet and rolled off the rubber band. She opened the card, and it was from her father to her mother, the signature simply, *Love, Don*.

She smiled. That would be her father. He was never big in the elaboration department, and her mother would have been happy just to have the card, on time. Ellen went through the other cards, all saved by her mother, but the last envelope wasn't a greeting card. It was an envelope of her mother's stationery, the pale blue of the forget-me-nots that grew by their sugar maple in the backyard.

Ellen knew what it was, instantly. She had gotten a note like that from her mother, too, written right before she died. The front of the envelope read, *To Don*. The envelope was still sealed, and she ran her fingertip along the back of the flap, double-checking. Her father had never opened the note.

Ellen didn't get it. Had he really not opened the note? Didn't he want to hear the last words of his wife, written after she knew she was going to die? She wasn't completely surprised, but she slid a nail under the envelope flap, and tugged the note out, its paper thick and heavy. The top flap bore her mother's embossed monogram, MEG, in a tangle of curlicues, and she opened the note, welling up at the sight of her mother's handwriting.

Dear Don,
I know that you have always loved me, even if you have forgotten it from time to time. Please know that I understand you, I accept you, and I forgive you.
Love always, Mary

Ellen took the note and went to sit down in the dining room. The house was still and quiet. Oreo Figaro was nowhere in sight. The windows were inky mirrors, the dark sky moonless. For an odd moment she felt as if she were suspended in blackness, connected to nothing in this world, not even Will, asleep upstairs. She held the note in her hand and closed her eyes, feeling its heavy paper beneath her fingers, letting it connect her to her mother through space and time. And at that moment, she knew what her mother would say about Will and Timothy, in that soft voice of hers. It was what she had written to Ellen in her final note.

Follow your heart.

And so there in the quiet room, Ellen finally let herself listen to her heart, which had been trying to tell her something from the moment she first got the card in the mail. Maybe her father thought it was crazy to worry, but inside, she knew better. She couldn't pretend any longer and she couldn't live the rest of her life looking over her shoulder. She couldn't feel like a criminal when a cop pulled her over. She couldn't hide Will from his friends and neighbors.

So she vowed to follow her heart.

Starting now.

Chapter 40

Ellen entered the lawyer's office and took a seat, surrounded by bronze, glass, and crystal awards, like so many blunt instruments. She had met Ron Halpren when she did the series on Will's adoption, having interviewed him for his expertise on family law, and she counted herself lucky she could call on him on such short notice.

"Thanks for meeting me on a Saturday," she said, and Ron walked around his cluttered desk and eased into his creaky chair.

"That's okay, I'm in most Saturday mornings." Ron had light eyes behind tortoiseshell glasses, a halo of fuzzy gray hair, and a shaggy graying beard to match. His frame was short and pudgy, and he looked like Paddington Bear in his yellow fleece pullover and thick jeans. "Sorry we're out of coffee. I was supposed to bring it in, but I forgot."

"No problem, and thanks for accommodating Will." Ellen gestured to the secretary's desk outside, where Will was eating vending-machine Fig Newtons and watching a *Wizard of Oz* DVD on the computer.

"It's great to see him so healthy. What a difference, eh?"

"Really." Ellen shifted forward on the chair. "So, as I

said on the phone, I'm seeing you in your official capacity, and I want to pay for your time today."

"Forget it." Ron smiled. "You made me look like Clarence Darrow in the paper. I got tons of clients from that press. I owe *you*."

"I want to pay."

"Get to the point." Ron gestured toward the door. "I hear the scarecrow singing. We don't have much time."

"Wait, let me ask you something first. Is what we say absolutely confidential?"

"Yes, of course." Ron nodded. "How can I help you?"

Ellen hesitated. "What if a crime is involved? I didn't commit it, but I know, or I suspect, that a crime has been committed by someone else. Can you still keep this confidential?"

"Yes."

"So if I tell you about this crime, you wouldn't have to report it to the police?"

"I'd be barred from so doing."

Ellen loved the authoritative note in his voice. "Here goes. I think that Will could be a kid named Timothy Braverman, who was kidnapped in Florida two years ago."

"Will? *Your* son Will?"

"Yes."

Ron lifted a graying eyebrow. "So the crime in question is the kidnapping?"

"Yes, it was a carjacking gone wrong, and the kidnapper murdered the boy's nanny."

"Those are past crimes, unless we consider the fact that you retain custody of a kidnapped child as a continuing crime, which I don't think it is. You did legally adopt him."

"Here's what I need to know. If Will is really Timothy, what are my legal rights? Could the Bravermans, his birth parents, take him from me? Would I have to give him up if they found out or if they came and found us? Wouldn't it matter to the court that he lived with me for two years?" Ellen had so many questions that they ran into each other on the way out of her mouth. "That I'm the only mother he's ever really known? Would that—"

"Please, slow down." Ron held up his hands. "Tell me how you found this out, about Will."

So Ellen told him the story from the beginning, showing him her adoption file, the composite drawing, and her computer printouts of Timothy and Will at their various ages. "By the way, my father thinks I'm crazy. He's the only other person I've told."

Ron studied the photographs on his desk, even placing the composite tracing over the photo enlargement of Beach Man. Finally, he looked up at her, his expression grave behind his glasses.

"What do you think?"

"You're not crazy, but you are speculating." Ron's gaze remained steady. "The composite drawing is the linchpin, and you can't support your belief that Will is Timothy Braverman by comparing the composite with a photograph. It just isn't reliable enough. I see some similarity, but I can't be sure it's the same person."

Ellen tried to process what he was saying, but her emotions kept getting in the way.

"I'm not an expert, and neither are you. Composites, as a legal matter, cannot stand alone. Any one of my first-year law students can tell you that a composite is merely an aid to the identification and apprehension of a suspect. They're not a positive identification." Ron shook his head. "You don't have enough information on which to base any conclusion that Will is the kidnapped child."

It was the same thing her father had said, only in lawyerspeak.

Ron continued, "Now, the first question you should

have is whether you have an obligation to go to the authorities with your suspicion. Answer? No, you don't."

Ellen hadn't even thought of that.

"The law doesn't impose responsibility on the citizenry to report crimes that are so speculative in nature."

"Good."

"That's not to say that you couldn't voluntarily report your suspicion to the authorities, if you wished. I'm sure there are fingerprints of Timothy Braverman on file, or blood tests that could be done, or DNA analysis that would determine if Will is Timothy." Ron tented his fingers in front of his beard and looked at her directly. "Obviously, you're concerned that if you tell the authorities and you're right, you would lose Will."

Ellen couldn't even speak, and Ron didn't wait for an answer.

"You're also concerned that if you're not right, you'd cause the Bravermans more pain and upset."

Ellen hadn't thought of them, but okay.

"Let's take a hypothetical. Assume for a moment that you're right. Will is Timothy."

Ellen hated the very sound of the sentence. "Could that even happen?"

"Hypothetically, it's easy, now that I give it some thought. All that is required for a valid adoption is a birth mother to produce a birth certificate, which is easy enough to fake. Unlike a driver's license or a passport, it doesn't even have a photo." Ron stroked his beard. "And she has to supply a signed waiver of her parental rights, from the birth father, too, which is also easy to forge, and she could make up the father's name. There are plenty of cases from mothers who put a child up for adoption without the father's consent. They're very common."

Ellen was remembering the elementary school, where Charles Cartmell's house was supposed to have been. The

Charles Cartmell that nobody had heard of and who didn't exist.

"The second question is what are your parental rights, if any? And what are the Bravermans' parental rights, if any? That's the question that's worrying you, isn't it?" Ron paused. "If you're right, who gets Will?"

Ellen felt her eyes well up, but kept it together.

"You raise an interesting question under Pennsylvania law, and one not well understood by laymen. It involves the difference between adoption cases and custody cases."

Ellen couldn't take the suspense. "Just tell me, would I get to keep Will or would I have to give him back to the Bravermans?"

"You'd have to give him back to the Bravermans. No question."

Ellen felt stricken. She struggled to maintain control, teetering on the fine line between crying and screaming. But Will was in the next room, lost in a world somewhere over the rainbow.

"The Bravermans, as the child's birth parents, have an undisputed legal right to their child. They're alive, and they didn't give him up for adoption. If he was kidnapped, your adoption is simply invalid. Therefore, as a legal matter, the court would return Will to them."

"And he would go live in Florida?"

"That's where they live, so yes."

"Would I have the right to visit him?"

"No." Ron shook his head. "You would have no rights at all. The Bravermans may permit you to, perhaps to wean him from you, so to speak. But no court would order them to permit you to visit."

"But I adopted him lawfully," Ellen almost wailed.

"True, but in the hypothetical, no one gave him up for adoption." Ron cocked his head, tenting his fingers again. "As you remember from when you adopted him, you presented the court with signed waivers, consents to adoption from his mother and his father. That's a prerequisite to any adoption. If the consents were false, forged, or otherwise fraudulent, the adoption is invalid, whether you knew it or not."

Ellen forced herself to think back to her online research, done last night in anticipation of this meeting. "I read online about the Kimberley Mays case, in Florida, do you remember that? She was the baby who was switched at birth in the hospital, with another baby. In that case, the court let her stay with her psychological parent instead of her biological parent."

"I know the case. It got national attention."

"Doesn't that help me here? Can't we do it that way?"

"No, it doesn't help you at all." Ron opened his hands, palms up. "That's what I started to tell you. There's a fundamental difference between adoption and custody. The Florida court in the Mays case was applying a custody analysis, which involves an inquiry into the best interests of the child. The court decided that it was in the child's best interests for her to stay with her psychological father." Ron made a chopping motion with his hand. "But we have an adoption case here. It has nothing to do with what's in Will's best interests. It's simply a matter of power. Your case is like those in which the father's consent to the adoption was forged by the mother."

"What happens in those cases?"

"The child goes to the biological father. It's his child, and he didn't validly waive his right to him."

Ellen tried a different argument. "What if Will were ten or older, you think he'd get sent back?"

"Yes. As a legal matter, time won't cure the fact that he was kidnapped, even though you were unwitting."

"So it doesn't matter that I'm the only mother he's ever known?" Ellen found it impossible to accept. "My house is the only house he's ever known. The school, the class-mates, the neighborhood, the babysitter. We're his world, and they're strangers."

"They happen to be his natural parents. It's a very in-teresting dilemma."

"No, it's not," Ellen shot back, miserably.

"Aw, wait." Ron's voice softened, transitioning from professor to friend. "We were speaking hypothetically. Come back to reality with me for a minute. I was there, when you were considering adopting him. Remember when we met, back then?"

"Yes."

"There was, and there still is, no reason in the world to think there was anything wrong with his adoption."

"But what about the mom with the twisted ovary? The lawyer's suicide?"

"People who can't get pregnant get pregnant, every day. My daughter-in-law, for one. And sadly, lawyers commit suicide. Life happens. So does death."

"I'm not crazy, Ron."

"I didn't say you're crazy. I don't think you're crazy. I think you got a bee in your bonnet, like my mother used to say. It's what makes you a good reporter. By the way, it's what made you adopt Will in the first place." Ron wagged a finger. "You couldn't get him out of your head, you told me."

"I remember." Ellen nodded sadly. Her gaze found a heavy crystal award, its beveled facets capturing a ray of sun, like an illustration of refraction in a physics book.

"You want my advice?"

"Yes."

"Good. Then listen to me."

Ellen felt as if it were a moment of truth. She hardly breathed.

"Take these papers and put them away, at the bottom

of the drawer." Ron slid the file, the photographs, and the composite drawing across his messy desk. "Your adoption was valid. Will is your child. Enjoy him, and invite Louisa and me to his wedding."

Ellen packed up her papers, wishing she could take his advice. "I can't do that. I want to know what's true."

"I told you what's true. You've elevated suspicion to fact."

"But it doesn't feel right." Ellen fought her emotions to think clearly, and it was clarifying to talk about it out loud. "You know what I really feel? I feel that my kid is sick, but the doctors keep telling me he's fine. Not just you, my father, too."

Ron fell silent.

"But *I'm* his mother. I'm Dr. Mom." Ellen heard a new conviction in her voice, which surprised even her. "Call it a mother's instinct, or intuition, but I have it inside, and I know better."

"I hear you. You believe what you believe."

"Yes."

"Nobody can tell you different."

"Right!"

"You feel certainty. You are certain."

"Bingo!" Ellen said, but a slow smile eased across Ron's face, spreading his beard almost like a stage curtain.

"But you have to have a valid proof to support your certainty, and you have none. Do you understand?"

"Yes," Ellen answered, and she did. She gathered up the photographs and papers, and rose with them. "If proof is what I need, then proof is what I'll get. Thanks so much for your help."

"You're very welcome." Ron rose, too, his expression darkening. "But be careful what you wish. If you find proof that Will is Timothy Braverman, you'll feel a lot worse than you do already. You'll have to make a choice I wouldn't wish on my worst enemy."

Ellen had thought of nothing else, when she was trying to sleep last night. "What would you do, if it were your kid?"

"Wild horses couldn't make me give him back."

"No doubt?"

"Not a one."

"Then let me ask you this, counselor. How do you keep something that doesn't belong to you?" Ellen heard herself say it out loud, though she hadn't thought of it that way until this moment.

"Och. My." Ron cringed. "Excellent question."

"And how do I explain that to Will, when he grows up? What if he found out? What do I say? That I loved you, so I kept you, even though I knew the truth? Is that love, or just selfishness?" Ellen heard the questions pouring out, her heart speaking of its own accord. "This is the thing, Ron. When I adopted him, I felt like he belonged to me because another mother gave him up. But if she didn't, if she had had him taken from her by force, then he doesn't belong to me. Not truly."

Ron looked away, hitching up his jeans by his thumbs.

"So what do you say to that?" Ellen felt her eyes well up, then blinked them clear. "What would you do then?"

Ron sighed. "Fair points, all, but I have an easy out. In that case, saner minds would prevail. Louisa would kill me."

"Well, I don't have a Louisa. There's no saner head around. It's the me show. I just can't forget about it. Put it back in the bottle."

"Did you try?" Ron smiled, weakly.

"I've been trying since the minute I saw the card."

"Give it time, then. You might feel differently, next month, or next year."

Ellen shook her head. She hadn't gotten this far in life without knowing herself. It was other people she had trouble with. "I'm not built that way. When I see a thread hanging from someone's clothes, I have to pull it. If I see trash on the floor, I pick it up. I can't step over it. I can't pretend it's not there."

Ron laughed.

"This is almost like that, only ten times more. A million times more. It'll be in the back of my mind for the rest of my life, if I don't resolve it."

"Then I feel for you," Ron said softly, meeting her eye.

"Thanks." Ellen managed a smile, picked up her papers and coat, and moved to the door, where the *Wizard of Oz* soundtrack grew louder. "I'd better go. Will hates the flying monkeys."

"Everybody hates the flying monkeys," Ron said, with a final smile.

Chapter 41

Ellen spent the afternoon in Quality Time Frenzy with Will, building a multicolored castle from Legos, stamping Play-Doh with cookie cutters, and making Boca burgers for dinner together. Will set the table, running back and forth with a squeeze bottle of ketchup and sliced tomatoes, and Ellen felt as if the kitchen were their domestic cocoon, with its soft lighting, warm stove, and chubby housecat curled up on the floor, in his tuxedo.

"I have a surprise dessert for you," Ellen said, but Will flashed her his picky-eater frown, as dubious a look as a three-year-old can muster.

"What is it?"

"I can't tell you, or it wouldn't be a surprise."

"Don't we have ice cream?"

"It's better than ice cream. Wait right here." Ellen got up, collected the dinner plates, and took them into the kitchen, where she set them in the sink. She fetched the dessert from the refrigerator, carried it to the dining room, and placed it on the table.

"Eeew, Mommy!" Will scrunched up his nose, the

only reasonable response to what looked like a bowl of green plastic.

"Give it a chance. It's Jell-O, in your favorite color." Ellen had spent last night rereading the Braverman website and had seen the detail that Timothy loved lime Jell-O. Will had never eaten it before, as far as she knew, and she wanted to see if he liked it. Her test wasn't scientific, but that would come later.

Will wrinkled his nose. "Is it spinach?"

"No, it's lime."

"What's lime?"

"Like lemon, but better."

"What's lemon?"

"You know lemon. It's yellow, like the water ice we get at the pool. Or like lemon sticks." Ellen let it go. "Did you ever have lime Jell-O before?"

Will shook his head, eyeing the bowl warily. "I had red. That was good."

"Red is cherry."

"Do we have red?"

"No. I made green."

"Can't you make red?" Will looked at her with plaintive baby blues, and Ellen managed a smile.

"Not this time. Today, let's try green Jell-O."

Will scrambled to a kneeling position in his chair and leaned farther over the table on his elbows, sniffing the bowl. "Why doesn't it smell?"

"Give it a try and tell me if you like the taste."

"Do you like it?"

"I don't know, I never had it either." Ellen hated lime Jell-O, but didn't want to prejudice him. "I like to try new foods." She couldn't resist propagandizing, but Will ignored her.

"Why is it all flat on top?"

"That's how it comes out. Grab the bowl and give it a little shake."

Will did, giggling. "It wiggles! Just like on TV!"

"Fun, huh? Food you can play with." Ellen scooped some Jell-O into his dessert bowl and held her breath as he picked up his teaspoon, dipped the tip into the shiny green mound, then touched the tip of his tongue to the spoon. She said, "Give it a real taste."

"Do I have to?"

"Please."

Will put the Jell-O in his mouth, and for a minute, didn't react.

"Well, do you like it?"

"It's good!" Will answered, his mouth full.

Chapter 42

Ellen spent the evening in her home office, figuring out where and how to find the proof that Will was or wasn't Timothy. It was nutty to try to prove something she didn't want to be true, but she didn't have to decide now what to do after she learned the facts. She could find out, then decide whether to keep Will or, inconceivably, to give him up. It was a process, and she could take it in stages. At stage one, all she wanted was the truth. And, happily, if it turned out that Will wasn't Timothy, she could stop driving herself crazy and put the whole thing behind her. She took her BlackBerry from the holster and pressed speed dial C, and Connie picked up.

"Hey, El, how are you?"

"Fine, thanks. I have a huge favor to ask you, Connie. Something big came up at work, and I have to leave town for a few days." Ellen hated lying, but she couldn't risk telling even Connie the truth. "Is there any way you can cover for me?"

"Sure. Where you goin'?"

"Couple of different places, I'm not sure yet. It's a big story, and I'm sorry, but it can't be helped." Ellen rarely went out of town on business, but she was praying she could sell Connie. She wasn't Don Gleeson's daughter for nothing. "I'll pay you overtime, whatever it takes. It's that important."

Connie hushed her. "I never worry about that. I can do it, but we're having people over tomorrow. Can it wait until Monday?"

"Yes, I really appreciate it."

"I'll pack my toothbrush. See you Monday, regular time. How many days will it be?"

God knows. "Just a few, the situation is fluid. Can you live with that?"

"Yep. See ya then."

Ellen hung up, with one more thing to do. She logged onto Outlook, skimmed her incoming email, and found one sender that surprised her. Marcelo. She clicked Open.

> Dear Ellen,
> I'm concerned about you. I hope you're feeling better. Please do call a doctor. We lack a human face without you! Best, Marcelo

Ellen felt a little thrill. He was such a great guy. It was worth fainting to get him to hold her. She smiled at the memory of being cradled against his chest, but it faded when she thought of what she had to do next. She hit Reply and started typing, then stopped. It was the point of no return, and the stakes were the job she loved and needed. Still, she typed on:

> Marcelo,
> Thanks for your nice note, but unfortunately, I need to take this week off. I have plenty of vacation time coming, and I'll take the time out of that.

Ellen paused, not knowing whether to mention the think piece, which was still due Friday. She continued, typing:

I'm not sure if I'll get my piece finished by dead-line, but I'll stay in touch with you about this. I'm sorry, and hope this doesn't cause too much of a problem. Thanks and best, Ellen

She clicked Send and swallowed hard. Taking a vacation with a layoff pending could be career suicide, but she had no choice. The situation with Will and Timothy put everything into perspective, and her job would always be second to her child.

"So be it," Ellen said aloud.

Oreo Figaro looked up at the sound, lifting his chin from his front paws, regarding her with disapproval.

Chapter 43

Ellen awoke to the ringing of her BlackBerry, which she kept on the night table as an alarm clock. She grabbed it before it woke Will. "Hello?" she asked, muzzy.

"It's Marcelo." His voice always sounded so soft on the phone, his accent more pronounced, and Ellen blinked herself awake, checking the digital clock. Sunday, 8:02 A.M.

"Oh, jeez, hi."

"Did I wake you?"

Yes. "No."

"Sorry to bother you, but I got your vacation request and I wanted to discuss it with you. It's a problem for us, right now."

"It's just that—"

"I'm going to be in your area tonight. I can stop by, if you like, and we can talk about it."

Marcelo, here? I'll have to vacuum. And put on makeup. Not in that order.

"Ellen? I don't mean to intrude—"

"No, it's fine, a great idea."

"What time is good?"

"Will goes to bed around seven thirty, so any time after eight o'clock."

"I'm free at nine. See you then."

"Great. Thanks." Ellen pressed End. Marcelo was coming here? Her boss, her crush? Was this a date or a firing? It was exciting and unnerving, both at once. At best, she'd have to lie to his face about where she was going on Monday, which wouldn't be easy. Especially if he wore that aftershave, eau d'eligible bachelor.

"Mommy?" Will called out, waking up in his bedroom.

"Coming, sweetie," Ellen called back, becoming a mom again.

Chapter 44

"Marcelo, hi, come in," Ellen said, opening her front door onto a living room that looked as if no one lived there. Will's toys, books, and DVDs had been put away, and the rugs had been vacuumed. Cat hair had been lint-rolled from the sofa cushions, and paw prints wiped from the coffee table. The house was so clean, it should be for sale.

"Thanks." Marcelo stepped inside, and Ellen edged back, suddenly awkward. She had fantasized about him walking through her door, though the fantasy didn't include vacuuming.

"Let me take your coat," Ellen said, but Marcelo was already sliding out of his black leather jacket, and she caught a whiff of spicy aftershave, a scent that spoke directly to her I'm-Very-Single cortex, bypassing the saner He's-Your-Boss lobe.

"What a nice house," he said, looking around. He had on a black ribbed turtleneck with nice brown slacks, and Ellen found herself wondering if he'd been on a date. He asked, "How long have you lived here?"

"Six years or so." Ellen brushed a stray hair from her eyes, surprised that even a single strand had escaped her product-heavy blow-dry. She had changed her outfit three times, only to end up in her trademark loose blue sweater, white tank underneath, jeans, and Danskos. She didn't want to signal that she considered this anything but a meeting between colleagues. "Would you like a Diet Coke or something?"

"Sure, great."

"Hang on a sec. You can sit down." Ellen gestured at the sofa cushion without hesitation.

"Let me help you. I'd love a house tour."

"Okay, but, it's a short one." Ellen waved awkwardly at the dining room. It was odd, having him in her house, standing so close to her when she wasn't even unconscious. "Speaks for itself, huh? And over here's the teeny tiny kitchen."

"Very nice." Marcelo followed her, looking around with his hands linked loosely behind his back. "It's warm and friendly."

"And clean."

Marcelo nodded, with a smile. "I was going to say it was clean. Very clean."

"Thank you." Ellen went into the cabinet, found a decent tumbler, then went in the fridge and got him ice and a soda. Oreo Figaro sat on the counter, watching the goings-on with interest.

"I like cats. What's his name?"

"Oreo Figaro."

Marcelo lifted an eyebrow. "Back home, many people have two names, like my brother, Carlos Alberto. But I didn't think that was so common in the States."

"It's not. He's Brazilian."

Marcelo laughed. He popped the soda and poured it fizzling into the glass. "I live in town."

I know. We all know. You're the hot, single Latin boss,

and therefore the most-talked-about person in the news-room, if not the Western Hemisphere.

"I think about moving out here, but I wonder how you meet women in the suburbs."

"At the sandbox, mostly."

Marcelo smiled.

"The men are short, but they're single."

Marcelo laughed again. "I was out here on a blind date. Can you imagine that?"

"Unfortunately, yes." Ellen liked the way his accent made it *e-magine.* "How was it?"

"Excruciating."

"Been there. Excruciating conversation, excruciating restaurant, excruciating kiss good night. It's excruciating."

Marcelo laughed again. "Glad to see you're feeling better."

I always make jokes when I'm nervous.

"It was very strange to have you faint, so suddenly." Marcelo frowned slightly, and Ellen recognized a flicker of concern behind his eyes, which made her warm all over.

"Thank you for being so kind about it."

"Give me no credit. I wanted to leave, but you were lying in my way."

Ellen laughed, and Marcelo sipped his soda and set it down.

"So, to your email."

"Yes."

"Please explain."

"I'm not sure where to begin."

"Let's be honest with each other. You're reliable. You make deadlines. You didn't take a vacation last year, I checked. All of a sudden, you're fainting and you need time off for a mysterious reason." Marcelo glanced away, then back again. "I will tell you, I usually keep my private life to myself, but my mother was recently diagnosed with breast cancer. She's at home, in Pinheiros, getting treatments, and she tells me they make her very tired."

Ellen felt for him, having been there herself, and the pain on his face was visible. "I'm sorry."

"Thank you. If that is what's going on with you, or if you have some other illness, you can be sure I'll keep it confidential."

Ellen felt touched. "I don't have cancer, but thank you for asking."

"Is it another illness? Is that it?"

Ellen didn't know what to say. His tone was so calm and the excuse so handy that she almost considered making up a short-lived disease. She could keep her job, if she lied.

"Do you have a drug problem, or alcohol? We have counseling for that, you know."

"No, that's not it, at all."

"Well, what then? Am I being too intrusive? I feel like I'm doing that a lot lately, with you, though I'm trying to help you. It's a difficult situation, having to make these layoff decisions, and I'm doing everything I can to save your job." Marcelo stood straighter, shaking his head. "But a vacation request, at a time like this, how do you justify that?"

"All I can tell you is that I need to take these few days off to settle something personal."

Marcelo looked at her, his regret plain. "That's it?"

Ellen was so tempted to tell him, but she couldn't. "Sorry," she answered. "That's it."

"Are you going somewhere or staying here?"

"I'd rather not say. I'm taking vacation time, is all."

Marcelo's lips pursed. "Will you get the homicide piece written on time?"

"Honestly, I don't know."

"How does your draft look?"

"I haven't started drafting yet."

"May I have your notes?"

"I haven't transcribed them yet." Ellen felt a wave of guilt at his dismayed expression.

"How am I supposed to give you an extension and no one else? How can I justify treating you specially?"

"If you have to fire me, I understand. But I need this time for myself."

"Would you rather get fired than tell me what's going on?" Marcelo asked, his eyes disbelieving. "Can that be what you truly want?"

"Yes," Ellen answered, though she hadn't thought of it that way.

"It matters *that* much to you, whatever you're doing?"

"It matters more to me than anything in the world."

Marcelo blinked.

Ellen blinked back. For a minute, they played eye chicken.

Marcelo sighed, and his expression softened. "Okay, you win. Take the time you need this week, but that's it. I'll tell everyone you're not feeling well. It'll make sense, after you fainted dead away."

"You're saying yes?" Ellen was dumbfounded. "Why?"

"I'm trying to show you that I'm not a jerk."

"I know that. I never thought you were."

Marcelo lifted an eyebrow, dubious, but Ellen knew she'd never convince him otherwise, after what Sarah had told him.

"What about the homicide piece?"

"It can wait a week. The fire in the Yerkes Building is the new story."

"What fire?" Ellen had been in the love cocoon with Will and hadn't heard. The Yerkes was one of the biggest buildings in town.

"Three people killed, cleaning personnel, so sad. The building burned to the ground. Police suspect arson."

"Wait a minute," Ellen said, as the truth dawned on her. "Does that mean you didn't really need my draft, just now?"

"Uh, yes." Marcelo looked sheepish. "Oh well."

"You rat!"

"You don't think I'm a rat. You like me."

Ellen was mortified. "How do you know?"

"I run the newsroom. You think I don't know the news?"

Ellen laughed, embarrassed. "Oh yeah, so what else do you know?"

"Is it true?" Marcelo's dark eyes glittered in a teasing way.

"You answer me. Then I'll answer you."

"I know everybody believes that I'm attracted to you, and that's why you're not getting laid off."

Ellen flushed.

"And I have to say, they're half-right," Marcelo answered, his voice suddenly serious. His eyes met hers across the counter, with a very adult honesty. "I would love to take you out, I admit it."

Ellen felt a smile spread across her face.

"But that's not the reason you're keeping your job. You're keeping your job because you're a great reporter."

"Thank you. And what if this crush is mutual?"

"So is it?" Marcelo was grinning, but she couldn't believe they were having this conversation. Oreo Figaro listened, in shock.

"Yes."

"That's very nice to hear, but it's too bad. Nothing will happen between us. It compromises you. It compromises me. This is romance in the time of sexual harassment, and that means nothing good happens, never ever. Except maybe this." In the next second, Marcelo leaned over and planted the softest, sweetest kiss on her unsuspecting lips, and when it was over, he pulled away. "Never ever again."

"Excruciating," Ellen said, meaning it.

Chapter 45

"Mommy, don't go!" Will wailed, grabbing Ellen around the knees and holding on for dear life. She was dressed for the early flight, her purse on her shoulder, her roller bag packed and ready, but she wasn't going anywhere, blocked by the Wall of Guilt.

"Honey, I have to." Ellen rubbed his little back. "Remember, we talked about this? I have to go away for work but I'll be back very soon, in four or five days, probably."

"FOUR DAYS!" Will burst into new tears, and Connie intervened, putting a hand on his shoulder.

"Will, you and me will have a great time. I brought ice cream, and we can make sundaes after school today. Won't that be fun?"

"Mommy, no!"

"Will, it's all right." Ellen had learned from experience that he would never calm down, so she gave him a last hug and kiss on the head while she pried his fingers off one by one, like the dewclaws of a kitten. "I have to go, honey. I'll call you tonight. You'll see, I'll be back soon."

"Say good-bye, Will." Connie had him in hand. "Bye, Mommy, see you soon!"

"Love you, Will," Ellen said, opening the door the second she was freed and running out into the cold with her bag.

Wondering if every mother felt like a fleeing felon, at times.

Chapter 46

The sky was a supersaturated teal, and kelly green fronds on the palm trees fluttered in the breeze. Lush olive green hedges lined the curbs, and thick lawns, edged to perfection, bordered dense reds of climbing bougainvillea, the orange and yellow of tiny lantana flowers, and dark purple jacaranda. And that was just the Miami airport.

Ellen slipped on a pair of sunglasses, driving a rental car, leaving the window open until the air-conditioning kicked in. She sweltered in her navy sweater and took it off when the traffic slowed to a stop. According to the dashboard, the temperature hovered at ninety-nine degrees, and the humidity mixed ocean salt, heavy perfume, and cigarette smoke like a beachside cocktail. In less than an hour, she'd be at Carol and Bill Braverman's.

She dug in her purse and found the paper with the home address, which she'd gotten online and MapQuested last night. The exit wasn't far up the highway. She leaned over the steering wheel, craning her neck like a sea turtle, not wanting to miss it. The traffic was stop-and-go, in impossibly heavy congestion that took up four lanes, wider than any expressway back home.

Traffic stopped again, and Ellen reflected on her mission. She'd have to wait for an opening to get the proof she needed and she couldn't predict when that would happen. She'd have to keep on her toes, and the hard part would be staying undercover. Nobody could know why she was here, least of all the Bravermans.

She left the highway, got off at the exit, and in time found herself cruising along a smooth concrete causeway over a choppy turquoise bay lined with mansions, many with glistening white boats parked along private slips. She reached the other side, where the traffic was lighter than it had been and the cars costlier. She took a right and a left, then saw the street sign outlined in bright green. Surfside Lane. She took a right onto the Bravermans' street.

Did Will start his life here? Was this his street?

She passed a modern gray house, its front a huge expanse of glass, then a Spanish stucco mansion with a red-tiled roof, and finally an ornate French chateau. Each house was different from the next, but she noticed right away that they all had one thing in common. Every home had a yellow ribbon tied out front, whether it was to a palm tree, a front fence, or a gate.

She slowed the car to a stop, puzzled. The ribbons were pale and tattered, like the one her neighbors, the Shermans, had back home, for their daughter serving in Iraq. But all these people couldn't have family serving in the war. She sensed the explanation before she saw it, cruising ahead to 826, then closing in on 830, which confirmed her theory.

HELP US FIND OUR SON, read a large white sign, festooned with yellow ribbons, and it stood planted in an otherwise picture-perfect front lawn. The sign showed the age-progressed photo of Timothy Braverman from the white card, and tiger lilies and sunny marigolds grew around its base, a living memorial to a son the Bravermans prayed wasn't gone forever.

Ellen's throat caught. She felt a pang of sympathy, and conscience. She had known from the Braverman website that they were missing Timothy, but seeing the sign with her own eyes made it real. The boy on the sign, Will or Timothy, looked back at her with a gaze at once familiar and unknown.

Please, no.

She set her emotions aside and looked past the sign. The Bravermans' house was like something out of *Architectural Digest,* a large contemporary with a crushed-shell driveway that held a glistening white Jaguar. Suddenly two women in tank tops and running shorts walked past the car, pumping red-handled weights, and Ellen hit the gas, not to arouse suspicion.

She circled the block, composing herself and cooling down as she eyed the homes, one more lovely than the next. She had expected that the neighborhood would be wealthy; any family who could afford that reward would live in a nice place, and her online research had told her that she was driving through a neighborhood of three-million-dollar houses. In fact, according to zoom.com, the Bravermans' house cost $3.87 million, which she tried not to compare with her three-bedroom, one-bath back home.

It's warm and friendly.

Ellen pushed that thought away. She took a left and another left, going down the next block, getting the lay of the land. No one was out except a gardener using a noisy leaf blower and a laborer edging a lawn. The sun beat down on the shiny foreign cars, dappling the lawns through the palm fronds, and she turned around and headed back to the main drag, Coral Ridge Way, the two-lane road that led back to the causeway. It was busy, and when the light changed, she parked across the street from the entrance to

Surfside Lane. She didn't park on the Bravermans' block for fear of being noticed.

She cracked open a bottle of warm water and checked the clock—1:45. She turned away when an older man strolled past with a chubby Chihuahua, and she watched the traffic to the causeway. By 1:47, her sunglasses were sliding down her nose, and the car had grown impossibly hot, proving that she was a stakeout rookie. She turned on the ignition and slid down the window.

She had barely taken a second sip of water when she saw the chrome grille of a white Jaguar nose out of Surfside Lane, pause at the stop sign, and pull a left. It had to be the Bravermans' car because theirs was the only Jaguar on the block. In the driver's seat was the outline of a woman, alone. She had to be Carol Braverman, herself.

Yikes!

Ellen turned on the ignition, hit the gas, and found a place in the brisk line of traffic to the causeway. Her heartbeat stepped up. Carol was two cars ahead as they picked up speed and soared over the causeway, the wind off the water blowing her hair around. She kept an eye on the white car as they wound through the streets, which grew increasingly congested, but she stayed on Carol as she turned into a strip mall and pulled into a parking spot.

Ellen parked several rows away and cut the ignition, then held her breath waiting for Carol Braverman to emerge. She remembered the photos of her online but was dying to see her in person, to see if she looked like Will, or vice versa.

The next moment, the driver's door opened.

Chapter 47

Ellen couldn't see Carol Braverman's face because she had on large black sunglasses and a hot pink visor, but she still felt a tingle of excitement at the sight of her. Carol got out of the car, tall and shapely in a white cotton tank top and an old-school tennis skirt. Pink pom-poms wiggled from the backs of her sneakers, and a bouncy dark blond ponytail popped out of her visor. She slipped a white quilted bag over her shoulder and hurried to the gourmet grocery, where she picked a shopping cart and rolled it inside the tinted glass doors of the store.

Ellen grabbed her keys and purse, got out of the car, and hustled through the parking lot to the grocery, snagging a shopping cart for show. The entrance doors slid aside, and the air-conditioning hit like January, but two women shoppers stood bottlenecking the entrance, looking at the green stand for cut flowers. She kept an eye on Carol but didn't want to draw attention to herself, especially when she realized how out of place she looked. Nobody else had on a thick white turtleneck, Mom jeans, and brown clogs accessorized with Pennsylvania mud.

She ducked into the back row of the flower department, going around the shoppers, and fake-lingered at the bird-of-paradise plants, then glanced over her shoulder. In the next minute, the women moved, leaving Carol right behind her, using the ATM machine, and so close that Ellen could almost hear her humming. She couldn't risk Carol seeing her and maybe recognizing her later, so she kept her head down and her sunglasses on her nose. The ATM beeped, and the humming grew fainter, so she knew that Carol had moved on.

Time to get stalking.

Ellen never knew when she'd get another opportunity and she had to see Carol's face, close up. She drifted sideways past a wall of nuts in plastic scoop-it-yourself canisters and fake-browsed the roasted unsalted almonds, raw salted almonds, and raw unsalted almonds. For a minute, she couldn't even fake-decide. Out of the corner of her eye, she could see Carol looking at the peppers, her back turned.

Ellen pulled a plastic bag from a perforated roll, picked up a plastic scoop, and dug out some raw almonds, then spotted Carol moving around the perimeter of the produce department, bagging a head of romaine and putting it in her cart, her back still turned. Ellen got a twist tie for her almond bag and crossed nearer to Carol, keeping her head down in the apple aisle, where rosy galas, fat Macintoshes, and Golden Delicious sat mounded like Egyptian pyramids. She positioned herself midway down the aisle, so that she could get a good look at Carol's face if she turned around.

Ellen picked up a Granny Smith and examined it with ersatz absorption, and in the split second she bent over to put it back, Carol spun around with her cart.

No!

The rest happened even before Ellen could process it. Carol's cart crashed squarely into Ellen's hip, startling her so that she backed into the apple pyramid, and before she could stop them, Gala and Fuji apples were rolling toward her in a pesticide-free avalanche.

"Oh no!" Ellen yelped, punching up her glasses.

"I'm so sorry!" Carol tried to catch the apples, but they hit the lacquered floor and shot off in all directions, like billiard balls.

"Oh, jeez!" Ellen bent over to hide her face, fake-collecting apples, just as Carol straightened up, her cheeks slightly flushed, her hands full of apples.

"I can't believe I did that! I'm so sorry!"

"It's okay," Ellen said, but she glanced up and almost gasped.

Carol had taken off her sunglasses, and in person, the resemblance between her and Will was obvious. She had Will's sea-blue eyes and creamy coloring. Her lips were on the thin side, like his, and her chin slightly pointed, too. Carol struck her instantly as being *of* Will, as if Ellen could smell the blood they shared. Stricken, she put her head down, but Carol knelt next to her, gathering apples in her tennis skirt.

"It was my fault. That's what I get for rushing."

"No, it was me. I knocked them over." Ellen collected the escaping apples, flushed with emotion, keeping her face to the floor.

"I was doing too much. I always think I can squeeze in one little errand. You ever do that?"

"Sure."

"Of course that's when things go wrong."

"Mrs. Braverman, let me help you," a stockboy said, hurrying over in a pepper green smock and checkered Vans. He bent down and corralled some of the apples, his fuzzy dreadlocks falling into his young face.

"Thanks, Henrique." Carol rose, brushing off a pair of tan, finely muscled legs. "I'm such a klutz today. I hit this woman with my cart."

"Really, I'm fine." Ellen rose, looking for the exit, but suddenly, Carol placed a manicured hand on her arm.

"Again, I'm so sorry."

"It's nothing, thanks." Ellen shed Carol's hand, turned away as calmly as possible, and walked through the produce department and out of the store. She hit the humid air and made a beeline for the rental car. Her eyes welled up behind her sunglasses, and her throat thickened. She fumbled in her purse for the car keys, let herself inside, then slumped low in the driver's seat.

She sat in the car, staring out the windshield. Cars broiled in the Miami sun, and pink flowers ringed the parking lot. She gazed at them without really seeing them, wiping her eyes and trying to process what she'd seen. Carol Braverman, a grieving mother. She seemed like a nice woman, she seemed like Will. She could be missing the child who was at her home right now, up north.

Ellen thought of Susan Sulaman, haunted by the loss of her children, and then Laticia Williams, bereft. She knew how they felt, and she could guess how Carol Braverman felt. A wave of conscience engulfed her, and she felt awful that she might be causing another woman that sort of pain. Another mother.

His real mother.

She reached for the bottle of water and took a sip, but it was hot and burned her throat. She couldn't help but feel it was a penance, of sorts.

A swinging white bag drew her attention, and Ellen looked out the window. Carol was leaving the grocery store and hurrying to her car, carrying a brown paper bag, then she chirped the car unlocked, got in the driver's seat, and reversed out of the space.

Ellen started the ignition, shaken.

Chapter 48

Carol drove faster than before, and Ellen had to concentrate not to lose her in the heavy traffic. The task checked her emotions and focused her thoughts. Her subjective sense that Carol was Will's mother wasn't scientific. She still had to get the proof she needed, despite what her heart was telling her.

The two cars threaded their way through the congested downtown, and Ellen stayed within three cars of Carol, not risking falling farther behind. The sidewalks were packed with tourists in bathing suits and cover-ups, and loud music *thumpa-thump*ed from a convertible. A sleek black Mercedes pulled up in the next lane, and its cigar-puffing driver grinned at her.

Ring! The sound jarred Ellen from her thoughts. It was her BlackBerry, and she kept an eye on Carol as she hunted for the device with her hand, fumbling around in her purse until she located it and checked the display. She recognized the number. It was Sarah Liu's cell number.

Ellen pressed Ignore and tossed the phone aside. She followed Carol through a fork in the road, then over a causeway, which was less busy. They drove out over a spit of land, where condos and high-rises gave way to suburban houses, with flowerbeds and manicured hedges. People strolled with small dogs, a young man pedaled a collapsible bicycle with tiny tires, and women power-walked, carrying water bottles.

Carol took a right and a left, with only one car between them, and Ellen spotted a sign painted melon, which read BRIDGES, and beyond it lay a small building with a red-tiled roof. A tall hedge concealed the building, but she guessed it was a spa or salon, and two women drove in ahead of her. She stayed behind Carol as they snaked through the tall hedge.

Ellen was last in the line of cars that trailed up the lovely winding drive, and the sight on the other side caught her by surprise. A large group of children toting backpacks clustered around several women, obviously teachers, under the shaded entrance to the building. The children couldn't have been more than five years old, so it had to be a pre-school.

Will could have a brother? Or a sister? Instead of just a cat?

She watched the scene with a sinking sensation. The teachers brought each child to the waiting car, waving a cheery good-bye, and she kept an eye on Carol to see which child was hers. Ellen hadn't thought about whether the Bravermans would have another child, or Timothy a sibling. The Braverman website hadn't mentioned another child. Maybe they hadn't wanted to risk his security, given what had happened.

Carol reached near the head of the line, but instead of going to the entrance, she peeled to the left and found a space in the parking lot. Ellen hung back, idling the car, and the next minute, Carol got out with her quilted purse and a black Adidas bag and hurried toward the entrance. The teachers waved to her as she jogged up to them, greeting her with smiles and chatter, but Ellen couldn't hear what they were saying.

She had to get out of the line for pickups. She took a quick right and parked at the far end of the lot, reversing into the space so she could have a clear view of the entrance, to see when Carol left with her child.

She lowered the car windows before she switched off the ignition, having learned her lesson, and waited. The dashboard clock read 2:55. It was a late dismissal for preschool, but if this school was like Will's, the parents could pick up at any time of the day.

But this preschool isn't like Will's. It's a lot nicer.

By three fifteen, she was sweltering in the parked car. The thermometer on the dash read 100°. Her shirt clung to her neck, and her legs were so hot that she wanted to tear her pants off. By three thirty, she'd rolled them up to capri length and wrapped up her hair in a messy topknot, having found a stray barrette in her purse. She waited, watching the entrance, but it seemed as if all of the kids had been picked up. By three forty-five, her sunglasses were melting onto the bridge of her nose, and she decided to take a risk.

She grabbed her bag, got out of the car, and walked through the parking lot to the entrance under a tall breezeway. There were no more teachers or children out front, and she walked to the front door and tried it, but it was locked. A VISITORS MUST REPORT TO THE OFFICE sign was taped to the glass, and she peered through. She could see the barest outline of a large entrance hall with a glistening tile floor, and colorful bulletin boards hung on the left wall, across from a glass-walled office on the right. Carol was nowhere in sight.

Ellen pressed a buzzer beside the door, and almost immediately a mechanical voice asked, "Can I help you?"

"I'm new to the area and I'd like to see the school."

"Come right in. The office is on your right." A loud buzz sounded, and she yanked on the door and let herself inside. A slim, attractive woman with dark, curly hair emerged from the office and strode toward her with a smile, extending a hand.

"Welcome to Bridges, I'm Janice Davis, the assistant director." She looked pretty in a pink cotton top, white pants, and light blue flats.

Ellen shook her hand. "I'm Karen Volpe, and I thought I'd stop in to see your school."

"Of course. Did you have an appointment?"

"No, I'm sorry." Ellen was wondering if Carol was in one of the classrooms. "My husband and I haven't moved down yet, and I wanted to see the preschools in the area."

"I see." Janice checked her watch, a slim gold one. "I don't have time now for the meeting we like to give with the tour. Let's make an appointment and you can return."

"I'm not sure when I can get back. Can you give me the quick version of the tour? We can chat as we walk."

"Sure, okay." Janice smiled. "You must be from New York."

Works for me. "How did you know?"

"Everything's quicker. You'll live here a week and your pace will slow down." The softness of her tone took the sting from her words, as did a hostess wave toward the hallway. "I'll show you our classrooms and our media center."

"You have your own library, in a preschool?"

"We all know how important reading and libraries are, and modesty aside, Bridges is the best preschool in south Florida, if not the entire state. We draw from three different counties." Janice went into lecture mode. "Now, when are you moving down?"

"We're not sure." Ellen scanned the hallway ahead, which was empty, with classrooms off to the side, five in all, their doors closed. She wondered which one contained Carol. "My son is three, and we like to be prepared, to do things in advance."

"You'd need to, for us." Janice stopped at the first door. "This is our classroom for two-year-olds, the ones who stay later, that is. We like to mix them with the older children, too, so they get the socialization that's so vital, especially for our onlies."

"Onlies?"

"Only children."

"Of course." Ellen looked through the window in the door, and inside was a sunny classroom with two teachers, finger-painting with toddlers in coral smocks. Carol wasn't inside.

"Admissions are very restrictive."

"My son is very bright." *He can trace all by himself.*

Janice led her to the next door. "The three-year-olds," she said, and inside sat a circle of children shaking tambourines, with two teachers standing in front of the room. Still no Carol. Janice showed her to the next door, where they paused. "And this is our classroom of four-year-olds. They're learning French right now."

"Really." Ellen peered through the window, where the kids and their teachers looked *très contents*. But there was no Carol.

"We believe that language skills should be taught early, and they take to it like ducks to water. I'll give you our literature on our postgraduate placement rates. We're a feeder for all the best private schools."

"Let's see the five-year-olds."

"What is it you do, did you say?" Janice asked, but Ellen walked ahead and peeked into the classroom full of five-year-olds in little chairs, books open in their laps. No Carol.

"Which language are they learning?" she asked, to avoid the question.

"Reading skills. We drill and drill."

Sir, yes, sir. "Good for you." Ellen straightened up. "And the media center?"

"This way." Janice led her down the hall to a double door. "This is one of the special enrichment events we have each day, for after-care. Monday is story time and on Tuesday we do science . . ."

Ellen tuned her out when she saw what was going on inside. A group of children sat in a semicircle, laughing and pointing while a teacher in a Mother Goose costume read to them. But a telltale pink pom-pom stuck from beneath the hem of her hoop skirt. It wasn't a teacher in the Mother Goose getup. It was Carol Braverman.

Janice said, "Here, you see story time, where we perform stories for the children."

"And the teachers do this?"

"No, she's not a teacher. She's one of our moms, who used to be an actress."

"An actress?"

"Yes. Her name is Carol Braverman, and she worked at Disney World. She was Snow White."

Of course she was. "Is her child in the class?"

"No, Carol just comes to read to the children." Janice paused. "She doesn't have a child in the class."

Ellen couldn't ask a follow-up without blowing her cover. "That's very nice of her, to do that. I guess you pay her very well."

"Oh, she won't take a dime for it. Carol does it because she loves children. Come with me." Janice took Ellen by the elbow and led her back up the hall. "It's actually a terrible tragedy. Carol's little boy, Timothy, was kidnapped a couple of years ago and they never got him back. That first year, she was a mess. Depressed, in hell. But she pulled herself together and decided that it actually helps her healing process to be around children."

Ellen felt a wave of guilt. "How can she do that? I would find that so painful."

"I agree with you, but do you want to know what she said to me, when I asked her that very question?"

No. "Yes."

"She said, 'If I'm around children, at least I get to experience what it would be like if Timothy were still with me. I don't miss out on everything this way, and when I get him back, I'll be right up to speed.'"

Ellen felt like crying. She didn't want to know this, any of it. She couldn't believe she was doing this to another woman. She wished she'd never come.

"I know, right? It's so sad."

"Think she'll get him back?"

"I'm sure the chances are low, but we're all pulling for her. If anybody deserves it, Carol does." They reached the office, and Janice brightened. "If you'll come in with me, I'll give you that literature I mentioned."

Ellen followed her inside the office, but her thoughts had skipped ahead.

She didn't know if she had the heart to stalk Carol to her next stop.

Much less to get the proof she didn't want in the first place.

Chapter 49

The late-day sun was even hotter, and Ellen was trailing Carol back through the luxurious suburbs when her Black-Berry started ringing. She plucked it from her purse and glanced at the display, which showed the newspaper's main telephone number.

Marcelo!

"Hello?" she said, picking up, but it wasn't him, it was Sarah.

"Marcelo told us you're taking a few days off. Listen, I won't keep you, but I wanted to apologize."

"That's okay," Ellen said, surprised. Sarah sounded genuinely contrite.

"I'm sorry I got so hyper about the story. When you fainted, I felt awful."

"Thanks. It's just this bug, I feel dizzy."

"Okay, so, we cool?"

"Sure." Ellen took a right turn, keeping up with Carol in rush-hour traffic. They were driving back through the congested part of the city, but she switched lanes, staying with Carol.

"I assume you heard, we got bumped for the Yerkes

fire." Sarah snorted. "One man's ceiling is another man's floor."

"Listen, I gotta go back to bed."

"Feel better. Take care."

"Thanks. See you." Ellen hung up and accelerated to make a green light as they wound left and right through traffic and finally traveled over the causeway to Surfside Lane.

Carol turned right onto Surfside, and Ellen drove down the main drag and took a U-turn, coming back to park in her position across the street, so that she could see if Carol went out again. She lowered the windows and twisted off the ignition, craning her neck to see down Surfside. If she tilted her head, she had a partial view of the Bravermans' house and driveway. More people were walking on Coral Ridge than before, but no one seemed to notice her. A man who looked like a model jogged past, and behind him, two Rollerbladers skated toward the causeway, their thighs pumping away.

Ring Ring! Ellen reached for her BlackBerry, checking the screen. HOME. It had to be Connie. "Hey, Con, how's it going?"

"Another day, another macaroni picture."

"Art you can eat, right?" Ellen smiled. Her thoughts traveled back to her snug little house though her gaze remained on the Bravermans'.

"I don't know if this matters, but I wanted to give you a heads-up. I think somebody just called here. Her name was Sarah. Is that someone from the newspaper or a story?"

"The paper." Ellen tensed. "When was this?"

"About half an hour ago. Will answered the phone and told her that you weren't home."

"*What?*"

"I'm sorry. He got to the phone before I did. He thought

it might be you. He talked to her and hung up. I heard him say Sarah. I didn't even get to talk to her."

"Will said I wasn't there?" Ellen couldn't process it fast enough. "Tell me exactly what he said."

"He told her you went on the airplane for work."

"Oh no!" It was exactly what Ellen had told him yesterday. She rubbed her forehead and came away with flop sweat. "This isn't good, Connie."

"Why doesn't she know what you're doing for work, anyway?"

The proverbial tangled web. "My editor wanted to keep it on the QT. We generally share our assignments, but Sarah is getting a little competitive lately, between you and me."

"Oh. Oops."

Ellen was trying to figure what to do. Sarah had caught her in a lie, then called her to confirm it. It was great journalistic technique, and it would get her fired for sure.

"Will wants to talk to you, okay?"

"Of course." Ellen could hear Will calling for her, so close he was probably reaching for the phone.

"Mommy, Mommy! When are you coming home?"

"Soon, sweetie." Ellen felt a pang at the sound of his voice, even as she slumped in the driver's seat, keeping an eye on the Bravermans' house. "Tell me about your macaroni picture."

"Come home soon. I have to go."

"Love you," Ellen called after him, and Connie got back on the line.

"We're about to have dinner. So how bad is it?"

"Don't worry. Just don't let him tell any more state secrets, okay?"

"Gotcha. Sorry."

"See you soon." Ellen hung up and called Marcelo for damage control, waiting nervously for the call to connect.

Another runner darted by on the sidewalk, glancing back at her. His shoulder cap bore a MOM tattoo, but she was pretty sure it was a coincidence.

"How are you?" Marcelo asked, his voice unusually cool, which took Ellen aback.

"Long story short, Sarah called my house and Will told her that I went away on business."

"I know. She just left my office. She came in to tell me that you lied to me."

Oh no. "What did you say?"

"What could I say? I couldn't admit that we confessed our mutual admiration in your kitchen, before we fabricated a story."

Ellen reddened. "I'm so sorry, Marcelo."

"I shouldn't have told them you were sick. So, in theory, you lied to me, and I lied to the staff, and Sarah came in to let me know. If I had just said that it wasn't their business, we'd be fine."

Ellen had undermined Marcelo's authority. A reporter couldn't lie to an editor without consequences. The entire newsroom would be talking about it and waiting to see what he would do. "So what did you say to her?"

"I told her I'd talk to you about it when you got back." Marcelo shook his head. "For an intelligent man, I act so stupid sometimes."

"No, you don't," Ellen rushed to say, hearing the subtext: *I never should have crossed the line with you.*

"I can't show you any favoritism, and I don't want to have to let you go." Regret freighted his tone, but Ellen straightened up, determined.

"There's no reason to do that, not yet. I'm still away, and that buys us a few days. I have to get clear of this situation."

"What situation?" Marcelo asked, a new urgency in his voice, but all of a sudden the white Jaguar was pulling out of the Bravermans' driveway and turning left toward the main drag.

"Uh, hold on." Ellen tucked the BlackBerry in her neck, twisted on the car's ignition, and hit the gas. She launched herself into rush-hour traffic, an overheated lineup of blaring music, cigarette smoke, and cell-phone conversations. She couldn't afford to let too much space get between her and Carol.

"Ellen? Are you there?"

"Marcelo, hang on a sec."

"Please tell me what is going on. I can help you."

"Sorry, but this isn't the best time for me and—" She lost her train of thought because Carol took an unexpected right turn before the causeway. Ellen steered her car into the right lane but the movement dislodged her BlackBerry, which slid off her lap and fell near the gas pedal.

"Good-bye, Marcelo!" she called out, then she hit the gas and swerved around the corner, in pursuit. She had to stay on track. She couldn't worry about her job now, or even Marcelo's. Sooner or later she had to catch a break. She ran the light, staying on Carol's tail.

Chapter 50

Ellen followed Carol through the carnation-and-canary-hued buildings of South Beach, where traffic on Collins Avenue was a sizzling stop-and-go. Between them was a white Hummer, like a giant bar of Ivory on wheels. Ahead, the Jag turned left, followed by the Hummer and Ellen. They traveled up a skinny back street lined with delivery entrances to a cigar store, boutiques, and restaurants. Dumpsters alternated with flashy cars parked so haphazardly that they looked strewn there. Carol pulled up behind a parked convertible, and the Hummer powered ahead, leaving Ellen no choice but to keep going or risk being recognized from the grocery store.

She cruised slowly ahead and watched Carol in her rearview mirror. The driver-side door opened, and Carol emerged, stepping out in a tight-fitting tomato red dress, her long dark blond hair loose to her shoulders. She chirped the car locked and walked around to its back fender, heading for the cross street on the far side.

Go, go, go!

Ellen parked illegally, turned off the ignition, grabbed her purse, jumped out of the car, and hustled down the street. Her clogs clopped along, and she made a mental note not to wear Danskos the next time she stalked somebody, unless it was a Clydesdale.

Carol took a left at the cross street, with Ellen tailing her on foot at a safe distance. They reached a street that was closed to traffic, Lincoln Road, and Carol plunged into the crowd of gorgeous models, crazies with face paint, gay men with matching mustaches, and European tourists speaking an array of languages. Pomeranians shared the packed sidewalk with a boa constrictor worn around the neck of a woman who had forgotten the feather part of her feather boa. Kiehl's, Banana Republic, and Victoria's Secret stores were interspersed with boutique and gift shops, and Ellen walked along, marveling. It looked like a street party, with merchandise.

She never lost sight of Carol, helped by the bright red dress. They threaded their way past Cuban, Chinese, and Italian restaurants, their tables spilling out onto large café areas for outdoor dining. Carol paused at a sushi restaurant and talked with a camera-ready maitre d', so Ellen slowed her step, watching them. In the next minute, a tall, dark-haired man slipped from the crowd and stopped beside Carol, kissing her on the cheek and encircling her slim waist in a proprietary way.

Bill Braverman.

She recognized him instantly from the online photos. He was slim, in a light gray sport jacket with jeans, but was too covered up to show the wiriness she'd seen online. Nor could she see his features clearly at this distance. She fake-read a menu posted in front of one of the restaurants, letting the crowd flow around her and waiting to see what the Bravermans would do. The crowd chattered away, and the sun vanished behind the palm trees, their spiked fronds waving. She glanced back at the Bravermans, and hidden by the crowd, edged closer to their table.

They were seated in the center of the outdoor dining area, and she got a good look at Bill's face. He was handsome, with his spray of black bangs over dark round eyes and a nose that looked like an older version of Will's. From time to time, he leaned back in his bistro chair, his cigarette smoldering between his fingers, and he spoke animatedly, laughing frequently.

Time to rock.

Ellen slipped her purse onto her shoulder, walked toward the maitre d' of their restaurant, and asked, "Is there a ladies' room inside?"

"In the back, to the right."

"Thanks." Ellen went inside the restaurant, and it smelled like Thai curry, reminding her that she hadn't eaten in ages. She found the ladies' room, went inside, and slipped off her sunglasses. She headed into one of the stalls, closed the door, and went into her purse. On the bottom was a white plastic bag, her DNA kit.

She took it out and checked the contents. Directions she'd downloaded, two pairs of blue plastic gloves she'd had under the sink, and two brown paper bags, which she used to pack Will's snack for school. She opened the directions and read them again, because she didn't want to screw up:

Our paternity test is the most accurate in the country! We analyze your samples at our state-of-the-art laboratory, using a 16-marker DNA test! Be thorough and collect all samples possible! Results are ready in 3 business days, but can be expedited for a small RUSH charge!

Ellen skipped the blah blah blah, which she'd read online. There had been plenty of DNA-testing companies on the web, including the one she was using. Her research had taught her that there were two testing options: the first was a standard paternity kit, which was admissible in court and required collection of the DNA by a cheek, or bucal, swab. She didn't need that one, and she doubted the Bravermans would offer up a sample. The second test was the one she was using, a nonstandard DNA test for paternity. Her gaze returned to the form:

For times when the bucal swab method just isn't possible, simply obtain one of the following items, place it in a brown paper bag, store it at room temperature, and send it to us. Follow precautions below!

Ellen read the precautions:

Must wear gloves so as not to get your DNA on the sample. Store at room temperature and do not get the sample wet. Must be put in a paper bag, not plastic.

She scanned the list of permissible collection items, just to make sure she remembered it correctly:

No need for silly collection kits! You can get DNA from a licked envelope, chewed gum, a soda can or any kind of can, including beer, glass, toothbrush, semen, dried blood stains (including menstrual blood), a strand of hair with the follicle attached, or a cigarette butt!

Ellen folded the papers up and put them in her purse, then slipped the plastic gloves into her jeans pocket. She used the bathroom and left the stall, washing her face and freshening her makeup, which made her feel almost civilized, then took a last look at herself in the mirror, letting her eyes meet their reflection. She had her mother's eyes, a fact that secretly made them both happy, as if it were confirmation of their closeness. Even now, looking at herself, she could still see her mother, within.

Follow your heart.

It was showtime.

Chapter 51

Ellen got a table in the outdoor dining area of the restaurant next door to the one with the Bravermans, with a clear view of their table. While the couple ate dinner, she checked her email on the BlackBerry, but there was nothing from Amy Martin. Then she'd called home and said good night to Will while she'd devoured a delicious seviche appetizer, a red-lacquered model boat of sushi, and a frothy cappuccino with almond biscotti.

She watched the Bravermans finish their coffee and share a tiramisu. Bill smoked a final cigarette, his third of the evening, but Carol didn't smoke, so Ellen would have to take her glass to get a DNA sample from her. The couple had laughed and talked throughout the entire dinner, cementing their qualifications as a happily married couple.

Which doesn't mean they're better parents than me.

Bill signaled for the check, so Ellen did the same, catching her waiter's eye. They paid at about the same time, and she rose right after the Bravermans, ready to swoop down on their table.

Now!

They left and threaded their way to the aisle, and Ellen

made a beeline for their table. Suddenly a group of tourists shoved in front of her, blocking her way, and she didn't reach the table until after the busboy had gathered the glasses.

Damn!

"Table no is clean," the busboy said in an indeterminate accent, picking up the plates and setting them with a clatter in a large brown tub.

"I'll just sit a minute." Ellen plopped into Bill Braverman's chair. "I only want dessert."

"No is clean." The busboy reached for the full ashtray, but Ellen grabbed it from his hands.

"Thanks." She checked it for gum, in case Carol had chewed some, but it only contained three cigarette butts, all Bill's. "I'll need this. I smoke."

The busboy walked away, but the maitre d' was craning his neck and peering at the table, along with a foursome of hungry patrons. She had to act fast. Her heart pounded. She slid the gloves from her pocket and shoved her right hand in one. The maitre d' was making his way over, with the foursome. She gathered the three cigarette butts from the ashtray, opened the paper bag under the table, tossed the butts inside, then closed it up and shoved it back into her purse.

"Miss, do you have a reservation?" the maitre d' asked, reaching the table just as Ellen rose, shaking her head.

"Sorry, I was just resting a minute, thanks." She headed out of the dining area to the sidewalk, crowded with dogs, skateboarders, Rollerbladers, and a tattooed man on a silver unicycle.

She melted into the crowd, exhilarated. Bill's DNA sample was safe in her purse. She wondered if she could get Carol's tonight, too.

One down, two to go.

Chapter 52

Ellen cruised around the block after Carol had pulled into her driveway, followed by Bill driving a gray Maserati. The sky was a rich marine blue, and the street silent, the fancy cars cooling for the night. Lights were on inside the houses, and high-def TVs flickered from behind the curtains.

She had a second wind, energized by her success with the cigarette butts, and was thinking of the other ways you could get DNA samples. Cans, glasses, licked envelopes.

Licked envelopes?

Ellen rounded the corner onto Surfside and eyed the Bravermans' green cast-iron mailbox. It was at the end of their driveway, but the red flag wasn't up, so there was no letter inside.

Rats.

She drove slowly past the house, reconnoitering. All the lights in the house were off, its modern oblong windows gone dark, and the only movement was the gentle whirring of its automatic sprinklers, watering the thick grass like so many mechanical whirligigs. Flowers bloomed at the foot of the HELP US FIND OUR SON sign, and the larger-than-life face of Timothy, or Will, floated ghostly in the dark.

Maybe not tonight.

Ellen was about to leave for the hotel when a light from the Bravermans' first floor went on from on the far right. She slowed to a stop, just past the house. The window had no curtains, and she could see Bill walk through the room and seat himself at a desk, inclining forward. In the next minute, his profile came to life, illuminated by the light of a computer laptop.

Ellen pulled the car over and parked on the opposite side of the street, then lowered the window, turned off the ignition, and watched Bill. She could see bookshelves and cabinets in the room, so she gathered that it was a home office. Bill spent a few more minutes on the computer, then got up and moved around the room, doing something she couldn't see. In the next minute, the front door opened and he emerged, carrying a black trash bag.

Yikes!

She ducked in the front seat and watched in the outside mirror. Bill put the trash bag in a tall green trashcan and rolled it to the end of the driveway, then went back toward the house. She stayed low until she heard the front door slam, then she eased up in the seat, looking behind her. The light in the home office switched off, and the house went dark again.

Trash could contain DNA.

She scanned the street, front and back, but there was no one in sight. She slid off her clogs, opened the car door as quietly as possible, and jumped out, her heart pounding. She bolted for the trashcan, tore off the lid, plucked out two bags at warp speed, and dashed back to the car like a crazed Santa Claus.

She jumped in the car, threw the bags in the passenger seat, and hit the gas, then went around the block and ended up on the main drag, speeding to the causeway with her booty. She pulled over and cut the ignition, turned on the interior light, and grabbed one trash bag. She undid the drawstring and peeked inside, but it was too dark to see the contents. It didn't smell like garbage, so she dumped it out onto the passenger seat, dismayed at the sight.

The trash was shredded, and it tumbled out like a ball of paper spaghetti. She pawed through it anyway to see if there was any item that could contain Carol's DNA, but no dice. It was Bill's home-office trash, strips of numbers, portfolio statements, and account statements. She remembered that Bill was an investor, so it made sense that he'd shred his trash. She never shredded anything, but her home office trash consisted of Toys"R"Us circulars.

She gathered up the trash, stuffed it back into the bag, and tossed it into the backseat. Then she reached over and grabbed the other bag, which was heavier. She yanked on the drawstring and opened the bag, releasing the yucky smell of fresh garbage. She held the open bag directly under the interior light and peeked inside. On top of the trash sat a heap of gray-blue shrimp shells that stank to high heaven, and she pushed them aside, going through wet coffee grounds, the chopped bottom of a head of Romaine, a Horchow catalog, and underneath that, a mother lode of mail. None of this would yield a DNA sample for Carol.

Bummer.

She pulled out the mail on the off-chance there was a sealed envelope. She flipped through it, but no luck. It was all unopened junk mail from Neiman Marcus, Versace, and Gucci, plus a glossy copy of *Departures* magazine. Stuck inside the magazine was a pink card from the dentist, a reminder that somebody had to get her teeth cleaned next month. She flipped the card over. The front read, Carol Charbonneau Braverman.

Ellen blinked. Charbonneau sounded familiar. She couldn't place if she'd heard it or if she was imagining it, her exhaustion finally catching up with her. She rooted through the rest of the trash, but there was nothing yucky enough to contain Carol's DNA. She tied the drawstring tightly, so it wouldn't stink up the car, and hoisted the bag into the backseat with the other. She took off for the hotel and threw the trash in a Dumpster on the way.

But when she finally reached her hotel room, she checked her email.

Amy Martin hadn't written yet, but her sister Cheryl had.

And her email brought the worst news imaginable.

Chapter 53

Ellen felt as if she had been punched in the stomach. She sank slowly onto the quilted bedspread, staring at her glowing BlackBerry screen. The email from Cheryl had no subject line, and it read:

> Dear Ellen,
> I'm sorry to tell you that yesterday, we found out that Amy passed away. She died of a heroin over-dose in her apartment in Brigantine on Saturday. Her wake will be Tuesday night, but there will be a private one for the family before her burial, on Wednesday at ten o'clock in Stoatesville, at the Cruzane Funeral Home. My mother says you can come to either time, and she would like to see you.
> Sincerely, Cheryl

The thought overwhelmed her with sadness. Amy was too young to die, and so horribly, and Ellen thought of how Cheryl must be feeling, then Amy's mother, Gerry, who had been so kind to her. Her thoughts came eventually to herself and Will. She had just lost her chance to learn anything from Amy.

Her gaze wandered over the blue-and-gold bedspread, the photographs on the wall, of nautilus and generic conch shells, and the balcony sliders. The glass looked out onto a bottomless Miami night, the same night that was falling at home. The sky was dark and black, no way to separate earth from heaven, and she felt undone, again. Loosed, untethered. She had a nagging fear, gnawing at the edges of her mind.

Quite a coincidence.

It seemed odd that Amy would turn up dead now, just when Ellen had begun asking questions about her. It seemed stranger still, considering the suicide of Karen Batz. Now, both women with knowledge of Will's adoption were dead. The only one left alive was Amy's boyfriend, and he was the one who looked like the kidnapper in the composite.

Not just a kidnapper. A murderer.

Ellen started to make connections, but even she knew she was entering the wild-speculation realm. There were innocent explanations for everything, and she flipped it. Amy had lived a fast life. Heroin addicts overdosed all the time. Lawyers committed suicide. Not everything was suspicious.

God help me.

Ellen willed herself to stop thinking, because she was making herself crazy. This had been the longest day in her life. She had one DNA sample, which was one more than she thought she'd get the first day. Her job was in jeopardy, as was her love life, but that was back home, which seemed suddenly very far away. Another world, even. She flopped backwards on the bed, and exhaustion swept over her, mooting even her darkest fears.

In the next minute, she fell into a terrible sleep.

Chapter 54

The next morning, Ellen parked her car in the same spot on the main drag, perpendicular to Surfside Lane. It was another hot, tropical day, but she was dressed for it today. She'd stopped at the hotel's overpriced gift shop and bought a pink visor, a pair of silver Oakley knockoffs, and a chrome yellow T-shirt that read SOUTH BEACH, which she'd paired with white shorts from home. Inside her pockets were a plastic glove and a folded brown paper bag.

She took a slug from a bottle of orange juice, still cold from the minibar. She felt weighed down by the news of Amy Martin's death and couldn't shake the fear that the overdose wasn't accidental. She put aside her dark thoughts to tend to the task at hand, especially because she wanted to get back home in time for the funeral.

She set the bottle in the cup holder and scoped out the scene, which was quiet except for people exercising. Two older women power-walked around the block, carrying water bottles and yammering away, and a younger woman was running in a sports bra with a black bathing suit bottom. Yet a fourth woman walked her white toy poodle, her cell phone and pedometer clipped to her waist like so much suburban ammunition.

Ellen was trying a new tack, so she got out of the car, pocketed her keys, and started walking. She strolled ahead with purpose, scanning the houses on either side of the street. No one had any red flags up on their mailboxes, and she wondered what time the mail would be picked up. She hoped Carol would mail a letter, so she could get DNA from the envelope.

She picked up the pace, gaining on the two older women who motored ahead in their sneakers. They wore Bermuda shorts in pastel colors and patterned tank tops, and even at seventysomething, looked in terrific shape. Each had short silver hair, but the woman on the left wore a yellow terry-cloth visor, and the one on the right had a white baseball cap. Ellen fell into stride with them before the Bravermans' house.

"Excuse me, ladies," she began, and they both turned around. "Do you know what time the mail pickup is in this neighborhood? I'm house-sitting on Brightside Lane for my cousins, and I forgot to ask them before they left this morning."

"Oh, who are your cousins?" Yellow Visor asked pleasantly.

"The Vaughns," Ellen answered without hesitation. Earlier this morning, she had driven down Brightside, about eight blocks away, and picked a name from one of the mailboxes. "June and Tom Vaughn, do you know them?"

"No, sorry. Brightside's a little too far over." Yellow Visor cocked her head, eyeing Ellen with confusion. "So why are you walking here and not there?"

Uh. "There's a big dog on that street, and I'm afraid of dogs."

"I agree with you. We're cat people." Yellow Visor

nodded. "Mail gets picked up around eleven o'clock in the morning. I'm Phyllis, and you're welcome to walk with us, if you're all alone."

"Thanks, I appreciate that." Ellen hoped to pump them for information until Carol mailed a letter or her DNA otherwise fell out of the sky.

"Good, we like new faces. We've been walking every day, two miles for the past six years, and we're sick of each other." Phyllis laughed, and her friend in the baseball cap nudged her.

"Speak for yourself, Phyl. You're not sick of me, I'm sick of you." She looked at Ellen with a warm smile. "I'm Linda DiMarco. And you?"

"Sandy Claus," Ellen answered, off the top of her head. They approached the Bravermans, where Carol's car was in the driveway, but Bill's was gone. She gestured casually to the memorial on the lawn. "What's that sign all about, do you know? And all these yellow ribbons?"

"Oh my, yes," Phyllis answered. A petite woman, she had bright eyes, a hawkish nose, and deep laugh lines that bracketed thin lips. "Their baby was kidnapped several years ago and they never got him back. Can you imagine, losing a child like that?"

Ellen didn't want to go there. "Do you know the family?"

"Sure, Carol's a doll, and so is Bill. And that little baby, Timothy, he was adorable."

"Adorable," Linda repeated, without breaking stride. "That baby was so cute you could eat him."

Ellen hid her emotions. The brown bag crinkled in her pocket when she walked.

"What a shame." Linda shook her head, her rich brown eyes tilting down at the corners. She had an oval face with a largish nose, and a thick gold chain with a coral horn bounced on her bosom as they turned the corner, passing a large brick Georgian mansion, more Monticello than Miami.

"It's so sad." Phyllis made a clucking sound. "They shot the babysitter, too. It doesn't seem fair. It's like when people rob a store and shoot the clerk. Why do they have to shoot somebody? I don't know what gets into people nowadays."

Ellen didn't say anything. Phyllis and Linda didn't need the encouragement to keep talking, and she was running out of breath anyway. A fireball sun climbed a cloudless sky, and the humidity was 120,000 percent. They passed a woman walking a black poodle, and Phyllis waved to her.

"Carol and Bill were in terrible shape, after it happened. It just about killed them. There were reporters camped out on the street day and night, bothering them all the time. Cops and the FBI, always coming and going."

Ellen let her talk, to see what she could learn. They reached the next corner, turned around the block, and walked past a house intended to look like a Roman temple.

"Bill was a great father, too." Phyllis sipped from her water bottle. "You know, he has his own investment company, very successful. He makes a lot of money for people in the neighborhood, and he doted on his son. Bought him golf bibs and a golf hat, too. Remember we saw him, Lin?"

Linda nodded. "Carol had such a hard time getting pregnant. I'm not telling stories out of school here. She talked about it all the time, right, Phyl?"

"Yes, she had a *very* hard time." Phyllis's lips flattened to a lipsticked line. "They tried for a long time. She really wanted that baby, they both did. Now look what happened."

Ellen felt a stab of guilt, flashing on Carol as Mother Goose.

"The poor woman." Linda wiped her upper lip. "Isn't that just the worst luck? They finally had their miracle baby, then they never see him again. End of story."

"There's no justice," Phyllis said, puffing slightly.

"It's a sin," Linda added.

Ellen didn't know it was possible to feel more guilty than she felt already. She had always thought of Will as her miracle baby. But he could have been Carol's miracle baby. Only DNA would tell for sure. She needed that sample.

The moment passed, and Linda said, "You know, if you live long enough, you realize there's nothing you can't handle. I lost my husband and I lost my kid sister. If you asked me, I never would've thought that I'd be standing here afterwards. Life makes you strong, and death makes you strong, too."

Ellen was thinking of her mother.

Phyllis shook her head, which jiggled slightly as they rounded the block. "She always says that, but I think she's full of baloney."

"Ha!" Linda waved her off. "Go ahead, tell her about the waves."

"Okay." Phyllis looked over at Ellen and her lined face grew serious, even as she pumped her arms like a pro. "I lived in Brooklyn all my life. We couldn't believe it when we retired down here, everywhere with the water, the intercoastal, and the ocean. We loved it. My Richard used to fish, I went out with him on the boat. On the boat is where I get my best ideas."

"It's boring, take it from me," Linda stage-whispered behind her hand. "She makes me go. I wanna drown myself."

"Are you going to let me talk to our guest?" Phyllis asked, mock indignant.

"Go ahead, just don't take the long way." Linda turned

to Ellen. "I'm Italian, so I love to talk, and she's Jewish, so she loves to talk."

Phyllis smiled. "That's why we're best friends. No one else can put up with us."

They all laughed, passing Ellen's car on the main drag, then taking a left onto Surfside Lane again, lapping the block.

"Here's my theory about waves." Phyllis extended her arms, palms up. "Bad things are like waves. They're going to happen to you, and there's nothing you can do about it. They're part of life, like waves are a part of the ocean. If you're standing on the shoreline, you don't know when the waves are coming. But they'll come. You gotta make sure you get back to the surface, after every wave. That's all."

Ellen smiled, considering it. "That makes a lot of sense."

Suddenly Phyllis and Linda fell silent, their gaze on the open door of a wooden contemporary on the left side of the street, catty-corner to the Bravermans'. A pretty redhead was emerging in a crisp black dress, with a black bag on her arm. She locked the door, then clacked in stylish black pumps down a concrete path to her driveway and a silver Mercedes.

"Who's that?" Ellen caught the mischievous look Phyllis and Linda exchanged. "Someone we don't like, evidently."

Phyllis burst into laughter. "I forgot my poker face."

Linda looked over at her. "You don't have a poker face. I know, I play poker with you."

"Fill me in, ladies." Ellen smiled. "I love to dish."

"She's a big snob," Phyllis answered, with the trace of a smile. "Her name is Kelly Scott and her family has more money than God. She's from Palm Beach."

"Pink and green country," Linda added with a naughty giggle, and Phyllis nodded.

"I've met her at least four times, and she acts like she never met me before. I hate that."

"Me, too," Linda said.

"Me, three," Ellen said, and they all laughed again. But she was watching the Braverman house as they walked by, looking past the yellow ribbons and the Timothy memorial and the curtains. Inside was Carol Braverman.

And Ellen needed her DNA.

Today.

Chapter 55

The sky began to cloud over, cutting the temperature, and Ellen sat low in the driver's seat of the car with the window open, watching the Braverman house. It was 10:36 A.M., but there'd been no sign of Carol, and the red flag on her mailbox was still down.

Ellen was still hoping that she'd mail a letter. She checked her BlackBerry, and Marcelo hadn't emailed or called. She wondered if she still had a job to go back to, or a crush.

Please tell me what is going on. I can help you.

She kept an eye on the house and straightened up as a mail truck appeared on the main drag and began stopping at the houses, delivering packets of mail. No sign of Carol with an envelope to be mailed, and now it was too late. The mail truck turned onto Surfside, traveled up the street on the right side, and delivered the mail to the Braverman house.

Damn.

Ellen felt on edge. Hot and testy. She sipped warm juice, then dug in her purse for the notes from the DNA test, reminding herself of the sample possibilities. Gum, soda can, cigarette butt, blah blah blah. She tossed the list aside and glanced back at the Bravermans' house, where there was finally some activity. Carol was stepping out the front door.

Ellen's senses sprang to alert. She couldn't keep waiting for something to happen. She had to make something happen. She got out of the car in her sunglasses and visor and went into her I'm-just-a-walker routine, strolling across the main drag and entering Surfside. She walked slowly, staying on the opposite side of the street as Carol walked from the front door and disappeared into the garage.

Ellen cut her pace, taking smaller steps, and the next minute, Carol came out of the garage with a green plastic gardener's tote. She had on a cute sundress and another visor, with her dark blond hair in its ponytail again.

Ellen kept her eyes straight ahead, but watched Carol cross the lawn to the memorial to Timothy, then she knelt down, setting the gardener's tote next to her. She slid on a pair of flowery cotton gloves and began to weed in front of the memorial.

It's as if she's tending a grave.

Ellen felt a twinge of conscience as she turned the corner, and as soon as she was out of sight, she broke into a light jog. She didn't know how long Carol would be out front and she couldn't blow this chance. It was almost too humid to breathe, and she was panting by the time she lapped the block and reached the intersection of Surfside Lane and the main drag, where she knelt next to a tall hedge, pretending to tie her sneaker.

Carol gardened at a leisurely pace, pulling the weeds and putting them in a neat pile on the left. A small plastic bag of peat moss and a large flat of yellow marigolds were sitting on the lawn next to the memorial, and a full sun bathed the front lawn. Ellen's breathing returned to normal, but she was sweating behind her sunglasses, and Carol must have been feeling the same way, because in the next second, she took off her sunglasses and visor and set them down. Ellen flashed on the DNA list:

Hair with the follicle still attached.

She couldn't be sure there would be a hair on the sunglasses or visor, and she wouldn't get another chance, so she rejected the idea. She shifted her feet and fake-tied the other sneaker, watching as Carol moved to the marigold flat and twisted off a small packet of flowers. Ellen watched her from her crouching position, and Carol gentled the plant from the flat and set it on the ground. She reached into the gardener's tote and pulled out a can of soda, then popped the tab, and took a sip.

Bingo!

Ellen scanned the block, and there was no one in sight. She slid the plastic glove from her other pocket, put it on her hand, and rose slowly. Then she slid her BlackBerry from her pocket and pressed the number for information in Miami. She asked for the Bravermans' phone number, and while the call connected, she walked toward Carol, who was bent over her flowers, making a hole for the new marigolds with her fingers. The phone rang once in Ellen's ear, then again, and in the next second, Carol looked up at her house.

Get the phone, Carol.

Ellen slid the paper bag from her pocket and started walking down Surfside Lane, keeping her gloved hand at her side, out of view. In the meantime, Carol was rising, taking off her gardening gloves on the fly, and hurrying toward the house.

Yes!

Ellen crossed to the Bravermans' side of the street, her heart pounding. She hustled up the sidewalk, getting a bead on the soda can. There was nobody exercising or walking dogs, and she wouldn't get another chance. She broke into a light run, the ringing cell phone to her ear. Ten feet away, then five, then right in front of the Braverman house. Carol's soda was a Diet Sprite, sitting next to the tote.

Now, now, now!

She ran straight up the Bravermans' lawn, swooped down with her gloved hand, grabbed the Diet Sprite and took off like a shot, running down the block. She turned the can upside down so the soda poured out, and she ran like she'd never run in her life. She tore around the block, bolted all the way to the main drag, then darted across the street.

HONK HONK! went a truck, skidding to a stop behind her.

Ellen tore open her car door, jumped in, and dumped the can in the brown paper bag. She twisted on the ignition, floored the gas pedal, and headed straight for the causeway. She felt like cheering. Wind off the causeway whipped her hair around, and she hit a red light, taking off the glove and leaving it on the seat, its purpose served. She took off her visor and sunglasses, relieved to finally shed her disguise. She caught a glimpse of the street sign and did a double take.

Charbonneau Drive?

The traffic light turned green, but instead of going straight over the causeway, she turned right onto the street.

Chapter 56

CHARBONNEAU DRIVE, read the street sign, and Ellen flashed on the dentist's reminder from the Bravermans' trash bag. She had known that Charbonneau sounded familiar, though she couldn't remember how. She'd passed the street every time she'd driven back and forth to the causeway. Charbonneau Drive had to be connected to Carol Braverman. It was too distinctive a name not to be.

Curious, she drove along Charbonneau Drive, which was winding and pleasant. She passed a white stucco rancher, a fake French château, and a brick McMansion; the houses had the same variety as on Surfside Lane, but all of them were the same, more recent, vintage. Palm trees lined the road, throwing dappled shade on the street, but they weren't as established as the palms on Surfside, and the vegetation, white oleander and bougainvillea, looked newer. A woman in a running singlet and shorts jogged by, and two men walked matching dachshunds.

She followed the street, and at the end of a cul-de-sac stood an immense mansion of pink stucco with a clay tile roof. It was three stories tall, with at least thirty arched Spanish windows and a covered walkway that sheltered a

grand main entrance. A sign on the lawn read, CHARBON-
NEAU HOUSE, and underneath that, OPEN TO THE PUBLIC.

I'm the public.

Ellen pulled into a parking lot of crushed shells and
turned off the ignition. She'd make it quick, but she put
her DNA samples under the seat anyway, then got out of
the car and walked to the house. The stucco had been re-
painted and the tiles on the roof meticulously maintained,
but the mansion was much older than the houses surrounding it on the drive. The lot was at least three acres of lush
lawn, the breeze was fragrant, and the place a reminder of
a slower, older Florida. She walked up the breezeway,
climbed stairs of red Mexican tile, and went inside the
door, looking around.

The entrance hall had a black-and-white tile floor and
was dominated by a huge staircase, covered with an Oriental carpet. There were three large rooms off the hall,
furnished as meeting rooms, and she entered the center
room, which overlooked an expanse of green lawn and a
small circular fountain.

"May I help you?" a voice asked, and she turned around.
It was a woman with a dark brown bob, light eyes with
friendly crow's-feet, and a warm smile. "Were you looking
for something?"

"I was driving past the sign, and I'm not from around
here. I thought the building was so pretty, I wanted to see
it."

"Why, thank you. We're very proud of Charbonneau
House and the work we do here."

"What is that, may I ask?"

"We promote theater arts and other cultural events to
children in the community." The woman, professional in
a crisp white blouse and a khaki cotton skirt, with red es-
padrilles, gestured to the main hallway. "In addition to the
conference rooms and classrooms, we have a full theater in

the back, which seats seventy-five people. We have a large backstage and several dressing rooms. We stage three productions a year and we just finished our run of *Once Upon a Mattress.*"

"How nice," Ellen said, meaning it. "And I see there's Charbonneau House and Charbonneau Drive. I assume it's related to the Charbonneau family?"

"Yes, exactly. The Charbonneaus are one of the oldest families in the area, and they've donated the house for the community's use." The woman gestured to an oil portrait in an ornate golden frame, one of two flanking the windows. "That's our benefactor, Bertrand Charbonneau, who unfortunately passed away about five years ago, at the age of ninety-one."

"How interesting." Ellen looked at the painting, of a reedy, silver-haired man in glasses and a light green business suit, leaning against a wall of bookshelves. She tried not to stare at the picture, to see if there was any resemblance to Will. Her head was already swimming, and the bag in the car would eliminate any guesswork.

"Bertrand was a wonderful man, a friend of my father's. He was one of the community's first residents and developed much of the real estate here. This house, his childhood home, was only one of his many gifts to our community."

Ellen was trying to piece together where, if anywhere, Carol Charbonneau Braverman fit in, but didn't want to show her hand, especially since this woman knew the family. "I gather Bertrand Charbonneau had an interest in theater?"

"His wife Rhoda had a brief career as an actress before she retired to raise their children. Even then, she remained very active in children's theater." The woman strolled over to the other oil portrait, and Ellen followed her. The painting showed another man, this one in a casual brown sweater, by a pool. The plaque read Richard Charbonneau.

"So this must be Bertrand's son?" Ellen asked, scanning the man's features. He had the same blue eyes she'd seen on Carol, and Will. It was the tour of Will's bloodlines, maybe, but she'd know soon enough.

"Yes, Richard was my father's contemporary. He and his wife Selma continued their father's efforts. Unfortunately, they both passed away many years ago, in a car accident."

"That's too bad. Do you think the family will carry on this tradition? It really seems like a wonderful idea."

"No worries there." The woman smiled pleasantly. "Richard and his wife had a daughter, Carol, and she works with the children every Wednesday and Friday morning. She understands all aspects of children's theater and even directs a play a year."

"Well, that's wonderful." Ellen's chest tightened, and she looked away from the portrait, hiding her emotion. If Will was really Timothy, then Bertrand Charbonneau would be his great-grandfather and Richard Charbonneau his grandfather. Will would be part of a wonderful family, born to extraordinary wealth. She thought ahead, to the day she'd get the DNA results, when she'd have to make a decision, or not.

You'll have to make a choice I wouldn't wish on my worst enemy.

"Will that be all?" the woman asked, cocking her head.

"Yes, thanks," Ellen answered, turning away.

She said another good-bye, walked from the room, and hurried out the entrance hall to the door. By the time she hit the walkway, her pace picked up from a light jog to a full-out run, and her footfalls crunched the seashells. She wanted to forget Charbonneau House, Charbonneau Drive, and her DNA samples, which would answer a question she never wanted to ask. Her chest heaved and panted, and she reached the car out of breath, then she flung open the door, grabbed the paper bag from under the seat, and raised her arm to throw it across the gorgeous lawn.

Her hand halted in midair. She thought of Will, and stopped herself. It was his birthright, not hers. His truth, not hers. She'd come here to learn whether he belonged to her or to the Bravermans, but neither was true. He belonged to himself.

She lowered her arm. She walked back to the car, sat in the driver's seat, and stowed the bag on the passenger seat.

It was time to go home.

Chapter 57

The ticketing line wound back and forth, and Ellen assessed it, worriedly. She didn't want to miss the flight and she'd been lucky to get a seat. She couldn't wait to see Will, and she felt almost herself again, having changed back into her sweater and jeans, which she needed in the air-conditioned terminal anyway.

She checked her watch. She'd scarfed down a turkey sandwich in the first fifteen minutes of her wait in line, and now she had nothing to do but look at the other travelers who had nothing else to do. The girl in front of her bobbed to music playing on her iPod, and the man in front of her was a middle manager, his thumbs flying over his BlackBerry keyboard at the speed of carpal tunnel syndrome. A man before him talked on a cell phone in rapid Spanish, which reminded her of Marcelo. She'd called him this morning but he hadn't answered, so she'd left a message saying she'd be back to work tomorrow.

"Excuse me, is our line even moving?" asked an older man behind her, and Ellen stood on tiptoe to see the ticket counter. Only one agent was manning the counter, and two of the self-service kiosks bore Out of Order signs.

"Honestly, no." Ellen smiled, but the man grumbled.

"I can walk to Denver faster."

"You got that right." Ellen looked away, and her gaze fell to the first-class line, only four people deep. "I wonder how much first class costs."

"Highway robbery," the old man shot back, and the line shifted forward an inch.

Her gaze drifted back to the first-class line, where a pretty redhead had just arrived, rolling a Louis Vuitton bag behind her, her head held high. She looked vaguely familiar and when she dug in a black purse, Ellen remembered where she had seen her before. It was the young woman who lived across the street from Carol Braverman.

Her name is Kelly Scott and her family has more money than God.

Ellen watched the redhead fan herself with some papers, looking sexy in black stilettos and a cobalt blue dress, whose bold color stood out among the Miami pastels. Businessmen passing by gave her more than a second glance, running their eyes over her body and shapely legs.

The line shifted, and Ellen moved up. Another businessman strode past her, carrying a lightweight bag and moving so quickly that his tailored sport jacket blew open. He joined the end of the first-class line, and Ellen looked over.

She recognized him instantly, stunned.

Chapter 58

The businessman was Bill Braverman, and Ellen marveled at the odds that he would show up at the airport at the exact same time as his neighbor. She got a closer look at him than she had before, and he was an attractive man with a tall, wiry build, dark hair, and a nose that looked like Will's, even in profile. She tried not to stare as he took out his wallet and cleared his throat, and at about the same time, the redhead turned around and glanced behind her. She looked right at Bill, who stood behind her, but strangely, she didn't say hello. Instead, she turned away and faced the ticket counters.

Ellen didn't get it. The redhead had to have seen Bill. He was right behind her and the tallest man in the line, not to mention her neighbor.

"We're moving," the old man said, and Ellen shifted forward, glued to the goings-on. Something was fishy between Bill and the redhead, but she wasn't jumping to conclusions. She stayed tuned as Bill took out his wallet and faced the front of the line, showing no sign that he recognized his neighbor, who was standing in front of him, with bright red hair and a killer dress. Men all over the terminal were looking at her, yet Bill was pointedly looking away.

Ellen considered it. These two people had to know each other, and they clearly had seen each other, but they were acting as if they were strangers. There was one possible explanation, but she resisted it.

"You can move up again," said the older man behind her, and Ellen filled in the gap. She kept watching, hoping that she was wrong. The redhead walked to the ticket counter, and the balding ticket agent brightened immediately. Bill looked in her direction, and the redhead got her ticket, bunny-dipped for her Vuitton bag, and rolled it away. Bill seemed not to notice her as she sashayed off, and Ellen lost sight of the redhead as she walked toward security.

The coach line shifted forward, and one of the ticket agents walked to the front of the line, made a megaphone of her hands, and called out, "Anyone for Philly? Philly, come on up!"

"Here!" Ellen ducked the tape to get out of line and hurried to the front, maneuvering to stand next to Bill, standing so close she could smell the residual cigarette smoke wreathing him. As casually as possible, she said, "Hard to go back to Philly in the cold."

"I bet."

"Where are you headed?"

"Vegas."

"Wow. I've never been. Have fun."

"You, too. Safe trip." Bill flashed her a grin, then went to the front desk, got his ticket, and walked off toward security, his jacket flying open.

Three people later, Ellen got her ticket and hurried ahead to security, but lost sight of Bill and the redhead.

She found herself again at the back of the line and in time made it through security, then took a quick look at the lighted departure signs for Las Vegas. The Vegas gate was two down from hers. She hurried toward the gate, scanned the passengers waiting for the flight, and spotted them in no time.

Bill sat reading a *Wall Street Journal* in one of the wide gray seats, and directly across from him was the redhead, flipping through a thick copy of *Vogue* and crossing and uncrossing her legs. It was a game they were playing, frequent-flier foreplay.

Ellen lingered behind a round pillar and watched Bill and the redhead until it was time for first class to board. They joined the line, leaving a few travelers between them. The redhead got her boarding pass swiped, and just as she entered the jet way, she turned behind her, ostensibly for her bag, and flashed Bill the briefest of smiles.

He's cheating on Snow White?

Ellen went ahead to her gate, disgusted and sad. She boarded, and her heart went out to Carol, planting marigolds on Timothy's memorial on the front lawn. Being nice to the grocery stockboy. Playing Mother Goose to toddlers. Teaching children's theater at Charbonneau House. Ellen was so preoccupied that she barely heard the ticket agent asking for her boarding pass.

She boarded, found her seat, and stowed her roller bag in the overhead, then sat down, suddenly exhausted. Outside on the tarmac, a baggage train chugged past, but Ellen closed her eyes. She didn't want to see anything anymore. Not Miami or its heat. Not Bill Braverman or his mistress. Not Charbonneau Road. Not the marigolds.

She felt awful inside, raw and depressed. She didn't want to think about letting Will go to the Bravermans. She didn't want to think about letting Will go at all. Will

was her son and he belonged with her. And her father, and
Connie. And Oreo Figaro.

Ellen stopped herself in mid-dwell. There was no point
to making herself crazy until she had the DNA results.

She vowed to keep the melodrama to a minimum until
then.

Chapter 59

"Mommy!" Will shouted, leaving his Legos and running to meet Ellen just as she closed the front door against the cold.

"Honey!" she called back, hoisting him up and hugging him close, ambushed by a fierce rush of emotion. She kissed him on the cheek and tried to pretend this was a homecoming like any other.

"I'm making a castle! A big castle!" Will kicked to be let down.

"Good for you." Ellen set him on the ground with his feet still kicking, and he hit the hardwood floor like a windup toy. He ran back to his Legos, hit the rug, and sprawled on his tummy in his overalls. Ellen wished she could take a mental snapshot and keep it forever.

"Welcome home!" Connie smiled, wiping her hands on a dishcloth as she came into the living room. "You made it early, huh?"

"Got it all done early." Ellen slid out of her coat, shaking off the unaccustomed cold, and felt happier than ever to be home. Oreo Figaro looked up from the back of the sofa, where he sat with his front paws neatly underneath him. The living room smelled deliciously of hot coffee and chicken with rosemary. "Connie, am I dreaming or is that dinner?"

"It'll be ready in ten minutes, and Will took a good nap, so he's up and at 'em." Connie met her eye meaningfully, and Ellen impulsively grabbed her and gave her a huge hug.

"Will you marry me?"

"Anytime," Connie answered, releasing her with a grin, then she went to the closet, got her coat, and put it on. Her overnight bag, purse, and tote sat packed on the windowseat. "You got a sunburn, eh?"

"I know." Ellen's hand went to the tip of her nose. It would be hard to explain at work tomorrow. Then again, everything would be hard to explain at work tomorrow.

"One last thing." Connie picked up her bags, and her smile vanished. "I'm sorry about the phone business. Hope I didn't get you in too much trouble."

"Don't worry, I can deal with it," Ellen said, though she didn't know how. "You took great care of him, and that's what matters."

"Thanks." Connie turned to Will. "See you later, alligator!"

"In a while, crocodile," Will called over his shoulder, playing happily on the floor, his world order restored.

"See you!" Connie let herself out, and Ellen went over and touched Will's hair. The dark blond filaments felt soft under her fingertips, and she tried not to notice his hair color was almost the same as Carol's.

"Please say thank you to Connie."

"Thank you, Connie!" Will scrambled to a standing position, then ran over and hugged his babysitter, and Ellen could see how happy it made her. She didn't want to think about how Connie would react if Will turned out to be Timothy. She put it out of her mind as she let Connie out the door, then kicked off her clogs and got down on the rug to play with Will.

She still had one DNA sample to collect, but she could do that after the Lego castle.

Chapter 60

Ellen scanned the directions for the DNA sample while Will stood at the kitchen sink and rinsed his mouth with warm water, his small fingers wrapped like a gecko's around the glass tumbler. Though she had to use the non-standard test for Carol and Bill, she was collecting Will's sample by the conventional method, and she had to get it tonight because all the samples had to be sent to the laboratory together.

"Spit, Mommy?" Will asked, his eyes trustful over the rim of the glass.

"Two more times, pal."

Will took a second gulp of water and spit it into the sink. "Is this good?"

"Yes, and we have to do one more thing."

"Okay." Will took his third gulp, letting the water dribble out of his mouth and down his chin for fun.

"Good, thanks." Ellen wiped his wet grin with a napkin, then took the glass from his hand, set it on the counter, and turned to face him, placing a hand on his little shoulder. "Now open up, sweetie, just like you do for the doctor."

"Is it gonna hurt?"

"No, not at all." Ellen took the Q-tip in hand. "I'm going to rub the inside of your cheek with a Q-tip, that's all. It's the same kind of Q-tip we use to clean your ears."

"Are you cleaning my mouth?"

"Yes." *Sort of.*

"Why is my mouth dirty? I brushed my teeth this morning."

"Ready to open up?"

Will opened his mouth like a baby bird, and Ellen rolled the swab on the insides of both of his cheeks for about a minute, making sure to cover most of his inner cheek. Then she withdrew the swab and set it on a folded piece of paper to dry, according to the instructions.

"Good job, sweetie."

Will began jumping up and down.

"We just need one more, okay?"

"Why?" Will opened his mouth again, and Ellen picked up another Q-tip and swabbed the inside of his cheek.

"Just to be sure. All finished. Great job."

"Now can we have dessert?"

"We sure can."

Anything but lime Jell-O.

Chapter 61

Ellen had just stepped out of the shower when her cell phone started ringing. She ran into her bedroom, picked up her BlackBerry, and checked the display screen. It was a 215 area code, a Philly phone number she didn't know. She pressed Answer.

"Hello?" It was Marcelo, and Ellen warmed to the sound, sinking onto her bed and drawing her pink chenille robe closer around her.

"Hey, hi."

"I got your message. Sorry I couldn't get back to you until now. Are you at home?"

"Yes, I'll be back to work tomorrow, like I said. If you're free, we can meet in the morning and talk over this thing with Sarah."

"I don't think it can wait. I'd like to come over tonight, if I may."

Wow. Ellen checked her watch—9:08. Will was in bed, fast asleep. "Sure."

"It's not a social call," Marcelo added, and she felt herself flush.

"Understood . . ."

"I'm on my way. I'll be there in half an hour."

"Great," Ellen said, and as soon as they hung up, she bolted to the closet. She changed her clothes four times, ending up with a light blue V-neck and jeans, but instead of a tank top underneath, she went with a lace-topped ivory camisole.

Though her underwear was the last thing on her mind.

Chapter 62

By the time Marcelo knocked on the door, Ellen's hair had dried loose and curly to her shoulders and she had doused herself with perfume, made up her eyes, and patted concealer on her telltale sunburn.

"Hello," Marcelo said, unsmiling as he came inside.

"Good to see you." Ellen knew she couldn't kiss him hello, but she didn't want to shake his hand, so she settled for closing the door behind him. "Can I take your coat?"

"That's okay, I won't be staying long."

Ouch. "Would you like a drink or something?"

"No, thanks."

"Do you want to sit down?"

"Thanks." Marcelo crossed to the couch and sat stiffly down, and Ellen took the chair catty-corner to him. He said, "I thought it would be better to talk here than in the office, since we're conspiring."

"I'm really sorry about what happened."

"I know." Marcelo looked tense, a new tightness around his mouth. "I've been struggling with what to do, how to handle the situation." He linked his fingers between his legs, leaning forward slightly. "To start with, I shouldn't have done what I did . . . started anything romantic with you. It was wrong, and I'm sorry."

Ellen swallowed, hurt. "You don't have to say you're sorry, and it wasn't so terrible."

"It was, especially considering how it turned out."

"But we can set it right."

"No, we can't."

Ellen felt like they were having a lovers' quarrel, and they weren't even lovers.

"I'm your editor, and there's no way we can be together, in the end."

"But we just started." Ellen was surprised at the emotion in her voice. "Other couples at the paper date."

"Not editor and staffer. Not a direct report." Marcelo shook his head, downcast. "Anyway, to the point. I lied to my staff. I've never lied to my staff, ever. I showed you a favoritism I wouldn't have shown anyone else, and I did it because I care for you." His voice softened, but his gaze remained firm. "But now I know what to do."

"I do, too." Ellen had thought about it on the plane, but Marcelo held up his hand.

"Let me, please. That's why I came here tonight. I don't want you to come in to work tomorrow morning."

No. "Why not?"

"I'm going to hold a meeting of the staff and I don't think you should be there. I'm going to tell them what happened. Not about my . . . feelings, I'm not that crazy." Marcelo smiled. "I'm going to tell them that I lied about your whereabouts because you had a personal matter that you didn't want me or them to know about, and I thought it was the best way to handle the situation."

"You're going to tell the truth?"

Marcelo chuckled. "It's not that crazy. We're a newspaper. We care for truth."

"But not now, not this way." Ellen couldn't let him do it. It was career suicide.

"I'm going to apologize and say that I realize, in retrospect, that it was poor judgment on my part."

"You can't do that, Marcelo." Ellen didn't know where to begin. "It undermines your credibility forever. They're already talking about you, and this will only add fuel to the fire. You'll never live it down."

"Reporters are intelligent and verbal people. They talk, they speculate, and they gossip. There's nothing to be done about it."

Ellen leaned forward, urgent. "That's not the way to handle this. One of us has to admit that they were lying, and that person can't be you."

"If I tell the truth, it will pass."

"No, it will follow you forever. I can't let you do it."

"You have no say," Marcelo said with a sad smile, and Ellen realized that if he wouldn't do it for him, maybe he'd do it for her.

"You'd hurt me more if you did that. They'll think we're sleeping together, and I'll be branded forever. It's better for me if you suspend me for lying to you."

"You *want* that?" Marcelo frowned.

"It's the only way. If you suspend me, I look like just another employee who lied to the boss. Everybody lies to the boss."

"They do?" Marcelo looked horrified, which Ellen thought was adorable.

"If we tell them I lied to you, then I'm just somebody who played hooky."

"Hooky?"

"Ditched work for the day. I even have a tan. But, on the other hand, if you tell them you lied for me, it makes it a bigger deal and it never goes away."

Marcelo pursed his lips, searching her face, and Ellen could see she was making headway.

"You're a journalist, so you should know. Employee lies to boss. That's no story. Boss lies *for* employee? A headline."

"I don't know." Marcelo ran his fingers through his hair, muttering. "*Que roubada.* What a mess."

"Marcelo, if you care about me, you'll suspend me without pay."

"Is that what you want?"

"Yes. For a week."

Marcelo's lips flattened to a sour line. "Three days."

"Done."

Marcelo eyed her, his regret plain. "It's a disciplinary action against you. It jeopardizes your job."

Ellen knew that, but this wasn't the time to cry about it. She'd gotten them into this mess and she was going to get them out. "Look on the bright side. If you fire me, you have to take me out. I could lose a job, but gain a boyfriend."

"You're killing me." Marcelo winced, rising, and Ellen stood up, too. They were standing about three feet apart, so close they could embrace, but nobody was touching anybody.

"I'm joking," she said, but Marcelo turned away and walked to the door, where he stopped and flashed her a final, sad smile.

"Then why aren't we laughing?" he asked.

For that, Ellen had no answer.

Chapter 63

Ellen set her DNA instructions on her bedspread and unpacked the two paper bags from her suitcase, the one containing Bill's cigarette butts and the other Carol's soda can. She set them next to the white business envelope that contained the Q-tips with Will's sample. From the corner of the bed, Oreo Figaro watched all of her movements with concern.

Ellen sat down beside the cat, petting his spiny back idly and picking up the Paternity Testing Form she had downloaded. She scanned the first few paragraphs that contained legal terms and conditions, then the form authorizing how to send the results.

The form contained various lines to fill out to identify the sample; name, sample date, race, and relationship, Suspected Mother, Suspected Father, Suspected Grandfather (paternal or maternal), Suspected Grandmother (paternal or maternal), and Other. She filled in Suspected Mother for Carol's sample, Suspected Father for Bill's, and Child for Will's. Then she made matching labels that the form requested, cut them out with a scissors, and taped them on the two brown paper bags and Will's envelope, like the arts-and-crafts project from hell.

She gathered the brown bags, the envelope, and the forms, and placed them in a padded FedEx Pak. She filled in the address slip, sealed the FedEx envelope, and set it on the nightstand. She would mail the FedEx Pak after she dropped Will at school, not that she wanted to think about the juxtaposition of those two events.

She sat back down on the bed and petted Oreo Figaro, but he declined to purr. In three days, she could find out that Will didn't belong to the Bravermans and she could keep him happily for the rest of their life together. Three days seemed forever to wait, and at the same time not nearly long enough. Because in three days she could also find out that Will did belong to the Bravermans, then . . .

That was where Ellen stopped her thinking. She had promised herself on the plane.

And Oreo Figaro withheld his purr.

Chapter 64

The next morning was freezing, the sky an opaque gray and the air holding a wet chill in its clenched fist, and Ellen was sitting in her car in the parking lot of a local strip mall. Traffic rushed back and forth on a busy Lancaster Avenue, the car tires stained white with road salt and their back windshields still deicing. She watched idly, and her car grew cold, the last heat dissipating. She had dropped Will off at school only half an hour ago, but it seemed longer. The FedEx Pak containing the DNA samples sat next to her like an unwanted hitchhiker.

Ellen was stalling, and though she knew it, she couldn't stop herself. All she had to do was slide down her car window, pull up the metal handle on the FedEx mailbox, and toss the package inside. As soon as she did that, it was out of her hands. The deed would be done. The lab would charge her credit card, process the samples, and email her the results. Yes or no. Hers or theirs.

Ellen couldn't believe she was still hesitating, not after she'd stalked the Bravermans and placed her professional career in jeopardy, in addition to losing a man she was profoundly attracted to, before she'd even had him. She

reminded herself that she didn't have to do anything with
the test results once she had them. Even if it turned out in
the Bravermans' favor, she didn't have to tell a soul. It
could stay her secret forever. Why should she stall, given
all she had gone through?

Her gaze shifted to the FedEx mailbox, and she reread
its pickup sticker for the umpteenth time. The stores in the
strip mall hadn't opened yet, and the glass front of a Sub-
way remained dark, the display counters and cash registers
shapeless shadows. She took a sip of coffee but couldn't
taste it, and set it into the cup holder. Hot steam curled
from her travel mug, which had no lid. She'd been too distracted to find it this morning, dreading the task at hand.

I can forget the whole thing.

Ellen turned on the ignition, and the car turned over,
throaty. Her coffee vibrated in the cup holder, a tiny rip-
ple appearing on its surface. She didn't have to mail the
samples. She could just drive away and let them decom-
pose or whatever they did. She could stop this insanity
right now. Her lawyer, Ron, would approve, and so would
her father. He'd kill her if he knew what she doing. The
car idled, and the heat vent blew cold air. Still she didn't
hit the gas.

I can't forget the whole thing.

She pressed the button and lowered the car window,
struck by the frigid blast, then she yanked the handle on
the mailbox and tossed the FedEx Pak inside. The drawer
closed with a final *ca-thunk*.

So be it.

Ellen hit the gas, knowing the day was about to get
even worse.

Chapter 65

Ellen pressed thoughts of the DNA samples to the back of her mind, trying to ignore the irony as she drove to Amy Martin's funeral. She steered through the run-down neighborhood outside Stoatesville, its residential blocks struggling to survive after all the manufacturing had gone, leaving behind corner bars and empty storefronts. She took a left and a right among the streets, finally spotting the converted rowhouse that stood out because of its freshly painted façade of ivory stucco, the only well-maintained place on the block. She knew it must be the funeral home, because they were always the prettiest buildings, even in a terrible neighborhood. The thought depressed her. You shouldn't have to die to be in a nice place.

She found a space on the street, parked, and got out of the car. Cold air blew hard, and she drew her black dress coat closer as she walked down the street. Her boots clacked against the gritty pavement, and she reached the funeral home, with a fake gold sign beside the door. The glass door was smudged, and she yanked on the handle and went inside, warming up momentarily and getting her bearings. An entrance hall contained a few oak chairs and a fake walnut credenza, on which rested a maroon vase of faded silk flowers and an open guest book with a vinyl cover. The place looked empty, and the air smelled dusty, only vaguely perfumed with flowers. A burgundy rug covered the floor and a long corridor to the left, leading to two louvered doors. Only the second door was open, and light spilled from the room. No sign indicated it was Amy's viewing, but it was a safe assumption.

Ellen crossed to the guest book and looked at the open page, scanning the list of names: Gerry Martin, Dr. Robert Villiers and Cheryl Martin Villiers, Tiffany Lebov, William Martin. It gave her pause. Amy had been so disconnected from these people in life, but they had gathered here to mourn her, death having mooted the estrangements and differences, the angry words or hurt feelings. Ellen felt moved to be among them, connected in the most tenuous of ways, if at all. She picked up the long white pen next to the book and signed her name.

She walked down the hall toward the open door, lingering for a moment on the threshold. The room was rectangular and large, but only two rows of brown folding chairs had been set up toward the front, where a group of women huddled together. The casket was closed, and she felt macabre admitting to herself she was almost disappointed. She wouldn't get a chance to see what Amy Martin looked like, even in death, to compare her features to Will's. But it didn't matter now anyway. The DNA samples would solve the mystery that was Amy Martin.

Ellen walked toward the group at the front and when she got closer, saw that Gerry was being comforted by Cheryl, who caught her eye and smiled.

"Ellen, how nice of you to come," she said softly, and Gerry turned in her embrace and looked up. Grief deepened the folds bracketing her mouth, which tilted down, and she looked like she was sinking in an oversized black pantsuit.

"I'm so sorry about your loss." Ellen approached, extending her hand.

"Real nice of you to come." Gerry's voice sounded hoarse, and she blinked tears from her eyes. "I know Amy woulda wanted to meet you. Someday maybe you can bring your little boy over to the house."

Behind her, Cheryl nodded. "I'd like to meet him, too, when he's feeling better."

"I'd be happy to do that," Ellen said, with a twinge. She'd forgotten that she had lied to them about needing Will's medical history.

Cheryl said, "Too bad you missed my husband and my brother. They were here last night and earlier, but they had to go." She gestured next to her at another mourner, a young woman. "This is a friend of Amy's."

"Melanie Rotucci," the girl said, extending her hand. She looked to be in her twenties, and on another day, would have been pretty, if a little hard-looking. Her gray eyes were red and puffy from crying, and her fair skin pale and wan. She had a cupid's-bow mouth, and her best feature was long, dark hair that spilled over the shoulders of her black leather jacket.

Ellen introduced herself, surprised to meet her. Cheryl and Gerry had told her that Amy didn't have girlfriends.

Cheryl must have been reading her mind. "Melanie met Amy in rehab, and they were really good friends."

"Amy was in rehab?" Ellen asked, confused. It was all news to her.

"We didn't know until we met Melanie. It turns out Amy was really trying to turn her life around. She went to rehab twice, for heroin. She was almost better, right, Melanie?"

"I really thought she was going to make it." Melanie's

mouth made a resigned line, in dark lipstick. "She was clean for thirty-five days the second time. At ninety days, she was going to tell everybody, all of you."

"My poor, poor baby," Gerry whispered, collapsing into new sobs, and Cheryl hugged her closer.

Strain etched Melanie's young face. "I need a cigarette," she muttered, rising.

"I'll keep you company," Ellen said, intrigued.

Chapter 66

"This must be hard on you," Ellen said as they stepped outside the funeral home and shared a grimy top step, its small size forcing them close together. Melanie cupped her cigarette against the cold wind, firing it with a thumb flicked on a yellow plastic Bic lighter.

"It's the worst."

"Were you good friends?"

"I mean, we didn't know each other that long, but when you meet people in rehab, you get tighter a lot faster. Amy said that rehab was like dog years, one is like seven." Melanie dragged on the cigarette, and smoke leaked from her sad smile.

"Where is the rehab center?"

"Eagleville, in Pennsylvania." Melanie leaned back against an iron rail and crossed long legs, in skinny jeans and black boots.

Ellen had heard of the place. "Can I ask, how old are you?"

"Twenty-two."

"A lot younger than Amy."

"I know. She took care of me like a big sister, or a mom or something."

It struck a chord. "Did Amy ever mention to you having had a child?"

"No way!" Melanie looked at her like she was crazy. "Amy didn't have a kid."

"I think she did and she put it up for adoption." Ellen almost didn't believe it herself, after Miami. "She had a baby, but I guess she didn't mention it to you."

"It's possible, I guess."

"It was a very sick baby, with a heart problem."

"I didn't know *everything* about her." Melanie's eyes narrowed behind a curtain of cigarette smoke. "Amy was her own girl, that's for sure, but we went through group together, the seminars they make us take, the lectures, rec activities all day long. We even spent our smoke breaks together. She never mentioned a sick baby."

Ellen set her emotions aside. "She ever mention a boyfriend? His name could've been Charles Cartmell."

"No. She used to date a lot, but she was changing that, too. She said in group that she was sick of hooking up with abusive guys. She wasn't going there, anymore."

"Did any of them visit her at rehab?"

"No. We're allowed visitors on weekends but she never got any. Neither did I, which was fine with me. If my mom came, I'd a kicked her ass."

Ellen let it go. "I'm wondering about one guy in particular, someone Amy was dating about three or four years ago. He wasn't a bad-looking guy, on the short side, white, with longish brown hair. They might've gone on a trip together, to someplace warm. Did she ever mention a vacation with a guy, at a beach?"

Melanie paused a minute, frowning. "No, but I know

that a while ago, she used to see a guy named Rob. Rob Moore."

Ellen felt her heartbeat quicken. "What did she say about him?"

"Just that he was a jerk."

"How long ago was this, that she saw him?"

"I don't know, but it was old news."

"Three or four years ago?"

"Yeah. Really in her past."

Ellen gathered that if you were in your twenties, three years ago was history. "Did she mention where he was from?"

"Not that I remember."

"Did she tell you anything else about him, like where he lived or what he did for a living?"

"No, nothing like that." Melanie blew out an acrid cone of smoke.

"How about his age? Or what kind of car he drove or where he was from? Anything like that?"

"No, just that he was a bad dude. Used to smack her around, and she dumped him. She wouldn't take that, forever. That was the thing about Amy. She was the one we all thought would make it." Tears glistened in Melanie's bloodshot eyes. "Two of the counselors came by earlier this morning, they woulda told you the same thing."

Ellen's thoughts raced ahead. "I hate to ask you, but I feel like I need to know. What was it that happened to her? How did they find her?"

"I was the one who found her," Melanie answered flatly.

"That must have been awful for you."

Melanie didn't reply.

"So she overdosed on heroin? How do you know something like that? Was there a needle in her arm?"

"No. She didn't shoot it, neither of us did. She snorted it. There was junk on the table and the credit card she used, a Visa." Melanie tossed her hair over her shoulder. "Anyway, we were supposed to go out that night, but she never met me, so I went over around nine the next morning. She was on the couch, dressed to go out."

"How did you get in?"

"I have a key. She was all stiff. The family thinks she overdosed, but I wonder if it was bad junk." Melanie faltered, then took a drag. "The cops said that she died the night before."

Ellen processed the information. "Why do you think it was bad junk and not just an overdose?"

"You never know with street junk."

"She lived in Brigantine?"

"Yeah."

"By herself?"

"Yeah. She got a room in a nice house and a new job, waitressing at this restaurant. She was going to meetings, too, every day. She never missed." Melanie shook her head sadly. "She's the one who told me to carry Subutex."

"What's that?"

"A pill. If you take it and you do H, you don't get high. Amy always carried two pills with her."

Ellen had heard of drugs like that. She'd done a story once involving Antabuse, a drug that made alcoholics sick if they drank.

"But that night, she didn't take a pill. The bottle was right on her nightstand with the two still in it."

Ellen thought it sounded strange. "So why did she take heroin instead of Subutex?"

"She musta missed it so much. Heroin's like that. You love it and you hate it, so much. She shoulda known better than to buy off the street, even in a nice neighborhood."

"Wouldn't she have mentioned to you that she was thinking of using again? How often did you speak to her, generally?"

Melanie tossed her cigarette butt to the sidewalk. "We talked on the phone, like, every day, and she was queen of texting. She texted all the time."

"Did you look at her texts from before she died?"

"Whoa, weird. I didn't. I totally forgot." Melanie was already reaching into her purse and extracting a silvery phone with a fake-jeweled face, which she flipped open. She pressed several buttons to retrieve the texts, then started scrolling backwards. Ellen edged close to her, and they read the text together:

scored new 7 jeans on sale. wait till u see them! xoxo

Ellen glanced at the top of the screen, which showed the time the text had come in—9:15 P.M. "She sounds happy."

"Yeah, mos def." Melanie pressed a few more buttons. "Here's another one, from earlier that day, around five o'clock."

Ellen and Melanie put their heads together, and read the previous text, which said:

$228 in tips, my best day ever! going to the mall 2 celebrate! see u soon! xoxo

"That's so random." Melanie shook her head. "It doesn't sound like she was thinking about using."

"It sure doesn't." Ellen thought about it. "Recovering addicts get sponsors, right? Did Amy have a sponsor?"

"Sure, Dot Hatten. She was here this morning. I don't know if she got a call from her that night. I was too much of a wreck to ask her, and she might not say anyway. They keep everything confidential, like lawyers or something."

"You don't think she'd talk to me?"

"I know she wouldn't."

"Do you have her phone number, anyway?"

"No."

"Where does she live?" Ellen could get the number online.

"Jersey, but if you want to know more about Amy, you should ask Rose. She was here before. She's another friend of ours. She's older." Melanie wrinkled her nose. "She was in rehab with me and Amy."

"Great, can I have her phone?"

"I have her cell number right here." Melanie pressed a few keys on the phone, found a number, and rattled it off.

"Hold on, I have to get a pen." Ellen rooted around in her purse, but Melanie dismissed her with a wave.

"You don't need one. Give me your cell number, and I'll text it to you."

"Of course," Ellen said, a reminder of her age, as she stood on the front step of mortality.

Chapter 67

Rose Bock turned out to be a middle-aged African-American woman with oversized aviator glasses and a sweet smile. She wore her hair cut natural and had on a blue-checked Oxford shirt underneath a navy suit, looking every inch the accountant. Ellen had reached her on her cell phone, and she was in Philly, so they'd met at a burger joint full of noisy students near the Penn campus.

"Thanks so much for meeting me." Ellen took a quick sip of a Diet Coke. "My condolences about Amy. Melanie told me that you two were close."

"We were." Rose's smile faded quickly. "So how did you know her? You didn't say on the phone."

"Long story short, I adopted a baby that I think was hers. At least that's what the court papers say."

"Amy had a baby?" Rose's eyebrows rose, and Ellen grew officially tired of the reaction.

"Hi, ladies." The waitress arrived with a cheeseburger in a blue plastic basket, set it down on the table, then went off. Rose picked up the burger and smiled sheepishly.

"I can't resist the double cheeseburger here. I traded one addiction for another."

"Enjoy yourself." Ellen managed a smile. "If you don't mind my saying so, you don't look like the typical drug addict."

"Yes, I do," Rose said, without rancor. "I was addicted to prescription drugs, Vicodin and Percocet, for almost nine years. I started with a back injury and never stopped."

"I think of Vicodin as in a different category from heroin."

"You shouldn't. They're both opiates and they work the same way. I might have been in a different income bracket from Amy, but we're both junkies. It could just as easily have been me, lying there today in a box." Rose picked up her heavy burger and took a bite in a way that looked almost angry to Ellen, but she wanted to stay on point.

"I'm trying to learn about Amy's death. The family told me she overdosed accidentally, or that it was bad heroin, street heroin."

"She didn't overdose." Rose shook her head, and laughter burst from a nearby table, a group of caffeinated undergraduates. "More likely, the junk was bad. Street junk gets cut with strychnine."

Ellen shuddered. "Poison."

"Yes."

"Melanie told me that Amy still had her Subutex on her, which she didn't take, and we both read her last texts, which were upbeat. Amy didn't mention to Melanie that she was looking to start doing drugs again. Had she mentioned anything like that to you?"

"No, not all." Rose finished chewing, then reached for her coffee and took a sip.

"I wonder why she didn't call you or Melanie, if she felt tempted to do drugs again."

"*You* wonder?" Rose winced, between bites. "I'm not her sponsor, but I am, I was, her friend. I would think she'd call me if she wanted to use. I'll never get over this, until I go to my own grave."

"I'm sorry. You can't blame yourself."

"That's what my husband says, and thanks for it, but it doesn't help." Rose set the sandwich down. "I would have bet a thousand bucks on Amy. She had relapsed twice, but that's part of the process, for some of us. She was finally able to get clean."

"So she never called you, to say she was tempted?"

"No, never." Rose's face fell into pained lines. "We talked on the phone every couple days, and all the talk was easy. She got a new job and she was getting ready to reconcile with her family. So that she started using again, two days after we spoke, well, it was a real blow." Rose shook her head.

"Melanie told me about a guy named Rob Moore, who Amy dated three or four years ago. He was abusive and she got away from him. You know anything about him?"

"Not really. Amy told me that she had a toxic relationship once, that much I know. I never knew his name. She talked about him in group. The therapists might know more, but they won't tell you, that's confidential."

Ellen tried another tack. "Did Amy say where he was from or where he lived? Anything that he might have done for a living? I ask because there's an outside chance that he's the father of my son."

"I wish I could help you, but I can't."

"Wait, maybe this will help." Ellen picked up her purse and pulled out a flurry of papers, one of which was the photo of Amy and the man on the beach, then handed the picture to Rose. Luckily, she hadn't cleaned out her purse after the Miami trip. She pointed at Beach Man. "I think this man might be Rob Moore. Did you ever see him?"

"No."

"She ever show you a photo?"

"No, just told me that he was a jerk." Rose handed back the picture, then paused, her eyes narrowing. "Hold the phone. Last week, she called me on my cell. I wasn't there to take the call, but she left a message, saying something about a 'blast from the past.'" Rose looked away, her lips parting slightly as she reached for a thought. "What was it she said? She had a visit from a blast from the past."

Ellen met her eye, and her blood ran cold.

"Do you think she meant Rob Moore?"

"Maybe." Ellen's thoughts came fast and furious, but it was risky to tell her much more. "What did she say when you called her back?"

"She said she was fine. I forgot about the message, and we started talking about other things." Rose's mouth tilted down, and the realization dawned on her. "You think that this guy came back in her life, but she didn't want to let on? Or she thought better of it?"

"I don't know what I think. I'm trying to figure out what happened. What day was it that she called you?"

"Friday. I missed the call because I was at my son's piano recital."

Ellen thought back quickly. She had met with Cheryl on Thursday night, after which Cheryl sent Amy the email telling her that Ellen was looking for her. Friday would be the night after Amy got the email, assuming she checked her email with any frequency. Ellen felt an ominous tightening in her chest, trying to put two and two together on the spot.

"Why does any of this matter? Do you think Rob Moore had something to do with Amy's using again?"

"I don't know," Ellen answered, feeling an odd momentum building within her. She wished she could tell Rose that she intended to find out, but she was too stricken to speak. Too many things weren't making sense, or maybe they were. She sensed it wasn't speculation. That Amy's death was connected to her visit to Cheryl. That she had set it all in motion. And that Rob Moore had everything to do with Amy's death.

"You there?"

"Sorry." Ellen fake-checked her watch, then rose. "Jeez, I'm late, I should probably get going, thanks so much."

"Now?" Rose blinked in confusion. "We're in the middle of a conversation."

"I know, but I have to go." Ellen grabbed her coat and purse from the seat. "I'll follow up and let you know if I learn anything new. Thanks again."

"You think we should call the police?"

"No," Ellen said, too quickly. "I'm sure it's speculation, but I'll give it some thought. Have to go now. Thanks again."

She turned and fled the restaurant.

Chapter 68

Ellen hurried from the restaurant, her head swimming. She broke into a light jog, pulling her coat around her with a shaky hand. Her heels clacked along the frozen concrete, and she almost ran into two students who came suddenly out of a bookstore. She hurried ahead, ignoring their laughter. Her breath came in short, ragged bursts, fogging from her mouth. Her eyes stung, and she blinked the wetness away, telling herself it was the cold. She reached her car, fumbled for her keys, jumped in and turned on the engine, then lurched into the lane of traffic.

HONK! HONK! A van driver blared his horn, but Ellen didn't look back. It was late afternoon and a premature night was falling, frigid as black ice. Cars clogged the street in both directions, their headlights aglow. She drove on autopilot, through a world that had gone topsy-turvy around her.

She had thought that Will was hers and would be forever. She thought that he had a young mother somewhere and a wandering father. She thought that they were gone for good, a young couple who made a mistake. But it had been a fantasy, created by a writer's imagination. All of it was fiction. And now Ellen was deathly afraid of what was true.

Her hands gripped the wheel. Her heart thundered. She skidded to a stop at a traffic light, the burning red circle searing into her consciousness like a hot poker. She was too emotional to think straight. She didn't know where to go or what to do. She couldn't go to the police because she'd lose Will. She had been going it alone for so long, she couldn't do it for another minute. She picked up her cell phone and pressed in a phone number.

"Please be there," Ellen was saying, when the call connected.

Chapter 69

"Come in, what's the matter?" Marcelo swung open his front door, and Ellen hurried past the threshold, compelled by a force she didn't understand completely, whether pulled or pushed inside she didn't know. It had taken her an hour to get to his house in Queens Village, but the ride over hadn't calmed her down. It had been all she could do to hide her panic when she'd called Connie and asked her to stay late.

"There's a problem but . . . I don't know where to begin." Ellen raked a hand through her hair and found herself pacing back and forth in his neat living room, a blur of exposed-brick walls, glass tables, and black leather furniture. Marcelo closed the front door behind her, and she spun on her heels to face him. "I don't even know where to begin."

"It's all right," Marcelo said softly, his dark eyes steady. "Try the beginning."

"No, I . . . can't." Ellen didn't know why she'd come here. She wasn't sure it was the right thing. She knew only that she needed to talk to someone. "I think I'm in the middle of something . . . I don't know what."

"Did you do something illegal?"

"Yes, and no." Ellen didn't know how to answer. She didn't know what to think. Her hands flew to her face, and she felt her fingerpads burrow into the flesh of her cheeks. "No, but . . . I think I stumbled onto something . . . I wish I never started. It's the worst . . . the worst thing that could happen."

"What could be so bad?" Marcelo asked, disbelieving, stepping closer to her and taking her by the shoulders. "What is it?"

"It's too awful, it's just . . ." Ellen couldn't continue, afraid to give it voice, as if she'd fall into an abyss, a darkness that would follow as inexorably as nightfall. She felt something tear loose in her chest, as if her heart were actually ripped from its moorings, untethered from everything that held it in place, everything that kept her alive, and she heard herself erupt in a sob that came from deep within and burst free. The next thing she knew, she was crying and Marcelo had put his arms around her, wrapping her in a strong embrace, and she could feel herself sagging against his soft shirt, hiccuping in the civilized office smells clinging to him, the remnants of her life before.

Marcelo was saying, "Whatever it is, we can figure it out. Everything is going to be all right, you'll see." He held her tight, rocking her slightly, and she heard him saying again that everything was going to be all right, and she listened to his words as if she were a small child, permitting herself to be told a fairy tale.

"I made a . . . a mistake, a terrible mistake." Ellen looked up at him through her tears and she could see in his expression that he had let his guard slip away, and all that was left was a naked pain that must have mirrored her own. He stroked her cheek gently, brushing away her tears, and Ellen felt his other arm behind her back and leaned against it fully, letting him support her. His eyes met hers, so full of feeling that she felt a kind of wonderment, and she couldn't remember anyone ever looking at her that way, and in the next instant he lowered his face and kissed her softly on the lips, once, and then again.

"Everything's going to be all right," he murmured. "You're here now, and we'll make it right."

"Really?" Ellen asked, still wondering, and when Marcelo leaned down to kiss her again, more deeply and with urgency, she had her answer. In that moment she gave herself over to him and her own emotions, kissing him back deeply, drawing from him comfort and strength, escaping into the delusion of his embrace, just for now, for the few moments before he learned the truth and understood that everything was most decidedly not going to be all right, but that all of her worst fears were about to happen and there was nothing and nobody who could stop them.

And in the next minute Ellen felt her own hands reaching up Marcelo's back, her fingers rough against the thin fabric of his shirt, pulling him as close as she possibly could, and he responded, holding her tighter, kissing her with more urgency, his breath quickening as they sank, fumbled, and stumbled together onto the couch.

Ellen felt him press her backwards against the leather, or maybe she pulled him up and onto her, almost embarrassingly eager to lose herself in him and forget about everything else. About Amy. About Carol. Even about Will. For a moment she wasn't a mother anymore but simply a woman, and the heat of Marcelo's kiss and the weight of his body chased every thought from her head and obliterated every worry. In the soft light, she saw him smile with pleasure as he helped her wriggle out of her coat and they shoved it slip-sliding off the couch and onto the rug.

"Here, allow me," Marcelo whispered, and Ellen eased

partway up and put her arms in the air, letting him pull her sweater over her head, and when her head popped out of the black neckline, she saw the softest expression cross his face, and he stopped for a second, halting the urgency of before, and his gaze traveled from her face, lingering at her neck and finally coming to rest on the black lace of her bra.

"*Meu deus, voce tao linda*," Marcelo said softly, and though she didn't know the translation, the way he said it communicated so much desire that it slowed her down and stopped her teenaged clawing. She eased backwards against the cool leather and lay with her head back and throat open, her chest rising and falling with need, her heart pounding in her ears, looking at him through tears that had stopped flowing, taking him in with her eyes.

"You are so beautiful," Marcelo said, and for a second, they were both suspended in place and time, letting the frank lust of their first kisses cool and ebb away, and they regarded each other as two mature adults, each sensing that they were starting something real by whatever came next. Marcelo looked down at her with a grave smile, then he cocked his head in what could only be a question, silently asked.

"Yes," Ellen whispered, raising her arms.

Marcelo lowered himself onto her in reply, and they kissed deeply and slowly, wrapping their arms and legs around each other, their tongues flickering and teasing, and in time, their clothes peeled off layer by layer until skin met skin, warmth met warmth, and heart met heart.

Until there was nothing between them at all.

Chapter 70

Ellen woke up naked, her limbs intertwined with Marcelo's and her head resting on a musky patch of his chest. She wondered what time it was, disentangling herself. Marcelo had turned out the lamp at some point, leaving the room dim except for the glow of a streetlight, bleeding through the slats in the window shutters. She propped herself up on an elbow and squinted at her watch. Nine o'clock. Her life rushed back at her like a freight train, full of noise, power, and something else. Fear. Suddenly she knew what had happened, all at once, as if she had seen it in a nightmare.

Amy was murdered. So was Karen Batz. Rob Moore is killing everyone who knows that Will is really Timothy.

Ellen sprang from the couch, looking for her clothes. She wiggled into her skirt, slid into her sweater, jumped into her boots. Marcelo slept on, his snoring soft and regular, and she didn't wake him to explain. She didn't have a minute to lose. She grabbed her coat, found her purse, and fumbled for her car keys, her heart beginning to beat fast. She crossed to the front door, and something was telling her that she had to hurry home.

Right now.

Chapter 71

Ellen shut Marcelo's front door behind her, clutched her coat closed, and hurried down the stoop into a snowstorm, keeping her head down. Flakes fell like hail, driven by an angry wind, biting the flesh of her cheeks as she hustled down the sidewalk. Snow covered the sidewalk, and she almost slipped on the way to the car.

She chirped the door open, jumped inside, and turned on the ignition and windshield wipers. Ice clung to the windshield in patches, but she wasn't waiting for it to thaw. She cranked the defrost, backed out of the space, and reached into her purse for her BlackBerry. She pulled it from her purse and pressed speed dial for Connie as she pounded the gas. The car zoomed down the dark street, and the call connected.

"Connie? You hanging in?" Ellen asked, trying to keep the nervousness from her tone. She didn't even know what she was nervous about. She just knew she had to get home.

"Sure. I'm watching TV. You said you might be late."

"Not this late." Ellen felt a twinge of guilt, but tried to pay attention to her driving. She switched lanes to pass a truck, took a right, then a left in slow traffic, everybody cautious in the snowstorm. Her windshield wipers flapped madly, a frantic beating that reminded her of her own heart.

"Take your time, El. Chuck had to work late, too."

"How's my boy?"

"He's out like a light."

"Good." Ellen waited for the familiar easing in her chest when she heard that everything was fine, but there was no easing tonight. She steered around a sluggish Toyota and switched lanes, heading for the cross street to the expressway.

"Oh yeah, the cat's throwing up, so I had to put him out back for a while."

"Okay. I'll be home in less than an hour."

"Drive safe. It's really coming down out here. We already have six inches."

"I hear you, 'bye." Ellen pressed End, tossed the Black-Berry aside, and flew around a pickup truck pulling into a parking space. She fed the car gas to the intersection, where the traffic light was turning red, then blasted through the intersection, heading home.

By the time she reached the highway, she knew exactly what he was going to do.

Chapter 72

Ellen hurried to her front porch in a full-fledged snow-storm, keeping her head down and barreling into the wind, her heels punching footfalls into the freezing, wet snow. She'd thought about calling the cops but didn't want to blow her cover. She was on her own.

She ran up the snowy porch steps and willed herself to get calm, arranging her face into a mask of normalcy. She plunged her key into the lock and twisted, opening the door onto a comforting scene that brought her no comfort.

Connie greeted her from the couch, with a big grin. "It's Nanook of the North!"

"Cold out there." Ellen fake-smiled and slid out of her coat. The lamps lent the living room a homey glow, the toys had been put away, and the TV played on mute, a plastic-surgery show. She grabbed Connie's coat and handed it to her, barely able to hide her urgency. "You'll be safe going home, right? You have four-wheel drive?"

"Sure, it's no problem." Connie put on her coat, flip-ping her ponytail over her collar, then got her tote and purse from the windowseat. "No way he's having school tomorrow."

"Then it's good I'm home, huh?" Ellen opened the door to let Connie out. "We'll just hibernate and make some cookies."

"I vote for chocolate chip."

"You got it." Ellen managed another smile as Connie picked up her stuff and crossed to the door. "Seriously, be careful out there."

"No worries, I'm invincible." Connie flashed her a final smile and headed outside, and Ellen shut the door, locked it, and threw the deadbolt.

Go go go.

Ellen didn't know how or why, but she knew what she felt inside. If Rob Moore was killing people who knew about Timothy, then she and Will had to get out of there immediately, tonight. She hurried up the stairs, hustled into Will's room, and hurried to the bed.

"Will, wake up, honey." Will slept on his back, his arms open and askew, stirring. Oreo Figaro didn't move, a black-and-white ball at the foot of the bed. She lifted Will up, hoisted him to her shoulder in his Elmo thermal pajamas, and he made a snuffling noise.

"Mommy?"

"Hi, honey." Ellen rubbed his back. "You can just stay asleep, I want to put you into something warmer."

Will put his arms around her neck, and Ellen moved quickly to the bureau, dipped sideways to yank open the bottom drawer, and grabbed one of his snowsuits. She crossed back to the bed, unfolded the snowsuit with a quick snap, and fumbled to stuff Will's feet into the legs. "Mommy, what?"

"Everything's fine, sweetie. We're just going out for a little bit." Ellen pulled the snowsuit up and unwrapped his arms from her neck, then stuck on his sneakers. "Hold on around my neck. We're going for a ride."

"Okay," Will said sleepily, holding tighter as she picked

him up again, left the room, and hurried down the stairs, keeping a steadying hand on his back. She reached the bottom and glanced at the clock on the entertainment center—10:15. She had to get going. She grabbed her purse from the windowseat, then remembered she needed cash. She kept two hundred bucks in the kitchen drawer for emergencies and she was pretty sure this qualified.

She hurried through the living room, noting that the Coffmans' station wagon wasn't in the driveway and their windows were dark. It was a lucky break that they weren't home, because if they spotted her going out this late in a snowstorm, they might have a question or two. She hurried with Will through the dining room and turned the corner into the dark kitchen.

She went to flick on the light switch, but all of a sudden there was a shadowy blur and the back of her head exploded in pain.

Her arms released their grip. Will slipped through her fingers. Everything went dark, and the last thing she heard was Will's scream.

"Mommy!"

Chapter 73

Ellen regained consciousness, lying on her side on the kitchen floor. Her head thundered and she tried to scream. Tape covered her lips. She tried to move her hands but they were wrenched behind her back, stuck together. Pain arced through her shoulder joints. Her ankles were bound. She was facing the dining room, her back to the kitchen.

Will.

Ellen felt a bolt of terror rattle through her very bones. Her BlackBerry rang in the living room, the sound of another place and time. She heard a noise behind her, a harsh ripping sound. She rolled herself over on the floor, in horror at the sight.

Will lay on his side facing her, a strip of duct tape over his mouth. He was crying hard, his small body shaking with sobs. A man bent over him, wrapping duct tape around his ankles in his blue snowsuit.

"Good morning," the man said, looking up with a sly grin.

It was the man from the beach. Rob Moore. He had a droopy brown mustache and he looked older and craggier than he had in the photo with Amy, but it was the same man. Shaggy brown hair curled over the collar of an old black coat he had on with jeans and snowy Timberlands. A red plastic jug with a long spout sat next to him on the floor. It had to be gasoline. The kitchen reeked of it. Ellen screamed in her throat, a mother's howl of outrage and dread.

"I second that emotion," Moore said, chuckling again as he tore off the duct tape with the side of a crooked incisor.

Tears poured from Will's eyes, and they widened in fear. Ellen shimmied closer to him, making noises.

Moore straightened, a smile twisting his lips. Suddenly he lifted his foot in the heavy boot and put it down hard on Will's head. "Move and I'll squash him like a bug."

Ellen felt paralyzed by fear. Will burst into new tears, his cheeks turning a violent red. Moore leaned forward and stepped harder on his head.

Will squeezed his eyes shut, his small forehead buckling with pain. Dirt and snow from the boots dumped onto his little face. Moore was crushing his skull.

Ellen screamed and screamed, shaking her head frantically.

"Lady, get back and shut the hell up."

Ellen scrambled backwards, writhing this way and that, finally bumping the back of her head on the stove. She looked up at Moore, begging him to stop.

"Is that the look of love you're givin' me?" Moore kept his boot on Will's head but eased backwards slightly. The redness ebbed from Will's cheeks. He was choking under the duct tape.

Ellen prayed to God he could breathe. That his skull wasn't injured. That his heart could withstand the pressure.

Moore said, "I woulda thought you got your fill with your boyfriend."

Ellen struggled to think through her panic. Moore must have been following her. Had he been to the funeral? What was he going to do with the gasoline? She refused to go to the obvious answer. Her throat emitted primal noises.

"Oh, shut up." Moore took his foot from Will's head, leaving him crying hysterically, his tears mixing with the mud on his face.

Ellen silenced herself, making eye contact with Will, trying to tell him that everything would be all right. She had to figure out what to do. Her thoughts raced. Nobody was coming for help. The Coffmans weren't home. Her neighbors on the other side were never home. Everyone else was hunkered in their beds for the snowstorm.

Moore picked up the plastic jug and twisted off the lid, releasing the unmistakable odor. He tipped the container over on top of Will, and gasoline spewed from the spout, splashing onto Will's legs in the snowsuit, the solvent darkening the material from blue to black.

Stark cold horror paralyzed Ellen's thoughts. Moore was going to set them on fire. He was going to kill them both. She started screaming behind the duct tape.

Bing Bong!

Suddenly, the doorbell rang in the living room.

Ellen screamed louder behind the tape, even though she knew it was useless.

"Shut up!" Moore set down the gasoline jug and stepped hard on Will's head.

Ellen shook her head back and forth like a madwoman. She prayed frantically that Moore would stop hurting Will. She didn't know who was at the door. It was too late at night for a visitor, unless it was Martha Coffman. Maybe they'd come home in the meantime and needed to borrow something. Maybe one of her boys was sick.

Bing Bong!

Moore grimaced, angry. Will's face turned blue-red before her eyes. A silent scream contorted his features. Tears poured from his eyes. Snot streamed from his nose over the duct tape.

Bing Bong!

"Give it up!" Moore whirled around, finally taking his foot off Will.

Ellen willed herself to think. If it was Martha Coffman, maybe she had seen something from her kitchen. She would call 911 if Ellen didn't answer the door.

Bing Bong!

"Shit!" Moore flew into a rage, his eyes wild and out of control. He plunged his hand into his coat pocket, and when he withdrew it, he was holding a large revolver with a steel barrel.

Ellen froze.

Chapter 74

"You see your kid?" Moore bent down and drilled the barrel of the gun into Will's temple. "I'll blow his head clean off."

Ellen was too terrified to cry, her emotion strangling the sounds in her throat.

"I'm gonna cut you loose, only because they're not goin' away. You answer the door and tell whoever's there to go. Do one thing wrong, just one, and I blow this kid's head offa his shoulders."

Ellen nodded frantically. This could be her only chance. She had to make something happen. Could she risk it? Could she not?

"I'll kill him. You understand?"

Ellen pumped her head, yesyesyes.

Bing Bong!

"All right then." Moore raised the revolver, sprang over to Ellen, and reached behind her back. He yanked her into the air by her wrists, hissing into her ear. "Up to you, bitch. One word and I shoot the kid."

Ellen shook her head, desperate to reassure him. In the

next second, her hands were cut free and she fell like a broken doll to the hardwood floor.

Moore cut loose her ankles, flipped her over, and tore the duct tape from her mouth. It stung until he drilled the gun between her eyes.

"Don't hurt him, don't hurt him," Ellen heard herself whisper over and over, like a prayer.

"No tricks." Moore's face was six inches from hers, a close-up of bloodshot eyes, greasy mustache, and breath foul with beer.

Ellen scrambled to get her feet under her, her knees jelly. Her thoughts clicked ahead, running the possibilities. "What if it's my neighbor? What if she won't go?"

"Make her." Moore shoved her from the kitchen, and she half walked, half stumbled through the dining room, glancing quickly out the windows. The lights still were off at the Coffmans'. Connie would have let herself in. So who was ringing the bell?

Marcelo!

He was the only possibility. He would help her. Together they'd get Will out of this. She hurried through the dining room. Her heart thundered, and she crossed the living room toward the door.

Bing Bong!

Ellen couldn't see the face at the door, but a shadow stood silhouetted in the yellowish porch light. She opened the door and stood stricken against a blast of frigid wind.

At her front door was the last person in the world she ever expected to see.

Chapter 75

It was Carol Braverman, standing in a long black coat, a quilted purse slung over an arm. Her hair was slicked back in a chignon, her eyes glittered with emotion, and her mouth made a glossy line. She asked, "Ellen Gleeson?"

Ellen nodded, stunned as Carol entered the house and began looking around the living room.

"I'm Carol Braverman, but you knew that already." Carol turned on her heel, the coat making a chic swish. She looked at Ellen with determined blue eyes. "You adopted my son."

"What? I'm sorry?" Ellen struggled to react. A million thoughts flooded her head. She couldn't process any of them fast enough.

"I came as soon as I had it verified. He's my son Timothy. He was kidnapped in Miami right after his first birthday."

"I don't know what you mean," Ellen said, beginning to think clearly. Will was in the kitchen under a gun. Moore could hear every word through the other entrance to the kitchen, over the landing. She had to get Carol out of here. One distraught mother was enough. Carol was a variable she couldn't predict right now.

"Sorry, but I think you do." Carol's eyes softened slightly. "I can only imagine what you must be going through, and I feel sorry for you, I really do. But we both know the truth. You have my baby, and I want him back."

"No, I don't." Ellen stepped toward her, leaving the front door open, filling the room with frigid air. "Please, leave my house."

"You have my son, don't pretend you don't know. You were in Miami two days ago."

"No, you're wrong." Ellen's mouth went dry. How did Carol know? No matter, a plan was coming together in her mind. She wasn't tied up anymore. As soon as she got Carol out of the house, she'd be free to move. She said, "I don't know what you're talking about. Leave my house, right now."

"Let me explain." Carol put up a hand. "A reporter who works with you called me at home and told me everything. Sarah Liu is her name. She told me about you and the boy you call Will."

Ellen felt it like an electric shock. Sarah had called the Bravermans? How? Why?

"She caught you on our website, printing out my son's picture. She called your house and verified that you were out of town. She figured out you'd come to Miami." Carol paused, cocking her head. "Why did you? Did you want to check us out?"

Ellen's mind reeled, then she fought to recover. She had to save Will. Moore would be waiting, the gun to her son's head.

"Sarah claimed the reward, of course." Carol smiled in gentle triumph, her diamond earrings flashing. "It's a million dollars, life-changing money. That's why we set it so

high. We knew that sooner or later it would bring somebody out of the woodwork, and it did."

"This is insane. Get out."

"I Googled you online, I found the articles you wrote
about him. I know you didn't know he was kidnapped, but
that's not my problem. He's mine, and I want him." Carol's
tone turned indignant. "My husband's on the way. His
plane was delayed in the snow, and I didn't want to wait."

Ellen almost spiraled into an emotional stall. She used
to think this was her worst nightmare, but now she knew
better. Her worst nightmare was in her own kitchen. She
had to get Carol out of here. Suddenly a noise came from
the stairwell, and they both turned. Oreo Figaro appeared
on the stair landing, where he stopped and sat down with
a yawn, curling his inky tail around him.

"Where is Timothy?" Carol demanded. "I demand to
see him."

"He's not Timothy, he's my son, and he's at a sleepover."

"A three-year-old, at a sleepover?" Carol moved toward
the stairway, but Ellen shifted over and blocked her way.

"Stop right there. You have no right to walk around my
house." She raised her voice to regain some authority. If
Carol took one step closer to the stairway, she'd be able to
see the kitchen from its other entrance. She'd smell the
gasoline, and they'd all end up dead. Ellen put a firm hand
on Carol's coat sleeve. "Get out, right now!"

"I thought we could do this without the police, but
maybe not. You have my son, and I won't leave here without him." Carol tried to wrench her arm free, but Ellen held
on to it with all her might. She was trying to save Carol's
life, but the woman was endangering the son they both
loved.

"I don't know who you are. I don't know what you're
talking about."

"You know he's mine, and I'm appealing to you, mother to mother." Carol's eyes filled with sudden wetness. "I held out hope, all this time, I *knew* he'd turn up. I knew he was alive. I could *feel* him."

"Get the hell out!" Ellen fought a rising panic. She could imagine Moore listening. They were running out of time. She could stand losing Will to Carol, but she couldn't stand Will leaving this earth, not while she drew breath.

"We hired a detective, and he confirmed everything Sarah said, including your plane ticket down and back."

"Go!" Ellen shoved her to the threshold, but Carol shoved back, her expression fierce.

"I'm not going!" She braced herself in the threshold, rooted as a tree. "I've waited two years to see him and that's long enough. I'll stand on your porch all night if I have to. I want my *son*!"

"He's not here!" Ellen shouted, loud enough for Moore to hear. "Go! NOW!"

"Call the police then." Carol folded her arms. "But you won't do that, will you? Because you know that you're keeping my child."

"Get OUT!" Ellen shouted louder, fighting a wild impulse to run to the kitchen, grab Will, and go like hell, but Carol's eyes narrowed with a new suspicion.

"Your eyes just moved. You just looked somewhere in back, behind you. He's back there, isn't he?"

"No, I didn't. Now—"

"I know he's here!" Suddenly Carol hit Ellen in the face, and she reeled backwards, off-balance, recovering too late.

"No, stop!"

"Timothy!" Carol broke free and bolted for the dining room.

"NO! STOP! WAIT!" Ellen chased her, took a desperate flying leap, and caught Carol by the hem of her long coat. The two women fell to the dining room floor, sliding on the hardwood and knocking into the dining room chairs like bowling pins.

"I want my son!" Carol screamed, as the two mothers wrestled on the dining room floor, bumping the chairs aside.

"NO!" Ellen struggled with all her might to pin Carol to the floor and had almost succeeded when they both heard the sound of raucous laughter.

"What was *that*?" Carol asked, her back on the floor.

Ellen felt her heart stop with fear, and she twisted behind her.

Rob Moore stood over them, his legs spread like a commando. He aimed his gun down at them. "Girl-on-girl action," he said.

"*You!*" Carol said, hushed, and Moore smiled slyly.

"Carol? Long time, no see."

Chapter 76

"Let's get this party started." Moore gestured toward the kitchen with the muzzle of his revolver. "In the kitchen, ladies."

"I could kill you!" Carol shot back, scrambling to prop herself up on an elbow. "You kidnapped my baby!"

"Boo hoo, princess." Moore snorted.

"I got you the money, and you were supposed to give the baby back! That was the deal. You were never supposed to keep the baby. Never!"

"The deal changed."

Ellen looked from Moore to Carol, dumbfounded. They had a deal? She straightened into a sitting position, incredulous. Meanwhile she wracked her brain for a way to save Will. She had to get him out of this alive.

"Why did you do it, why?" Carol cried. "All you had to do was give him back to me. You got your money."

"My girlfriend wanted him. She was always sayin' she couldn't have a baby, and when I tol' her no, she split with him."

Ellen needed to stall, to give herself time to think. "Was that Amy? Was Amy Martin your girlfriend?"

"Yeah. The dumb bitch."

"You killed Amy?"

"Duh," Moore answered.

"And the lawyer, too? Karen Batz?"

"Sure."

"But why? Did she know?"

"I wasn't leavin' a loose end. If she figured it out, she woulda squawked. Carol woulda had the best lawyers money could buy, and I woulda gone to the joint."

"You bastard!" Carol's gaze bored into him. "That was my baby! I thought about him every minute! You ruined my life!"

"You ruined your own life, you brat. You went through your money like water."

"This isn't about me, it's about you. You told me you'd give the baby back. You lied! You took him!"

Ellen kept thinking about how to save Will. Sooner or later, she'd get an opening.

"Do you know what you did?" Carol scrambled to stand up, and Oreo Figaro walked into the dining room. "You almost *killed* my husband. You *ruined* my marriage."

"You shoulda told him the truth, then. You shoulda said to him, 'Honey, wifey-poo isn't the good girl you think.' 'I used our kid to pay for my little hobby.'"

"She used her kid?" Ellen said, stalling. "*She* did it?"

"Yeah, it was all her idea." Moore sneered. "You didn't think that, did you? You didn't figure that out. Little Miss Goody-Goody here, she gambled up all her money, so she needed to tap her kid's."

"Shut up!" Carol shouted, but Moore ignored her.

"She knew me from the casino, Miccosukee. I was parkin' cars for rich bitches, and she hired me to kidnap her kid. She got the ransom from the kid's trust fund. She told me the nanny would be there and—"

"Stop it, stop it!" Carol shouted louder, startling Oreo

Figaro, who ran under the dining room table. "You weren't supposed to kill her. You weren't supposed to keep the baby!"

"Enough!" Moore gestured with the gun, his gaze shifting toward the kitchen. "You wanna see your son? He's in there."

"He is?" Carol's face flooded with happiness. She rushed to the kitchen, and the sudden movement sent Oreo Figaro scooting to Ellen.

Just then a lethal glimmer flickered through Moore's eyes. Ellen didn't have time to think, only to act.

And everything happened at once.

Chapter 77

Carol reached the kitchen threshold and saw Will, lying on the floor. "My baby!" she cried.

Moore raised the gun and aimed it at the back of Carol's head.

Ellen scooped Oreo Figaro off the floor and threw him right at Moore's face.

"Reowwh!" The fat cat screeched in protest, his thick body twisting this way and that, and the surprise knocked Moore off-balance. He raised his hands and fell backwards. The gun fired into the ceiling. Oreo Figaro fell to the floor, righting himself and scampering off.

Ellen launched herself like a missile, aiming for Moore's gun. She barreled into him, and he staggered backwards into the kitchen. She grabbed the gun with all her might and struggled to wrest it from his grip.

"Get offa me!" Moore howled. He held on to the gun, whipped Ellen around, and slammed her into the doorway. Her head banged against the wood but she hung on to his wrist, fighting for the gun even as he pointed its muzzle at Carol, who had picked up Will and was taking him out the other doorway.

"RUN!" Ellen screamed.

"Shut up!" Moore threw her against the stove, shaking her hand loose and training the gun on Carol.

Carol looked over her shoulder, and in one motion, put Will on the landing behind her, blocked him with her body, and raised her arms protectively, facing Moore. She shouted, "Don't you dare hurt my son!"

Moore squeezed the trigger, firing point-blank, and Ellen screamed in horror.

Carol's chest exploded in wool tatters. Her mouth dropped open. Her head snapped forward. She dropped onto the kitchen floor, crumpling at the knees, her legs grotesquely askew.

"NO!" Ellen hurled herself at Moore, but this time, in her hand was the cast-iron burner from her stovetop. She swung the burner as hard as she could into Moore's face. The spiked end speared his forehead, and a gaping hole appeared. In the next second, it spurted a gruesome freshet of bright red blood. Moore's eyes flew open, and he slumped against the wall, then slid down, insensate.

Ellen heard herself shouting something, but even she didn't know what she said. The gun fell to the floor, and she picked it up and aimed it at Moore as he landed in a sitting position. She pointed the gun at him, not knowing whether to shoot him or save him. A crooked grin crossed his face before his eyes cut away and his gaze fixed.

Ellen hurried over to Carol, picking her up with care and feeling under her chin for a pulse. There was none. Blood soaked her coat from the hole in her chest, right over her heart.

Ellen leaned Carol back down on the floor, bent over her and listened for breath. No sound. She opened Carol's mouth and began to breathe air into her, but it was too late for CPR. She tried anyway, but it was no use. Carol's head fell back, too loose on her neck, her mouth hanging

open, and Ellen heard herself moan, stricken. She set her
down on the floor carefully, saying a silent prayer.

Will.

Ellen half crawled, half stumbled to the landing, where
Will lay bundled, sobbing. His terrified eyes met hers, so
much like Carol's that for a minute, it gave her a start. She
picked him up and hurried out of the kitchen with him,
shielding him from the grisly scene and telling him everything was going to be all right. She hurried him into the
living room and sat with him on the couch, putting him
on her lap and comforting him as she unpeeled the duct
tape from his mouth. She started slowly, but he cried even
harder, his nose bubbling.

"Hold on, sweetie, it'll only hurt for a second." She
yanked off the duct tape, letting it fall, and he erupted in
the full-blown wail of a newborn.

"Mommy! Mommy! It hurts!"

"It's all over now, it's all over." Ellen kept talking to
him, grabbing a Kleenex from the coffee table and wiping his nose. The tape had pulled some of the skin around
his mouth off, leaving it irritated and sticky, and the adhesive made an ugly pattern around his lips.

"It hurts!"

"Here we go, it'll stop soon." Ellen dried his eyes with
a new tissue, then tried to comfort him as she untaped his
hands and feet, the stench of gasoline filling her nostrils.
She was sliding him out of his wet snowsuit when she
caught a glimpse of blood dripping behind his right ear.

God, no.

"It's okay now, honey," she said, but his tears kept
flowing. She pulled a Kleenex from the box, held it to the
wound, and flashed on Moore's big boot crushing Will's
face in the same spot. She felt stricken, but masked her
emotions. She didn't know if Will was bleeding inter-
nally, inside his ear or even behind his eye. He needed an

ambulance. She pressed the tissue to his wound, hurried with him to the living room phone, and called 911 with Will crying in her arms.

"What is your emergency?" the dispatcher asked, and Ellen collected herself, composing a lead paragraph on the spot.

"An armed intruder broke into my house tonight. He tried to kill me and my son, and I killed him in self-defense." Ellen felt her throat catch. She couldn't believe her own words. She had never harmed another human being, much less killed one. "He shot and killed a woman named Carol Braverman. He also injured my son, who's three, and he's bleeding from behind his ear. I need an ambulance right away, and the police."

"You say there were *two* people killed?"

"Yes. Listen, I need an ambulance for my son. His head was . . . stepped on and it's bleeding. He's crying, and I'm worried."

"Mommy!" Will cried harder, and Ellen struggled to hear the dispatcher.

"Keep him awake, and the ambulance will be there right away. You can stay on the line until they get there."

"Mommy! Mommy!" Will cried, louder.

"No, that's okay. I'd rather take care of him. Just hurry, please, hurry!" Ellen hung up, hugged Will close, and rocked him a little like the old days until his tears finally slowed. She grabbed a few more Kleenex and cleaned him up, then got a fresh one for the wound behind his ear. "What hurts, honey? Tell me."

"My head!"

Please, God, no. "That's why we're going to the doctor, so he can fix it."

"Dr. Chodoff?"

"No, a special doctor."

"I want Dr. Chodoff!" Will sobbed.

"Let's get your coat," Ellen said, narrating her actions to calm them both as she walked to the closet, took his corduroy hoodie from a hook, and sat back down on the couch with him, slipping his arms into the puffy sleeves, getting him ready. His sneakers reeked of gasoline, so she took them off.

"Stinky shoes, huh?" Ellen asked, as part of the narration, and Will nodded, his small chest shuddering from his final sobs. She touched lightly behind his ear, and in the lamplight she could see a large cut on his scalp, bleeding. She prayed there wasn't a skull fracture and reached for another tissue, pressing it over the wound.

"Mommy, what?"

"You have a boo-boo behind your ear. We're going to take a ride to the doctor. We have to get you looked at."

"Who was that man?"

"In the kitchen? A very bad man. A terrible man, but he's not going to hurt you anymore."

"Did he hurt you, Mommy?"

"No, I'm okay. So are you. You're going to be fine after we see the doctor." Ellen cuddled him, and Will rubbed his eye with a balled-up fist.

"My head hurts."

"Stay awake, okay, honey?" Ellen jiggled him a little and talked to him about nothing, even as the bright red blood from his cut soaked Kleenex after Kleenex until they looked like the tissue-paper poppies he made in school. She hid them from his view until the bleeding finally slowed, which only worried her more. Oreo Figaro wandered in, sat down in front of the couch, and tucked his legs underneath him.

Will sniffled. "You hurt Oreo Figaro, Mommy."

"No, I didn't. I knew he'd be okay."

"You throwed him."

"I know." Ellen didn't correct his English. He could

make all the grammar mistakes he wanted, from here on out.

"That wasn't nice."

"You're right." Ellen turned to Oreo Figaro. "I'm sorry, Oreo Figaro."

The cat signified his forgiveness by looking up and blinking, and he kept watch over them both until the police cruisers arrived, their red lights slashing the cozy living room with bloodred splotches, spattering the stenciled cows and country hearts.

"What is that, Mommy?" Will asked, twisting to see.

"It's the police, here to help us, buddy." Ellen rose and looked out the windows to the street, which had been transformed to a staging area. Police cruisers were parking out front, their exhausts billowing into the snowy air and their high beams slicing the dotted darkness. Uniformed cops sprang from the cars, black figures against the whiteness, running up her front walk to the porch.

"Here they come, Mommy."

"Right, here they come." Ellen crossed to the door as the cops hustled onto the porch, their shoes heavy as soldiers as they reached the front door.

They were coming to save Will.

And to destroy the only life he knew.

Chapter 78

Ellen opened the door, and police filled the living room and immediately began looking around, hurrying into the dining room and toward the stairs, their shoes heavy on the hardwood. Outside the window, she saw flashlights flickering as cops searched her front and side yards. Will quieted in her arms, gazing wide-eyed at an older cop with wire-rimmed glasses who took her aside, his hand on her elbow.

"I'm Officer Patrick Halbert," he said. Snowflakes dusted the shoulders of his nylon jacket. "You're the home-owner who called 911?"

"Yes." Ellen introduced herself. "Where is the ambulance?"

"On its way. Are you injured, ma'am?" Officer Halbert looked at her coat, and she realized that there was blood all over her.

"No, this isn't my blood. It's my son who's hurt. When will the ambulance get here?"

"Five minutes, tops." Officer Halbert's tone sounded official, but under the wet patent bill of his cap, his eyes looked concerned and they scanned Will, up and down.

He asked, "Now, you told our dispatcher it was a home invasion?"

"Yes, it was."

"Is there anyone else in the house?"

"Pat!" one of the cops called from the kitchen. "We got two in here!"

Ellen said, "We need to get going, he's bleeding from the head. Can't you take us to the hospital?"

"It's best to wait, so they can treat your boy on the way." Officer Halbert chucked Will's stocking foot. "No shoes, fella?"

Will recoiled, and the cop plucked a Bic from inside his jacket, slid a notepad from his back pocket, and flipped open the pad. "Ms. Gleeson, why don't you fill me in on what happened?"

"Can't we talk about this after my son is treated? That's my priority, and it's not good to talk in front of him, anyway."

"This won't be your formal statement, we'll talk later at the station house. I know who you are, my wife reads you in the paper." Officer Halbert smiled, more warmly. "We'll talk until the ambulance arrives."

"It's a long story, but there was an intruder in my house. He had a gun. He broke in and tried to kill me and my son. He poured gasoline on him." Ellen glanced at Will, whose gaze remained on the cop, though she knew he was listening. "Then a woman named Carol Braverman came in and interrupted him, and he shot her when she tried to save Will. I tried CPR on her but it was too late." Ellen felt a stab of guilt but stayed in control. It wasn't the time to break down. "They're in the kitchen."

"They're the bodies?"

"Yes." Ellen caught a glimpse of bright red lights in the street. It was the ambulance pulling up, spraying snow from its back tires. "They're here."

"Let's go." Officer Halbert quickly put away his pen and pad. "We'll escort you to the hospital, Ms. Gleeson."

Ellen was already out the door, cuddling Will against the storm, and he held her tight as Halbert and some other cops fell in beside them, and they descended the porch stairs into the snowy night. A paramedic jumped out of the cab and flung open the ambulance's back doors, spilling harsh fluorescent light onto the snow.

Ellen hurried down the walk with Will, plowing through wet snow in her boots. "Lots of snow, huh?"

"So much!" Will answered agreeably.

"Already eight inches," Officer Halbert added, steadying Ellen by the arm as the paramedic rushed to meet them.

"This the boy?" the paramedic shouted over the idling engines. He held out his arms for Will, and Ellen handed him over.

"Yes, he's three, bleeding from behind his ear. His head was . . . pressed from the side."

"You ride in back, Mom." The paramedic hustled Will to the back of the ambulance and climbed inside, and Ellen followed, stepping up onto the corrugated metal floor.

"Here we go, Will," she said, putting a hand on his stocking foot. She must have been crazy not to get him another pair of shoes. "We're riding in an ambulance. Cool, huh?"

"Wait, wait!" came a shout, and they all looked back. A black sedan had pulled up behind the police cruisers, and a man was running toward them in the snowstorm, waving his arms, his sport jacket flapping in the whirling snow. Cops surged toward him, blocking him, but in the light from the open ambulance, Ellen recognized his agonized features.

It was Bill Braverman.

"Stop, wait!" He fought the cops to get to the ambulance,

but they held him back, the melee silhouetted in the high beams of the cruisers. A bitter wind picked up, and the snow swirled as Bill struggled free of them and reached the ambulance doors, shouting, "Wait, stop, let me see!"

"Mister, get outta here! We gotta go!" the paramedic shouted back, pushing him away, but Bill took one look at Will and his expression filled with joy.

"Timothy, it's *you*! Thank God, it's you!" Bill held out his arms, and Will burst into terrified tears.

"Mommy!" he screamed, and Ellen jumped up, blocking the way.

"Bill, we'll sort this out later. I have to get him to the hospital. He has a head injury."

"*You!*" Bill went wild with outrage. "*You're* the one! You're the woman who adopted our son!" He started to climb into the ambulance, hoisting himself up by the open door, but the cops pulled him back and the paramedic held him off. He shouted, "That's *my boy*! That's Timothy! Where's my wife? What did you do to my wife?" He turned angrily to the cops flanking him. "I'm Bill Braverman! Where's my wife, is she here? Is she all right?"

"She's right here," the paramedic answered, gesturing in confusion at Ellen, who had turned to calm Will.

"Mommy! Mommy!" Tears spilled from his eyes, his lower lip shuddering.

Officer Halbert put a hand on Bill's arm. "Sir, is your wife Carol Braverman?"

"Yes, where is she? Is she all right?"

"Sir, please come with me," Officer Halbert said. "I need to speak with you." The other cops crowded around, clearing the ambulance as snow whirlpooled around them all.

"But that's my son! My son! Is he hurt? Where's my wife? That's our *son*!"

"Mommeeee!" Will screamed, confused, and Ellen

smoothed the hair back from his head. Blood leaked down the back of his neck, and bright red drops stained his hoodie.

"It's all right, baby, it's all right."

"We gotta go!" the paramedic shouted, buckling Will onto the gurney, then he shifted over to shut the back doors and twisted the handles closed. He climbed around Ellen and leaned toward the driver in the cab. "Locked and loaded, Jimmy!"

"It's all right," Ellen kept saying, holding Will's hand. She looked back through the windows, and just before the ambulance pulled away, she heard an anguished cry through the howling storm. Bill Braverman had lost his wife on the very night he'd found his son.

"Okay, little man, this won't hurt a bit," the paramedic said to Will, wrapping a child-size pressure cuff around his arm.

"It's all right, honey," Ellen said, holding his hand, but Will cried harder. "It's all right, everything's going to be all right."

Through the back window, the cops became stick figures against the whirling white, and Ellen felt a wrench of deep sadness. For Bill, for Carol, and for herself.

And especially, for Will.

Chapter 79

Ellen slumped in the cloth-covered chairs of the waiting room of the emergency department, ignoring the back issues of *People* and *Sports Illustrated*. The place was empty except for two young cops, who watched TV on low volume. The doctor had sent her out to the waiting room while Will was taken up to MRI and X-ray.

She closed her eyes, tilting her head back on the hard edge of the chair, trying to block out the images. Will, with gasoline on his snowsuit. Rob Moore, looking excited as he aimed his gun at Carol. Carol, raising her arms to protect Will. Bill, screaming against the snowstorm. The blood on her shirt.

Ellen looked down numbly, and the blood had dried to a stiff, oddly shiny patch of red-black. For some reason, it bothered her that she didn't know whether the blood was Moore's or Carol's.

She sank deeper into her chair. She had set out to find the truth, and she had her truth. She'd have to give Will up, when the time came. She understood it on an intellectual level, but couldn't begin to let herself feel it. That would come later, after she finally handed him over. Then she could lose it, after she knew he was alive and well. Healthy, again. She heard a noise and looked up.

The doors of the emergency room whooshed open, and through the glass she could see Bill Braverman, his sport coat bloodied, entering with Officer Halbert and another cop. She felt a sinking feeling in the pit of her stomach as they spotted her, then came into the waiting room.

"Ms. Gleeson?" Officer Halbert's smile was wearier than earlier. "How's your son?"

"Not sure yet."

"The docs here are great, you'll see." Officer Halbert pulled up a chair opposite her, while the other cop took a seat to the side. Bill Braverman sat with them, glaring at her. His eyes flashed with hostility, and his mouth became a straight line. He had probably gotten the blood on his coat holding Carol, and Ellen couldn't help meeting his eye.

"I'm so sorry about your wife," she said to him.

"Thank you," Bill answered, hoarsely, but his dark eyes, puffy and red, didn't soften. "I'd like an explanation from you."

Officer Halbert raised a hand. "Mr. Braverman, we'll get her statement later, as I told you."

"I'd like to know now," Bill shot back. "She's sitting here, my son is in the hospital, and my wife is dead. I want to know what happened."

"That's not our procedure, Mr. Braverman."

"Ask me if I care about your procedure."

Officer Halbert was about to reply when Ellen raised a hand.

"It's okay," she said. "He has a right to know and there's no reason to stand on formality."

Halbert pursed his lips. "We'll still need your statement. Later."

"Fine." Ellen took a deep breath and shifted in her

chair to face Bill. "It all started with a white card I got in the mail, about a kidnapped boy." She filled them in on what she'd figured out about Amy Martin and Rob Moore while Officer Halbert took notes, and she brought them up to date, telling them how she'd rushed home tonight. "I was worried that Moore might come after Will and me, and I was trying to get us out when he showed up."

Officer Halbert broke in, "We were wondering, how did Rob Moore get into your house? There was no sign of forced entry."

"I think the back door was left open. The cat goes in and out a lot, and we leave it unlocked sometimes. It's Narberth, after all."

"I hear that." Officer Halbert smiled. "We've never had a murder in the borough."

"Now you have two," Bill interjected, but Officer Halbert continued:

"If I may get a few things out of the way, did Moore attempt to rob you?"

"No, he was there to kill me and Will. He had us taped up and was pouring gasoline over my son."

"We saw the plastic jug." Halbert checked his pad. "Now, can you tell us what happened earlier, when Carol Braverman came over?"

Bill said, "Yes, do tell."

Ellen nodded, suddenly shaky. She hated him to find out this way, but it couldn't be helped. "Well, evidently, they had planned to kidnap the baby together. Carol paid Moore to do it."

Bill reddened. "*What?*"

"It's true."

"The hell it is!"

"I swear it—"

"How do you know?"

"Carol said so. She said Moore was supposed to give

the baby back but he didn't. That she had gambling debts and had to use her son's trust fund to pay them off."

"That's not possible!" Bill shot back, and Officer Halbert looked over at him, but didn't say anything.

Ellen said, "I was surprised, too, but she did. Moore said it was all her idea."

"How would she even know Moore? There's no way she knew such trash."

Ellen thought a minute, remembering the ugly scene, her stomach tense. "She said they met at a casino. Miccosukee, I think they said. Does that name mean anything to you?"

Bill blinked.

"What is Miccosukee?" Halbert interjected.

"It's a casino, on an Indian reservation outside of Miami," Bill answered, and Ellen breathed a relieved sigh.

"Moore said he was a parking valet there."

Bill asked, "He said she had gambling debts?"

"Yes." Ellen could see he didn't believe her, but something she said had hit home, she just didn't know what. She continued and told them every detail of what had happened, from Carol's entering the house to when Moore pulled the gun on them in the dining room. "He said that Carol had used up her trust fund money to pay her gambling debts and that she wanted to use Will's, er, Timothy's money."

Bill's eyes narrowed. "Who said that?"

"Moore did, and she didn't deny it. How else would I have known it?"

Bill had no reply, and Officer Halbert remained silent, watching the two of them.

Ellen continued, "She said you didn't know anything about the plan. She said you were so upset when he kept the baby that it almost killed you, and that it ruined your marriage."

Bill scoffed. "We have a wonderful marriage."

Ellen hesitated. "I saw you catch a plane a few days ago, from Miami to Vegas."

Bill's eyelids fluttered when he got her meaning, and he raked a hand through his hair. "Okay, well, we did have problems. We tried so hard to have Timothy, and after we did, it was like Carol didn't want anything to do with him. She had postpartum depression, I guess that's what it was. She'd always gambled, poker on the computer, but then it got worse. I confronted her, and she told me she was going to casinos. She told me she would stop. I thought she had." Bill's eyes glistened, and he hung his head. "I told her if she kept gambling, I'd leave her and take Timothy."

"Maybe that's why she kept it from you."

"I'm sure," Bill said, suddenly subdued, and Ellen saw a change in him, as if together, they were solving a puzzle, each providing some of the pieces.

She asked, "I'm curious, how would she pay the debts off with the ransom? How did that work?"

Officer Halbert and the other cops seemed to wait for his answer, and Bill rubbed his face.

"Lemme think. The kidnapper, when he phoned—this Moore—said that no FBI or police could be involved, and we went along with it. He also said the mother had to deliver the money. I said no, I was worried about her safety. I didn't want to send my wife out there to meet a killer." Bill's lips flattened. "But Carol said she wanted to do it by herself. She said she felt responsible because she didn't get Timothy out of the car in time, and I believed her."

Ellen could see why he'd believed her. She looked like the perfect wife and mother. The Mother Goose outfit; the children's theater at Charbonneau House. After her scheme had gone awry, Carol must have been expiating the guilt of a lifetime.

Bill shook his head. "We got the money from Timothy's trust, which was set up by my in-laws. They were very wealthy. The executor is a lawyer in town and he approved it, and before Carol made the delivery, she must have taken some cash off the top. God knows how much or where she hid it. That must be what she used to pay off her debts."

Ellen considered it, and it made sense. "She skimmed the money before she turned it over, and Moore must have agreed. How did she deliver it?"

"In a gym bag, he specified that."

"Did you check the bag?"

"No, why would I?" Bill kept shaking his head. "We packed it, she took it, and she left with it."

Ellen had no answer. It was an ingenious scheme, until it wasn't.

"If Moore had given Timothy back, the plan would have worked. It would have been fine. But he killed our babysitter and he kept Timothy. God knows why."

Ellen told him that Amy wanted the baby because she couldn't have one herself, and Bill's eyes widened in disbelief.

"So why not keep him then?"

"He got sick, as you know. Carol said she'd read my articles about him."

"I read them, too."

"So when I wanted to adopt him from the hospital, Timothy Braverman became Will Gleeson."

Bill's upper lip curled in disgust. "Someone can put a baby that isn't theirs up for adoption and get away with it? You'd think that somebody, the state or some agency, would catch that. You think they'd do background checks or something so this doesn't happen."

Ellen agreed. "They do background checks on the adopting parent, like me, but they don't do them on the women putting their baby up for adoption. Funny, huh?"

Bill sighed, his shoulders slumping. "I just cannot believe that Carol did this to me and Timothy. For money."

"Desperate people do desperate things." Ellen paused, feeling an odd sort of peace that came either from perspective or exhaustion. "She's beyond judgment now. She came up with a terrible solution to a terrible problem, one that resulted in a murder, and eventually, even her own."

Officer Halbert interjected, "I'm looking at two parents, and both of you love the same boy. Neither of you did anything wrong. It's a lose-lose situation, and I'm sorry for you both."

"Thanks," Ellen said, having nothing better to say, and Bill sighed again, looking at her with new eyes. He had learned the truth, and his truth was as terrible as hers.

"I'm sorry," he said after a moment, and Ellen nodded, trying not to cry.

"Me, too." Then she added, because it needed saying, "It sounds awful now, but I want to tell you how Carol died, because she redeemed herself. She gave her life, for Will. For Timothy. She saved his life."

"What happened?" Bill's lip trembled, and Ellen told him the story, after which he heaved a great sob, then collapsed into hoarse, choking sounds that hunched his broad shoulders, collapsing his frame and driving his face into his hands, in his own private hell.

There was a soft knock at the doorway, and the emergency-room nurse appeared, leaning into the room. "Ellen, your son is back from X-ray."

"How is he?" she asked, rising.

"The doctor will give you a full report," she answered, and Ellen went to the door.

"No, wait." Bill looked up from his hands, his eyes red and his cheeks tear-stained. He gave a mighty sniffle. "I'm his father. Can I go in, too?"

Ellen turned to him. "If you don't mind, Bill, would

you not? It might upset him. I'll be sure to come out and tell you."

"He's all I have, now. For God's sake, I just lost my wife."

"This isn't about you or me. It's about Will."

"Timothy," Bill corrected, rising. He wiped his face with the back of his hand.

"Whatever his name, he needs comfort now. He needs me." Ellen watched as Bill's eyes hardened, even wet. "Please, be realistic. He doesn't know who you are yet. You're a stranger to him."

Officer Halbert stood up, too. "Mr. Braverman, she adopted him, and she's still his mother."

"She was never his real mother," Bill shot back, and Ellen swallowed hard, but the ER nurse raised an authoritative hand in Bill's direction.

"Sir, are you listed as next of kin on the intake form?"

"No."

"Well, Ms. Gleeson is. She's on the form as his mother, and only she can be admitted to the unit, per this hospital's regulations. You are not permitted back with us."

Ellen turned to go. "Bill, I'll ask someone to come out and tell you how he is," she said, following the nurse, who led her to the emergency-unit door, pressing in the code to unlock the door.

"What was that all about?" the nurse asked.

"It's a long story." Ellen only shook her head. "I just want to see if my son is all right."

Chapter 80

They reached Will's examining room, and Ellen felt a wave of déjà vu. Will lay under the covers, wearing a print hospital gown, looking tiny in the adult-size hospital bed. His head was bandaged with gauze, and he lay on the pillow with his eyes closed. Another nurse was putting up the guardrails of his bed, next to the ER doctor, a young man with rumpled hair who stopped writing on his clipboard to flash Ellen a reassuring grin.

"Don't worry, he's fine," the doctor said quickly, and she almost cheered with relief.

"What did the X-ray show?" Ellen went to the bed and held Will's hand, which felt oddly cool to the touch. His eyelids looked bluish, and she assumed that was okay, if scary.

"There's no fracture. Children's bones have a lot more give than adults, and it served your son well. The cut behind his ear is all stitched up."

"Thank God. How about his heart?"

"All good." The doctor looked sympathetic. "You've gotta get over that, Mom. He's fine now. Don't worry so much."

I'll get right on that.

"I'd like to admit him and keep an eye on him overnight."

"Sure, better to be on the safe side. I can stay, right?"

"Yes. We'll get him a room and put in a cot for you."

"Great." Ellen looked down at Will. "He's sleeping so soundly."

"I gave him a light sedative, and he'll rest until morning."

"Good, thanks." Ellen pulled up a chair. "You know, he saw terrible things tonight, people getting shot right in front of him, and in the next few weeks, there will be a major disruption in his life. Can you give me the name of some counselors that can help him?" Her throat went tight. "With the transition?"

"I'll have the social worker make some recommendations." The doctor moved away, touching her lightly on the shoulder. "Take care."

The nurse left with him, saying, "We'll let you know when we have a room for him."

"Good, thanks." Ellen turned to the other nurse. "Would you tell the man in the waiting room that he's okay?"

"All right, but only as favor to you. Don't like him, myself." She scuffed off, and Ellen took Will's hand.

His breathing was slightly congested, and his crusty nose bubbled away.

Ellen closed her eyes, to listen better.

The sound of him breathing.

It was the sweetest thing she had ever heard.

Chapter 81

Two hours later, Ellen cuddled Will in a private room, holding him close in the darkness while he slept and the TV played on mute, showing photos of Ellen's own house. DOUBLE HOMICIDE IN BABY DRAMA, said the red banner on the screen, and she read the closed captioning, its spelling occasionally funky:

> Police report that Narberf resident Ellen Gleeson was attacked in her home in an attempt to kill her and her baby, who she adopted but who was really Timothy Rravermark, a child kidnapped from wealthy Miami socialites . . .

Ellen looked away to the snow swirling outside the window. The hospital was quiet, and the only sound was the faint talking of the nurses down the hall. The door was partway closed, and she felt the world at bay. Snow inched up the panes, making a drift with an icy edge, thin as a knife. Steam heat fogged the glass, blurring the lights outside. She and Will had come full circle together, ending up in a hospital. She wondered how they could ever be separated, if that were even physically possible, but she'd insulate herself from thinking about that as long as she could, surely as the snow insulated the room, the hospital, and the world entire.

Somewhere out there was Marcelo, who had been trying to call her, but she couldn't take the call and had switched off the cell phone. Hospital signs read that cell phones interfered with the equipment, and she wanted to spend the time alone with Will.

She thought fleetingly of her father, still off in Italy, but she'd call him tomorrow when they got home. She wasn't sure when he was coming back. She had no idea how she'd tell him the news, which would crush him. She'd have him over to say good-bye to Will and she couldn't imagine that scene.

He's Will. He's ours.

She thought of Connie, too, and how upset she'd be. The babysitter loved Will and would feel his loss almost as acutely as Ellen would. There would be no see-ya-later-alligator, this time. She worried most of all about how Will would cope. He loved Connie, as surely as he loved her, and he would need help to deal with the trauma and the transition. The child had known, and lost, three mothers in three years. She would get one of those therapists that the doctor recommended as soon as she got him home.

Will stirred in her arms, breathing deeply, and Ellen gazed down at him, his bandaged head on her chest. Multicolored lights from the TV flashed across his face, mottling his features like a kaleidoscope, but she could make out the gentle hillock of his cheek, his cheekbone still buried under baby fat, the contours of his face yet to be formed by time. She tried not to think that she wouldn't know what Will would grow up to look like. Or how he'd do in school. Who his friends would be, or his wife. Or the minutiae, like if he'd always love cats or would dogs count, too? How would he dance at a party? What about later, when SATs came, and shaving, and college? What would he be when he grew up? All the stuff of a boy's life. Her boy's. Not her boy. Her boy no longer.

She held on to Will while a Bowflex commercial came on, and in time she drifted into an anguished sleep, wondering about the thousand other questions to which she would never know the answer.

And someday, wouldn't permit herself even to ask.

Chapter 82

Dawn came late, the sky dark until well after six, when the winter gloom lifted like a black velvet curtain, revealing yet another curtain, one of dark pewter. Ellen woke up slowly, still cuddling Will, and waited, lying in bed, listening to the hospital come slowly to life, with the nurses talking in low tones about the snowstorm, the skeleton crew, and the mom with the kidnapped baby in Room 302. Today, the reporter was the news.

"Mommy, when we get home, can we make a snowman?" Will asked, after the doctor had cleared them for discharge.

"We sure can." Ellen zipped his hoodie, and he was dressed to go, except for being shoeless. All he had on was a pair of blue cotton socks, stretched out of shape. "What was I thinking last night? I forgot your feet!"

Will giggled, looking down, so that their heads almost touched. "My feet are in my socks!"

"They are? Show me, just to make sure. Wiggle them for me."

"Look." Will's tiny toes popped around in their socks. "See, there they are. Under."

"What a relief. Whew. You know what that reminds me of?"

"What?"

"Of Oreo Figaro, when he's under the sheets. Remember how every time I make the bed, he gets under the new sheets and runs around?"

"He gets lost."

Ellen popped on his hood. "Right, he doesn't know how to get out, and we have to get him out."

Just then the nurse came in with the discharge papers on a clipboard. "Can you give me your John Hancock?" she asked, handing the clipboard to Ellen and smiling at Will. "How you doing?"

"I have my feet."

"Good." The nurse smiled. "You need your feet."

Ellen stuffed her purse under her arm, took the pen the nurse was offering, and scribbled her name. "Thanks."

"Just to give you a heads-up, there are reporters out front."

"Great." Ellen managed a smile for Will's sake, then turned to him. "Hear that, pal? You know what a reporter is, don't you?"

"*You're* a reporter!" Will pointed at her, smiling, and Ellen grabbed his finger and gave it a quick kiss.

"Right, and there'll be lots of people like me out front, only they might shout your name and take your picture. You ready for that?"

"Ready!"

"Good. Let's go home."

"I want to make a snowman!" Will shouted, and Ellen hushed him.

The nurse asked her, "Do you have a ride home?"

"I called a cab. I used my cell phone, so please don't throw me in hospital jail."

"Don't worry." The nurse waved her off. "If I were

you, I'd call the cab back and tell him to go to the emergency exit, not the main entrance. The security guard can give you the heads-up. His name is Mel."

"Good idea," Ellen said, grateful. "I'll stall in the gift shop."

"Gift shop!" Will cheered, and both women smiled.

"You know what that is?" the nurse asked him.

"Toys!"

Ellen picked Will up. "Thanks."

"Good luck," said the nurse, her eyes compassionate.

Ellen knew the nurses were feeling terrible for her, but she wasn't feeling terrible because she was still insulated. And she realized then that it wasn't the snow or the hospital that insulated her. It was Will himself. As long as she had him with her, she would keep it together, because she had to, for him. That was what it meant to be a mother.

"Let's go home, Mommy!" Will kicked his feet.

"First, say thank you to the nurse."

"Thank you," Will shouted, waving.

"You're very welcome," the nurse said, leaving.

"Thanks," Ellen said briefly, then carted Will out of the room and down the hall, where he waved and thanked the nurses, all of whom waved back with brave smiles.

"Bye, Willie!" the last one said, sitting at the desk nearest the elevator.

Will scowled. "That's *not* my name."

Ellen hit the button to go down. "Let's forgive her and go to the gift shop."

"Yay!" Will said, and the elevator came, the doors opening. "I want to push the button!"

"What do you say?" Ellen stepped inside, and Will twisted himself to lean down toward the button panel.

"Please!" he said, and the doors slid closed. When they opened again, Ellen stepped out of the cab and looked for a sign to the gift shop.

"There she is!" a man said, and she looked over, startled. People were rushing toward her, and she raised a hand.

"I have no comment, boys. Not now, not ever."

"We're not the press, Ms. Gleeson," the man said. "I'm Special Agent Manning from the FBI and this is Special Agent Orr."

Chapter 83

"Oh," Ellen said, surprised. She noticed for the first time that a few uniformed cops stood behind them, one of whom she recognized from last night. The young one. Something was wrong. Her mouth went dry.

"Mommy, where's the gift shop?"

"In a minute, sweetie." Ellen asked the first FBI agent, "What are you doing here?"

"Is this boy Will Gleeson?"

"Yes."

"We're here to take him into protective custody."

"What? Why?" Ellen was dumbfounded. "He doesn't need protecting. He's with me."

"As you know, he's Timothy Braverman, a child of Carol and William Braverman, kidnapped in Miami, and we're here to facilitate his return."

"What? Here? *Now?*" Ellen's arms tightened on Will. Her thoughts tumbled one over the other in confusion. She hadn't expected this, not yet. "He hasn't even eaten. He has no shoes. We have to go home."

"Ms. Gleeson, we are authorized to take the child. Here are the papers, you can take a look." Special Agent

Manning extended a packet of blue-backed paper folded in thirds, and Ellen glanced at the caption. The letters WARRANT and SEIZURE swam before her eyes. She found herself looking for an exit, but the only one lay ahead. The press clustered outside. Reporters watched them through the glass doors. Camera flashes fired like explosions. Ellen started to panic.

"Wait, listen, I know Bill Braverman. I was going to get his number from the police and set up a timetable that's best for Will."

"Ma'am, we're here at the request of Mr. Braverman. I'm sorry but, by law, you can't keep the child. We have to make certain that you don't abscond with him."

"We're going to the gift shop, Mommy!" Will said loudly, his voice trembling with new anxiety.

"I won't abscond with him, I promise. I know I have to make a transfer, but just not yet. Not this way. I wanted to explain it to him, and he hasn't even had breakfast, and my father—"

"Ms. Gleeson, we have to take him now. Please don't make this harder on the child than it already is." Special Agent Manning held out his hands, but Ellen stepped back with Will.

"I'm not giving him up this way. I'm still his mother. I have a lawyer. I would have called him last night, but I wanted to make sure Will wasn't hurt."

"I told you we'd have a problem," said a voice from behind the FBI agents, and Bill Braverman emerged from the back of the group, flanked by an older man in a suit. "I told you she'd try to run."

"I'm not trying to run!" Ellen shouted, shocked. "I just didn't think we'd be doing it this morning, right now. He just got out of the hospital. I need to talk to him, to prepare him—"

"Mommy, who are they?" Will asked, clutching her shoulder.

Bill pushed next to the FBI agents, his dark eyes cool and his expression hardened. He had on different clothes from last night, and he was all business. "I'm his father, and I have a legal right to him. Right now."

"We have to talk about it. The timing, I mean."

"No, we don't."

"Mommy, what?" Will started to cry.

"Bill, look at him, think of *him*," Ellen said, desperate. She couldn't believe this was happening. It was her against all of them. "This is the craziest way to do this. This is the worst possible thing for him."

"You mean for you," Bill shot back, and Ellen's heart pounded.

"He doesn't know what's going on. I have to explain it to him. I was going to call a therapist when we got home."

"I'll call a therapist. We have them in Miami, too. I'll take good care of him. He's mine." Bill advanced a step, but the man in the suit restrained him and turned to Ellen.

"Ms. Gleeson, I'm Mike Cusack and I'm representing Bill. You have no right to the child by law, and we have reason to believe you will leave the jurisdiction with him."

"I won't, I swear. I wasn't going anywhere but home."

"You tried to flee last night, didn't you? That's what you told the police."

"That was different." Ellen tried to think through the panic. "That was when I thought he was in danger, but not now."

"You didn't return him to the Bravermans after you knew he was Timothy. You intended to keep him."

Ellen felt accused and convicted, both at once. Everyone watched. The photographers outside fired away. "I wasn't sure what to do, I wasn't sure he was theirs and—"

"My client wants his child back, and the police are here to enforce his legal right. Please, don't be selfish. Do the right thing."

"Mommy?" Will sobbed. "Mommy!"

"Honey, it's all right." Ellen patted his leg, frantic inside. She turned to the FBI agents. "I'll turn him over, I promise, just not this minute. Come to my house. Follow me home. You'll see, I'm not going anywhere."

"We can't do that, Ms. Gleeson. We're here to take him, whether you cooperate or not. If you have a complaint, you can call—"

"Call who?" Ellen exploded, losing control. "I don't need to call! I'm going to give him up, later! I just want to make this orderly! He's a boy, a little boy!"

"Mommy, no!"

"I'm sorry, Ms. Gleeson." Special Agent Manning reached for Will, and the cops advanced behind the agents as if on cue.

Ellen shouted, "We're not doing it this way! Not this way!"

"Ms. Gleeson, please." Special Agent Manning grabbed Will by the shoulders and he screamed.

"Mommeeee!!"

"Don't touch him!" Ellen stepped back with him, but the elevator door was closed behind her. Will cried louder, and she whirled around holding him tight, looking for the emergency exit, but one of the FBI agents grabbed her elbow, and Special Agent Manning wrenched Will from her arms, "He's my son!" she screamed, suddenly empty-handed.

Will wailed louder. "MOMMEE!"

"We're moving, people!" Special Agent Manning called out, carrying a hysterical Will out toward the exit.

"No!" Ellen screamed, trying to grab Will's foot but coming away with his blue sock. "Will! It's all right!"

"MOMMEEEE!" Will's eyes widened with fright, and he reached for her over the FBI agent's shoulder, his bandaged head bobbing as they swept him through the entrance hall in a moving phalanx.

"WILL!" Ellen lunged after them, but two cops held her back as she torqued this way and that, then another cop joined them, and she fought them all while Officer Halbert tried to get her attention, his eyes sympathetic.

"Ms. Gleeson, please stay here. Please, stop. Don't make us arrest you."

"MOMMEE, COME!" Will screamed, before the hospital doors slid closed behind him and a thousand lightbulbs went off.

"Let me go, you bastards!" Ellen screamed, out of control. Will was gone, just like that, and it hit her. She couldn't stop screaming. She couldn't breathe. The room spun around, a blur of polished floors, shocked faces, camera flashes. She felt as if she were going crazy. She flailed out with the court papers, then her open hand. "They just can't take him, just like that! Just like that!"

"Ellen, no!" a man called out, and the next thing she knew, Marcelo appeared next to the cops, and she reached for him.

"Marcelo! They took Will! Call Ron Halpren! Call Ron!"

"Let her go!" Marcelo shoved the cops aside. "Are you guys insane? You're hurting her! I have her, I've got her now."

"She has to let the kid go!" one of the cops shouted.

"She did! What, are you trying to kill her?" Marcelo circled an arm around Ellen, and in one sure motion, ran her away from the cops and the entrance. She half stumbled and half sagged against him, her brain finally giving up and her heart taking over. There were too many tears to see anything clearly. There was no air to breathe.

"WILL!" She heard herself howl at the top of her lungs, a sound she'd never heard come out of her; it didn't even sound human, and she was going insane, she could tell by the stunned expression on the nurses walking by and an old man carrying a stack of morning newspapers and another woman so upset her hand flew to her mouth.

Ellen screamed again but Marcelo kept her from falling, and suddenly security guards in dark blue uniforms were running beside them and Marcelo said something to them, and they all ran down one shiny hallway then another until they hit doors and freezing air and a parking lot and a red-lighted sign that read EMERGENCY, and there was a maroon car with the engine running and another security guard sitting in the driver's seat.

Marcelo shoved her into the backseat and she landed screaming with her wet face and snotty nose against the cold leather seat and Marcelo threw himself in after her, holding her from behind as she fought and howled and choked and cried, and the car lurched finally off.

Chapter 84

When Ellen woke up, she was lying in her clothes in a bedroom she didn't recognize, and Marcelo was sitting at the end of the bed, holding on to her hand. Her head felt fuzzy and strange, her thoughts blank. The room was very dark. The wood blinds were closed, the walls covered with black-and-white photographs, and the dresser a lacquered black, under a mirror of onyx.

Marcelo focused on her, a tiny buckle creasing his forehead. His expression looked strained, the corners of his lips turned down. He had on an open white shirt, and the edges of his body blurred in the darkness.

"You awake?" he asked softly.

"What time is it?"

Marcelo's gaze shifted to his left, then back again, presumably to check a bedside clock. "Seven thirty at night. You've been asleep since this morning."

Ellen tried to understand. "I slept the whole day?"

"You needed to."

"Where am I? I feel funny."

"You're at my house, and you took a Valium."

"I did?" Ellen didn't remember.

"Yes, you were so . . . upset. I offered one to you, and you said yes. I drug my women only with their consent."

"Why do you have Valium?"

"An old girlfriend. The relationship expired, but the pills didn't." Marcelo smiled, and Ellen sensed from under her pharmaceutical cloud that he was trying to cheer her up. She didn't dare rewind the day's events to remember why she was here. She knew, but she didn't want to know. She had traded in one insulation for another.

"Why did you bring me here and not home?"

"Your house was a crime scene."

Of course.

"Though it's since been released. Also, there was press out front."

"Who did we send?"

"Sal."

Ellen lifted an eyebrow.

"Who better?"

"Make him tell it right, Marcelo. Tell it true, all of it. I'm fine with it."

"Good."

"Just so it's not Sarah." Ellen felt bitterness even through her drug haze. "She's the one who called the Bravermans, you know, for the reward."

"I heard from the police." Marcelo's smile vanished. "Which would probably explain why she quit the other day."

"She did?"

"Walked in and quit, packed up her desk, and left. No notice, nothing."

"Did she say she didn't need it, because she's rich now? She won the lottery."

"No, she said I was the worst editor in the country and I was just"—Marcelo paused a minute, smiling—"a pretty boy."

"She said that?"

"It's not that funny. I am pretty." Marcelo stroked Ellen's cheek, and she started to feel something, which worried her. She didn't welcome any emotions right now, even good ones.

"Do you have another pill?"

"Yes, but I don't think you should take it yet. Your lawyer's here."

"Lawyer?"

"Ron. You asked me to call him, and he came over at the end of the day."

"He's here?" Ellen started to get up, but Marcelo gentled her back down.

"Stay put. I'll have him come up." He rose and left the room, and Ellen lay still, trying to maintain an equilibrium. It wasn't time for emotion, but action. Maybe there was still something that could be done. In the next minute, footsteps scuffed on the stair and Marcelo came back into the room, followed by Ron Halpren, in a dark suit and tie.

"Hi, Ron," Ellen said, to show that she was a functioning human being. "Please don't say anything nice or I'll lose it."

"Fair enough." Ron sat down on the bed, his beard grizzled and his crinkly eyes soft.

"Also don't look at me like that."

Ron chuckled, sadly. "Okay, I'll be the lawyer, not the friend. I heard what happened, I read the papers."

"Papers?"

"The court papers they gave you at the hospital," Marcelo said, standing behind Ron, his arms folded.

Ellen thought back. Whatever. "So is there anything I can do?"

Ron hesitated. "Nothing."

Ellen tried to stay in control. "I mean, just about the timing."

"What about it?"

"It's so . . . soon. Abrupt. He has clothes at home, and toys, and books, and DVDs, and a cat." Ellen stopped herself. Will would miss Oreo Figaro. Maybe she could get the cat to him. "Why can't we ease the transition? And for his benefit, not mine." She was remembering what they'd said at the hospital.

"It doesn't work that way, at least not with Braverman. I spoke with Mike Cusack, a big gun at Morgan, Lewis. I gather Mr. Braverman has some dough."

"Yes."

"Well, he got out the heavy artillery, and as a legal matter, you can make a transition, as you say, only if they agree, and they're not agreeing. They don't trust you or the situation."

"It's not about me."

"I know that, and you should hold on to that thought. It's not personal." Ron patted her hand. "Braverman has to go home and bury his wife, and his lawyer says that he wants to start over. Pick up the pieces."

Ellen's heart sank. "I can see that, but what if that's not what's best for Will? Sending Will into a funeral, his father a grieving widower, right off the bat? He'll freak."

"You're talking best interests again, and remember, that's not the law. It's a power notion. Braverman has absolute power and he's wielding it." Ron's gaze rested on hers. "I think you need to pick up the pieces, too. You need to understand that Will will be loved and very well cared for. They already contacted a pediatrician and a therapist specializing in young children."

Ellen felt tears fighting to surface, but held them back. Will would have medical experts, but no mother. She couldn't even say the words.

"In time, he'll be fine."

"He's not property, to be delivered. He's a child, with feelings."

"Kids are resilient."

"I hate when people say that," Ellen shot back, more harshly than she intended. "It's like we'll all pretend that the kid's feelings don't matter, because they get in the way. But you know what happens, Ron? Kids swallow the hurt, and sooner or later, it comes out. One way or the other, the hurt comes out. And you know who gets hurt then? Not the adults. The kid. *Will.* Someday he'll be hurting and he won't even know why." Ellen gave a little hiccup and covered her mouth, holding back a sob. "He lost a mother at a year old. Now he's losing another. Can't we be a little sensitive? Is it so much to ask?"

"We have no choice, and he will be fine, in the end." Ron patted her hand, then squeezed it, as Marcelo left the bedroom for a minute, then came back with a glass of water.

"Have another pill," he said, offering her the tablet in his open palm, and Ellen raised herself, popped the Valium, and drank the water like she lived on the Sahara.

"Ron, can I call Will? Can I talk to him at least?"

"No."

"You're kidding."

"No." Ron shook his head. "They think a clean break is best."

"For who? Them or him? They accused me of being selfish, but they're the ones who're selfish."

"I hear you, but there's nothing we can do."

Ellen hoped the pill worked fast. "Where is he now, do you think?"

"Will? In the city, still. They'll be in town until the coroner releases Carol Braverman's body."

Ellen felt a pang. "When will that be?"

"A couple of days."

"So knowing Bill, they're at the Ritz or the Four Seasons. I say the Ritz."

"I say the Four Seasons," Marcelo said, but Ron frowned.

"Don't even think about it, either of you. Cusack told me if you try to see Will, they'll take out a restraining order."

Marcelo frowned. "These people, they're cruel beyond belief."

"There it is." Ron shrugged. "Cusack said, and I believe him, that this guy is just trying to protect his kid."

"From me?"

"Yes."

Ellen tried to process it. "I really can't call Will?"

"No. Their child therapist said it would be confusing for him and prevent his bonding with his father again."

"An expert said that?"

"You can find an expert to say anything."

"Then we should find our own expert."

Ron shook his head. "No, there's no trial here, and no judge. They won. They win. On the good-news front, I asked if they'd give you an update on his condition, physical and emotional, next week, and they agreed."

"Big of them." Ellen felt anger flare up, muted by the drug.

"We'll take what we can get and go from there."

"They need to know his medical history. They didn't even know that. I have his records."

"I'm sure we can send it to them or his pediatrician."

Ellen slumped back into the pillow, trying not to hit somebody. Or cry. Or scream. Or turn back time, to the day she read that awful white card in the mail.

"Try to rest, Ellen. You know what Shakespeare says. 'Sleep knits up the ravell'd sleave of care.' "

"Shakespeare was never a mother."

Ron rose. "Call me if you have any questions. Hang in there. I'll be thinking of you. So will Louisa."

"Thanks." Ellen watched Ron go to the door, followed by Marcelo, and she called out after them, "Ron, thanks for not saying, I told you so."

Ron didn't answer and they walked down the steps, the footsteps scuffling again, and in time, Marcelo came back upstairs with another drink.

"Please tell me that's whiskey."

"Coke."

"Or not." Ellen raised herself and took a sip, tasting the sweetness.

"Are you hungry?"

"No." Ellen gave him the glass and lay back down, her head mercifully fuzzy again. Thoughts of Connie and her father popped through the oncoming clouds. "I have to tell the babysitter what happened."

"She probably knows. It's all over the TV."

"She'll be so upset." Ellen felt a deep twinge. "She shouldn't have to find out that way."

"I'll take care of everything." Marcelo put the glass on the night table. "I don't want you to worry about it. What's her phone number?"

"It's in my phone, in my purse. Her name is Connie. Also my father needs to know. He's in Italy. Getting married."

Marcelo frowned. "When does he get home?"

"I forget."

"It'll wait, then."

"I need to feed the cat."

"Let it go. Time to rest." Marcelo squeezed her arm.

"Thank you for being so nice."

"Ron's right, you have to pick up the pieces. I'll help."

"You don't have to."

"I want to. I'm privileged to." Marcelo stroked her arm, and Ellen felt her body relax.

"Am I staying here tonight?"

"Yes."

"Where are you sleeping?"

"You tell me. I do have a spare room, but I'd like to stay here with you."

Ellen's head started to fog. "Is this a date?"

"We're beyond dates."

Ellen closed her eyes. She liked Marcelo's voice, nice and deep, and the accent that made his words sibilant, his speech more like a purr than words. "But what about work? I mean, you're my editor."

"We'll figure it out."

"You were so worried about that, before."

"Let's just say that since then, I've gotten a better perspective."

And whether Marcelo kissed Ellen on the cheek or she just dreamed it, she couldn't tell.

Chapter 85

Ellen woke up, and the bedroom was still dark. She was lying on top of the comforter in her clothes, and Marcelo was spooning her, fully clothed, his arm hooked over her waist. The bedside clock glowed 3:46 A.M., and she waited for sleep to return, but it was as if a switch had been thrown in her brain. A light seared through the dark room of her mind, illuminating every corner, flooding every crack in the plaster, filling the grain in the floorboards, setting even the dust motes ablaze.

Will is gone.

Ellen imagined him in a hotel. He'd be wondering where she was, what had happened, why he wasn't home, why he wasn't with his cat, why he wasn't going to school. Bill would be calling him Timothy and smiling in his face, and there would be lawyers and pediatricians and shrinks, but there would be no mother. His world had been turned upside down and stood on its head. He'd gone from life with a single mother and no father, to a life with a single father and no mother, like the negative to his positive, his existence in obverse.

He's just a little boy.

Ellen knew what she had to do next, or tears would flow and engulf her. She plucked Marcelo's hand from her hip, edged toward the side of the bed, and rolled out as quietly as she could. She padded downstairs in the dark, running her fingertips along the rough brick wall to guide her way. Her feet hit the floor, and she crossed the room to the glass coffee table, where a black laptop sat with its lid open. She hit a key, and the screensaver appeared, a color photograph of an old wood fishing boat at ebb tide, its orange paint weathered and peeling, with a tangle of worn netting mounded from its bow, in a twilight sun.

She opened Microsoft Word and pressed a key, so that a bright white page popped onto the screen, then slid the laptop around and sat down on the couch, pausing a second before she began. The title came easily.

Losing Will

She stopped a minute, looking at it in black and white, the faux newsprint making it real. She swallowed hard, then set her feelings aside. She had to do this for her job. And for Marcelo. And mostly, for herself. Writing had always helped her, before. It always clarified her feelings and her thoughts, and she never felt like she could understand something fully until the very minute that she'd written about it, as if each story was one she told herself and her readers, at the same time. In fact, it was writing that began her relationship to Will, and she found herself coming full circle again, so she began:

Last week, I was asked to write a story about what it feels like to lose a child. We were concerned that, among all of the statistics and bar graphs attending an article about the city's escalating homicide rate, the value of a child's life would be lost.

So I set out to interview women who had lost children.

I spoke with Laticia Williams, whose eight-year-old son Lateef was killed by stray bullets, a victim of violence between two gangs. I also spoke with Susan Sulaman, a Bryn Mawr mother whose two children were abducted by their father several years ago.

And now, to their examples, I can add my own.

As you may know, I lost my son this week when I learned that, unbeknownst to me, my adoption of him was illegal. My son is, in fact, a child by the name of Timothy Braverman, who was kidnapped from a Florida couple two years ago.

I hope you don't think I'm being presumptuous in inserting my own experience into this account. I know that my child is alive, unlike Laticia Williams. But forgive me if I suggest that how you lose a child doesn't alter the fact that, in the end, he is lost to you. Whether you lose him by murder, abduction, or a simple twist of fate, you end up in the same place.

Your child is gone.

What does it feel like?

To Laticia Williams, it feels like anger. A rage like a fire that consumes everything in its path. She feels angry every minute she spends without her child. Angry every night she doesn't put him to bed. Angry every morning that she doesn't pack him his favorite peanut-butter-and-banana sandwich and walk him to school. In her neighborhood, all the mothers walk their kids to school, to make sure they get there alive.

Of course, that the children remain alive after they get home is not guaranteed.

Her son "Teef" was shot in his own living room,

while he was watching TV, by bullets that flew in through a window to find their lethal marks in his young cheek. The funeral director who prepared Lateef's body for burial took all night to restore the child's face. His teacher said he was the class clown, a leader among his classmates, who stuffed his desk with posthumous Valentines.

To Susan Sulaman, losing a child feels like emptiness. A profound vacancy in her heart and her life. Because her children are alive with their father, or so she assumes, she looks for them everywhere she goes. At night, she drives around neighborhoods where they might live, hoping for a chance sighting. In the daytime, she scans the small faces on school buses that speed past.

Susan Sulaman is haunted by her loss.

I asked her if she felt better knowing that at least the children were in their father's hands. Her answer?

"No. I'm their mother. They need me."

I know just how she feels, and Laticia, too. I'm angry, I feel haunted, and it's still fresh. It's so new, a wound still bleeding, the flesh torn apart, the gash swollen and puffy, yet to be sewn together or grafted, years from scar tissue, bumpy and hard.

Losing Will feels like a death.

My mother died recently, and it feels a lot like that. Suddenly, someone who was at the center of your life is gone, excised as quickly as an apple is cored, a sharp spike driven down the center of your world, then a cruel flick of the wrist and the almost surgical extraction of your very heart.

And like a death, it does not end the relationship. I am still the daughter of my mother, though she is gone. And I am still the mother of Will Gleeson, though he is gone, too.

I have learned that the love a mother has for her child is unique among human emotions. Every mother knows this instinctively, but that doesn't mean it doesn't need articulating.

And it remains true, whether the child is adopted or not. That, I didn't know before, but I've learned it now. Just as it doesn't matter how you lose your child, it doesn't matter how you find him, either. There's a certain symmetry in that, but it's no comfort now.

I didn't give birth to Will, but I am tied to him as surely as if we shared blood. I am his real mother.

It's the love, that binds.

I fell in love with Will the moment I saw him in a hospital ward, with tubes taped under his nose to hold them in place, fighting for his life. From that day forward, he was mine.

And though, as his mother, I certainly felt tired at times, I never tired of looking at him. I never tired of watching him eat. I never tired of hearing the sound of his voice or the words he made up, like the name of our cat. I never tired of seeing him play with Legos.

I *did* tire of stepping on them in bare feet.

It's hard to compare loves, and it may be silly to try, but I have learned something from my experience in losing Will. Because I have loved before, certainly. I have loved men before, and I might even be falling in love with a man now.

Here is how a mother's love is different:

You may fall out of love with a man.

But you will never fall out of love with your child.

Even after he is gone.

Ellen sat back and read the last line again, but it began to blur, and she knew why.

"Ellen?" Marcelo asked softly, coming down the stairs.

"I finished my piece." She wiped her eyes with her hand, but Marcelo crossed to her through the darkness, his mouth a concerned shadow in the glow of the screen. He reached for her hand.

"Let's go lie down," he whispered, pulling her gently to her feet.

Chapter 86

The next morning dawned clear, and Ellen rode in the passenger seat of Marcelo's car, looking out the window, squinting against the brightness of the sun on the new-fallen snow. Its top layer had hardened in the cold, and the crust took on a smooth sheen. The streets on the way to her house had been plowed, leaving waist-high wedges beside the parked cars.

They turned a corner, and a trio of kids in snowsuits and scarves played on the mounds. One child, a girl named Jenny Waters, was from Will's class, and Ellen looked away, pained. They left Montgomery Avenue, and she noticed how the landscape had changed with the snow. It made unrecognizable blobs of shrubs, lay like a mattress on the roofs of parked cars, and lined the length of barren tree branches, doubling their thickness. Everything familiar had changed, and she tried not to see it as a bad metaphor.

Last night after she'd finished her piece, she'd fallen back to only a restless sleep and felt raw and nervous inside. A morning shower had helped, and she'd changed her top, slipping into an old gray sweater of Marcelo's.

Her hair was still wet, falling loose to her shoulders, and she didn't bother with any makeup. She took it as a measure of confidence in her new relationship, and she didn't want to see her own face in the mirror, anyway.

"I should call my father," Ellen said, mentally switching topics.

"Your phone's in your purse. I charged it for you."

"Thanks. I feel bad that I didn't call Connie, either. She's probably at a football game today. She loves Penn State."

"She called you, and I spoke to her. She's meeting us at your house. I hope that's okay with you. She thought it would be."

"It is, sure." Ellen felt her heart gladden. "How is she? Is she okay?"

"She's very upset, but I think it will do you good to see her." Marcelo swung the car onto her street, and Ellen swallowed hard as she looked at her house. Newsvans parked in every available space, with microwave towers that pierced the blue sky. Reporters with videocameras mobbed her sidewalk.

Ellen said, "I hate the press."

"Me, too." Marcelo's gaze shifted to her, worried. "Would you like me to go around the block, one time?"

"No, let's do it." Ellen pulled her coat closer around her.

"Looks like national, too, and TV." Marcelo craned his neck, slowing the car as they neared the house. "I'll let you read Sal's piece before we file."

"You filing this afternoon, by two?"

"It can wait. I'll email it to you."

"Thanks." Ellen knew he was pushing the deadline for her. "Are you coming in?"

"If you would like. I'm happy to meet Connie."

"Come in and meet her, then I think I'll be okay." They approached the house, and to Ellen's surprise, her neighbor Mrs. Knox was out front, ignoring the reporters and shoveling her walk for her. The sight gave her a sudden pang, of guilt and gratitude. Maybe she wasn't such a busy-body, after all.

"Here we go." Marcelo pulled up, double-parked, and hit the emergency lights. "We'll have to do this fast."

"Okay." Ellen grabbed her purse, and they both opened the doors and jumped out. She hustled around the front of the car, almost slipping on the snow, and Marcelo took her arm and they hurried together to her front walk. The reporters surged toward them almost as one, brandishing microphones, aiming videocameras, and shouting questions.

"Ellen, when did you know he was Timothy Braverman?" "Ellen, were you gonna give him back?" "Marcelo!" "Hey, El, how did the FBI find out who your son was?" "Ellen, aren't you gonna make a statement? Marcelo, give us a break! You're one of us!"

Ellen hurried up her walk with Marcelo right behind her, keeping the press at bay. She hustled to the porch steps, spraying snow, and crossed to the front door, which Connie opened for her.

"Connie!" she cried, more in anguish than in greeting, and the women fell into each other's arms.

Chapter 87

After Marcelo had gone home, Ellen sat with Connie in the living room, telling her everything while they shared a box of tissues, and they cried all over again when they came to the same awful conclusion, that Will was gone from both their lives.

"I can't believe this happened." Connie mopped up her eyes with a Kleenex, her voice raspy. "It's unreal."

"I know." Ellen kept stroking Oreo Figaro, who sat in a silky ball on her lap.

"I hope you don't mind, but I got here early and I went up to his room. I looked around at all the stuff, all his toys, all his books." Connie sighed, her chest heaving in her sweatshirt. "I put his books away, force of habit, and I closed his door. I didn't think you'd want to go in. Is that okay?"

"It's all okay. Anything you do is okay."

Connie smiled sadly, her ponytail on her shoulder. "I should've read to him more. I didn't read to him enough."

"You read to him plenty."

"You thought I should read to him more." Connie

looked at her directly, cocking her head, her eyes glistening. "You used to think that, didn't you?"

"You were the best babysitter I could have ever asked for."

"Really?" Connie asked, her voice breaking, and she dabbed at fresh tears.

"Really. You can't imagine how grateful I am to you. I could never have done my job without you, and I needed to do my job. For Will and for me."

"Thanks for saying that."

"I should have said it before, a thousand times. It's true." Ellen scratched behind Oreo Figaro's ear, and he began to purr happily, his chest thrumming against the palm of her hand. "You know, I used to be a little jealous."

"Of what?"

"Of you, of your time with Will. Of how close you were. I used to not like it that you loved him, and he loved you. It threatened me."

Connie remained silent, inclining her head, listening. The sun coming through the living room windows was too bright to bear, and Ellen didn't really understand what was powering her confession. But it didn't matter why she said it, only that it needed saying, so she continued.

"I'm sorry about that, because now I know better. The more people who loved that boy, the better. We loved him up, really, between the two of us." Ellen felt her eyes fill again, but blinked them clear. "I used to think that kids were like a glass or something, that they'd break if you poured too much love into them. But they're like the ocean. You can fill them up with love, and just when you think you've reached the brim, you can keep on pouring."

Connie sniffled. "Agree, but here's the thing. Will may have loved me, but he always knew who his mother was. He knew the difference between you and me, and he never forgot it."

"You think?" Ellen asked, though the words only hurt more now that he was gone.

"I know. I've sat for kids all my life, and take it from me, the kids always know who Mom is. Always."

"Thanks." Ellen set the cat aside on the couch and rose slowly, on joints that seemed suddenly stiff. "Well, I guess I have to go see what the kitchen looks like."

"No, you don't." Connie wiped her eyes with finality. "I went in there. It made me sick to see it, and it'll make you even sicker."

"I have to live here. I thought about moving, but no way." Ellen walked into the dining room, which was still in disarray. She flashed on Carol on the floor next to her, the two of them looking up at Rob Moore, standing behind the muzzle of his gun.

"I know it's not a crime scene anymore. But I didn't know whether to put the chairs in order or not."

"I will." Ellen picked up a chair from the floor and slid it noisily into place under the table, then did the same to the other, feeling the beginning of an odd sort of satisfaction. Maybe this was what everybody meant by picking up the pieces. She took a deep breath, braced herself, and headed for the kitchen threshold. "Let's see how bad it is."

"Right behind you," Connie said, and they both stood together, eyeing the kitchen.

My God.

Ellen supported herself against the doorjamb, scanning the scene. A large, shiny pool of black-red blood had dried into the floorboards, filling the grain and knots in the hardwood, making a macabre drawing etched in ink. It must have been where Carol had died.

"Disgusting, huh?" Connie asked, and Ellen nodded, her chest tight. She flashed on poor Carol, her arms raised protectively, then chased that thought away.

Across the room, near the back door, lay another island

of blood, smaller but just as nauseating, where Moore must have fallen. The stink of gasoline hung in the air, and a dozen yellow spots stained the floor where the solvent had splattered. She squeezed her eyes shut against an instant replay of Will's mouth taped shut, his snowsuit drenched with gasoline.

"I told you it was bad."

"It's worse than bad." Ellen bit her lip, thinking. "Do you think I can scrub the blood out?"

"No, and I swear I smell it."

"There's only one solution."

"Cover it with a rug?"

"No." Ellen crossed to the window and opened it, then fumbled around for the metal slides and threw open the storm windows, letting in a blast of fresh, snowy air that somehow felt cleansing. "I'm going to rip up the whole damn floor."

"You mean do it yourself?" Connie smiled, surprised.

"Sure. How hard can it be? It's just destruction. Any idiot can destroy something." Ellen went to the base cabinet, found her orange plastic toolbox, and set it out on top of the stove, trying not to notice that one burner was missing. She opened the toolbox and took out her hammer. "I'm no contractor, but the sharp end looks like it could do the trick. If I start now, I can get it done by tonight."

"You want to do it *now*?"

"Why not? One way or the other, this floor is getting thrown away. I don't want it in my house another minute." Ellen took a gulp of fresh air, wielded the hammer, and bent down over one of the gasoline stains. She raised the hammer high over her head and brought its sharp end down with all her might.

Crack! The edge of the hammer splintered the wood, but unfortunately embedded itself there.

"Oops." Ellen yanked on the handle of the hammer,

and its head came free, splintering the wood. "Looks like it works, but at this rate, I'll be finished by next year."

"I have a better idea." Connie stepped around her, opened the door to the basement, and went downstairs, and by the time she returned, Ellen had destroyed only part of a single floorboard. She looked up to see Connie hoisting a crowbar like the Statue of Liberty on *This Old House*.

"Way to go!" Ellen said. "I didn't even know I had one of those. Thanks." She rose, delighted, and reached for the crowbar, but Connie held it tight.

"I'll use this. You use the hammer. We'll get this done together. It'll go twice as fast, and besides, I wanna destroy something, too."

"Isn't there a football game?" Ellen asked, touched.

"No matter." Connie got down on her hands and knees, then wedged the end of the crowbar underneath the splintered floor. "Mark will have to win without me this time."

Tears came to Ellen's eyes, and she didn't know what to say. For once, she didn't say anything. She got back down on her hands and knees, raised her hammer, and the two women worked together for the next several hours, grimly destroying the evidence of a nightmare, with the only tools they had on hand.

A hammer, a crowbar, and the human heart.

Chapter 88

After Connie had gone home, Ellen piled the last of the broken floorboards on her back porch because reporters were still camped out front. She stepped back inside the kitchen, shut the door against the cold, and closed the window, breathing in deeply. The gasoline smell was gone, but the subfloor was a mess. Removing the top boards had only exposed the older floor beneath, and she hadn't been able to pull out all the nails. They popped up here and there, making an obstacle course for Oreo Figaro, who walked gingerly to his food dish.

Ellen crossed to the refrigerator, careful not to step on a nail or a cat, and opened the door. She was about to reach for a bottle of water when her hand stopped in midair. Staring her in the face was the Pyrex bowl of lime green Jell-O, with a shiny cavern dug in the middle.

It's good, Mommy!

She grabbed the water bottle and slammed the door closed, determined to get through the rest of the day. The house had fallen quiet, a hollow echo of how she felt. She checked the clock on the wall—2:25. Odd that Marcelo hadn't called, and she had yet to call her father. She left the room with the water, twisted off the cap, and took a slug, then went into the living room, hearing only the sound of her footsteps on the floor. She found her purse and dug inside for her BlackBerry, but it wasn't there. She must've dropped it in Marcelo's car.

She looked up, aggravated, and through the windows she could see a commotion on the sidewalk. Reporters and photographers clustered around a taxi pulling up in front of the house, and in the next second, emerging from the crowd was her father.

Dad?

Ellen ran to the door as he waved off the press, taking the arm of an attractive woman in a chic white wool coat, probably his new wife, whose name Ellen had almost forgotten.

"Honey, what the hell?" her father asked, stepping inside, his hazel eyes round with disbelief. He stamped snow from his loafers. "This is crazy!"

"I know, it's awful." Ellen introduced herself and extended her hand to his wife. "Barbara, right?"

"Hello, Ellen." Barbara smiled with genuine warmth, her lipstick fresh and her teeth white and even. She was petite with smallish features, tasteful makeup, and highlighted hair coiffed to her chin. "Sorry we have to meet in these circumstances."

"Why didn't you call?" her father interrupted. "Thank God for the Internet, or we wouldn't have known a damn thing."

"It just got so crazy, all of it."

"We're in the hotel, and I went online to check the scores, and there's my daughter's picture and my grandson's gone! We got on the next plane."

"Why don't you go sit down, and I'll explain everything." Ellen gestured them toward the couch, but her father waved her off, agitated and acting oddly like a much older man.

"We came straight from the airport. I've been calling your cell."

"Sorry, I left it in a car." Ellen had to catch them up but she wasn't going to begin with Marcelo. "It's been difficult, Dad."

"I can imagine," Barbara said with obvious concern, but her father was distracted to the point of disorientation.

"So where's Will?" He looked around the living room, his head wobbling slightly. "Is he really not here?"

"He's really not here." Ellen stayed calm, only because he was so upset. She'd never seen him so shaken, so out of control.

"That can't be. Do the cops have him or what?"

"He's with his father, and they're already talking to shrinks and pediatricians, so I'm praying he'll be okay."

"Where is he? Where'd they take him?"

"He's in a hotel in town."

"I want to see him." Her father set his jaw, the soft jowls bracketing his mouth like a bulldog's.

"We can't, Dad."

"What do you mean, we can't?" Her father's eyes flared. "He's my only grandchild. He's my *grandson*."

"If we try to see him, they'll get a restraining order. I'm hoping that if we work with them, then we can—"

"That can't be legal! Grandparents have rights!" Her father's face reddened with emotion. "I'm calling a lawyer. I won't put up with this. Nobody takes my grandchild away from me!"

"I have a lawyer, Dad. He says what they're doing is legal."

"Then you didn't get yourself a good enough mouth-piece." Her father jabbed his finger toward her chest, but Barbara put her hand on his jacket sleeve.

"Don, don't yell at her. We talked about this. You know what she's been through."

"But they can't take him away!" Her father threw up his hands, his expression caught between bewilderment and pain. "I go away for one minute and when I come home, my grandson is gone? How can this be legal?"

"Dad, relax." Ellen stepped forward. "Sit down, have a cup of coffee, and I'll tell you the story. You'll understand the situation better."

"I understand the situation just fine!" Her father whirled around, his finger pointing again. "I remember when you came to see me, you thought that kid in the picture was Will. So I got it wrong. Ya happy, now?"

"What?" Ellen asked, stricken.

"Don!" Barbara shouted, so loudly that he stood stunned for a moment. "Shut up. Right now." She faced him head-on, despite her tiny frame. "I can't believe what I'm seeing. I can't believe this is the man I just married. I know you're a better man than this."

"Wha?" her father said, but accusation had left his tone.

"This isn't about you, or even Will." Barbara raised a manicured hand. "This is about your daughter, your only daughter. Start focusing on the child you have, instead of the one you don't."

"But she shouldn'ta said anything. She shoulda just shut up!"

Ellen felt slapped, and Barbara's mouth dropped open.

"Don, she did what any good mother would do. She did what was right for her child, even though it cost her."

Ellen recovered, listening. Barbara had given the clearest and best statement of why she'd followed up on that damn white card. She'd never thought of it exactly that way.

Her father's gaze shifted from Barbara to Ellen, suddenly very sad. He raked his thin hair with trembling fingers. "I'm sorry, El. I didn't mean it."

"I know, Dad."

"It's just that Will was my . . . chance."

"What do you mean?" Ellen asked, mystified, and tears came to her father's eyes. The only other time she'd seen him cry was at her mother's funeral, and the sight caught her by the throat.

"He was my chance, El. My second chance."

Ellen touched his arm, sensing what he'd say before he said it. She gave him a big hug, and he eased into her arms, with a little moan.

"Everything I did wrong with you, I was gonna do right with him. I wanted to make it up to you. To your mother."

Ellen thought her heart would break, and in the next minute, her eyes brimmed with tears, and she found herself crying like a baby in her father's arms.

"I'm so sorry, honey," he whispered as Ellen sobbed and breathed in his expensive aftershave, and she drew real comfort from his embrace in a way she never had before. The deepest pain in her heart eased just a little, and she let herself feel how very powerful is something so simple, yet so profound, as a father's love.

And she thanked God he was alive.

Chapter 89

It wasn't until they had gone and Ellen was rinsing their coffee mugs that the phone rang in the kitchen. She turned off the faucet, crossed the room, and checked caller ID, which showed the newspaper's main number. She picked up. "Hello?"

"Ellen?" Marcelo asked, worried. "Are you okay? I've been calling your cell."

"I think I left it in your car. I was going to call you, but my father and my new stepmother just left."

"How are you?"

"Good, okay." Ellen glanced over and saw that the Coffmans still weren't home, their house dark. "You probably want me to look at that story, huh?

"Only if you feel up to it."

"I'm not sure."

"Then let it go. I loved what you wrote for the homicide piece."

"Good, thanks." Ellen felt a warmth she couldn't deny.

"I'll be done here around nine. Happily, there's news besides you."

"You'd never know it from the crowd outside."

"Would you like company tonight? I don't think you should be alone."

"I'd like that."

"I'll be there." Marcelo's voice softened. "Take care of yourself, 'til then."

"See you." Ellen hung up and left the kitchen by the other exit, feeling an odd sensation when she reached the upstairs landing. It was exactly the spot where Carol had set Will down, before she'd made her final stand.

Ellen felt a tightness in her chest, then forced herself to step over the spot and climb the stairs. She caught a glimpse of the scene outside on the sidewalk, and the reporters were still there, smoking cigarettes and holding cups of take-out coffee against the cold. The afternoon sky spent its last hour before twilight descended, dropping purple and rose streaks behind the cedar shakes and satellite dishes, a suburban night in winter.

Ellen's clogs clattered on the wooden stair, echoing in the silent house, and she wondered how long she'd go on noticing every noise that she'd never noticed before. She lived in a house of echoes now. She'd have to exchange her clogs for slippers if she wanted to keep her sanity.

She reached the top of the stair, which ended in front of Will's room, and faced his door, which was closed. Not that it helped. Butterfly stickers, scribbled drawings, and a WILL'S ROOM license plate covered the door, and Ellen reached almost reflexively for the doorknob, then wondered if she should go in.

"Mrrp?" Oreo Figaro chirped, rubbing against her jeans, his tail curled around her leg.

"Don't ask," she told him, twisting the doorknob. She opened the door, and the Cheerios-and-Play-Doh smell caught her by the throat. She willed herself not to cry, and her gaze traveled around the room, dark except for the white rectangle of the window shade, bright from the snow and the TV klieg lights outside. She didn't know how long she stood there, but it was long enough for the daylight to leak away, so stuffed animals dematerialized into shadowy blobs and the spines of books thinned to straight black lines. Stars glowed faintly from the ceiling, and the WILL constellation took her back in time, to the countless nights she'd held him before bed, reading to him, talking or just listening to his adorable up-and-down cadence, the music of his stories from school or swimming, told in his little-boy register, like the sweetest of piccolos.

She watched almost numbly as Oreo Figaro leapt noiselessly to the foot of Will's bed, where he always slept, curled next to a floppy stuffed bunny whose ears were silhouetted in the light from the window shade. Will had gotten that bunny at a party that Courtney had thrown for her at work, when she adopted him. Sarah Liu had given it to him.

Anger flickered in Ellen's chest. Sarah, who was supposed to be her colleague. Sarah, who would later sell both of them out, for money. Sarah, who stole from her the choice about when or whether to give Will up. He could be here right now, home where he belonged, cuddled up with his cat, instead of in a strange hotel room, lost and confused, in all kinds of pain, going home to a house without a mother.

"You bitch!" Ellen heard herself shout. In one movement, she lunged into the room, grabbed the stuffed bunny, and hurled it into the bookshelves, where it hit a toy car. Oreo Figaro leapt from the bed, startled.

Anger flamed in Ellen's chest, and she hurried from the room.

On fire.

Chapter 90

Ellen stood on the snowy brick doorstep and knocked on the front door of the gorgeous Dutch Colonial. The ride to Radnor hadn't dissipated her anger, even with newsvans trailing her, and she knocked again on the door, drenched in the calcium white light of the klieg lights. Reporters recorded her every movement, but she didn't care. They were doing their job, and she was doing hers.

"Hello?" Sarah opened the front door, and her dark eyes flared in alarm. She shielded her eyes from the klieg lights with a raised hand. "What are you doing here?"

"Let me in. We're on TV, girlfriend."

"You have no right to come here!" Sarah tried to shut the front door, but Ellen straight-armed it open.

"Thanks, don't mind if I do." She powered over the threshold into a warm, well-appointed living room, furnished with gray suede sectionals and a thick pile matching rug, where two young boys were sitting on the floor, playing a noisy video game on a widescreen TV.

"Wait! My kids are here."

"I can see that." Ellen masked her emotions to wave to them. "Hey, guys, how you doing?"

"Fine," one answered without looking up, but Sarah shut the door and motioned to them.

"Boys, go to your room," she said, staccato, and they set down the game controllers and rose instantly, astounding Ellen. She couldn't get that kind of obedience from her hair, much less her son. They left the room, and Sarah picked up the controller, hit the red button for off, and set it down on top of the TV, which had gone black.

"Sarah, how could you do it?" Ellen kept her temper in check. "Not just to me, but to Will? How could you do that to Will?"

"I didn't do anything to him, nothing wrong anyway." Sarah edged backwards, tugging at the corner of her skinny black sweater.

"You cannot believe that."

"I do, and it's true. Your son is where he belongs, with his real parents." Sarah didn't look regretful in the least, her mouth still tight. "I did the right thing."

"You didn't do it because it was the right thing. You did it for the money." Ellen took a step closer, fighting the impulse to hit Sarah in the face. "You couldn't wait to quit your job, now that you're rich."

"It doesn't matter why I did it, what matters is that he wasn't legally yours. He was Timothy Braverman."

"I might have told them, but you took it out of my hands."

"No, you wouldn't have. No mother would."

"Maybe you wouldn't, but I might have, and because of you, Will was taken in the worst possible way." Ellen's anger bubbled to the surface. "No explanation, no phasing in, just *taken*. It's the kind of thing that can mess him up for life."

"All I did was tell the truth."

"Don't pretend you have the moral high ground, because you don't. Was it moral to spy on me? To search my computer? You even tricked my son into telling you where I was!"

"He wasn't your son. He was their son."

"He was *my* son."

"Not legally."

"He was my son until I said different." Ellen felt angry tears, and at some level, even she knew she was yelling at the wrong person. She wasn't angry at Sarah, she was angry at everyone and everything. Angry that it had happened in the first place. Still she couldn't stop herself. "I would never do anything to hurt your children, no matter what."

"You're not worried about Will. You're worried about yourself."

"You know what, you're right. I love my son and I want him home and I'm never going to have him again. But most of all, I want him to be happy. If he's happy, I'm happy, and thanks to you, he's in pain and—"

There was a noise behind them, from the other end of the living room, and Ellen turned around, shocked at the sight. It was Myron Krims, Sarah's husband, but he was in a wheelchair. She had met him only once, years ago, and he had been walking fine. Then he was one of the top thoracic surgeons in the city, but he was clearly ill. His black sweater and khakis were swimming on him, and his hair had gone completely gray. Circles ringed his eyes, and his aspect looked vague.

"Dear?" Myron asked, his voice shaky. "I've been calling you."

"Excuse me." Sarah hurried to her husband, and Ellen watched as she bent over him, whispered something in his ear, then wheeled him out of the room. Sarah returned after a moment, her face a tight mask. "So. Now you see."

For a minute, Ellen didn't know what to say. "I had no idea."

"We don't advertise."

"What happened?"

"He has MS." Sarah straightened a suede pillow that didn't require it.

"For how long?"

"For the rest of his life."

Ellen reddened. "I mean, how long has this been going on?"

"None of that is your business. It's nobody's business but ours."

Ellen saw a premature fissure in Sarah's forehead and wondered why she'd never noticed it before. All this time she'd thought she was the only one on a single income, but she'd been wrong.

"I was doing what was right for my family." Sarah's voice remained controlled, and her gaze unwavering. "I was doing what I had to do."

"You could have told me." Ellen felt disarmed, grasping. "You could have warned me."

"What would you have said? Don't take the money?" Sarah snorted. "It was my family or your family. I chose my family. You would have done the same."

"I don't know," Ellen answered, after a minute. She was thinking back to what the cop had said at the ER waiting room. *It's no-win.* Suddenly she didn't know anymore what was right or moral, what was legal or fair. She no longer took satisfaction in confronting Sarah. She wasn't composed enough to analyze the situation. She couldn't even tell what she would have done in Sarah's position. She knew only that Will was gone, and there was a deep rent in her chest where her heart had been. Her shoulders sagged, and she felt herself sinking onto the couch. Her face dropped into her hands, and in the next second, the cushion dipped down as Sarah sat beside her.

"I tell you this," Sarah whispered. "I am sorry."

And at that, Ellen let slip the few tears she had left.

Chapter 91

Ellen got home, hollow and spent, raw and aching. She tossed her bag and keys on the windowseat, and stamped powdery snow from her snowy clogs. She took off her coat and hung it up, but it fell onto the closet floor. She didn't have the energy to pick it up. She was thirsty but didn't get anything to drink. She was hungry but didn't bother to eat. She didn't even have the strength to be mad at the reporters, following her back from Sarah's, plaguing her with questions. Oreo Figaro came over to rub against her shins, but she ignored him and went upstairs to read Sal's piece.

She clopped slowly up the stairs, the sound of her clogs like the ticking of a clock slowing down. She had never felt like this in her life. She was empty, a ghost of a person. She went into her office on autopilot, flicked on a light, and crossed to the computer. She sat down and moved the mouse, and her computer monitor woke up with a screensaver of Will posing with Oreo Figaro.

Please, no.

She opened up Outlook and watched the boldfaced names pile into the Inbox. She waited for Marcelo's email to load and braced herself to read the article. But Marcelo's wasn't the email that caught her eye. She moved the mouse, clicked on another email, and opened it, reading quickly.

And then she screamed.

And when she stopped screaming, she reached for the phone.

Chapter 92

Ellen shot up like a rocket, sending her desk chair rolling back across the floor, and ran to the door, then tore down the stairs.

Clop, clop, clop, clop, like a racehorse she sounded. She reached the living room, grabbed her purse and keys from the windowseat, snatched her coat from the closet floor, then flung open the door and hit the icy air.

She slammed the door shut behind her and went flying down the steps, spraying snow everywhere, her heart in her throat, heedless of the reporters, who surged forward as they had five minutes ago, raising cameras that had been at rest and flicking on generators to power up klieg lights and microphones.

"Hey, where you going now?" a reporter called out, filming her, and the others joined in. "Ellen, what's going on?" "You going back to Sarah's?"

Ellen tore through the snow on her front yard, staying on her property where the press couldn't follow, struggling in the deep snow to get to her car, as the reporters shouted questions from the sidewalk.

"Can't you give us a statement?" "Ellen, come on, give

us a break!" "What's all the activity? You going to see Will?"

Ellen chirped the car door open, jumped in, and switched on the ignition. She threw the car in reverse while she hit the button to lower the driver's window. "Move, move, everybody!" she hollered, gesturing frantically out the window, her heart pounding. "Get out of the way! Get out of my way!"

"Where are you going?" "Have you heard from your son? Are they letting you see him?"

"Move, move, MOVE!" Ellen reversed out of the driveway, hitting the gas until they jumped out of the way. Some shouted questions while others sprinted to their cars and newsvans, ready to follow her again.

"Ellen, they're staying at the Four Seasons, did you know? Is that where you're going?"

"MOVE!" Ellen put the car in drive and hit the gas, spraying road salt and snow, speeding to the corner, and turning left so fast that she almost fishtailed on Wynnewood Road. She kept control of the car and accelerated up the plowed street in almost no traffic, and by the time she hit City Line, she was being followed by newsvans with microwave towers and an array of pursuit vehicles. The traffic light ahead turned red, but she hit the gas and powered through the intersection. She passed a snowplow, a bus, and even an ambulance at speed.

Nothing was going to stop her.

Not now, not ever.

Chapter 93

Ellen hurried from the waiting room behind Special Agent Orr, passing the thick gold seal of the FBI, the framed picture of the president and the attorney general, the Ten Most Wanted posters, and whatever else was hanging on the off-white walls. She followed Special Agent Orr down the glistening hallway and reached a wooden door with a plaque that read CONFERENCE ROOM.

Special Agent Orr twisted the knob. "Here you go, Ms. Gleeson," he said, admitting her, then leaving.

Ellen stepped inside, getting her bearings. She had driven the farthest to get here, so they were all already in place. Special Agent Manning stood up at the head of the table, and on the near side, Ron Halpren stood up, too, with an uncertain smile. He was dressed in a tux from a benefit dinner, and Ellen shook his hand.

"Sorry to disrupt your night, gentlemen," she said, sitting down next to Ron. She nodded at Special Agent Manning, who retook his seat at the head of the table. "Thank you, too, Special Agent."

"It's my job." His smile was only polite and he was dressed casually, with a blue FBI windbreaker over a light

Oxford shirt. Behind him was a large smoked-glass window that overlooked the snowy city at night. "I just hope this isn't a wild goose chase."

"It isn't." Ellen looked at the other side of the table, where Bill Braverman sat glaring in a sport jacket and polo shirt, next to his lawyer, Mike Cusack, who dressed like him.

"So why are we all sitting here?" Bill demanded, his eyes flashing with anger.

Ellen composed herself, folding her hands on the conference table, and took a deep breath.

Chapter 94

"Okay, here goes." Ellen paused, her heart in her throat. She was about to drop a bomb, and she met Bill's eye with sympathy. "The fact is, you're not Will's father."

"That's a lie!" Bill shot back.

"It's true, and I have proof."

"You're insulting me *and* my wife!"

Cusack placed a restraining hand on Bill's arm. "Please, allow me."

"Why should I?" Bill tore his arm away, glaring at Ellen. "You don't fool me for one minute! What kind of scam is this?"

"It's not a scam."

"Ms. Gleeson," Cusack broke in, looking askance. "You should be aware that intentional infliction of emotional distress is civilly actionable, and we won't hesitate to file suit against you."

Ron frowned. "I won't let you threaten her, Mike."

"But this is an Internet scam, obviously." Cusack raised a graying eyebrow. "Don't tell me you were taken in by that stupid email. Are you sending money to Ethiopian ambassadors, too?"

"It's not a scam, I assure you," Ron said, his tone even and reasonable.

Special Agent Manning cleared his throat. "Let's settle down and let Ms. Gleeson tell us what this is all about."

"Thank you." Ellen gathered her thoughts. "To make a long story short, when I was in Miami, I got DNA samples from both Carol and Bill Braverman. I followed them to a restaurant, and I collected some cigarette butts that Bill left in an ashtray—"

"You did *what*?" Bill interjected, rising, but Cusack pressed him back down.

"—I also got a Diet Sprite can that Carol drank from, and I sent them both to a lab that I found on the Internet."

"This is ridiculous!" Bill slammed the table with a heavy hand, but Ellen stayed the course. She couldn't blame Bill for his reaction, but neither was she backing down.

"I got the results emailed to me, and Ron forwarded the email with the results to you. Honestly, I'd forgotten about the tests, and I had no doubt that Will was really Timothy, after that night in my kitchen. Rob Moore said that his girlfriend was Amy Martin, and I knew that Amy was the one who put Will, or Timothy, up for adoption."

Next to her, Ron added, "It's a perfect chain of custody."

"It is," Special Agent Manning said, and though Ellen didn't speak law enforcement, she got the gist.

"The results of the test came back, and they show that Carol was clearly Will's biological mother. But Will has none of Bill's DNA. The results are that Bill is not Will's father."

"You're saying that Carol cheated on me?" Bill's eyes flew open.

"I'm sorry, she must have." Ellen felt terrible for him, but still. "You said your marriage wasn't the best."

"She wouldn't!" Bill flushed red. "She didn't, and she

certainly wouldn't fool me into thinking another man's child was mine!"

"I'm sorry, I really am." Ellen took a second to compose herself, then said the words she'd been rehearsing all the way here. "Will is not your son, so you have no legal right to him. My adoption remains legal, and I want my son back."

Ron added, "My research showed the law would be the same in almost all jurisdictions, including Florida. As Carol has no living parents, Ellen is entitled to keep Will."

"This is a trick!" Bill shouted, jumping to his feet.

"Based on an *Internet* DNA test?" Cusack remained in his chair, his expression only slightly less hostile. "What do you take us for?"

Special Agent Manning waved Bill into his seat, and he complied, albeit angrily.

"It's a legitimate lab," Ellen said, willing herself to remain calm. She had discussed the way this meeting would go with Ron, who was her first phone call after she read the email. "But if you want to run another test to confirm the results, you're welcome to."

"I'm *welcome* to?" Bill repeated, incredulous.

"I will agree to a lab of the FBI's choosing, with the test to be administered under their supervision."

"I won't take any damn DNA test!" Bill's jaw set with determination. "Timothy's *my* son, and I'm keeping him!"

Ron raised a finger in his professorial way. "As a legal matter, we could require you to take a DNA test. If we take this matter to court right now, any judge would order you to do so, and my client and I are more than prepared. In fact, bear with me." Ron reached into an accordion-style briefcase sitting on the floor, extracted a manila folder, then opened it, slid out some papers, and handed them to Special Agent Manning, Bill, and Cusack. "These papers are ready to file. I have an emergency judge standing by. It's your choice, Mr. Braverman. If you and Will don't voluntarily take the DNA test, the court will order you to do so. I'll also ask the court to place Will in protective custody in the interim, so that you don't leave the jurisdiction with him."

"You *have* to be kidding!" Bill grabbed the papers from the center of the table and skimmed the front page, his eyes darting rapidly left and right, his mouth pursed in fury.

But Ellen could see that Cusack, sitting next to him and reading the papers, lifted his eyebrow again.

Ron added, "Mike, if you'd like a minute alone with your client, Ellen and I would be happy to step outside."

Cusack looked up after a minute, deep in thought. "Yes, thank you. I'd like to confer with my client."

Ellen and Ron rose from the table, left the conference room, and went into the hallway, where they closed the door behind them and Ron placed a fatherly hand on her shoulder.

"Ellen, don't get excited." His brow furrowed. "You have to remember that the Internet lab could be wrong. Even the most reliable labs get false results on tests, all kinds of tests, and I don't want you to get your hopes up."

"They're *not* that fly-by-night," Ellen said, but she knew better. "Jerry Springer uses them."

Ron smiled. "Remember, plan for the worst and you'll be happily surprised."

"Way to kill the mood, counselor."

Fifteen endless minutes later, the door to the conference room opened, and Special Agent Manning stuck out his head. "We're ready for you," he said simply.

Chapter 95

Ellen filed into the conference room with Ron behind her and took her seat at the table across from Cusack. Bill had deserted his chair but was standing by the window, his arms folded and his expression grim. Ellen saw the strain around his eyes and knew that he was more anguished than angry, and her heart went out to him.

Cusack began, "We've decided, in a spirit of cooperation, to undertake a DNA test. The FBI has recommended a lab that it uses all the time, and we'll be taking the samples of Bill and Timothy tonight."

"We'll fast-track it," Special Agent Manning interjected. "We should have the results by Monday."

Ellen felt her heart pounding but didn't show any emotion, for Bill's sake.

Cusack continued, "However, we don't believe it's necessary to place Timothy in protective custody with the Bureau, pending the results. Timothy is at the Four Seasons with a babysitter that comes highly recommended. Bill would like to keep the boy with him at the hotel and he won't leave the jurisdiction. We trust you'll agree." Cusack fell silent, awaiting Ellen's response.

So did Bill, by the window, his arms folded, and Ron, who cocked his head, his smile characteristically gentle.

"What do you want to do, Ellen?" he asked. "You can leave him with Bill until the tests come back, or the FBI can make him comfortable in a hotel."

Special Agent Manning added, "The Four Seasons isn't in our budget." He chuckled, *huh huh,* but nobody else did.

Ellen's eyes met Bill's from across the room, and she felt their shared bond. This situation was no-win, at every turn. As for protective custody, it had been Ron's idea. She didn't really want Will to stay with a cop. It only took Ellen a minute to make her decision:

"I trust that Bill will take good care of him, and right now, that's what's best for him. I don't want to disrupt him again if the test is wrong."

"Thanks," Cusack said, and Ron nodded.

But Bill didn't reply, just turned away and gazed out the window into the cold, dark night. He was facing the prospect of losing his son.

And Ellen knew exactly how he felt.

Chapter 96

A new snow had fallen, covering the minivans, swing sets, and lawn furniture in pristine white. The afternoon sky was sunny and bright blue, and the wind frigid and fresh, as if the deep freeze had killed every last germ, leaving only the healthiest and most wholesome air. Ellen breathed it in, standing on her porch with no coat like a crazy lady, folding her arms against her chest, her hair freshly shampooed, her sweater dry cleaned, and her socks laundered and matching. She even had on new clogs.

"Ellen, we could wait inside," Marcelo said, standing on her right.

"Nah, let's stay here," her father said, on her left.

"I agree," Barbara said, next to her father in her lovely white coat.

Behind them, Connie stood with her husband, Chuck. She said, "Wild horses couldn't drag me off this porch."

They all smiled, Ellen most of all, despite the reporters, TV anchorpersons, and photographers who mobbed the sidewalk in front of her house and spilled into the street, shouting questions, taking videos and pictures, and requiring five uniformed cops to keep traffic moving.

Marcelo smiled, puzzled. "Let me get this straight. It's freezing outside, but we're on the porch?"

"Right," Ellen and her father answered in unison, then they looked at each other.

"Great minds," her father said, and Ellen laughed.

Marcelo threw an arm around her shoulder. "You know what? I like it."

"Good," she said, snuggling against him.

Suddenly a black sedan turned onto the street, and Ellen felt her heart start to thunder. She stepped forward for a closer look, and the sedan slowed when it reached the photographers, who started hoisting videocameras to their shoulders. The sedan's emergency lights went on, flashing yellow as it braked in front of the house.

"My God," Ellen said under her breath, already in motion, and the press surged forward, pointing their cameras and microphones to the sedan. The doors were opening, and Bill emerged from the driver's side and Cusack from the passenger's. Reporters swarmed them with cameras and microphones, and Ellen ran down the front walk toward the crowd, and in the next instant she heard a little voice from its center.

"Mommy! MOMMY!"

"WILL!" Ellen shouted, tears blurring her eyes as she hit the crowd and elbowed her way through, reaching the sedan just as Bill unlatched Will from the car seat and carried him through the crazed reporters to her.

"MOMMY!" Will screamed, his arms reaching for her, and Ellen took him in her arms and hugged him so tightly she almost squished him.

"It's all right, it's all right now," she said, as Will burst into tears and wrapped his arms around her neck. Reporters shouted questions and stuck cameras in their faces, but Ellen caught Bill's eye, and his expression was pained. She called to him, "Want to come in, have a soda?"

"No thanks," Bill called back, then gestured vaguely at Will. "I got him new shoes."

"Thanks." Ellen felt a stab of sympathy. "Another time, then?"

"See you," Bill said, his eyes on Will's back. Grief flickered through his expression, then he turned away amid the clicking cameras, and so did Ellen, with a guilt that vanished in happiness when Marcelo, her father, and Chuck arrived at her side and ran interference as she hurried back up her front walk, hustled across the porch to the open front door, and swept inside the warm, snug house.

Will didn't touch the ground until half an hour later, after being passed from mother to grandfather to mother to new stepgrandmother to mother to Marcelo to Connie and Chuck then back again to Ellen, until he had stopped crying and everybody held him tight, kissed him too much, and reassured themselves by feeling his weight in their arms that he was, really, safely, and finally back home.

Ellen felt her heart truly at peace for the first time since she'd first seen that white card, so long ago. She set Will down in the living room, but, oddly, he frowned, even as he stood at the center of an adoring circle. His glistening eyes scanned the room, ignoring the twisted streamers of green crepe, the green helium balloons on the ceiling, and even the pile of wrapped gifts from a love-crazed family.

"What's the matter, sweetie?" Ellen asked, puzzled. She reached down and ruffled his soft hair with her fingers. She thought she might never stop touching his hair.

"Where's Oreo Figaro, Mommy?"

"Oh. He was here a minute ago," Ellen answered, looking around, and in the next second, they both spotted the cat under the dining room table, running from all the commotion, a black-and-white blur with a tail like an exclamation point.

"There he goes!" Will hollered, taking off after the cat, who bounded into the kitchen.

"Uh-oh." Ellen went after Will, and everyone watched him, collectively holding their breaths. They had all discussed how he would react to seeing the kitchen again, and she had talked to a child psychologist who'd told her to let Will take the initiative in asking questions. The therapist had also approved her redecorating idea, and she prayed Will would, too. She held her breath when he reached the kitchen threshold.

"Mommy!" Will hollered, surprised. "Look in here!"

"I know, it's a surprise for you." Ellen came up behind him and rested a hand on his head. She and Marcelo had worked in the kitchen all weekend, installing laminated wood over the subfloor and painting the walls to cover the bloodstains. The wall color had been the easiest choice, although when sunlight flooded in through the back window, the room looked like it was growing. She doubted she'd ever get used to a bright green kitchen, nor should she.

"It's my favorite!" Will exclaimed, then grabbed the cat, and gave him a kiss. "I love you, Oreo Figaro."

"I love you, too," Ellen replied, in her Oreo Figaro voice.

Will giggled and set the cat back on the floor. "Can I open my presents now?"

"Yes, but gimme a kiss first." Ellen bent over, and Will threw his arms around her neck. If she was expecting a big reunion kiss, she wasn't getting one, not when there were gifts waiting to be unwrapped. Will ran out of the room, and she called after him, "Love you!"

"Love you, too!"

Ellen went to the cabinet and got a trash bag for the gift wrap, then straightened up, remembering that the last time she had stood here, she had killed a man. She turned to the wall where Moore had slid down, as if to reassure herself that it wouldn't still be bloodied.

But it was.

A sudden horrific flashback shot out of nowhere. Before her eyes, Moore slumped against the wall. Bright red blood spurted from a deep hole in his forehead. A crooked grin crossed his face.

Ellen froze, remembering. That smile was crooked because it turned down on the right. Like Will's.

She put it together, stunned. She hadn't noticed it then, because she was sure that Bill Braverman was Will's father. But now that she knew that he wasn't, the crooked grin assumed a new significance. Then she remembered what Moore had said that night to Carol.

You shoulda said to him, "Honey, wifey-poo isn't the good girl you think."

Ellen stared at the wall, but it had turned green again. She stood a moment, shaken, trying to collect her thoughts, trying to process what she had just learned.

If Bill wasn't Will's father, she had at least a guess who was.

Epilogue

About a year later, there was another winter snow and another party with wrapped presents, balloons, and crepe streamers crisscrossing the living room, which this time was packed with noisy, sugar-fueled classmates of Will's. They ran back and forth, played with new toys, ate grocery-store sheet cake, and generally wreaked havoc for his fourth birthday.

"Watch out!" Will shrieked, running with a new laser sword, and Ellen grabbed it from him on the fly.

"Don't run with this."

"Please!"

"No, you'll hurt somebody."

"Aw, Mom!" Will took off after his friend Brett, and Ellen's father came over, his eyes glittering with mischief.

"I'll take that weapon, my lady."

"What for?" Ellen handed it over.

"You'll see. This will do nicely." Her father examined the laser sword, and Barbara joined him in her elegant white pantsuit, a multicolored party hat perched atop her head.

"Ellen, don't let him have that. He'll embarrass us all."

"Too late for that," Ellen said with a smile. She had come to love Barbara, who wisely hadn't tried to replace her mother, because no one could. But somewhere along the line, she had opened her mind to the possibility that if you could love a child no matter how he came to you, then you could also love a mother, no matter how she came to you.

"I need this for my golf lesson." Her father gestured across the crowded room to where Bill Braverman and his pretty date were talking with Connie and Chuck. Her father called to him, "Bill, come here. I need your expertise."

"Coming." Bill strode over in his out-of-place linen jacket, pants, and tassel loafers, making his way through the kids and ruffling Will's hair.

"Look how fast I go, Bill!" Will called after him.

"Good for you!" Bill entered the dining room, grinning, but her father was all business.

"Show me what you were saying before, about my grip." Her father flipped the sword around so that the point faced the floor, then wrapped his fingers around the hilt, swinging it like a golf club. "You said it was my elbow, right? Not tucked in enough?"

"Not exactly, let me show you." Bill focused on his task, and Barbara moaned.

"Please, guys, anything but golf."

"There is nothing but golf," Bill said, smiling, then turned to Ellen. "By the way, I have those papers for you to sign, for Will's trust. When he's of age, he can decide how much he wants to set aside for Charbonneau House."

"Great, thanks." Ellen smiled, and in the next second she felt an arm encircle her waist and tug her into the kitchen. Before she knew it, Marcelo had taken her into his arms, hugged her gently, and given her one of his best kisses.

"This is a wonderful party," he purred into her ear. "Very romantic."

"It's the Snickers bars. Snickers equal romance." Ellen put her arms around him, stretching out her hands over his shoulder. Her engagement ring sparkled prettily in the sunlight, and she never would have guessed that green would make such a nice backdrop for a diamond. It gave her a new appreciation for photosynthesis.

"You're doing it again, aren't you?" Marcelo asked, chuckling.

"Doing what?"

"Looking at your ring."

"Just kiss me," Ellen said with a smile, but suddenly Will burst into the kitchen and stopped himself before he ran into them.

"Marcelo," he said, looking up, "are you gonna kiss Mommy?"

"If you say it's okay, Will."

"Do it! She likes it!" Will hugged Marcelo around the leg, then ran out of the kitchen, and Ellen smiled.

"Good move, asking permission."

"I know who the boss is." Marcelo kissed her softly and sweetly, then whispered, "*Eu te amo.*"

And for that, Ellen didn't need a translation.

Acknowledgments

I have always been a fan of "write what you know," and this novel arises from a new sideline of mine: newspaper columnist. More than a year ago, I began writing a weekly column for *The Philadelphia Inquirer* called "Chick Wit." (Check it out online at my website, www.scottoline.com.) To stay on point, this novel grew naturally from my observations of the rewards and stresses of a reporter's life—especially in bad economic times—but it's important to head this disclaimer: *Look Again* is fiction.

I made it up, every word.

The newsroom herein is not *The Philadelphia Inquirer*'s, and the fictional owners of the newspaper, as well as its reporters, staff, and editors, are not anyone at the *Inquirer*. And though, like every newspaper, *the Inquirer* has suffered in this economy, the paper is nevertheless thriving due to the talent, hard work, and business savvy of its amazing publisher, Brian Tierney, with the help of Pulitzer Prize winner and great guy Bill Marimow and marketing whiz Ed Mahlman, as well as my friend and editor Sandy Clark, who has been a warm and loving guide in new terrain. I owe much to her, so thanks, Sandy.

I needed to do lots of research for *Look Again,* and I owe a huge debt to the following experts. (Any and all mistakes are mine.) A big hug to brilliant Cheryl Young, Esq., a divorce and family lawyer who is an expert on the intricacies of the law, as well as having an understanding of its very human implications. Big thanks, as always, to Glenn Gilman, Esq., and detective extraordinaire Art Mee. Thank you very much to Dr. John O'Hara of Paoli Hospital, as well as Brad Zerr, who put me in touch with Dr. Glenn Kaplan, head of Pediatric Surgery at Paoli Hospital in Paoli, Pennsylvania, and Tina Saurian, nurse manager of the Maternity Unit. Thanks, too, to Dr. Paul Anisman, chief of Pediatric Cardiology at Nemours/Alfred I. Dupont Hospital for Children in Wilmington, Delaware. Dr. Anisman showed me around and answered all my dumb questions, so I got to see firsthand the wonderful work he and his staff do for babies and children from around the world.

Thanks, too, to Rosina Weber of Drexel University, as well as dear pal and now Harvard prof. James Cavallaro, Esq., and his great wife, Madja Rodigues. Thanks to Dr. Harvey Weiner, director of Academic and Community Relations at Eagleville, for his expertise and for the good work he does for those suffering from drug and alcohol addiction. Thanks, too, to William Fehr, consultant and pal of Mama Scottoline. Thanks to Barbara Capozzi, Karen Volpe, Joey Stampone, Dr. Meredith Snader, Julia Guest, Frank Ferro, Sandy Claus, Sharon Potts, and Janice Davis.

I owe biggest love and thanks to the brilliant and enthusiastic gang at St. Martin's Press, starting with my editor, Jennifer Enderlin, whose comments on an early draft of *Look Again* improved the novel a thousandfold. (Not to mention that she thought of its terrific title, after I had been tearing my hair out for weeks.) And massive hugs all around to genius CEO John Sargent, ultrachic publisher Sally Richardson, the indomitable Matthew Shear, marketing maven Matt Baldacci, musical sales whiz Jeff Capshew, dynamic duo John Murphy and John Karle in publicity, Courtney Fischer, and Brian Heller. I've been overwhelmed by the wonderful energy, talent, and teamwork that St. Martin's has shown me; it's not a publishing house, it's a powerhouse, and they pull together like crazy for a common goal, namely this book. I couldn't feel happier or luckier to be at SMP, and I am indebted to all of you. Thanks so very much.

Deepest thanks and love to my genius agent and dear friend Molly Friedrich, Amazing Paul Cirone, new mom Jacobia Dahm, and to our newest addition, the lovely and talented Lucy Carson! Welcome, Lucy! This little tribe at the Friedrich Agency has nurtured me for a long, long time, and I feel enveloped in their embrace.

Thanks and big love to my wonderful assistant, Laura Leonard, who helps me in every single thing I do and is simply indispensable to my life.

And to my family, who are my life.

Reading Group Questions

1. *Look Again* really examines the notion of parenthood. What do you think makes someone a parent? Do you think the bond a child has with a nonbiological parent can be as strong as one they would have with a biological parent? Why?

2. Lisa's favorite quote is one from Eleanor Roosevelt: "A woman is like a tea bag. You never know how strong she is until she's in hot water." How does Ellen prove that she is a strong woman? Does Ellen remind you of anyone you know? Could you relate to Ellen, and did you like her? Why or why not?

3. As a journalist, Ellen has a heightened need to find the truth. In this circumstance, was this a good thing, or a bad thing? What would you have done in Ellen's place? Would you have looked for the truth, even if it meant losing your son? What do you think were Ellen's motivations?

4. The idea of "letting go" a child helped shape the whole premise of the book for Lisa, which led her to thinking

about who really "owns" a child. Who do you think "owns" a child, and what exactly does that mean? If children actually "own" themselves, what then is the role of parents, and what are the limitations on parenthood?

5. If the child you raised and loved with all your heart actually belonged to someone else, and you were the only one who knew, would you give the child up? How do you think those around you would react? Who in your life would agree with your decision, and who would have done the opposite?

6. How would you describe Ellen's relationship with her father and how do you think it changed over the course of the book? Ellen considered her mother her go-to parent. Do you think everyone has a go-to parent, and what defines them as such?

7. What effect do you think all the drama in Will's life will have on him in the future? Do you think things ultimately worked out to his benefit or detriment and why?

8. How do you feel about single parents adopting children? What kind of, if any, additional requirements do you think should be put on single parents before they can adopt? How do you feel about open adoption? Is it better or worse for children? Is it better or worse for the adoptive parents? The biological parents? At what age do you think a child should be told they are adopted?

Read on for an excerpt from Lisa Scottoline's

COME HOME

Available in hardcover from St. Martin's Press

Jill stopped on the stairway, listening. She thought she heard a voice calling her from outside, but she'd been wrong before. It was probably the rushing of the rain, or the lash of the wind through the trees. Still, she listened, hoping.

"Babe?" Sam paused on the stair, resting his hand on the banister. He looked back at her, his eyes a puzzled blue behind his glasses. "Did you forget your phone?"

"No, I thought I heard something." Jill didn't elaborate. She was in her forties, old enough to have a past and wise enough to keep her thoughts about it to herself.

"What?" Sam asked, patiently. It was almost midnight, and they'd been on their way to bed. The house was dark except for the glass fixture above the stairwell, and the silvery strands in Sam's thick, dark hair glinted in the low light. Their chubby golden retriever, Beef, was already upstairs, looking down at them from the landing, his buttery ears falling forward.

"It's nothing, I guess." Jill started back up the stairs, but Beef swung his head toward the front of the house and gave an excited bark. His tail started to wag, and Jill turned, too, listening again.

Jill! Jill!

"It's Abby!" Jill heard it for sure, this time. The cry resonated in her chest, speaking directly to her heart. She turned around and hurried for the entrance hall, and Beef scampered downstairs after her, his heavy butt getting ahead of him, like a runaway tractor-trailer.

"Abby who?" Sam called after her. "Your ex's kid?"

"Yes." Jill reached the front door, twisted the dead bolt, flicked on the porch light, and threw open the door. Abby wasn't there, and Jill didn't see her because it was so dark. There were no streetlights at this end of the block, and the rain obliterated the outlines of the houses and cars, graying out the suburban scene. Suddenly, a black SUV with only one headlight drove past, spotlighting a silhouette that Jill would know anywhere. It was Abby, but she was staggering down the sidewalk as if she'd been injured.

"Sam, call 911!" Jill bolted out of the house and into the storm, diagnosing Abby on the fly. It could have been a hit-and-run, or an aneurysm. Not a stroke, Abby was too young. Not a gunshot or stab wound, in this neighborhood.

Jill tore through the rain. Beef bounded ahead, barking in alarm. The neighbor's motion-detector went on, casting a halo of light on their front lawn. Abby stumbled off the sidewalk. Her purse slipped from her shoulder and dropped to the ground. Abby took a few more faltering steps, then collapsed, crumpling to the grass.

"Abby!" Jill screamed, sprinting to Abby's side, kneeling down. Abby was conscious, but crying. Jill reached for her pulse and scanned her head and body for signs of injury, and there were none. Rainwater covered Abby's face, streaking her mascara and blackening her tears. Her hair tuck to her neck, and rain plastered her thin sundress to her body. Her pulse felt strong and steady, bewildering Jill. "Abby, Abby, what is it?"

"You have to . . . hold me." Abby raised her arms. "Please."

Jill gathered Abby close, shielding her from the rain. She'd held Abby so many times before, and all the times rushed back at her, as if her very body had stored the memories, until this very moment. Jill flashed on the time Abby had fallen off her Rollerblades, breaking an ankle. Then the time Abby had gotten a C in her trig final. The time she didn't get picked for the travel soccer team. Abby had always been a sensitive little girl, but she wasn't a little girl anymore, and Jill had never seen her cry this hard.

"Abby, honey, please tell me, and I can help."

"I can't say it . . . it's so awful." Abby sobbed, and Jill caught a distinct whiff of alcohol on her breath and came up to speed. Abby wasn't injured, she'd been drinking. Jill hadn't seen her in three years, and Abby had grown up, she'd be nineteen now. Abby sobbed harder. "Jill, Dad's dead . . . he's dead."

"*What?*" Jill gasped, shocked. Her ex-husband was in excellent health, still in his forties. "How?"

"Somebody . . . killed him." Abby dissolved into tears, her body going limp, clinging to Jill. "Please, you have to . . . help me. I have to find out . . . who did it."

Jill hugged her closer, feeling her grief and struggling to process what had happened. She couldn't imagine William as a murder victim, or a victim of any kind, for that matter, but her first thought was of his daughters Abby and Victoria, and her own daughter, Megan. The news would devastate all of them, Megan included. William was her stepfather, but the only father she'd ever known. Her real father had died before she was born.

"Babe, what are you doing, let's get her into the house!" Sam shouted, to be heard over the rain. He was kneeling on Abby's other side, though Jill didn't know when he'd gotten there.

"William's been murdered," Jill told him, sounding numb, even to herself.

"I heard. We're not calling 911, she's just drunk." Sam squinted against the brightness of the motion-detector light. Raindrops soaked his hair and dappled his polo shirt. "Let me take her arm. Lift her on one, two, three," he counted off, tugging Abby's arm.

"Okay, go." Jill took Abby's other arm, and together they hoisted her, sobbing, to her feet, gathered her purse, and half-walked, half-carried her toward the house, sloshing through the grass, with Beef at their heels.

Jill tried to collect her thoughts, in turmoil. She'd always dreamed of seeing Abby again, but not in these circumstances, and she dreaded telling Megan about William. But as agonized as she felt for the girls, Jill wouldn't shed a tear for her ex-husband. There was a reason she had divorced the man, and it was a whopper.

And evidently, not only the good died young.

Coming soon from *New York Times* bestselling author

Lisa Scottoline

DON'T GO

Available in April 2013, in hardcover,
from St. Martin's Press